THE SWEDISH PRINCE

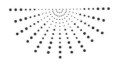

KARINA HALLE

METAL BLONDE BOOKS

Copyright © 2018 by Karina Halle

First edition published by Metal Blonde Books March 2018

All rights reserved.

No part of this book may be reproduced in any form or by any electronic or mechanical means, including information storage and retrieval systems, without written permission from the author, except for the use of brief quotations in a book review.

Cover by: Hang Le Designs

Photography by: Photo P

Model: Miles Reza

Edited & Proofed by: Roxane Leblanc & Kara Malinczak

To my Norwegian father, Sven, and my Finnish mother, Tuuli, who would always speak Swedish to each other when they didn't want me to hear what they were saying. Thank you for keeping Scandinavia alive in your hearts and mine.
PS I wish you had taught me Swedish.

"What the world needs is a return to sweetness and decency."

— AUDREY HEPBURN AS PRINCESS ANNE IN
ROMAN HOLIDAY

PREFACE

A NOTE FROM THE AUTHOR

A very, very long time ago, in a galaxy far, far away…

Just joking.

But a very long time ago in a studio apartment in Vancouver there was a young woman who was obsessed with the Golden Age of Hollywood. Originally, she was at school for screenwriting and a fellow student introduced her to *The Philadelphia Story* and she fell so in love with it that she became gleefully obsessed with the films of the old days.

Anyway long story short, though she loved Jimmy Stewart and Cary Grant, in the end Gregory Peck won her heart and Audrey Hepburn was one of her favorite actresses and hey, you can bet she saw *Roman Holiday* countless times.

Anyway that young woman is me and, yes, I've seen *Roman Holiday* a hell of a lot. It's my go-to. It's hilarious and the acting is not stuffy and rigid as it often was in the day, but very quick and natural and authentic. Gregory and Audrey (and Eddie) had amazing chemistry together, the dialogue by Dalton Trumbo sparkled and it was shot entirely

PREFACE

on location in Rome, which meant it brought the atmosphere with it. No fake sets here, this was the real deal.

The only problem I always had with *Roman Holiday* was the ending. Now if you've seen it, you know the story: Audrey is the drugged runaway princess who escapes the embassy one night and passes out on a public bench, only to be discovered by the very handsome, very sexy, gravelly-voiced Gregory Peck.

He's the American journalist slaving to his boss, low on funds, just wanting to get out of Rome. When he discovers the drugged girl is not "Anya" as she tells him but the missing Princess Anne, well now he has the story of a century to write. So as long as he doesn't let her know he knows who she is.

But will he write the story? That's his plan but it's how they discover each other, even under the false identities, that's the fun part. The only problem with the whole wonderful film though is…the ending.

Now I'm not going to spoil it but that ending always leaves me frustrated. I get that in the film they only actually knew each other and fell in love in ONE DAY but I still bought it. Insta-love? I'm down with it. It's alive and well in The Swedish Prince too. Romance with a capital R. Love with a capital L.

But in the film, I just wanted…more.

Always more, never less?

Anyway, I always said to myself, one day I'll write something inspired by this and change the ending. I'm going to write a REAL sweep-you-off your feet, charming, romance and give the characters a HEA you will swoon for.

So that's what The Swedish Prince is. A reverse twist on *Roman Holiday*! But I was picturing Armie Hammer the whole time as Viktor (sorry Mr. Peck).

I even went specifically to Stockholm in the middle of

PREFACE

winter to do research for this book. Being a Scandinavian myself (Finnish and Norwegian) I felt right at home.

But next time I'm going in the summer. Because...it was colder than a polar bear's toenail.

I should also note that while there IS a real Swedish Prince (Prince Carl Phillip) and while he IS outstandingly hot and sexy (look him up), I took many, many liberties with the Swedish Monarchy. In the end, this book is complete fiction. And if any Swedes are offended, or find some mistakes regarding Sweden or the language, I apologize. I also blame my parents (see dedication).

(PS Tehachapi, the other location that features in this book, is a beautiful town and worth a visit. One of my favourite places/passes to drive through in California.)

And if you're a sensitive reader, I should also point out this romance does contain an ample amount of swearing and graphic sex, so keep that in mind, please.

With all of that said, I hope you are ready to get swept away with the utterly romantic The Swedish Prince...

PROLOGUE

MAGGIE

New York City

"That is the absolute last time I'm trying online dating," Sam says to me with an exaggerated sigh as she leans back in the couches we've taken over in the corner of the bar.

"What happened this time?" I ask her this out of courtesy because I know she's going to tell me anyway. Plus, Sam is a pro at online dating at this point. It doesn't matter how many times she says she's quitting, the next day she's back in the proverbial saddle, swiping left and right and complaining about dick pics. I should probably note that she doesn't exactly complain about getting them, it's just that the dicks in said pics aren't up to her standards.

"What didn't happen?" she says, brushing her bangs out of her eyes. "I mean, we just met up for drinks down in the village, which is fine. Super casual, you know? And in person he was a tiny bit more attractive than his picture online."

"Which pic? The one in his profile or his unsolicited dick pic?" I ask.

"For your information, no dick pics were sent, unsolicited or not. Anyway, so he wasn't bad looking though I could already tell we didn't have that easy chemistry I hoped we would. Halfway through the date, I was pretty sure I wasn't going home with him. Then he showed me his sex playlist."

I raise my brows. "Sex playlist?"

"Yeah. On his phone. And the music was really good." She shrugs. "So I slept with him."

"You're insane."

"I know. I know." She shakes her head before picking up her margarita and leaning over to take a loud slurp of it. "Worst part is, he put it on shuffle and I hadn't seen the entire list. So when he was going down on me, *Never Going to Give You Up* came on."

I burst out laughing. "You were Rick-Rolled during sex?"

She nods frantically. "I couldn't come if my life depended on it! So I said I had to leave and quickly got out of there. Highlight of the night was getting a kebab on the way home. My life is a never-ending cycle of bad decisions and falafel."

She's kind of right about that. Sam is my closest friend here in the city, which counts for a lot since I've been living in New York for nearly two years now and making friends is harder than you think. Luckily we're both in the same journalism program and we've bonded over hating most of our teachers and the dismal dating scene.

At least Sam is putting herself out there night after night. I won't even look at Tinder or Huggle or any of those oddly-named apps, even though Sam has created a profile for me absolutely everywhere. I may be just twenty-two years old but I'm pretty old fashioned when it comes to dating and still have it in the romantic recesses of my heart that I can meet someone in real life, rather than online.

Of course, this has proven to be nearly impossible in this

city. Don't get me wrong–NYC is a million times better than my hometown of Tehachapi, California. The only guys in that town are ex-convicts from the state prison, and with my father being a prison guard there, there would be some definite disapproval.

But New York is just too big and chaotic to date. Everyone looks like a model, first of all, and while I'm fairly thin and not too hard on the eyes, I look like some tiny, cute, big-eyed pixie. Looks wise, I'd like to say I'm about an eight out of ten in Tehachapi, probably a six out of ten in the Midwest, but in the supermodel streets of Manhattan, I'm pretty much a chihuahua. Woof.

Still, I'm holding out hope. Hope that one day, while I'm in a bookstore, I'll be reaching for the last copy of the new Neil Gaiman just as someone else is and my fingers will brush his and I'll look up and find the man of my dreams. I know that's a terribly optimistic way to look at love, but I can't help it. I'd never held out for a prince charming until I moved here, where a new beginning seems to be waiting around every corner.

Hell, I don't even need love right now. What I really need is to get laid and I know I don't need Prince Charming for that. We might reach for the same book in a bookstore but I'd be just as happy if he slammed me up against those bookshelves and fucked me senseless. Sam's been getting dick left and right–dicks flying all over the place–and I'm hard up for even just one.

"You'll find someone," I say to Sam. "And he'll have a better sex playlist than that guy. Here, let me buy you a drink."

"Don't be stupid," she says, putting her hand on my arm and forcing me to stay seated. "You know you're broke as fuck and this is one pricey drink."

Also true. I got a scholarship to NYU and the journalism program, thanks to studying my ass off for years, but I could only afford to move here thanks to working my ass off for years. My family doesn't come from money–that's putting it mildly–and even though my parents both work, my father as a prison guard, my mother as a hotel housekeeper, they still have six kids, including me, to support.

The only reason I'm here right now is because I spent my evenings during high school working with my mom at the local La Quinta. Even now I'm working most nights and weekends as a barista at a coffee shop around the corner from the residence halls, and I'm barely scraping by.

I give Sam a grateful look, though I honestly wish I could do more. "How about I just sprinkle good blessings on you?" I reach into my purse I picked up from the thrift shop, a terrible fake of a Gucci that's made from plastic rather than leather, and take out a small jar of gold glitter eye shadow. I dip my fingers in, and before she has a chance to object, I sprinkle some on her head.

"What are you doing?" she shrieks, trying to get out of the way, but she's laughing. Soon she's covered in a very light dusting of gold.

"I used to do this to my sister April all the time," I tell her, putting the shadow back. I don't want to waste it. "She believed it."

"And where is your sister now?"

"Well she's only thirteen and I think if I tried this again she'd give me the evil eye and never speak to me again. Teenage angst, you know." Actually, at this moment, all of my siblings are out with my seventeen-year-old brother Pike, the oldest after me. There's a fair or something down in Bakersfield that they've made the trek to, I guess to give my parents a night of peace for once.

Knowing that my siblings are all together like that makes my heart ache, just a little. I don't get homesick often. I mean, I'd been dreaming about leaving that town for most of my life. But every now and then it hits me for a moment, usually passing quickly. Tonight is one of those nights.

In fact, I've had this weird feeling in my chest for most of the evening, a sense of unease. I'm prone to worry about things like money and school and my lack of love life but this is something different, something I can't put my finger on. I consider myself to be quite intuitive so I probably should pay attention, but I just don't know how.

"Are you okay?" Sam asks me, staring at me inquisitively. "Why don't I buy *you* a drink?"

"I'm fine," I tell her. "Just vibed out for no real reason."

"It's not the company, is it?"

I grin at her. "No, not tonight."

"Then you look like you could use a drink. I'll be right back."

Normally I would protest a bit but Sam comes from money and is quite generous with it. It makes me feel small sometimes that she often has to pay for me to do the things she wants to do, but that's just my own pride. And tonight, I do think I could use a drink to settle my nerves.

I watch her as she goes to the bar, her lithe, barre-class sculpted body capturing the eyes of every guy in the room. You wouldn't even think she'd need Tinder and all those dating apps, but most guys are too intimated to talk to her.

Then there's me. Guys will sometimes approach me once I smile at them (I have a pretty severe case of resting bitch face otherwise), but once I open my mouth, I usually say something awkward or off-putting. My sense of humor can be odd and I'm not always on everyone's frequency.

I lean back into the couch, doing that thing where I'm

scoping the crowd but trying not to make eye contact with the wrong guys. And by wrong guys, I mean the ones you have no interest in, ones who take a mere meeting of the eyes to mean something a whole lot more. I don't know why simply looking at someone means you want to have sex with them but anyway.

My phone vibrates in my purse and I fish it out.

It's a call from April which is weirder than weird. Maybe she could sense I was talking about her?

But even as I'm about to answer it, the unease in my chest builds and twists and I know this isn't a matter of her checking in with me and seeing how I'm doing. That's not like her. Something is wrong.

And usually when something is wrong, Pike or my parents would call me, not her.

My heart races as I press the talk button.

"April?" I ask, plugging my other ear and turning away from the noise of the bar.

Crying. I hear crying on the other end, sobbing, a kind of crying that doesn't come from a teenager getting dumped or bullied, but from something unfathomably worse.

"April? Is that you? What's wrong?" I ask, trying not to sound panicked.

"Maggie," she sobs. "Oh my god, oh my god. Maggie, they're dead!"

Time seems to fold in on itself in slow motion.

The terror flowing through me is spreading, slow sticky fingers that take over every muscle.

"Who is dead?" I cry out softly.

Oh god.

Who?

Who?

"They were murdered!" she cries, then erupts into even louder sobs. "The guy, he came for Dad."

Oh my god.

"He came for him and we weren't there," she goes on in hysterics. "Maggie, he shot them both. They're dead! Mom and Dad are dead."

"I..." I don't know what to say, what to feel. Surely this isn't actually happening. This isn't happening. This has to be a joke or a misunderstanding or maybe I'm dreaming? I look around me and I just see blurs and colors. I must be dreaming. "Are you...are you sure? Where's Pike?"

"Pike is talking to the police," she says. "They're dead, they're dead, they're dead!"

I shake my head, unable to understand any of this. "But they can't be dead, April. They don't die, this doesn't happen. It isn't happening. It isn't..." I try to swallow. "Who shot... who shot them? I don't get it."

"They're dead!" she screams and then breaks off into loud sobs that seem to shake the phone and then there is silence.

In the silence I realize I'm not breathing.

My heart is barely beating.

I feel outside of my body and inside my body all at once, reality of whatever this is refusing to set in.

"Hello?" someone says into the phone. I forgot I was even holding it to my ear and it takes me a moment to recognize the voice.

"Pike? Pike, what's going on?" I manage to say.

He clears his throat, his voice shaking as he says, "There was a guy, from the prison. He'd been out for a few months, I guess he hated Dad. He, uh...he came into the house and shot him. And Mom. As they watched TV in the living room. We were all at the fair, the neighbor heard the shots and called me."

To hear it from Pike, quiet, dependable Pike, suddenly makes it real.

"I can't believe this," I whisper. Because I can't. "Dad

would have shot back. Dad has his guns. How could he have walked in, wouldn't Walter have barked?"

"He shot Walter too."

Our beloved dog.

Somehow this is making it hit home, suddenly this seems like it could be real. An ex-convict broke into our house and shot our dog. Our wonderful dog.

But how could he shoot my parents? How could they be dead?

This isn't happening.

"The guy was arrested not too far from here," Pike says and I'm wondering how he's staying so calm. I guess he has to. Our parents are dead and I'm not there. He's the oldest.

But I'm their legal guardian.

"They're gone, Maggie," he says. "Gone." He takes in a deep breath and a small whimper comes over the phone. "I think you need to talk to the cops. Hold on."

Hold on.

Hold…on.

To what?

What is there to ever hold on to again?

What in this world will ever be solid and stable and good again?

"What happened?" Sam whispers as she sits down across from me, placing my drink in front of me. The drink. She bought me a drink. I would give *anything* in my power to go back in time, just five minutes, to that moment where my biggest worry was my lack of love life and money. To that time where my parents were alive.

"They're dead," I say to her, voice barely a whisper— flat, dull. "My parents are dead."

My world, my wonderful, crazy, hopeful little world, was forever gone.

Gone.

Gone.

"This can't be happening," I tell her, the shock starting to wear off, letting in tiny slivers of pain that I know will rip me apart, never to be put back again. "This can't be happening."

But it is.

PART ONE

CHAPTER ONE

MAGGIE

ONE YEAR LATER

TEHACHAPI, CALIFORNIA

"Where the hell are the Frosted Flakes?"

"Rosemary, don't say hell."

"We just have Cornflakes."

"Okay, who drank the last of the orange juice and put the carton back in the fridge?"

"Why don't you just sprinkle sugar on the Cornflakes, it's the same as Frosted Flakes."

"These aren't even Cornflakes. They're called Flakes of Corn. We can't even afford real Cornflakes."

"Did you know that Cornflakes were invented to stop masturbating?"

"April! Not in front of Callum."

"What's masturbating?"

I close my eyes and try to will myself back into the happy peaceful place that the yoga and meditation YouTube videos have been telling me about. I've been using them for months now to help my stress and anxiety, and I think I have to face facts that my happy peaceful place just doesn't exist.

"Guys, everyone shut up," Pike says in his deep voice, making everyone in the kitchen hush. "You're going to give Maggie an aneurysm."

A brief pause.

I can hear the grandfather clock in the hallway tick.

Finally, Callum asks, "What's an aneurysm?"

I open my eyes and can't help but smile at my youngest brother. He's only seven but he's bright and always asking questions. Always getting into trouble too, which I've been discovering lately.

"It's what I'll get if you guys don't behave."

"Then what's masturbating?"

"It's what you do when you can't get laid," April says under her breath.

"April," I reprimand her, but she doesn't shrink at all from my glare. She never does. Pisses me right off.

I sigh and mix some instant oatmeal into the boiling water on the stove and the kitchen dissolves into chaos again.

I never asked to be the legal guardian of my siblings. I never asked for my parents to be brutally murdered in the very home that we're all in. I never asked to give up my dreams of a career and a better life to come back here to Tehachapi and pick up the pieces of all the lives that were completely shattered.

I never asked for any of this. None of us had. But I'm here and I'm doing the best I can every day to ensure a brighter future for my brothers and sisters.

But...shit. It's hard as hell. I was close with my mother, though we had many years of ups and downs as all mothers and daughters do. But I never once thought about how hard it must be to raise us all. I knew she worked her ass off, I knew my father did too. I knew that we always just scraped by. I grew up in a world where if something broke, you either fixed it or waited years for a replacement that wasn't much better. Where bargain bins and thrift stores and generous neighbors were our only real source of goods.

But I never realized how emotionally tiring and complex it is to actually raise a family, especially one of this size with so many different, and often times conflicting, personalities.

There's Callum, who is the youngest. But when I say he gets into trouble, I mean the moment you tell him not to do something, he'll do it. And as bright and curious as he is, he's struggling at school and getting in fights with kids. He may smile a lot and have big sparkling blue eyes but I can see the pain and frustration underneath.

There are the twins, Rosemary and Thyme (yeah, yeah I know), who are eleven years old. Despite their names, which makes many eyes roll, the twins are smart, hard-working and diligent. They don't "match" either–Rosemary is a jock-in-training, Thyme is a goth-in-training. Contrary to what you might think, Thyme is the outgoing one and Rosemary can be competitive and sullen. But other than Pike, they're the biggest help to me in this house.

April is fourteen, boy-crazy, pretty—and she knows it—but angry too. All of that combined makes for a lethal force. My biggest fear is that she's going to get pregnant at some point, or maybe start doing drugs if she hasn't already. Maybe something worse. I worry about her the most and she seems to hate me the most, so I guess that's kind of how this relationship works.

Then there's Pike. Now eighteen and out of high school, Pike is old enough to be their legal guardian, so we kind of share the duties. He was all set to go to university on a scholarship except our parents death threw his last bit of high school out of whack and he pretty much bombed all the classes he needed to ace. He won't even try again. He now has his sights set on being a tattoo artist instead of the paleontologist he originally wanted to be. Talk about a one-eighty. He's quiet, doesn't talk much, and spends a lot of his time smoking cigarettes and putting ink on himself.

My family was always kind of complex before my parents died, so you can imagine that everyone here, including me, is still deep in the thick of it, each trying to deal with the loss the best we can.

"Hey," Pike says, coming over with some papers in his hand. "R and T are going on a field trip to the air force base and need a signature. Oh, and Callum's teacher wants us to have a meeting with her."

I sigh, stirring the oatmeal vigorously. "Why are we doing this now? Where were those papers last night?" I glance at the clock. I have to drop them all off at their schools before I head into work.

"Rosemary forgot," Thyme speaks up, looking sheepish.

"Oh and you didn't?" Rosemary says snidely.

I don't even bother looking at Callum. I know he's got a mischievous grin on his face. Don't know why he loves being in trouble so much.

"You know you can sign these," I tell Pike, snatching the papers from his hands and, oh jeez, I think he just added knuckle tattoos. "What are those?" I gesture to the fresh tattoos.

"Ink," he says simply, handing me a pen. "And they're hieroglyphics."

"Of what?"

"What are hieroglyphics?"

"Oh come on, Callum, don't be a dummy, you know what those are," Rosemary says.

"Rosemary, don't call him a dummy," I tell her and then

raise my brow at Pike. "Just promise me you won't start tattooing your face. You have a nice one."

He gives me a rare smile. "I do?"

"Don't get a big head about it, but yeah. You're the only hope this family has to go off and marry a sugar mama. Or daddy. We won't judge as long as you pass the coin down our way."

"What's a sugar–?"

"Callum, stop asking so many questions!" someone yells.

I quickly sign the forms and then stride over to the calendar on the fridge where I make a note of an after-class meeting with Callum's teacher.

"Do you want to go or should I?" I ask Pike. "It's in the evening."

He shrugs. I know he doesn't want to go and I also know that he will if I ask him. But he just started a job as a mechanic at a local garage and he's often exhausted. And the kids are legally my problem, not his.

"I'll go," I tell him.

"You sure?"

I give him a tired smile. "We could both go together but we don't have money for a babysitter." *And someone refuses to babysit*, I finish in my head.

He nods. He doesn't even have to look at April to know she's who I'm thinking about. If I was a better mother–scratch that, I am not their mother—but if I was better at setting down rules and discipline, then maybe I could convince April to watch her siblings.

But I'm not those things. With this family now, I have to pick my battles.

"Are you both still talking about me?" Callum asks innocently.

I give him a look that I hope will freeze him in his chair but like April, he's immune. He shovels Cornflakes–or No

Name Flakes of Corn–into his mouth and smiles, the milk dripping out of the ends.

I roll my eyes.

"Your teacher is unhappy with you, Callum," Pike says, pouring himself a cup of coffee and sitting down next to him. "Again."

Callum shrugs, eats more cereal, smiles.

Kid is going to grow up to be a sociopath.

"Maggie," April practically snarls as she dumps her plate in the sink. "We're going to be late."

I glance at the microwave clock. She's right.

I quickly get half my oatmeal down, grab an apple, and then yell, "Okay everyone, the bus is leaving now!"

When my parents died, we all inherited money. Unfortunately, my parents didn't have a lot of money in general and didn't get the best insurance plan. I got my money six months ago and it was only enough to buy us a much-needed minivan to take place of the broken-down piece of shit we had before, plus a little extra to put into savings. Pike also put his money in savings after buying himself a used motorcycle, which he then fixed up. Everyone else has to wait until they're eighteen to claim theirs, though I have a feeling April's will be for a one-way ticket out of here.

I don't blame her.

Thankfully the mortgage on the house is fully paid, and even though the big sprawling place is run down and sits on a hill above both Highway 58 and busy train tracks, providing rumbling and endless noise all hours of the day and night, it's home. Plus, the property taxes are cheap and manageable.

The twins fight over who gets shotgun, with Rosemary winning out in the end because of her supreme elbowing, while Thyme, Callum and April climb in the back. I honk goodbye to Pike, then wave at our closest neighbors, the

Wallace's, who are out gardening. They're old as sin and now that it's May and the scorching summer weather is already here, they can only be found outside in the early morning hours.

I drop off Callum first since his grade school is closest, then the girls, and take a deep, long inhale before I head to work.

After I got the news about my parents, there was no more university, no more journalism degree. I grabbed the first flight out and had Sam ship all my stuff back home. Good friend that she is, she even came a few days later with most of it, to be my support during the funeral.

The minute I arrived back in Tehachapi, chaos carved a permanent place in my heart, sometimes overshadowing my grief. Sometimes they would tag team me together and on those days I just wanted to lock myself in the bathroom, get in the bathtub and cry. I did that a few times, wanting to drift away to a place where the pain couldn't get me, where sorrow didn't reside in my bones, where I wasn't always so overwhelmed.

But I couldn't do that for long. I had to hold it together for the sake of everyone around me. There were meetings with lawyers and insurance companies, police and coroners, teachers, schools, funeral homes, neighbors. While my parents were always just getting by, they were well liked in the community, and everyone was grieving.

I don't feel like I even had the chance to grieve. I went to a therapist here in town but even that was a bit much since she was friends with my mother. So I've just dealt with their death the way I've been dealing with it.

Including breaking down in tears between dropping my siblings off and getting to work. It's only a ten-minute drive from one end of town to the other, but I feel it's the only time I have time to myself, time to think.

Inevitably, my thoughts turn to Mom and Dad and all that I've lost. In some ways, it's good to be insanely overworked and busy at all times because you don't have to feel the grief as much, but when I do find those moments alone, in the car or in bed at night, sometimes it can overwhelm me. Instead of a slow trickle, it's a tidal wave.

This morning though, I'm running late for work. I have no time to reflect and feel sad or wallow in self-pity. I got my old job back as a housekeeper at the local La Quinta hotel but at least I'm a step above where I used to be when I was a teenager. Actually, I've taken over my mom's old position, which is totally morbid, but hey it keeps food on our table.

I park the van in my usual spot, grab a spare uniform I keep shoved in the glove compartment (because of course I forgot mine in the wash at home), then climb into the backseat and get dressed. I've become a pro at this, like Clark Kent changing into Superman in a phone booth, except I'm turning into a maid in a minivan.

Then I'm rushing into the hotel through the back entrance, hoping to head straight into housekeeping without being spotted.

Of course, I run right into Juanita, my boss.

"Five minutes late, Maggie," she says to me in her no-nonsense voice. "This better not become a problem."

"I know, I'm sorry," I tell her, frantically tying my hair back. I hate that this has happened so often.

"You really oughta get that brother of yours to be dropping off the kids," she says, the stern features of her face melting into sympathy. "I honestly don't know how you do it."

"I barely do it and you know that," I tell her wryly. "Also, I wouldn't be able to do it without this job. So thank you, it won't happen again."

She just nods and I get out of her way and right to work.

As one can imagine, there has been a gargantuan learning curve when it comes to my new life, but thankfully everyone has been really supportive and understanding, Juanita included. I just know that their sympathy won't last forever. In the end, I'm either cut out for something or I'm not.

I'm still not sure what the verdict is.

I just know I can't afford to fail.

Even though being a housekeeper at a hotel isn't a glamorous occupation, especially a no-frills one by the highway that counts their breakfast waffles as a selling point, I don't hate it. Okay, that's a lie. There are many parts of it I hate, but they aren't what you think. The whole cleaning up after people, washing the shit out of the sides of the toilets (literally), finding used condoms, dealing with the overall grossness of errant body hair and fluids and whatnot, that's tolerable. Maybe it's because I grew up in a big family, maybe it's because I used to have this very job when I was a teen.

What I do hate is something that didn't even cross my mind when I was younger. When I was younger, being on the poor side didn't affect me as much as you would think. This isn't a prosperous town and there are many families struggling to make ends meet. My story isn't anything new.

But now that I left, that I've lived in New York, that I've seen the world out there, the world I could have had…I hate how society looks down on people like me. Housekeepers, cleaners, waitresses, blue-collar jobs, we're only given a fraction of the respect that we deserve.

This is most apparent when you have brazen businessmen (and women) treating you like dirt when you're on the job, making snide comments, giving you dirty looks when you're just trying to get by, complaining about a non-existent mess that maybe another housekeeper did and then, of course, not tipping.

Today I work as quickly and efficiently as possible,

keeping my mind free of distractions as best I can and just losing myself in the process. I have to admit, there is something rewarding about it, the fact that when you step into a room that looks like a bomb went off and you manage to make it look completely new again, you're able to see the improvement. And at the end of the day, I can look at the work I've done and feel like I've accomplished something.

I'm at the last room in my section on this floor and knock quickly on the door.

"Housekeeping," I say loudly.

No response.

I knock again and notice there is no "Do Not Disturb" sign on the doorknob. "Housekeeping," I say again, getting out my key.

I slide it in and the door opens with a beep.

I step inside to do my overall inspection, just to make sure that there isn't anyone inside. Happens more often than you'd think.

And as I do so, I nearly run into a man walking out of the bathroom.

A tall man. Like, a fucking giant.

A giant, naked, beast of a man.

I freeze on the spot and gasp and the guy keeps walking away from me into the room. He doesn't seem to hear me. In fact, I swear he's got swagger. Hot, naked-guy swagger.

I know I should quickly run out of there before he turns around and spots me. This might even be one of those encounters that I've heard about from other housekeepers, where there's a naked guy who "pretends" he didn't hear you knocking and your best bet is to leave immediately.

But this guy…

I can't take my eyes off of him.

I really, really should but he's just so…tall.

Large.

Smooth, tanned skin, impossibly broad shoulders, sinewy muscles that ripple down his back.

Then his ass.

Oh my god, his ass.

The fact that there's a bit of a tan line against his tawny skin makes it seem extra firm, like a juicy peach I just want to get down on my knees and bite into and–

He turns around.

I barely have enough time to remove my eyes from his nether regions and bring them up to his face where I glance those damn wireless earbuds in his ears.

He's listening to music.

Of course he is.

And he's staring at me with beautiful, sky-colored eyes open wide in shock.

"I'm so sorry," I blurt out, fighting like hell to keep my eyes at his level and not on his dick, which he's attempting to hide with his hand and even though it's only in my peripheral, and he has large hands, his attempt is futile. You cannot hide that thing.

"I didn't hear you come in," he says loudly, a hint of an accent on his words, and then he takes out his earbuds with his hands, leaving his dick to hang freely.

Don't stare, Maggie, don't stare.

Instead, I gawk.

That's one hell of a dick.

I swear I even see it twitch under my gaze—this long, dark, meaty-looking python that has me wishing this was a porno so I could drop to my knees. I've never had a penis that large and beautiful near the vicinity of my mouth before but I bet I could figure out what to do with it.

And while I'm staring dumbly at it, my key card slides out of my hands and onto the floor.

"Shit." I snap out of it and bend over to pick it up.

Just as he bends over to pick it up.

Frightened by the proximity of his giant penis, I flinch and straighten up.

Banging the top of my head against his jaw.

"I'm so sorry!" I yell again while simultaneously backing up, holding the top of my throbbing head.

He's even more dumbfounded than before, grabbing his jaw with one hand, staring at me in confusion.

"I'm so sorry!" I say again, aware that I'm yelling and I manage to turn around and head toward the door before I can assault him again.

"Uh, miss," he says just as I'm almost free, "your key."

Fuck!

I turn around and see him walk toward me, that fucking dick of his swinging freely like a battle-axe, holding out my key between his long fingers.

I slap my hand over my eyes so I can't see anything at all, manage to grab the key from his fingers, and then quickly turn and scuttle away. I'm pretty sure I mumble something like "I'm sorry," or even "penis" as I go, but thankfully I make it to the hallway and pull the door shut.

"Holy shit," I mutter to myself before pushing my housekeeping cart down the hall as fast as I can, my face burning up. "Holy shit."

God, I hope he doesn't lodge a complaint that says that I'm some maid that tried to see him naked or something. There was no "trying"—I couldn't not see him even if I wanted to.

You should have tried harder.

And I'm right. I should have. I guess it's a testament to either how lonely or how horny I am. My sex-life, my love-life, it's all been put on the backburner ever since I moved back to Tehachapi. It wasn't even anything great in New York, but at least I had gone on a few dates, gotten laid a few times. Now, I've been a sex camel for the last year and I think it's starting to weigh on me. Apparently, strange, naked men are enough for me to lose my fucking mind.

But he wasn't just some average man. He was well over six feet tall, with hands bigger than my face and a body that looked sculpted from bronze. He had eyes that reminded me of the sky on a summer day and an accent that spoke of a refined upbringing somewhere far more interesting than here.

He was honestly the most gorgeous, beguiling man I'd ever seen and that's not even including his penis.

I lean against the wall outside the housekeeping room and try to shake some sense into myself, shooting up a silent prayer. Hopefully that's the last time I see that guy.

CHAPTER TWO

MAGGIE

"Who listens to their earbuds when they get out of the shower?" Annette says to me, smirking over her beer as she does so.

"To be fair, I don't think he just got out of the shower," I tell her. "He wasn't wet at all. He was completely dry." And smooth. And clean. Every taut and tawny inch of him.

"Even so, it's La Quinta, not the Four Seasons," she says. "Who wants to walk around naked in their hotel room listening to music?"

She shudders and I reach over and lightly punch her on the arm, almost making her spill her beer. "Hey. I clean those rooms. You can rub your naked butt up and down that carpet. It's clean as a whistle."

"I'm only joking," she says with a tsk of mild disgust, picking up a napkin and wiping down the side of her beer bottle. "I guess I should watch what I say around you today, Miss Sensitive."

I roll my eyes and take a sip of my glass of wine. "I am not Miss Sensitive. I just had an off day."

"Which is why we're here," she says brightly, gesturing to

the Faultline Bar. The Faultline is one of the nicer bars in town. It's nothing fancy but at least the drinks are good and the staff is polite. Bonus points for not crawling with prison workers and ex-convicts. Not that I ever went in those bars before but I definitely couldn't handle it now. That's where you'd often find my dad after his shift and I'm sure I would feel him in the walls, not to mention the patrons there would probably love to talk about him to me, bringing up the ghosts.

Not that I often come out to the bars anyway. I don't have the time or the money. But I haven't caught up with Annette for a few weeks now and she said she was buying me a drink and Pike said he'd watch everyone while I was out. He didn't even hesitate. Maybe the stress is causing my face to crack.

Annette is in her fifties—she's actually my mother's best friend. Or was. It's always hard to talk about that because do you really stop being someone's friend when they've died? She's never stopped being my mother, even though she's not here anymore.

Anyway, I've always known Annette and always liked her, despite her being crass and crude, or maybe because of that. After my parents died, we started getting closer. She's a great person to talk to because she's still grieving in the same way I am, plus she's going through a bitter divorce and could use a friend. Her soon-to-be ex also works at the prison as the warden and he's very respected, so I think Annette is slowly losing her friend pool in this town, with most of them siding with him.

I sigh and lean back against the booth. "I need to get out of this town," I tell her ,and then I'm immediately hit with a million pangs of guilt and regret. There's no leaving, not now.

"You know, anytime you want time off, you can go," Annette says. "I'll keep saying it until you believe me, but I would be more than happy to watch the kids for a weekend. Go drive down to LA and live it up. Act like the twenty-three-year-old that you are. You're too young to have to deal with all of this."

"I can't take time off work," I tell her.

"Bullshit," she says, tapping her hot-pink nails against the table. "You've worked there for a year, you can get your two weeks. You just need to take them."

"But I'll probably need them for an emergency," I tell her. "What happens when April graduates and wants to go to college and I have to take her there, wherever that is." I pause. "Fuck, she probably won't even go to college. She won't get a scholarship, not with the way she's been acting and we all know we can't afford to pay right now. She might not even graduate."

"Regardless, Maggie," she says with emphasis. Even though she quit smoking years ago, her voice still sounds like she smokes five packs a day. "That's the future, and you know there's no point in getting upset about something that far ahead. Things change."

"But they don't change," I tell her. "Callum is only seven. I'm his guardian for another eleven years. Tehachapi is my prison until then."

"Look, Maggie. It's a prison for a lot of people. Literally."

I don't want to talk about it anymore. It feels futile and more than that, I feel rotten for even wanting to leave. Without me, my brothers and sisters have no one to keep their lives running. We're all in this together, whether we like it or not. And not one of us likes it. Every one of us wishes and prays every night that we could get our parents back, but wishing and praying doesn't change a thing.

"So how is your writing going?" Annette asks, quickly changing the subject.

It's not a better one. It's literally the worst question you can ask a writer.

"It's going...okay," I say slowly after I take a gulp of wine. It's a lie. It's not okay. Every night after everyone goes to sleep I try and steal an hour for myself to write but it's becoming harder and harder. I'm not inspired–I'm tired.

"And you've given up on the local paper?"

Ah yes, the local paper, The Tehachapi News. Not exactly what I was aiming for when I went to NYU, but now I'd die for an opportunity to write for them, even if I'm just covering the local mountain bike races. But as many times as I've shown up at their office and emailed my resume and samples and inquired about writing for them, it doesn't seem to go anywhere. I get the brush-off in a form letter without so much as an explanation.

"I've given up on a lot, Annette," I tell her, smiling as I do so because I don't want our outing to turn into gloom and doom. *Quit complaining and live in the moment*, I tell myself. *Enjoy this time out of the house and with your crazy friend while you can.*

"Looks like you're not the only one who has given up," she says, nodding to the bar.

My eyes drift over to a man who is hunched over the counter, seemingly sleeping or passed out. I had seen him earlier when I walked in here, my mind registering him as piece of the background. But now that Annette has brought him to my attention, I find myself focusing on him differently.

There's something about this man's shape, maybe even his vibe, that calls out to me. Impossibly broad shoulders. Long legs tucked under the stool. Only the nape of his tanned neck exposed along with his shiny, golden brown hair, his face buried by his arms. He's a big guy, a guy that's not from here, well over six feet tall and...

Oh my god.

"Oh my god, I think that's *him*."

"What?" Annette asks.

I stare at her with my mouth agape, noting the look of suspicion on her face. "I think that's him."

"Him who?"

"The guy. The naked guy."

"Mr. Magic Dick?"

I roll my eyes and lower my voice, my body somehow lowering against the table as I speak. "I didn't say it was magic, just that it was large."

"Same thing, sweetheart," she says.

I look back at the guy passed out at the bar and this time it's all clicking into place. It's him. I've seen him naked, so I can recognize him clothed.

What the hell is going on? What are the odds that I'd see him here, tonight?

Well, actually they're pretty good since Tehachapi doesn't have a thriving nightlife scene.

"You'd think a man of his size, and I mean his height, get your mind out of the gutter, would be able to handle his liquor a little better," Annette comments and as she does so, my eyes drift up to meet the bartender's. She's someone I went to school with, two years younger, and though I don't really know her she's looking at me pleadingly, like she needs help.

I should probably stay in my seat but something is compelling me to check out this situation a little closer. Probably because this stranger has made his second appearance in my life and once again it's in a state of vulnerability. Not that he seemed overly vulnerable when I saw him naked —actually it was more like he was owning the moment.

Yet here I feel like I need to do something, like I'm the one who's responsible for his ass. His very firm, gorgeous ass.

"I'll get you another beer," I tell Annette as I get up.

"Uh-uh," she says. "Make sure you get yourself something too."

I'm driving so one glass of wine is my limit.

I make my way over to the bar, smiling at the bartender. "Can I get another Bud Light?" I ask her before sneaking a glance at the guy. Now that I'm closer to him, I feel a rush of energy run through me, a feeling that takes me by surprise, like every nerve in my body is alive and dancing.

"Sure," the bartender says then glances at him warily. "Do you know him?"

"He's staying at the hotel I work at. That's all I know," I admit. Well, that and the fact that he looks fantastic naked. "I'm guessing he had too much to drink?"

She shrugs as she gets me the beer. "I guess so. When he came in here he seemed fine. Ordered a glass of vodka on the rocks and that was it. Next thing I knew he was just fucking passing out right there. I've shaken him a few times but he just groans."

Hmmm. A little concerning. "He didn't talk to you about anything?"

"No," she says, sliding the beer my way. "Asked for the drink and that's all. Definitely not from here, though. Has an accent. Scandinavian for sure, which makes it weirder. I spent a few weeks in Sweden and Norway last year, and let me tell you, those people can handle their liquor. This guy, not so much."

A customer appears at the other end of the bar, getting the bartender's attention and leaving me alone with the drunken Scandinavian mystery man.

I should get this beer right back to Annette who is watching me expectantly, but I take a few extra seconds to take him in.

My eyes slowly absorb all his details. The gleam of his hair, bronze and gold intertwined with the rich brown, just long enough that you could give it a good tug, to slide like silk through my fingers. The nape of his neck, lightly tanned with fine blonde hair, a spot that seems achingly exposed and secretly sensitive, that disappears into the collar of his black leather jacket. It fits his broad shoulders like a glove, the leather seeming both soft and well-crafted. As my attention drifts down to his dark gray jeans and boots, I'm realizing how well-tailored and expensive all of his clothes look. He doesn't seem like the type of person who would stay at La Quinta for fun. He's someone better suited for the fancier hotels and places. A businessman.

But what business could he be in?

Porn. With that dick, it's gotta be porn.

"Hey," I find myself saying softly, reaching over to nudge his arm with my elbow. A low rumble emits from him but he doesn't move. "So I'm the girl who walked in on you naked earlier today and I just wanted to apologize. It wasn't intentional." I pause, aware that there's a chance he might be listening, also aware that Annette is still staring at me questioningly from across the bar. "To clarify, this happened at the hotel. I was the maid and you were, well, you were walking out of the bathroom totally naked. I guess you didn't hear me. Why were you listening to music anyway? What music was so important that you had to stick in your earbuds and strut around like you were at home? Speaking of home, where the hell are you from?"

I stare at him for a few more minutes, watching his back rise and fall. Finally, he makes a breathless sound and moves his head back and forth until it settles with the side of his face tilted toward me, eyes closed.

I'm struck by the intimacy of the moment, dazzled by how gorgeous he looks up close. It was hard to focus on his face earlier for obvious reasons, but now I feel like I can really drink him in.

Though his jaw is strong and wide and dusted with stubble, there's something almost innocent about the way he looks. Maybe everyone looks this sweet when they sleep but his eyelashes are definitely enviable and his full lips seem curled into a soft smile, contrasting with the hollowness beneath his sharp cheekbones.

Even fully clothed and passed out drunk on a bar, he's still the most gorgeous man I've ever seen.

"Guess I'll be calling the cops later," the bartender says with a sigh, breaking the spell as she comes over to me and stares at the sleeping giant with disdain.

"Why? What did he do?"

She folds her arms and gives me an *are you kidding me* look. Suddenly I know what April is going to look like when she's older. "The guy is *huge*. And I might be tougher than I look but I'm not about to drag his ass out of here by myself at the end of the night."

"But he hasn't done anything wrong," I say feebly.

"If you want to take care of him, be my guest," she says before turning her back to me.

I take another glance of him and head back over to Annette.

"What. On. Earth. Were you doing?" she asks as she snatches the beer out of my hand. "That wasn't just getting me a beer."

I shrug and slide into my seat across from her. "I don't know, I wanted to see what the situation was."

"And?"

"And I don't know. He's drunk."

"I can see that."

"But something doesn't fit here," I tell her, jerking my chin toward him. "The bartender says he had one drink and it was lights out. Plus, she says he's all Scandinavian and shit and probably drinks vodka for breakfast. Then there's the fact that he's rich."

She cocks her penciled brow at me. That has her attention. "Rich?"

"His clothes are expensive. He's well-put together."

"And so what's a rich man doing in Tehachapi?"

I shrug. That part has me stumped. "I don't know. Passing through maybe."

"And Scandinavian?"

"That's what the bartender thinks. Swedish or Danish or something."

She purses her lips and looks me over.

"What?" I ask, automatically feeling defensive over the way she's looking at me.

"You're taking far too much interest in this person."

I frown. "Earlier you were talking about his magic dick."

"I didn't expect to see him here. Honey, I'm just looking out for you. Don't get involved with someone staying at your hotel."

"How am I involved?" I ask incredulously, throwing my arms out for equal measure. "I'm a concerned citizen."

She shrugs and settles back in her seat, the bottle at her mouth. "He's none of your concern, and you've always been one to go out of your way to help people but honestly, you're already spreading yourself too thin." She pauses and then says, "Did I tell you what Hank said?"

Hank is her soon-to-be ex-husband and he's never not saying or doing something. She launches into the latest tirade which I make myself listen to. I know she needs a friend and an ear as much as I do.

But my eyes are almost always finding their way back to the drunk foreign dude. I find myself wondering how he got so drunk–someone that tall and well-built isn't a lightweight–then why he's here in Tehachapi with his Scandinavian accent and pricey clothes. And, yeah, my mind keeps bringing up the image of him naked. Over and over again.

Maybe it's the sob story or the fact that neither I nor Annette have been out in a while, but she has more beer and I end up having another glass of wine that she so graciously buys for me. By the time we're ready to go, the bar looks close to closing.

I'd been keeping an eye on the guy all night. He hasn't moved at all. Now it looks like he has to and the bartender is shaking him awake while shooting me a worried look, as if it's also my problem now.

"Can you take him back to the hotel?" she shouts across the room at us as we're heading to the door. "Or I'll call the cops to give him a lift." It almost sounds like she's threatening me, like the fact that I'd met the guy earlier in the day meant that he was somehow mine.

Annette snorts and says to the bartender. "Honey, this ain't our problem. We don't know him."

"And he's not my problem either," she says.

The man grumbles something in a foreign language, and for the first time actually sits up in his chair, waving the bartender's arm away.

Annette takes a step backward while I stare at him in surprise.

"I'm calling the cops if you don't get your ass out of here!" the bartender rallies at him, sounding tough though her voice is shaking.

The guy can barely open his eyes, but he seems to understand. He slurs more foreign words, most of which I think are swears, and tries to get to his feet.

Then he sways unsteadily, and without thinking I rush over to him, my hands going to his chest to push him back, and keep him upright. It's like trying to keep a redwood tree from falling over, and yet somehow it works and he slumps back onto the chair. If he truly was dead weight, I would have been crushed.

"We'll take him," I say, my heart racing at my proximity to him, the crazy strength I just pulled out of me.

I'm surprised I said it.

So is Annette.

She reaches out and grabs my arm, tugging me away from him. "What the hell is wrong with you? We'll take him? He's not a dog you adopt from a shelter, Maggie."

"Good luck," the bartender mutters, walking back down the bar with a flourish like a teacher passing off an unruly kid to its parents.

Now I'm committed.

To what, I don't know.

I wave my arm at him. His eyes are still closed, and his chin keeps dipping down into his chest. His chest. Hard as cement. I can't believe I was just pressing my hands into it moments ago. He didn't even smell like alcohol, just something musky and woodsy, cozy and comforting.

"We can't leave him here," I tell her.

"Yes we can," Annette says, looking around the bar for someone else to save us from this situation, but we're the last ones in here. "It's not your problem. It's definitely not my problem. Let the girl call the cops. They can deal with him."

It's definitely the easier, saner option. I can't say why I feel like I have to be this stranger's knight in shining armor tonight, but I do. "Either you help me get him to the hotel or I do it alone."

Annette stares at me.

I stare right back at her.

I've made up my mind.

Finally, she sighs, rolls her eyes, and taps her pink nails along her arms. "Fine. But I'm trying to think like your mother. She would not approve of this."

"My mother would be proud that I'm going out of my way to help a stranger. That's exactly the kind of thing she would do." Her comment has me on edge, defensive. My mother was always the one to come to someone's aid.

"Well now I'm worried you're dazzled by his cock and not thinking right," she says.

"Shhhh," I tell her sharply, looking over at the guy to see if he heard. I can't tell. It does look like he's about to slide off the bar stool at any moment.

She sighs again. "Okay, let's go. You take one side, I'll take the other."

We flank him on both sides, I lift his arm up over my shoulder, pressing my fingers into his chest again and give Annette a nod. With a groan, we both pull the guy up to his feet. It's not easy given that he's over a foot taller than I am but he's somewhat supported.

Luckily I'm parked by the entrance, and working together in unison we manage to walk the guy outside, even though he almost takes a tumble once or twice, nearly bringing us down with him.

We get him into the back seat of the van where he immediately collapses and then I drive us off toward the hotel.

"I can't believe we're doing this," Annette says in a low voice, shaking her head as she watches the streetlights pass by. "You haven't even thought this through. How are you going to get him to his room? You going to go through his pockets for a room key?"

"I'll use my housekeeper card."

"What if someone from your work sees you?"

Hmmmm.

Maybe I haven't thought this through.

"I'll be sneaky."

"No, *we* will *try* and be sneaky and try is the operative word because it's not going to work because clearly you've never lugged around Andre the Giant before. You're going to get caught. Then what?"

I give a half-hearted shrug. "Tell them the truth?"

"Won't it look like you're sleeping with the guests or something? Don't you have a no fraternizing rule?"

"Not on paper," I say slowly though now I'm remembering when I was in high school, one of the housekeepers got caught having sex with someone in the hotel room and she was fired. I think she tried to pass him off as a boyfriend but it was clear that he was just a guest and they didn't really know each other.

Shit.

Getting fired is the last thing I need, let alone having rumors fly about me sleeping with the guests.

"I say we just pull up to the hotel, slide open the door, and kick him out," she says. "He'll roll down the hill toward the hotel. Piece of cake."

"Like we're dumping a dead body?" I cry out softly, mouth agape.

She throws her hands up. "Well, honey, I don't know."

I sigh and quickly make a U-turn in the middle of the road. Luckily it's late and pretty much deserted.

"Where are you going?" Annette asks, looking around wildly.

"Taking him to your house."

"My house?" she shrieks which makes the stranger in the backseat stir and yell something that I'm still certain isn't English before he passes out again.

I eye him in the rearview mirror, wondering if I've made a colossal mistake. I mean, what if he realizes where he is and starts freaking out while I'm driving? I don't know this guy, I don't know how he reacts. Suddenly I imagine us re-enacting that scene from *Tommy Boy* when the deer wakes up in the back of the car.

All the better to drop him off at Annette's.

"Yes, your house," I repeat.

"No way. No. Nope. Maggie, I have spies."

"*Spies?*"

"Hank still comes by unannounced. We're still in divorce proceedings. The neighbors are on his side. What will it look like if I bring some guy home?"

"You're not doing anything wrong."

She just stares at me with devil eyes. "It doesn't matter. I'm not taking any chances, especially not for someone I don't know."

I sigh, my hands squeezing the steering wheel. She's right. I don't want to get her in trouble and I don't want this to hurt her divorce in anyway. People can be vicious here.

At the same time, I can't take him to the hotel. It will look wrong and I'll get in shit, I just know it.

And I don't feel right about getting him put in a drunk tank either.

I exhale again noisily, knowing what I'm about to do.

"What?" Annette says, frowning at me.

"I'm taking him home."

"Maggie."

"I'll put him in Mom and Dad's room," I tell her. "He can sober up."

"Maggie," she says again, voice sharper now. "No. You don't know this guy. You can't bring him in your house. Not with your brothers and sisters there."

I know she has a point. "They're all asleep right now. I'll tell Pike about it. Pike is big enough to handle him."

She shakes her head. "No."

"Annette. It's happening. Now do you want me to drop you off first?"

"Oh, like I'm letting you do this on your own."

"Look, we'll get out his wallet and you can keep it as

collateral or something. Just in case something goes wrong."

She stares at me, and I know she's wondering what the hell is going on in my head. I don't know. Lately I feel like I'm knowing who I am less and less, so maybe it shouldn't be surprising that I'm acting out of character. Or maybe this is my character now. Maybe I'm so starved for something different and new that I'm willing to haul a drunk guy to my house and use my parents old bedroom as a drunk tank.

"I should stay the night," she says.

"It won't be a problem," I tell her.

"Famous last words."

Five minutes later I'm pulling the van outside of the house. I peer up at it through the windshield. The lights are all off except for the lamp in the foyer and Pike's room. We run a really tight ship when it comes to the electric bill, so lights out really means it's lights out.

"This is ridiculous, you know that," Annette says as she gets out.

"I know."

Being as quiet as possible, we slide the van door open and manage to get him out and into the house.

We whisper to each other as we attempt to get him up the stairs, trying to keep our voices down even though at one point the dude tilts to the left and nearly flattens me against the wall. It would almost be comical if it wasn't such hard work. It would be even sexy under any other circumstance.

Finally, we get to the second floor and stagger down the hallway and around the corner to my parent's old bedroom. I open the door and quickly flick on the light.

I don't come in here very often. It's like a tomb in some ways. The curtains are usually closed and everything is as it was before they died. None of us have the heart or the nerve to move things around much. I know the bed linens have been changed because we've had guests over and I've occasionally come in here to dust, but I don't spend much time. The memories hurt.

Even now it feels like their ghosts are in the walls, shadows in the dark. Loving ghosts, but ghosts all the same. Reminders of lives that once were, a love I'd do anything to have back.

I swallow hard and bring my focus back to the guy as we get him backward onto the bed where he falls like a sawn tree, making the bed shake from the impact of his large frame.

Annette flips him over so he's on his side and then brings out the wastebasket from the ensuite bathroom, placing it below him while I undo his boots.

"Don't tell me you're going to undress all of him," she asks, brow raised.

"Shhh," I say to her in a hush. "Keep your voice down."

"Not answering my question."

I ignore her and finish taking off his boots and with a sigh she starts struggling with his leather jacket, trying to remove it. He moans something softly, his eyes still closed, head flopping against the pillow as she finally gets it off of him.

She sighs, folding the jacket up in her arms and staring down at him. "He really is handsome, isn't he?"

I don't say anything to that. I also don't mention he's wearing size fifteen boots. I didn't even know that size existed but it seems to coincide with the size of his dick.

When the other boot is off, I take the giant pair and place them against the wall as Annette puts the jacket down on the chair across from the bed. My mother always used that chair as a place to throw her uniform and clothes before crawling into bed. It was the only place and time she allowed herself to be messy and free. When morning came, everything was always neatly put away.

Annette gets an impish look in her eyes and suddenly

reaches across the guy, her hands going for his pants.

"What are you doing?" I whisper harshly.

She bites her lip as she reaches around underneath his ass and then triumphantly pulls out his wallet.

"Ta-da."

She flips it open and I come over to her side to peer at it.

There isn't much to it. A Visa debit card with no name on it, a couple of bucks in cash, and picture ID. Annette takes it out of the slot and flips it over and back. It looks brand new, the black and white picture recent. It says Körkort Sverige on top, whatever that means, and below that Andersson Johan.

"Is Andersson his first name or last name?" she whispers to me. "Or his address?"

"Maybe his name is Körkort Sverige?"

"I think that's Russian."

"No, Russian uses a totally different alphabet."

"What the fuck is going on here?" Pike's voice bursts through the room and both of us jump in surprise, the wallet flying out of Annette's hands and onto the bed, landing right on Körkort Sverige's broad chest.

I suck in my breath, waiting for him to wake up, but he only stirs slightly.

I turn to look at Pike who is staring at both of us incredulously, his hair mussed from sleep. "Why are you…" He takes a step toward us and his eyes go to the stranger's legs sticking off the end of the bed. "Who the hell is that?"

"It's a long story," I tell him. "And keep your voice down."

Pike looks to Annette expectantly. "What's happening? Why are you both in here and who the hell is this guy on the bed?" He comes over to us and stares down at him. "Shit, is he dead?"

"No," I tell him, putting my hands on his shoulders and pushing him back. "He's very drunk and he's sleeping it off here."

"But *who* is he?"

"Körkort Sverige," I tell him. "He's foreign, he's drunk, he was staying at the hotel and we saw him at the bar and it was either he stays here, or the cops put him in the drunk tank."

He stares at me blankly. "And what was wrong with the drunk tank?"

"Look, I'm sure he'll just wake up in the morning and be on his way."

Pike is not convinced. I don't blame him. I am absolutely crazy for doing this. Funny thing is, I haven't felt this engaged about something in, well, in a long time.

"If you think I'm going to sleep a wink tonight with a stranger in the house, you are sadly mistaken," he eventually grumbles. "I'm going to be stationed outside his door with a gun."

I glare at him. I hate that he's kept my parents guns, considering what happened to them. "It'll be fine."

"Well, since Pike's got a handle on this, I'm heading home," Annette says. She puts her hand on my shoulder and squeezes it. "And I'm calling a cab. It's probably best you stay here in case he wakes up. At least you'll be a familiar face."

If I am, it won't be in a good way. "Are you sure?"

She's already bringing out her phone and dialing as she walks past us. "I'm sure. Call me tomorrow and let me know how it goes, okay honey?" She gives Körkort one last look over her shoulder. "And good luck. I don't approve of any of this but I suppose you have to make your own mistakes."

When she's left the room, I exchange a glance with Pike.

"What's gotten into you?" he says to me.

"I honestly don't know," I say with a sigh. I reach over and pluck the wallet from his chest, holding it to me. If he tries anything, does anything, then at least I have proof of who he is.

Whoever he is.

CHAPTER THREE

VIKTOR

THREE WEEKS EARLIER

STOCKHOLM, SWEDEN

"Your Royal Highness?"

The phrase strikes fear in my heart, prompting a rush of bitterness to flow through me like bile. I glare at Dr. Bonakov, a warning in my eyes. "Please don't call me that," I tell him, my voice hard. "I've been seeing you practically my whole entire life and you've always called me Viktor."

He gives me a placating smile, seeming unsure how to deal with me now, and hastily pushes his glasses further up his nose. In some ways, Dr. Bonakov has been more of a father figure than my actual father, so to hear him speak to me so formally, stings.

"You were always addressed as Your Royal Highness before," he calmly points out.

"But not by you. That's what you called Alex. I was always Viktor. I wish to remain Viktor to you."

"All right, Viktor," he concedes. He clears his throat, a sign of the lecture that's about to follow. Maybe one reason he feels like a father figure is that he advises as much as he listens. "You know you're supposed to contact me when things become too much. I shouldn't have to hear it from your mother herself."

I let out a sour laugh, adjusting myself on the couch. "One month ago my brother died. One month ago I became the heir to the throne, something you know I've never wanted. Things are permanently *too much*. Every second of every day. Do you seriously want a phone call every minute of every hour? Do you really want the agonizing play-by-play of how my life is fucking falling apart?"

He watches me carefully for a few moments, tapping his pen against his notepad. He's seen my outbursts before but not like this. I'm not myself lately. I'm not sure I'll ever be myself again.

Then he sighs, looks down at his paper. I relax a little now that his gaze is off of me. "I know this is a big transition for you. I know you're grieving. Not only your brother but the loss of the life you had before. Things will take time."

I grunt. How he can try and sum everything up so neatly is infuriating. Everyone always doles out words of apparent wisdom, catchphrases they think either encompass your whole experience or they say things that make themselves feel better.

It will take time.
You will come out stronger.
One day at a time.
He is always in our hearts.
Life isn't a bed of roses.
Time heals all wounds.
It's all bullshit.

"But," he continues, "the only way that you'll be able to get through this is to realize when you're on the verge of losing control. When you're drowning. When it overwhelms you, not just your new responsibilities, but the grief. The sorrow. If you don't learn to manage it now, you'll never be able to move forward."

"I don't fucking want to move forward," I snap at him, the blood pounding hot in my head. "I want things to go back. I just want everything to go back."

Silence fills the room. Because there's nothing Dr. Bonakov can say. Nothing anyone can do. If I drown, I drown.

Tomorrow it will have been exactly one month since my older brother Alex died. He was only thirty-four. The public has no idea how he died. They have been fed neat little lies, something tidy enough to appease them. But I know the truth and that the burden I carry, as we all carry, as loved ones who didn't do enough to save him.

None of us have been given enough space and time to grieve. I was never the media darling before. That was all Alex. Composed, kind, the stature of a king, it was Alex that everyone loved, that everyone wanted a piece of. I was always left more or less alone. I was a prince but he was the heir apparent, the future king. As long as I behaved myself, the people, the press, the world, took little interest in me.

All of that has changed. Been flipped on its head. My grief, my taking over *his* role, has caused a firestorm that is constantly trying to burn me down. Everywhere I go, everywhere I turn, people are there, eyeing me up like some exotic dessert that they want a bite of before anyone else. They want to see the sorrow in my eyes, they want to know how I will handle being the future King of Sweden. They want to see me rise to the challenge just as much as they want to see me fall.

I don't think I can rise. I can barely get to my knees.

The doctor sighs and starts scribbling something quickly on his prescription pad. "With what happened to your brother, you know I'm wary about giving out strong medication, but I do think this will help you over the next coming while."

He leans over and hands me the slip of paper. As usual, I can't read his writing.

"Here," he says as he gets up and goes over to his desk. He brings out a pill bottle and shakes two out into his hand then comes back over to me and places the pills in my palm.

"Take one when you need peace," he says. "See how it goes at first. You might not even need the prescription. But heed the warnings, please. Don't take it with alcohol. Take it when you're alone and needing comfort of the heart."

He takes a long pause, breathing in, breathing out, studying me as I stick the pills in the pocket of my jeans. "I know that talking to me is the last thing you want to do, Viktor. I know that's why it's your mother calling me, worried. But even though she is a queen, she is still your mother and she is suffering just as much, or more, as you. Please, for her sake, try not to add to your worries. Talk to her and if you can't, reach out to friends. I know King Aksel suffered a similar loss when the queen of Denmark died. People like that can help you get through it."

I swallow, feeling guilt wash over me. The last thing I want is for my mother to worry. I know she's struggling, I know she's turning to my father and finding little comfort, I know she worries I might suffer a similar fate.

I get up and thank the doctor, my voice barely audible, and grab my coat before stepping out of his office and into the waiting room. My private secretary, Frederick, gets up, his messenger bag slung over his shoulder, his iPad out with all of the day's schedule on it.

"How did it go?" he asks politely as we walk to the lift.

Freddie is a few years younger than me and has been my private secretary, personal assistant, and constant companion since the moment he graduated from university in England. He's smart, fluent in several languages besides just Swedish and English, efficient, incredibly well-organized and in some ways, is probably the person closest to me.

He was also close to Alex but unlike me, he's thrived under the grief and the pressure of his job as I've been catapulted in a new direction. My public appearances and engagements before were very limited. Now, I'm shuffled along on a packed schedule that he meticulously maintains. Without him I would be even more lost.

Without him I would be free.

"It was fine," I mumble to him, not wanting to get into it.

"Good to hear," he says simply as the lift doors open

Sometimes I wish there was a bit more warmth from Freddie–he's polite to a fault, never one to pry into your feelings or private life, never one to open up about his own–but I'm used to it.

"So the rest of the day," Freddie says, launching into it the moment the doors close. I also wish Freddie would give me some space, but he's under orders of the king and queen to keep me going and in line. These days, that means never giving me a break, just sending me to a therapist instead, as if that will change a thing. "In an hour there's a press conference just outside the palace, so we'll need to get you home to change."

I glance down at myself. I'm in gray jeans, boots, a navy fisherman's sweater and a long, gray wool coat that I carry folded up in my arms that wasn't needed on this mild spring day. "This won't suffice?"

"You have to be in the formal garb."

I groan. "Not even a suit? Alex did all his interviews in a suit."

Freddie gives me a furtive glance underneath his sharp glasses. A tight smile follows. "Your parents want to ensure that the public knows you're the new heir."

My heart starts to race again. "But everyone fucking knows by now. The fucking funeral was *televised*."

The doors to the ground floor open and Freddie gives me another look, this one to remind me once again who I am, where I am.

He grabs me by the arm and leads me away from the front doors. Stationed there are members of the royal patrol, my bodyguards, but even so, we go in and out through the back entrances so that no one knows I've been here. I can't imagine how it would look to know the Prince of Sweden was seeing a shrink. Though, fuck, we all have. It's practically a requirement for royalty.

"Didn't I just do a press conference?" I add as we step out into the back alley and get in the waiting car.

"Sorry," Freddie says, buckling himself in with one hand while scrolling through his iPad with the other. "After the press conference you'll have a meeting with the literacy charity that Alex founded, then you have a radio interview with the national broadcast in Helsinki. Tonight there is a ball held by the Countess at the Alandel Palace. You must go to that one. It's in honor of your new role, and the daughter of the countess would make an ideal girlfriend. Those are your mother's words, of course."

I can scarcely breathe. The walls of the car seem to close in around me, a black haze that quickly thickens. I'd barely woken up this morning before I was shuttled off to a meeting with my parents and the royal advisers, then was sent straight to Dr. Bonakov. The rest of my day is never-ending, just like it was yesterday, just like it will be tomorrow.

Just like it will be for the rest of my life.

"Pull over," I tell Kris, the driver. "Pull over!"

We've only made it a block from the doctor's office, still in the alley.

Kris pulls the car over.

I open the door and get out, walking, stumbling down the lane.

I don't know where I'm going.

I don't know what I'm doing.

I just have to get out of here.

And that's when I have an idea. I can just keep walking. Walk until this alley turns into the street, walk down the street until it turns into the sea. Keep going until I'm in its icy depths, until I'm with Alex.

"Your Highness!" Freddie yells after me.

I don't stop. Fuck that term. Even in a state of panic, I'm not Viktor to anyone. The formalities remain. The constraints. I keep walking, faster now, the end of the alley shining like a beacon under a burst of sunlight. I fish out that pill that the doctor gave me and force it down my throat.

Two of my guards suddenly appear at the end of the alley, blocking me in.

I would never ever have dreamed of fighting them before.

But I am a great deal taller than they are, and larger and stronger than at least one. They have been trained to protect me, but training has no match for raw emotion, for pure anger and desperation unscripted.

I could do a lot of damage.

I stop in front of them, feeling cagey, my fists opening and closing. I think one is Tor, the other is Gustav. I look in their eyes. They're determined to keep me in line though a bit wary of the force they'll need to use in order to do it.

I just don't fucking care anymore.

"Let me pass," I growl at them.

They exchange a worried glance. Good. They should worry about me. I'm worried. Everyone is fucking worried.

"We're here for your protection, your highness," Gustav says. I can hear Freddie's shoes slapping on the ground behind me as he gets closer, echoing against the buildings.

"I'm going for a walk," I tell them, looking them dead in the eyes and trying to keep my voice steady.

"Your Highness," Freddie says from behind me, breathless. I don't even glance at him.

"As Your Royal Highness, the Crown Prince of Sweden, heir to the throne, I command you to let me pass. I don't want to be at your mercy anymore. I don't wish to do anything you have planned, Freddie, and that means everything. I just want to be alone, to do what I fucking please."

"Your highness," Freddie says again, nearly chiding me. Now I'm looking at him. At six-foot-five I'm just a foot over him though he barely shrinks away. Just adjusts his tie and gives me a stern look that could rival my father's. I wonder if he's been giving him tips. "I don't think it wise for you to cancel any of today's engagements," he goes on. "Your parents would be very upset, and it would look terrible for the monarchy."

I frown at him, my fists still balled until they feel tight and numb. "What looks terrible for the monarchy is having me paraded around town acting like everything is fine when it's not fine. My brother is dead. We should all be allowed to grieve."

"It's been a month, your Highness," he says carefully, looking away as if he's ashamed he said it. Well he should be ashamed. It's the most awful thing I've heard in a long time.

"Have some respect for who would have been your future king," I sneer.

"Have some respect for yourself," he says, boldly. "You have been nothing but a handful and I know that this is grief and I know this is normal, but you are not a normal citizen, your highness. You are the Crown Prince, you are the heir to the throne, you are all of these things and more, and if you don't learn to control yourself, to put on a mask and act out your roles and your duties, then you'll never rise to be the man that your brother was."

I don't even think. All I do is feel.

I feel my arm swing back and my fist come forward.

Right toward Freddie's cheek.

Somehow Gustav is faster than I am.

Maybe this medication is already kicking in.

I clock Gustav in the jaw instead, my knuckles exploding against him as he falls back, knocking Freddie to the ground as he does so.

I'm instantly filled with both rage and regret.

An arm shoots out, Tor, attempting to hold me back from any further damage.

There's no point. Whatever fight I had in me is gone.

I can't even look at Freddie. Freddie who has been with me for so long, a man I've never been violent or rude to before in all my life, a man who is just doing his best to keep me in line. I can't look at Gustav either, a man hired to protect me and yet here I am hitting him. Accident or not, I had been ready to fight all of them from the start.

Handle me.

They can't handle me.

And I'm someone that needs to be handled. Not carefully, like some fragile gift, but with brute force.

I hate what I've become.

Freddie was right. I'll never rise to be the person my brother was. And the worst part of all that is, my brother couldn't rise to the person he was expected to be either.

I can't stay here.

I must keep moving.

I duck back away from Tor and walk past him to the street, grateful that no one saw the fight that just erupted here, a fight that would be splashed all over the papers, all over the world. They don't stop me this time.

I shuck on my coat, suddenly cold, and hail a cab passing by.

"Take me to the dirtiest bar you can think of," I tell the cab driver as I climb in the backseat, handing him a stack of kronor. "And don't take me back until I'm sufficiently drunk."

"Viktor."

My mother's voice rings through the fog in my brain, coming in like music in a dream. Something that you know isn't existing outside your brain and yet has a whole life of its own. So real.

"Viktor, darling, please wake up. You're safe now."

Safe?

I open my eyes and that in itself is a struggle. It's like they want to stay shut forever, like my body is already telling me to give up. Go back into that darkness. She lies. It's safer there, not here.

"There you are," my mother says softly.

And there she is, sitting on the edge of my bed in...

Wait, this isn't my bed. This is my old room in the palace where I grew up, the palace where my parents live. The king and queen.

She gives me a tight smile and I then notice my father

hovering by the door. It's closed. There's no one else in the room except for...

Oh wait, Dr. Bonakov. He's sitting in an ornate velvet chair by a desk, sipping a cup of tea.

"What happened?" I ask, my voice sounding groggy, foreign, far away.

I can't remember a thing.

And what I can remember is horrible. Getting out of the car. Fighting with Freddie. Punching Gustav. Escaping. Getting a cab to a dive bar in the worst neighborhood possible. Sitting alone in the corner, avoiding people's eyes, having shot after shot of vodka until...

This.

"You had a bit of an...episode," my mother says. "Luckily, the people who you had the episode around were the types to not remember any of it afterward."

I glance at the doctor. "I took one of the pills," I told him.

He nods. "I figured. Thankfully you're here now and all in one piece."

"But how did I get here?"

"The taxi driver that drove you to the bar kept coming around every hour to keep an eye on you. Finally, he phoned our press office. Didn't even take it to the tabloids."

"Proves that not all Stockholm cabbies do the devil's work," the doctor says impishly.

"Viktor," my mother says, her voice becoming more stern now, ignoring him. "We can't go on like this. We just can't."

I attempt to sit up in bed, my head ringing, pounding like a parade of horses is trampling over my brain. She slides a pillow behind me and through a wince, I get a better look at her. She's dressed in her nightgown and robe, her blonde hair in curlers, her eyes and nose red from crying. My father is in a suit, his face giving me nothing though I swear he's got a few more gray hairs than he did yesterday.

"I'm sorry," I say, clearing my throat. "I'm sorry I lost my temper."

"Lost your temper?" my father says gruffly. His words ooze with disappointment. "Losing your temper is snapping at someone because they gave you a hard-boiled egg instead of soft. What you did was act violently toward not only one of your guards that are charged with protecting you, a guard who would lay down his life for you, but with Frederick Vereberg, who is one of the few people left here with any brains. That wasn't losing your temper, Viktor, that was losing your goddamn mind."

I have no rebuttal to that. He's right. I have lost my mind.

"I don't know what to say."

My mother sighs and looks over at my father, raising her brows. He just scoffs and turns away, hands behind his back, acting like the crown moulding around the door is far more fascinating than what's to be done with his son.

His only son.

Once again, the sorrow hits me like an ice pick to the chest.

"Dear boy," my mother says softly, placing a frail hand on mine. I stare down at it, peppered with sunspots, with lines and veins, and I realize that no one else outside this room gets to see my mother this way. To the nation she is Her Royal Highness, Queen Elin of House Nordin. To me, she is a mother. A mother who just lost her oldest son, who is trying her hardest to hold it together for the good of her country.

"I've been discussing you with Dr. Bonakov," she goes on.

"You're sending me to a mental institution?" I ask.

She doesn't smile at that. It was a poor joke.

"I'm sending you somewhere," she says.

I cock my head at her, wondering what she means, as my father comes over and hands me a large yellow envelope.

"What is this?" I ask, opening it. Onto my lap falls a

driver's license, a credit card, a bank card and a passport. My picture is on all of them with the name Johan Andersson. My place of birth has changed from Stockholm to the city of Malmö. My birthday remains the same.

I stare at them blankly, my brain too drugged and sluggish to comprehend.

"This is your therapy, Viktor," my mother says. She looks at Dr. Bonakov who nods ever so slightly. "We know that you haven't been handling the changes here very well."

"So you're giving me a new identity?"

"Temporarily," the doctor says. "It's a break. A break that we would all rather see you take than abdicate."

"Abdicate?" Who said anything about abdicating?

"Look," my father says, walking over slowly, hands still behind his back. "We're no fools. We're not heartless either. You've gone your whole life knowing you'd probably never sit on the throne, never having to worry about anything beyond just showing up for photos. The press has left you alone for the most part. You've been in the military, you've gone to school, you've studied, you've planned a different future from the one you've been handed. Now you've had to re-route. Your freedom has been stripped. That's why you've been having a nervous breakdown."

"Getting drunk isn't a nervous breakdown," I protest, though even as the words leave my mouth they're already sounding like lies.

"Last week you swore during a live interview," my father says, ticking off his fingers like bombs. "The next day you proceeded to forget the names of our own government officers during your meeting with the Prime Minister. Followed by you getting…*ahem*…handsy with one of the women at the Estonian embassy's dinner party."

I shrug. "She was handsy first."

"She was the ambassador's daughter!" he snaps. "You grabbed her ass in front of him!"

"Arvid, calm down," my mother says, waving him away with her hand.

He lets out a huff of air and starts pacing.

She looks back to me, sympathy creasing her brow. "You don't have to do anything you don't want to. But we think the best way for you to deal with what happened to Alex, to deal with your new future, is to take a break. A real break. A holiday. Pretend to be someone else for a while."

I blink at her, still having a hard time letting this sink in. "Who will I be? Even under another name, people will recognize me."

"Here they will. Europe too. Go to America. Canada. Australia. Anywhere away from the continent. I promise you, they don't know who you are."

"For how long?"

"However long it takes you to get yourself together," my father says, pausing near the door.

"I would say three weeks," the doctor says after my mother looks at him for his opinion. "Maybe four. Any longer than that, and you might not want to come back."

"Oh, you'll come back, even if you don't want to," my father says. "You'll come back. Or we'll force you back here."

"Arvid," my mom chastises him. "Have a little kindness right now." She smiles at me gingerly. "Four weeks. That's about as long as we can cover for your lack of public appearances."

"What are you going to tell people?" I have to admit, there is a kernel of hope burning in my stomach, the idea of not having to do any appearances for four weeks. Not having to be the heir apparent. Not having to be a prince.

I'm not sure the last time I felt this much light inside me.

"We'll think of something," she says. "You just make sure

that you stay out of trouble, wherever you are. If it gets back to us that there is a prince on the loose," she stops to chuckle at her own words and I can't help but smile, "well, we'll all have a lot to answer for. Above all, my dear boy, I want you safe."

"Which means I won't have any guards…" I say slowly. I've never not had a bodyguard around me, even when I was at university, even when I was in the military.

"That's right."

"We're taking a big risk," my father adds. "What you did yesterday, you won't get away with over there. You understand?"

I look him in the eye and nod. "I understand." I glance at the doctor, at my mother, and do my best to hold back my smile. "When do I leave?"

"After you've apologized to Frederick and Gustav," she says. "In person."

"Of course, of course. I'll apologize right away. That was…what I did was beneath me."

She pats my hand. "Then if you do that today, perhaps you can leave tomorrow. Just let us know where and we'll arrange your ticket."

I pick up the passport, slowly flipping through the pages.

The pages are blank and waiting.

A clean slate.

CHAPTER FOUR

MAGGIE

I WAS TOSSING AND TURNING ALL NIGHT LONG, MY MIND racing, latching onto Körkort Sverige in my parents bedroom and then running wild with loose and erratic thoughts that didn't make much sense at all. At one point I got up to pee and spent a good five minutes standing in the dim light of the hallway, staring at my parent's door, daring myself to open it and see if the stranger was still in there. Maybe the whole thing had just been a dream, my underused imagination having concocted this mysterious man out of thin air.

It was probably an hour before my alarm went off that I finally did fall asleep, so that when I woke up again, I had that sticky panic that I didn't know where I was or what had happened.

I groan and look at my phone as everything comes flooding back to me again. It's six a.m., the sun is moments from rising, the dark gray light of dawn starting to brighten before my eyes. It's also Saturday, which means the house will be silent until around eight or nine when the first bleary-eyed kids make an appearance. I'm not even working today and normally sleep in for another hour before I get started on the day's chores, but suddenly I'm all too aware of the foreigner in the house.

I get up, slip on my robe and slippers and silently open my door, padding down the hall. Pike's door is still closed–so much for him spending the night outside his door with a gun–and I have no idea what to expect if I open the stranger's door. Should I wake up Pike just in case? Do I need a knife?

I quickly duck into the bathroom and grab one of my razors, the closest thing to a weapon, and holding it in one hand like I'm about to slice someone with it, I put my hand on the knob and gently open the door.

It doesn't creak. Everything creaks in this old house but for once the door opens silently and I'm able to take a few cautious steps inside the room.

It's completely dark inside, so I keep the door open so the light from the hall is able to flow in, a spotlight on his legs that barely illuminates the rest of him.

He's sleeping, I think. He's motionless anyway, though I can see the rise and fall of his chest. He's on his back, which in hindsight wasn't the best place to leave him since he might have gotten sick in the night and choked.

I realize I'm staring at him like a total creeper, mesmerized by his face even in the low light, the way that the shadows catch the hollows of his cheeks, the depth of his brows, the sharp angles of his jaw.

Then he stirs, just a little.

"Körkort?" I whisper, not wanting to startle him. "Mr. Sverige?"

He mumbles something in some language, his eyes still closed.

"I don't want to alarm you," I continue. "Just know that you're safe and sound."

God, do I ever sound like a moron.

I reach out and touch his foot.

His very long, very large foot. It sticks straight up off the bed like an Easter Island monolith.

He twitches.

I should probably stop touching his foot.

"Who is *that*?"

The voice makes me yelp, jump off my feet.

I whip around to see Callum in the doorway, rubbing his eyes and staring at the man.

Then I whip right back in time to see the man wake up.

Sit up.

Startled.

Sees me.

Sees Callum.

Starts yelling.

I don't understand him, but he is pissed and being pissed in a foreign language always sounds worse.

"Callum go back to your room!" I yell at him, waving him away frantically before I approach the guy, my hands raised, but of course one of my hands is holding the razor and it's gleaming in the light from the hallway like a guillotine blade about to fall.

The man's eyes widen and he moves back, rattling the headboard and somewhere down the hall I can hear doors open.

Oh crap. So much for keeping this under wraps.

"I'm not here to hurt you," I say, trying to sound assuring though my voice is cracking like thin ice.

"Then why do you have a razor?" he says, speaking English now. That same perfect English from yesterday, his accent seeming to melt away though his voice is booming.

I stare at the razor for a moment while he keeps talking. "Where am I? Did I have an accident?"

I shake my head. "No. No you're fine. You're safe."

"I'd feel safer if you dropped that weapon," he says, nodding at the razor, his words sounding more polished as he calms down.

I nod and can't figure out where to put it. I don't want to put it in the bathroom because I feel like he'll make a run for it when I do and the last thing I want is for this stranger to come barrelling down the hallway into everyone else. And I don't want to put it on the bedside table behind him in case this was a tactic on his behalf and then he'll be the one armed with the razor. And I'm definitely not giving it to Callum who I can tell is still standing right behind me.

So I chuck it across the room where it hits the window and drops to the floor.

"Callum don't walk over there," I tell him, still keeping my eyes on Körkort.

"Where am I?" Körkort repeats.

"You're in our house," Callum says.

"What is going on in here?" Now it's Thyme behind me. "Who is he?" she gasps.

I turn to look at her standing there in her pajamas. "Thyme, take Callum to the kitchen now. Please. And wake Pike up while you're at it."

"I'm already up," Pike says, not sounding impressed, not looking impressed. He comes into the room, arms crossed, eyes fixed dangerously on the stranger, Rosemary right behind him.

That doesn't put the stranger at ease. He immediately gets to his feet and everyone kind of goes *whoa* and takes a step back. Even though I know he's tall, he's just such a looming, formidable presence, he commands the entire room

"I need someone to tell me what the…" Sverige pauses, looks at Callum, "*heck* is going on here before I call the police."

"You should be grateful I didn't call the police on you last night," I can't help but retort.

The man flinches slightly, a cloudy look coming across his eyes.

"Now, if everyone will just calm down, I'll explain," say. "This is Mr. Sverige," I announce to everyone behind me, gesturing to him. "Mr. Sverige is staying at my hotel." And at that, a look of realization washes over his face, slowly at first, then like he's been doused in cold water. I clear my throat. "I was with Annette at the bar last night and recognized him. He wasn't feeling very well, to put it mildly, so I decided the best bet would be to bring him back here so he could, well, sleep it off."

I'm pretty sure my mother would have sugar-coated this whole situation to everyone, maybe to spare potential embarrassment on his behalf, but I've never been good at sugar-coating.

"Why didn't you take him back to his hotel?" Rosemary asks.

I lock eyes with him. Even in the dim light, they're the kind of eyes you get lost in.

Not here, I remind myself. Stay on task.

"Because," I say carefully, "the hotel doesn't like the staff and the guests to mingle outside of work hours. I could have gotten in trouble."

The guy nods, swallowing thickly. I watch his Adam's apple bob in his neck and feel a low hum in my core.

"Everyone up to speed now?" I ask in such a way that's basically telling everyone to get out.

I turn to look at them with wild eyes to coax them on their way. Rosemary and Thyme and Callum are still staring at Sverige, both fascinated and scared by him. With a grumble, Pikes steps in front of them and attempts to make them backup, ushering them into the hallway.

"You might as well wake up April too," I call after them.

"April never came home last night," Rosemary informs me as she disappears into the hall.

"What?!"

"I think I should go," the guy says, quickly grabbing his leather jacket from the chair, though he wobbles on his feet just enough to make him quickly sit back down on the bed.

I stare at him in confusion trying to make sense of two things at once. "No, I'll drive you," I tell him absently while my mind goes over what Rosemary said. April didn't come home last night? Why is no one more worried about this? Why am I the last to hear of it?

"I can get a cab," he says, searching his leather jacket pockets for his phone. When he finally locates it, he swears. "Shit." It looks dead.

"It's not a problem," I tell him. "I brought you here, it's only fair I take you back."

He looks up at me, his forehead creasing, and for the first time I feel like I'm really looking at him and he's really looking at me. We see each other, not in some awkward naked encounter or drunken mishap, but actually as two people, two strangers brought together in the strangest of circumstances.

"Is this your house?" he asks after a moment, breaking his gaze to glance at his blank phone again.

"Well I live here, so yeah," I tell him.

"And those are your…kids?"

"Siblings," I tell him, not wanting to get into it. "I'm the oldest."

He nods. "I see." He's staring at his hands now, shaking his head ever so slightly. "I'm really sorry for what happened last night. If I…if I hurt anyone, if I did anything, I can make it right."

"Hurt anyone?" His words make me stand up straighter.

"I don't know. I don't remember any of it and I was at a bar…"

"Well I can't tell you if that was your first bar of the night or not but from what the bartender said, you took a seat at the bar, ordered a drink and that was that. You passed out. Then my friend and I got there and I can confirm that you didn't hurt anyone, you were out cold. And when the bar was closing, well it was either I bring you here or the bartender was going to call the cops to put you in a drunk tank."

His eyes widen somewhat fearfully at that. "It would have been easier for you."

I shrug. "I don't know. I guess because I'd seen you earlier in the day…" Pause for awkwardness. "It just didn't feel right. Look, about that, I'm sorry I walked in on you naked."

"You are?" he asks, tilting his head ever so slightly to study me through his long lashes. "I could have sworn you enjoyed that."

Now my brows are raised.

A small smile tugs at the corner of his lips.

He's fucking with me.

"It was an accident," I tell him. "You oughta lock your door if you're going to be strutting around your room naked like that and can't hear if someone's knocking."

"But then I would have never met you, would I have?"

"That was scarcely a meeting."

"Sure, but then you never would have seen me later and felt bad enough about the whole thing to actually take me to your house to sleep off the drugs."

"Drugs?" I repeat. God, I should have figured it was drugs.

He frowns, getting back to his feet. "Prescription drugs," he says emphatically. "I, uh, took a pill or two I probably shouldn't have and then had something to drink, which I most definitely shouldn't have. The combination has been known to knock me out before. I'm not sure what I was thinking."

He stares past me at the wall and for a moment I think he's judging the stained and peeling wallpaper of my parents neglected old bedroom but then I realize he's lost in his thoughts, his gorgeous eyes running through an array of emotions I can't sort through.

"Well don't worry too much about it," I reassure him. "You weren't much of a problem at all."

I don't want to tell him that I felt strangely compelled to take care of him all night. That even though our encounter previously was anything but sexual and romantic, I couldn't stop thinking about him.

Even now, with him standing here in this room, pulling on that worn, butter-soft leather jacket over those thick arms, those broad shoulders, I wish there was something I could do to make him stay longer. I'm no longer holding onto a razor blade, he no longer seems like a dangerous stranger. I actually want to get to know him because even from this brief time I can tell there's a lot more to this man. Behind the movie star good looks, there's a man with a story, the kind you want to pull up a chair and get lost in.

I cough awkwardly, suddenly aware of how I've been staring at him. "Well, Mr. Sverige, I guess I'll take you on your way."

"Thank you, Miss America," he answers.

I give him a funny look. "Where are you from anyway?"

"You don't know?" he asks.

"I couldn't figure it out," I tell him. Then my expression turns sheepish. "Which reminds me, I better go get your wallet."

"My wallet?" he asks in surprise.

I point to his boots at the foot of the bed before I head out of the room. "Your boots are there. Let me just grab it."

He starts to sit down at the end of the bed and I quickly scamper to my room to grab his wallet.

Pike reaches out to grab me just as I curl my hands around the leather and step into the hall.

"What are you doing, Maggie?" he asks in a hush, pulling me toward him.

"I'm taking him to the hotel, chill out." I shrug myself out of his grasp.

"I'm coming with you."

I look him over. He's always been protective, but this is on another level. "I'll be fine. He's not going to murder me."

Not the best choice of words. They hang in the air between us.

"Don't joke about shit like that," he grumbles, his dark brows knitted together. "I don't know what I'd do without you."

"You'll never be without me," I tell him. "I promise you that. I promised Mom and Dad that when I agreed to be the guardian. I'm never leaving you guys, got that?"

He sighs, running his hands down his face. Then he stares at the wallet. "How much money does he have in there?" he asks quietly.

"Why?" I ask suspiciously.

"Maybe he won't miss it."

My jaw nearly drops. "Are you suggesting we rob him?"

"Actually, it was Callum's suggestion."

"What is wrong with you two? I'm helping someone and you're suggesting I rob him while I'm at it?"

"We need the money."

"Doesn't mean we take money from someone else. And what the hell is wrong with that kid to suggest that? Didn't our parents raise him better than that?"

Pike shrugs. "We'll find out at the teacher meeting."

"Everything okay?" comes Sverige's deep voice as he turns the corner, staring at us openly.

"Fine," I say quickly, glaring at Pike and his audacity before whirling around to hand Sverige his wallet. "Here you go. I was only holding onto it as collateral. In case you turned out to be a psychopath or something."

He takes the wallet from me, our fingers brushing against each other for a second that seems extra-long and drawn out in my head.

Yeesh.

"It's all in there," I tell him, nodding at it.

He holds it in his hands for a moment before he says, "I trust you" and slips it into his jacket pocket.

"We better go," I say, eyeing Pike to step out of the way.

"Are you going to get changed or drive him in that robe?" Pike asks.

I sigh. "Hold on. Stay there. Pike, be nice."

I turn and run into the room and pull on pajama pants and a sweater in seconds flat, returning to the hall to see them both where I left them, staring at each other awkwardly.

Pike looks at me. "Any idea where April is anyway?"

I shake my head with a groan. This isn't the first time April hasn't come home, but even so, we're going to have to find her soon. "Have you texted her?"

"Of course," he says. "Called her too. No answer. And the messages *are* getting delivered."

"She's probably sleeping," I say. And I hate that I think I know where.

I head down the stairs with the foreigner right behind me, his footsteps surprisingly light on the steps. Now that he's up and about, not drugged, not naked, he moves with a regal kind of elegance. His body seems to glide effortlessly through the space in front of it with a kind of confidence I can only dream of.

I bet he's a fantastic lay, flits through my head. I don't bat the thought away.

"Nice house," he says as we head down the hall toward the kitchen. I glance at him over my shoulder to see him looking over the walls, the crooked paintings, the old photos in broken frames.

"It's really not," I tell him, hoping if we move fast enough past the kitchen no one will stop us.

No such luck.

"Hey," Callum practically yells at us as I pass by the kitchen and the foreigner decides to stop in the doorway and peer inside at the scene.

"Callum, be polite," I warn, trying to glare at him over the guy's massive frame and failing miserably, even on my tip toes.

The guy moves over so it's the both of us in the doorway now and Callum, Thyme and Rosemary are sitting around the kitchen table with bowls of No Name Flakes of Corn. Callum is holding the container of sugar like a weapon, poised over the cereal and ready to let loose.

"What's your name?" Callum asks him, ignoring me.

"It's Mr. Sverige and I'm afraid we have to go," I interrupt. "Thyme, don't let him put that sugar in his cereal, do you understand?" I place my hand gently on Sverige's bicep. It's hard. So hard. "It's a trap. We should go."

"A trap?" he asks, glancing down at me and there's such intimate curiosity in his eyes that I suddenly feel hot under my skin, realizing the two of us are standing rather close to each other, and I'm *touching* him.

I have trouble swallowing, my eyes focused on his lips. "Yeah," I say softly, knowing I should take my hand away.

"She thinks we're going to say something embarrassing,"

Thyme says, almost proudly. It's enough to tear my eyes away from him and fix them on her in a warning. My hand drops to my side.

"She'll have an aneurysm," Callum adds, and I know I have to get this guy out of here before my brother starts talking about the other words he learned.

"Come on," I tell him, nodding down the hall.

"Okay, Miss America," he says, and I'm both flattered and confused by the nickname. "Very nice to meet you all," he says to them in his polished voice. "I bid thee farewell."

I give him an odd look at that one and as we continue down the hall I can hear Rosemary repeat to the others, mimicking his accent, "*I bid thee farewell?*"

"So, where are you from again?" I ask him as we head out to the minivan. I don't think he ever told me.

"I thought you knew," he says and stops in front of the van. "Is this your vehicle?"

I can't tell if he's being judgey or not. His damn poise and accent are making it difficult, as well as the fact that he said vehicle instead of car. "Yes. Get in, your highness."

His face goes white. He blinks at me. Is he having a seizure? The drugs kicking in again?

"Are you okay?" I ask.

He nods slowly, goes around to the side of the van and opens the passenger door.

"Why did you call me that?" he asks evenly as he sits down.

I shrug as I get in my seat and buckle up. "Because you looked like you were judging my ride, just as you were probably judging my house."

"Your ride?" He frowns at me. "I would never do that. I wasn't judging. I was interested in your house, that's all. I like it. It's charming. It's got life."

He's so sincere I can't help but believe him.

Good lord, he's so gorgeous and yet so, so *odd*.

"Okay, good." I sigh, turn the key and the van gives a bit of a cough and rumble before it purrs to life. "Sorry. I get defensive sometimes."

He presses his lips together, frowning. Those eyes of his skirt over every inch of my face, studying me. My stomach does a backflip. I can't remember the last time a man–hell, anyone–looked at me this way. "You know, it was really nice of you to do what you did," he finally says.

"No worries. I guess I felt guilty for seeing you, uh, vulnerable and stuff," I tell him as I turn the van onto the road, not comfortable with all this sincerity.

Out of the corner of my eye I catch a small smile on his mouth. "I didn't mind at all."

Nor should you, I think to myself, trying not to smile in return. "Anyway, so what are you doing here in ol' Tehachapi? It's not exactly the forefront of culture and civilization."

He licks his lips, just enough that I see the tip of his pink tongue, then turns his attention out the window. "I was just passing through when my car broke down on the highway. About thirty minutes east of here. Middle of the desert. *That* was a day."

"What's wrong with it? You know my brother works as a mechanic. He could help you out. You know, if you need it."

"We'll see. I've been trying to fix it myself for the last few days," he says with a shrug. "I think I need a new carburetor."

"You can fix cars too?"

"What? I don't look like I can?"

Well, no. Not with his elegant mannerisms, the way he holds himself, the fit of his clothes. It looks like he pays people to do everything for him and yet there's not an arrogant thing about him. A bit of cockiness from the way he bites his lip, a confidence that comes in knowing he looks like a god, but arrogance, no.

I end up shrugging. "I don't know. I don't know a thing about cars to be honest."

"Well I do," he says, almost defensively. "Been working on cars ever since I was a child, helping, uh, my father's friends with them. The problem with this car is it's an old car, a Mustang, nineteen sixty-five. Those parts take time, yes. Might be here for a bit longer."

Is it crazy that I'm relieved he's staying in this town for longer? It *is* crazy.

"Don't you have somewhere you need to be? Where were you headed?"

"Los Angeles," he says. "And no, I have nowhere I need to be. I'm…on vacation. For another week. Then I fly out of Los Angeles and back to Stockholm."

"Stockholm? So you're Swedish!" I knew it.

"Is that a surprise, Miss America?" he says, adjusting his seat to give his long legs more room. "You've been calling me Mr. Sweden this whole time."

"Huh?"

"Körkort Sverige," he says.

"Isn't that your name?"

He breaks into a grin, a movie star smile that shows off perfect white teeth, making him look simultaneously younger and even more handsome. My body is reacting to this faster than my brain can, my breath catching in my throat, my heart thumping harder in my chest.

"Sverige means Sweden in Swedish," he says. "Körkort means driver's license. I'm afraid you've been calling me Mr. Swedish driver's license."

I burst out laughing. "You're kidding me."

"I'm not," he says. "I quite enjoy it."

"So what *is* your name?"

"It's...," he pauses. "Johan. Johan Andersson."

Just like it said on his license, I just thought that was where he lived or something. He's also pronouncing the "J" like a "Y."

"Well don't I look like the horse's ass," I remark.

He frowns quizzically. "You have a very nice ass. Not at all like a horse."

I'm laughing again. "I can't tell if you're joking or not."

"I would never joke about a nice ass," he says, straight-faced though his eyes have a mischievous slant. "Miss America."

"You can stop calling me that now."

"Let me think about it. What is your real name?"

"Maggie. Maggie McPherson."

"Is that so?"

He extends his hand to me. I stare at it in surprise for a moment before I take my hand off the wheel and give him mine. My hand is so damn tiny in his and when he envelopes it with his strong, warm fingers, it practically disappears. "It's an honor to meet you, Maggie McPherson."

"It's nice to meet you, Johan Andersson. Though I must admit, I got used to calling you Körkort Sverige."

"You can call me anything you want," he says.

And, oh, dear god, is he *flirting* with me? Maybe. I feel like he's holding onto my hand for longer than he maybe should, even though I also want him to never let go.

As if he senses this, he lets go of my hand and brings it back to his lap, looking almost chagrined as he stares out the window at the town as it passes us by.

I'm about to ask what kind of business he's in when a text on my phone beeps in. I quickly glance at it. It's Pike. Says: **Still no sign of her**.

Meaning April.

"What is it?" Sverige–sorry, *Johan*–says, watching me.

My jaw feels like it's been clamped together. I wiggle it open and try to give him a smile. "My sister. April. She's fourteen and she didn't come home last night."

"Fuck," he swears, his accent seeming to thicken as he does so. "That can't be good."

"She's done this before," I tell him, just so he doesn't suggest we go to the police or something. "Once she was at a girlfriend's house after partying all night, or so she says. I've always thought differently though."

He looks at me expectantly. "Does she have a boyfriend?"

I nod. "Yes," I say grimly. "And he's the biggest douchebag on the planet. In fact, he lives just over there." I nod up ahead at a long dusty road that leads into the hills.

I was planning on dropping off the Swede and then cruising past the dickhead's house on the way back home, hoping to find April but suddenly I've flipped on my indicator and I'm making a turn.

This is either going to be a good idea or a very, very bad one.

CHAPTER FIVE

MAGGIE

"Are we paying him a visit?" the Swede asks, brows raised as I turn the van onto the bumpy road that might lead toward April.

I should feel bad that I'm not only delaying dropping off this guy but now I'm somehow involving him in my problems, but I guess I just feel safer with him in the van. April's supposed boyfriend, a guy that everyone calls Tito, isn't a tall guy, but he's big and he's vicious. He's one Colt 45 away from getting a face tattoo.

"I just want to see if she's there," I tell him. "Won't take a second."

A few beats pass, and I can tell he's mulling something over. Finally, he asks, his voice lower, "What do your parents think about all of this?"

I stiffen. This question. This fucking question.

And of course, he means no harm by it. No one ever does.

And yet this question always rips me apart at the seams.

"They're dead," I tell him bluntly. No use softening the blow. The more you soften it, the more they'll treat you with kid gloves, like you're some fragile snowflake moments from melting. Sometimes I am, but not today.

"I'm sorry for your loss," he says.

And that's all he says.

His voice carries weight and gravity to it that shows he understands and if he doesn't understand, he at least cares enough to try. But the simplicity of his response is freeing. I don't have to explain a thing.

We drive in silence for a few minutes, my brain jumping from one thing to the next. What I'm going to do when I find the house, if I'm going to get out and knock on the door, if I'm just going to park outside and wait and see. What I'll say to April. Will I be quiet and stern, dripping with the disappointment that my father was so good at doling out? Or will I yell and scream, like my mother might have when she lost her temper?

Then it's focusing on *him*, this gorgeous specimen of a man who is in my car and filling the space with his quiet energy and inquisitive eyes and his strong, capable presence. I shouldn't feel this comfortable with someone I don't really know, and yet I am.

Or maybe comfortable isn't the right word. I'm not exactly relaxed by him. My pulse is racing, my cheeks feel hot, my skin is dancing like electricity is flowing through the air. There's tension between us, maybe something that exists only in my head, but it exists all the same. I haven't felt a push-pull with anyone in…well, ever. Not like this.

You're a sad, sad girl, I tell myself. *This guy is not only passing through on vacation, but he's way out of your league and way too good for you.*

Fuck. The truth hurts.

For a moment there I forgot who I was.

I slow the car down in front of the house without even realizing I'm doing it.

Tito's house is blue, faded from the sun, two stories high, and nestled in a crop of dead pines. Five junk cars and an old station wagon litter the driveway, along with piles of garbage bags. Broken glass twinkles in the overgrown weeds that flank the gravel path to the house.

"This is it?" the Swede whispers as I park the car across the street. I can't bring myself to think of him as Johan. Somehow it doesn't fit. "Doesn't seem like the right place to raise children."

I give him a sour smile. "He's nineteen. Lives here with a bunch of other losers."

"Isn't that illegal? Your sister is fourteen, yes?"

"Yeah. It's illegal if…I don't want to think about it." I sigh, closing my eyes for a moment because there is a well of emotions inside me that are bubbling up and I know I'm about to unload on him. I shouldn't. I really shouldn't. This guy just wants to go back to the hotel, back to his car, back to his country.

And yet…

"Honestly, I just don't know what to do anymore," I tell him, shaking my head and then it all spills out. "And I feel like so much of it is my fault. The moment I was done high school and I saved up enough to leave this shithole, I was out of here. I just left, and I didn't look back. For those years I was in New York…I was in New York, by the way, studying at NYU, I just kind of forgot where I came from. I was a bad sister. A bad daughter."

Oh shit. Am I going to cry? I look up at the roof of the van and blink back any tears. "I didn't check in with the family much. Not as much as I should have. I was just so immersed with living this new life, trying to be the person I always dreamed I could be. I had no idea what was going on at home. The wedge between April and I grew stronger. I stopped knowing who she was, knowing the person she was growing into. Then, then my parents died, and I was back here, and I was thrust into the middle of this…this family that was mine and wasn't mine at the same time. And we're hurting, you know? We're all hurting and we're sad and we're picking up the pieces and yet we're also drifting even further apart. Now I look at April and I don't just see my sister, I see a stranger. And she hates me."

I take a moment to catch my breath. My heart is racing even faster than before. There's silence in the van except for the sound of the engine ticking. I sneak a glance at the Swede.

He's watching me with this quiet intensity in his eyes and sympathy etched in his brow. "It sounds like you're doing the best you can," he says, and though his voice is soft, it emits a low, deep rumble I feel in my bones. "You shouldn't be so hard on yourself."

He might be right. But if I'm not hard on myself then how will I ever get better? Be better? I have to be hard on myself in order to grow. I'm in charge of this family now and to fail is…not an option.

I open my mouth to tell him this but a movement by the house catches my eye.

I crane my neck past him to see the front door opening and April stepping out, walking toward the station wagon in the driveway. Her dark hair is hanging in her face and she's wearing the same jeans and cardigan I saw her in yesterday, dirty Converse on her feet.

"There she is," I say, and before I know it, I'm getting out of the van and storming across the street toward her. I hope the Swede has enough presence of mind to stay in the car while I deal with this.

"April," I bark, and in seconds I know I'm not taking my

dad's role of quiet disappointment, but my mom's volcanic one.

She jerks back in surprise, stopping in her tracks by some broken beer bottles. "What are you doing here?" she says, and I watch as her eyes go from shocked to angry. Angry that I've intruded into this part of her life, angry that I have the nerve to act like her parent.

"You didn't come home last night," I tell her, doing my best to keep my voice steady, to keep my emotions in check.

Think like Dad, think like Dad.

"So?" she answers defiantly. Hands go to her hips, hair gets flipped over her shoulder.

This is *not* going to be easy.

"So we were worried first of all," I tell her, "and second of all, what are you doing here? You know you can't spend the night anywhere without telling me first, especially not *here*!"

"If I told you, you wouldn't have let me come."

"I know. No one in their right mind would have," I tell her and reach out, grabbing her arm. "But now you're coming back home with me."

"Whatever," she says, ripping herself out of my grasp and fixing the most bitter, damaging eyes on me, the kind that really tell me how much she hates me. "You can't make me."

The front door to the house opens and Tito steps outside, immediately walking toward me with enough posturing and bravado to make me think he's going to fuck me up. "What the fuck is going on? Fucking,Maggie McPherson. You're looking good."

"Yeah, hi, Tito. Just claiming my *fourteen-year-old* sister here," I tell him, reaching for her again.

"Fuck off," April swears, immediately stepping behind the wall of Tito. "We're going to the mall."

"The mall?" I repeat. "The mall? There is no damn mall in this town."

"There is in Bako," Tito says, taking a step toward me. "She'd like some new clothes for school. Do you know how she gets bullied for wearing that shit you dress her in?"

"I don't dress her!" What the fuck. I look at April. "Bullied?"

She shrugs. "I'm tired of wearing second-hand shit. Tito is going to buy me a whole new wardrobe."

"Oh yeah, and what are you giving him in return?"

"Fuck you," April says.

I am seconds away from saying "fuck you too" but I can't, I can't. I have to push through this, be the better person, the older person, the guardian, the parent. Fuck, even the wise older sister will do.

I jerk my head to the van. "Please, April. Now."

"She's not going," Tito says putting his hand on my shoulder and pushing me until I have to take a step back. "You're not her fucking mother."

That shouldn't sting but it does. It does enough that I forget to be afraid that he just fucking touched me.

"I'm her legal guardian." I eke out the words, trying to hold back tears. "She's coming with me."

"Go home, Maggie," April says but now her tone is quiet and unsure. She actually looks a little scared until she pushes her hair into her face and hides behind him again.

"Yeah go fucking home you little bitch," Tito says, getting in my face. He reeks of pot, his eyes are bloodshot, his forehead pale and sweating. I don't care if I have to call the cops, but I am not leaving my sister here with him. She can hate me for the rest of my life, but I'm not backing down.

"Are you okay, Maggie?" I hear a voice from behind me and my stomach tightens. I look over my shoulder to see the Swede striding over to us. And while the sight of his gloriously tall and commanding frame coming this way feels something like a knight in shining armor, I know this isn't going to go well.

"What the fuck?" Tito snarls as he takes in the stranger. "Who the fuck is this?"

"A friend." The Swede cocks his head, stopping right beside me, observing Tito like an animal at the zoo. "And who might you be?"

"Fuck off," Tito says though I pick up a slight hesitation in his voice. The Swede towers over him and though Tito is packed with muscle, I know, personally, the Swede is too.

"Not the best manners," the Swede says, pretending to wipe spit off his face.

"Who is this?" hisses April as she looks him up and down.

"This is Mr. Sverige," I tell them because, shit, in my panic I've forgotten his real name. "A friend of mine."

Having him here now gives me the courage to step around Tito and reach for April again.

She shrinks back but I see the fear in her face again, like she's acting out of her own control and now Tito is stepping to the side, his chest blocking my view, his meaty, dirty hand on my shoulder, *shoving* me back.

"She doesn't want to—"

Before Tito can finish his sentence, the Swede is placing his hands on Tito's shoulder and pushing him away. He shoves him back so hard that he stumbles and almost falls down on the ground.

"Fuck!" Tito yells, throwing his arms out, one of his arms smacking into April's chest and knocking her over.

She yelps as she falls and I scamper over to her just as Tito lunges himself at the Swede.

"You fuck!" Tito roars, trying to tackle him, arms out, head first, but the Swede is quick and steps out of the way rather effortlessly. But instead of just avoiding contact, he then brings his elbow down on the back of Tito's head and the guy goes down in a second, sprawled out on the gravel.

"Oh my god," I say, and the Swede meets my eyes, breathing hard and looking somewhat ashamed. "Is he–?"

But my question is answered before I can finish my sentence.

Like the T-1000, Tito is suddenly up on his feet, coming to life again before my very eyes. The Swede barely has time to turn around before Tito is throwing a punch, getting him in the corner of his jaw.

I yell something.

April yells something.

The Swede barely reacts except for the look of pure fire in his eyes.

With one hard, smooth swing he punches Tito square in the face, making him spin and tumble to the ground yet again. He lands with a groan, head in his hands, trying feebly to get to his feet and failing.

The Swede shakes his hand out, wincing, and then looks around with a wild look in his eyes. "We should go, yes?"

I stare down at Tito. He seems okay but…

"Tito," April cries out pitifully, ready to fall to her knees by him like Broken Juliet over Thug Romeo but I grab her by the arm and yank her toward the van.

"He'll be fine," I tell her, my nails desperately digging into her cardigan.

"We need to go," the Swede says again and I'm wondering why he looks so cagey. Maybe getting busted for fighting when you're a foreigner means him getting deported, who knows. But I don't want to stick around here either.

"I don't want to go with you!" April yells at me, tears in her eyes, and for a second, I am struck with the deepest fear; what if she runs off? What if she physically won't go? I'm only five-foot-four. She's an inch shorter, and I have more muscle, but she can fight like a wild, cornered animal. If she's not scared of me, of my discipline, if she doesn't care and hates me and is full of spite, how will I survive this? How will I survive the next four years?

But for some reason—praise the lord—she relents. She lets me take her over to the van and I watch with my breath in my mouth as she climbs into the back seat, worried that at the last minute she's going to bail.

She doesn't. The door slides to a close with a punctuated click.

I let out a long, shaking breath and look up at the Swede who is standing right at my side.

"I am so sorry you had to see that," I tell him, my voice small. "That you had to witness that. Do that." I glance at his knuckles that are raw and bleeding. "Shit."

He quickly glances at his hand and shrugs.

"There's no cow on the ice," he says with a warm smile. "It's fine. I'm just glad I was here."

"There's no cow?" I repeat, dazzled by both that strange phrase and the way he came to my rescue, the way he's looking at me now, like it was his *honor*.

His smile widens, and he lets out a laugh that makes my stomach fill with butterflies. "Yes. Sorry. It is a saying we have. *Det är ingen ko på isen*," he says in Swedish, the language sounding so melodious and beautiful. "There's no cow on the ice. It means don't worry."

"Because you would worry if there was a cow on the ice?"

"Well yes. Wouldn't you?"

I laugh despite myself. "I guess I would." I reach out and touch his hand, his warm, strong hand, and hold it, examining his knuckles. "You need to get fixed up."

"Too bad there isn't a nurse at the hotel," he says in a low voice, still watching me intently. I'm not sure if it's because of the adrenaline running through our bodies or the way we're standing so close, but I swear his eyes seem to darken, like clouds coming over a summer sky. Nothing ominous, just mercurial, like an intensity is building.

I swallow. "I have to take April home. You don't mind coming along for the ride? Again?"

"Not at all. I have nowhere to be and you're the only person I now know in this town. I think it would be rather lonely if I went back to my hotel room right now. Not to mention boring. There are no fistfights there."

"No cows on the ice either," I point out as I walk around the hood to the driver's side.

"You're picking up on Swedish already," he says. "I'm rather proud."

Now I'm grinning like an idiot, and for a second, I forget all the horrible shit that just happened.

I'm reminded of it the minute I get back in the car.

April is crying in the back seat while simultaneously giving me the finger when I ask if she's okay. Outside, Tito staggers to his feet and goes back inside his drug den. Then there's the Swede buckling in beside me with his long legs and bleeding knuckles. I can't believe he just fucking took that beast Tito down like that. I'm having a hard time processing all of this, it all happened so fast.

But rather than an uncomfortable silence all the way back to the house, the Swede fills the air by talking about his trip in America so far. How he started out in New York City and spent a few days there before buying a vintage Mustang from a collector and driving across the Midwest, through the Rockies and all the way here before his car decided to bite the dust.

I hate to admit it, but I'm envious. Here's a man who

seems so self-assured, who is traveling by himself through America doing whatever he wants. Money doesn't seem to be an issue. Time doesn't seem to be an issue. I've never seen someone look so free.

I want that. I want the freedom to drop everything and just run away. Run away like a coward but at least I would feel the wind in my face and hope under my wings. At least for a little while I could live under the pretence that anything can happen until the guilt and shame and responsibility would drag me back home.

I hate that I feel that way. And then I hate myself for hating myself.

The cycle never breaks.

Before I know it, I'm pulling the van back up to the house and my heart feels waterlogged. April immediately jumps out and runs inside even before I've had a chance to cut the engine.

I sigh and look over at him with a weak smile before resting my head on the steering wheel. "Back again."

"Are you okay?" he asks, one brow delicately raised.

Funny how he asks it, his tone suggesting we've been friends for many years. We're not even friends. We don't even know each other. I barely remember his real name. And yet there's no denying this feeling.

It's only because you've seen him naked, I remind myself. *Don't be fooled by your hormones.*

But I know that's not the only reason.

I give a slight nod. "I'll be okay. I guess I better go inside and see how Pike is handling it. Who knows what version of our story she's giving him."

He studies me for a moment through those long lashes of his. Finally, he says, "You're a lot stronger than you think you are."

I flinch, taken aback. "What?"

"I just don't think you give yourself enough credit."

I can't help but frown. "No offense, Mr. Sweden, but you don't actually know me."

He rubs his lips together and shrugs. "No. I suppose I don't. And you don't know me either." He pauses. "Would you like to have dinner tonight?"

I blink, floored by the question. "Dinner?"

Dinner?

Is he asking me out for dinner?

Like…a *date*?

After all that, why the hell would he ask me out on a date? Shouldn't I be taking him out for dinner after the way he came to my defense and knocked Tito out?

"You do eat dinner, don't you?" he adds.

"Uh, usually."

He continues to stare at me expectantly. "So? Would you like to have dinner with me tonight?"

"But…*why*?" I blurt out.

"Because I like you," he says. He says it so simply, so earnestly, that it could be the most romantic thing anyone has ever said to me. "I find you very interesting. And it would be nice to not eat alone for once."

"There isn't anywhere nice to eat here," I tell him, aware that my palms are starting to get sweaty.

"But I'm sure there's somewhere good, yes?"

There are a few restaurants that I personally love, even if they aren't anything fancy, but I haven't gone out to eat in a year. Not since New York. "I'll have to ask Pike," I tell him. "He was stuck with the kids last night when I was…well, with you at the bar."

"All right," he says with a slow nod. "And if he says no to tonight, how about tomorrow night?"

God, he's persistent too.

I'm in heaven.

A sweaty-palmed, heart-racing, lightheaded kind of heaven.

"Maggie?"

My name on his lips sounds sweeter than a love song.

I come back to earth.

Give him a smile. "I would love to."

CHAPTER SIX

VIKTOR

I'm living a lie.

I'm living a lie, and for the first time in three weeks, I hate it.

Up until my damn dream car broke down outside of however you pronounce this town's name, I was reveling in the freedom that being Johan Andersson brought me.

It was fucking unbelievable.

From the moment I stepped on that private jet leaving Arlanda airport in Stockholm, to landing in Germany where I took one last glimpse of my bodyguard and started my journey under a fake passport, I've been living a life I'd only dreamed of.

I was no longer shadowed by guards. I was no longer recognized. I was no longer of interest to anyone. I was no longer on my best behavior. I was no longer conscious of anything other than remembering my new name and my new job. Johan Andersson, heir to a fictional Swedish pharmaceutical fortune. I was free.

There was no better place to land than New York City,

Manhattan, the city where dreams are made. It was everything I thought it would be. I was immediately enveloped by the bright lights and honking cabs and endless streets, swallowed by the pulse of millions of people. I was anonymous. I was free to be whoever I wanted.

The first day I slept in until past noon. No one was there to wake me up. I had a new mobile just for this trip and no one was calling it wanting anything. There was no Freddie making sure I was on task. There were no butlers knocking at my door. I got up when I felt like it, and even though I was groggy and jet-lagged, I went out onto the streets to a coffee shop and spent hours at the window just watching the world go by.

I've never been able to look at people that way. Unabashedly. Openly. Observing strangers like I'd never been around humanity before. No one noticed. No one minded. I was just another face in the crowd. I wasn't a prince at all, I was just a human being.

It felt fucking good.

That's pretty much all I did in New York. I wandered the streets, I watched people. I went to both rooftop bars full of the types of socialites I grew up around and I went to hipster bars where people pretended not to care but really did and I went to the dive bars where people sat in silence and drank until their minds were silent too. I sat on park benches, I watched dogs run around tiny dog parks, I saw tourists run from pigeons and drivers arguing about traffic.

I even tried to see *Hamilton* but lost patience trying to get tickets. Maybe next time.

After New York, I took the train to Chicago, something I'd always wanted to do after I saw the movie *North by Northwest*. And under a false identity, I really felt like Roger Kaplan. Then in Chicago I spent a few more days walking, observing, eating and found myself the car of my dreams from a private seller on Craigslist. A Caspian Blue 1965 Mustang hardtop in near mint condition. I handed over the money in cash and hit the open road. Windows down. Wind in my smile.

Smile. I hadn't smiled since Alex died and yet now I was. I was smiling and every time the guilt crept up on me, reminding me of what I lost, that I had no right to smile, I buried the feeling and pretended that Johan Andersson had never experienced loss. And I kept smiling.

With each day I spent driving across the States, the more into my new character I became. It was fairly easy. When you're thrust from one type of life, a very bizarre, very specific life that you've only ever known, and into one of the total opposite, it becomes easy to pretend to be somebody else.

It was working too, until I was driving between Las Vegas and Los Angeles. I'd always wanted to see Vegas so I got a room at The Venetian for a night. I'd barely given my car to the valet when I walked through the ornate lobby with its painted ceilings and got caught in the middle of a large wedding party that was passing through.

All the bridesmaids were clutching white lilies.

The groomsmen had them as corsages.

Their scent filled the air, as intoxicating as poison and within seconds it felt like my chest was closing up and I was close to passing out.

White lilies were everywhere at Alex's funeral.

I never really noticed until I smelled them again.

The smell of death.

It broke apart the mask I was wearing, and once again I was Viktor, a grieving prince, lost under foreign lights.

I got back in that Mustang and drove through the desert, escaping those lilies and the memories and the pain.

Or so I thought.

Just before the desert rose up into the rolling hills that surround this town, the Mustang sputtered and came to a crawl. I was lucky I didn't get smoked by a few semi-trucks while I was at it.

Fortunately, it didn't take long for me to call a towing company and for them to show up and take the Mustang to the nearest hotel, where I told them I would tinker with it in their parking lot.

By then it was late, I was stressed, sad, and tired, and I'd passed out without much time to think about anything. The next morning, however, I did my best to keep Viktor buried away. As annoying as it was to have my dream car break down like that, the car that had taken such good care of me on my trip across the States, it was good to have something to do, something to keep my mind occupied, something to fix since I sure as hell couldn't fix myself.

It was when I was a greasy mess and I realized I needed a new carburetor that I went back into my room to shower and eventually look for parts online. I was walking around naked, an audiobook playing in my wireless earbuds since audiobooks in English were the best way for me to perfect the language, that I realized I wasn't alone in the room.

The funny thing is, I'd gotten used to wandering around in hotel rooms naked. In Sweden nudity is barely an issue, but even so, back at home, I was constantly bombarded by people. In these hotel rooms I felt safe to do as I pleased.

That was until I turned around and discovered a maid staring at me with wide eyes and an open mouth.

One extremely pretty and young maid, the kind you have fantasies about. Dark hair loosely pulled back, a disarmingly sweet face with lush lips and eyes like black holes, eyes that tempted you to get close and tumble in, never to get out again.

She took me by complete surprise.

I definitely took her by surprise.

She yelped, mumbled something and looked like she couldn't get out of my room fast enough. I can't blame her. She was rather small and with my height and stature I'm sure my cock was looking positively monstrous in front of her.

I didn't expect to see her again. After she left, our little incident was the only amusing part of the day.

The day that crept into night.

The night that brought loneliness on a dry desert wind.

I could have sworn I smelled lilies in the air.

Maybe it was the overly-perfumed scent of a guest passing by in the hallway.

Maybe it was just in my head, conjuring up ghosts when I was alone and vulnerable.

Either way it struck me as hard as it had in Vegas, a bomb of sorrow that exploded inside me, shrapnel that made me bleed from the inside out.

I fell to my knees, overwhelmed, taken over.

I could have sunk right through the floor.

But I wouldn't let the tears fall.

I felt if I did, I'd be taking a step backward into Viktor again. Into the person I was running away from, into the role I knew I'd eventually have to succumb to, a role that would now hurt so much more after this taste of freedom.

In desperation I found the pills that Dr. Bonakov had given me. I took two.

They took too long to kick in.

With no fridge in the room and no bar or restaurant in the hotel, I walked the ten minutes into town and went into the first bar I saw. Sat at the bar. Ordered a vodka on the rocks.

And that was it.

Lights out.

Into the black.

But there were dreams. Wild and dark and confusing. I dreamed about Alex and a crown laced with razor blades, bearing his blood, blood that washed me away into the next morning.

Where I woke up.

In a dim room of gray light.

In a strange bed.

With a strange girl and a young boy staring at me.

My first thoughts were that I'd been in an accident of some sort, that maybe I was in a hospital. Then that thought turned to one of being kidnapped because I noticed the girl was holding a razor blade like she wanted to slice me, like the razor blades in my dreams. Somehow, she figured out who I was and was holding me for ransom.

Then I noticed who she was.

The maid.

Then I learned what she did.

Took care of me when I was unconscious at the bar. Took me home. Made sure I was safe.

Something she didn't have to do for a complete stranger.

And now I'm here, sitting in her kitchen at the worn wooden table while she's rifling through a first-aid kit she just pulled out from under the sink, about to treat the raw wounds on my knuckles. That guy had a face made of steel, I swear, and it didn't help that I'd punched Gustav in the face just a few weeks before.

We're not alone in the kitchen, of course.

On one side of me is a young boy who can't seem to stop smiling. I can't tell if he's just happy or he's plotting my death.

On the other side of me are a pair of twin girls, one with

her hair dyed jet black, black clothes, a hint of eyeliner. The other in no makeup at all and a bright yellow shirt. Both stare at me with identical expressions of dry amusement, like I'm some stray animal their sister Maggie found on the street.

Maggie. Miss America.

Now that I've spent the morning with her she's morphed from being the hot little maid that walked in on me naked to becoming the only person I know in this town, a person who went out of her way for me, a person who seems genuinely interested in me without knowing who I really am. I have to say, I'm enchanted by her.

Which brings me to my dilemma.

That I've fed her lies.

That I'll keep feeding her lies.

And I hate it.

"So what do you do?" the girl with the black hair asks me pointedly. "What is your job?"

Maggie is unscrewing a tube of ointment and quickly glances at me, listening.

"I'm part of a big company in Sweden."

"Is it IKEA?" the other girl asks.

I smile. If I had a kroner for every IKEA joke I've heard these last few weeks.

"No it's not IKEA."

"Volvo?" the dark-haired girl asks.

"It's not Volvo either."

"ABBA?" the boy says.

I raise my brow at him. "You think I'm part of ABBA?"

He just shrugs gleefully and starts wiggling in his seat. "See that girl," he starts singing to "Dancing Queen," the song horribly off-key, "watch that scene, oh no, she smells like pee."

"Callum," Maggie admonishes him while I burst out laughing.

"You know," I tell him, "that song was sung in honor of the Queen of Sweden the day before her wedding. You might want to show some respect."

"Why? Are you the King?"

Not yet.

"Ugh, Callum, please don't start insulting other people's countries," Maggie says again, pulling up a chair beside me and placing her fingers on my wrist. Her touch feels like a warm spark, soothing and electric all at once. She glances at me with a shy smile as she squeezes ointment onto her finger. "I'm sorry. He has this bad habit of changing song lyrics to anything to do with poo or pee."

"Is that so?" I say to him, and he just giggles in return. From the way he's bobbing his head, I can tell he's finishing the song in his head, probably adding another phrase about my mother.

"So," Maggie says, dabbing the cream on my knuckles. I hold back a wince. "What is the company?"

Curious bunch. Though I suppose I am in their home and they're trying to get to know me as more than some Swedish stranger.

"It's a pharmaceutical company," I tell her.

"Ah," she says with a nod. "That sounds…very important."

"It's okay," I tell her, wishing I didn't have to lie. I try and find my truth in it. "My whole family has worked there for generations. We made it everything it is today. I'm poised to take over the company after my father, uh, quits."

"Oh well that's exciting," she says. I watch as she takes her time dressing my wounds, the way her brows come together in concentration. I have to wonder if she's this attentive with everyone or if it's just for me.

But if it's just for me, it's not for *me*. It's for a persona I created, the future head of a big company. Johan Andersson.

If she knew the truth about me, would it matter? She doesn't seem that impressed by my fake job though I know a lot of people usually are. Pharmaceutical companies pull in a lot of money.

But if she found out who I really was…?

"Am I hurting you?" she asks, her voice sweetly concerned.

I meet her big brown eyes and realize I was tensing up. "No. I'm fine. Thank you." I force myself to relax. It doesn't help that the more she touches me, leans into me, looks at me, the tenser I get. She smells decadent and sweet, like sugar and cinnamon.

She nods, looking almost embarrassed, as if she realized how attentive she's been, how close we are. She straightens up, putting some space between us, and starts getting out a roll of bandages.

"Do you cook?" the dark-haired girl asks me as Maggie wraps the bandage around my hand.

"Cook?" I actually can cook, only because I find it soothing and it gives me a sense of control. Growing up, we had a whole arsenal of staff to do everything for us. "I do okay for myself."

The twins exchange a look, a playful smile.

"What? Why?" I ask, suspicious.

Then the dark-haired one launches into a fairly dead-on impression of The Swedish Chef from the Muppets. "Ooo-dee doo-dee bork bork."

I roll my eyes, sighing loudly. I grew up wanting to murder that damn puppet.

"Girls," Maggie says, but she's trying to bite back a smile, avoiding my eyes.

"It's okay," I tell her. "I've gotten a lot of that."

"Hurdy-schmerdy bork bork!" Callum yells. "Dancing queen, smells like pee!"

Maggie shakes her head. "I swear to god," she mutters under her breath before tucking the end of the bandage into the wrap and getting to her feet. "Okay. You're done. I'm taking you home now."

"Honestly, it's fine," I tell her, getting out of my chair. "You'll be glad to know most Swedes have a pretty good sense of humor." I raise my bandaged hand in her direction. "Thank you, by the way."

She shakes her head again, dark hair falling in her face, and waves me away dismissively. "No cow on the ice," she says.

I grin. Something in my heart shifts, something new, something...*soft*. The pain I've been holding inside starts to melt, just an inch. But an inch is enough to take me by surprise.

"So about dinner," I say to her. I know I'm being forward, maybe even annoying, but I'm chasing that feeling inside, that part of me that's melting away.

"Are you staying for dinner?" Callum asks me.

"*No*," Maggie says emphatically.

"Dinner?" a voice comes from behind us.

It's Maggie's oldest brother, or at least I assume he is. Who knows how many other people there are in this house. Again, I'm floored at the fact that she's the legal guardian of them all, that they're all under her care now. I know I have my own responsibilities I'm running from but at least I had the option to run. She can't. She's saddled with them. And so fucking young.

"Sverige...Johan," Maggie corrects, and it's almost like she doesn't believe my fake name any more than I do, "asked me out to dinner tonight."

Her brother stares at me, tattooed arms folded across his

chest. He looks like he can take care of himself in a fight and also looks like he'd have no problems *trying* to kick me out of his house. He definitely wants to.

But I'm not about to fuck up my hand again. I take a step away from him, holding my wrist to show him I'm not going to be a problem.

"Are you paying for her?" he asks me.

I blink at the question. "Pardon?"

"Are you paying for her?" he repeats.

"Of course, I am," I tell him, not understanding why he would think otherwise. What man wouldn't pay for a woman when he invites her on a date?

He thinks it over for a moment and then nods at Maggie. "It's fine. You deserve to be taken out for a night. And, frankly," he looks up to the ceiling, "I don't think you should be here tonight with her."

"What is she saying?" Maggie asks, wrapping her arms around herself like she's cold. "She hates me, doesn't she?"

He exhales, squeezing the bridge of his nose. "She hates everyone and everything. You can't really blame her…" He glances at the other kids who are all staring at him and nodding subtly. "Anyway, I know what happened. She's just pissed that your Alexander Skarsgård over here hurt her white-trash boyfriend." He looks to me. "By the way, if I were you, I wouldn't stick around here for too long. I'm impressed you were able to knock Tito out, but he's got a lot of friends in that crack house and they don't play nice."

I shrug. "That's fine. I don't play nice either."

"So you're really okay with looking after the kids tonight?" she asks him.

"You know we can take care of Callum if the both of you want to go out," the dark-haired girl says. "We're old enough."

"One step at a time," her older brother says. "I'm sure this won't become a habit for Maggie."

"Hey!" She chides him and then looks at me, clearly ready to get out of here. "Let's go."

We get out of the house and into the van before anything escalates and within no time she's pulling up a block away from the hotel.

"Sorry to drop you off so far away. I just don't want anyone at my work to see us," she explains as she shoves the van into park. "Not that we're doing anything wrong. I mean, nothing's happening, not in the way that they think. That they could think."

I study her face, the flush creeping into her cheeks, the slightly flustered way she's talking. "Define what wrong is."

She stares at me, frowning. "I mean like, uh…"

"Do you mean like me taking you out for dinner? Or do you mean me taking you to my room afterward?"

Her pupils enlarge, making her eyes glow. She's speechless. It's utterly charming.

"Maybe both," she finally says, her voice coming out in this low, breathless hush that makes me bite my lip. This isn't the right place to get an erection but if she keeps looking so flushed and innocent, it's going to become a problem.

"And what happens when we do go out for dinner?" I ask her. "When I do invite you back to my room?"

Those dark eyes of her widen even more. She swallows.

I grin at her. "I guess we'll cross that bridge when we come to it," I tell her, letting her off the hook as I unbuckle my seatbelt and open the door, getting out.

"No cow on the ice," she whispers, almost to herself.

"Not yet anyway," I tell her. Then I clear my throat. "I'll be by your place at seven to pick you up."

"What? I'm picking you up. You don't have a car that works."

"This is a date, Miss America," I remind her. "You're not driving. Neither am I. I'll call a cab for us. Simple as that."

She nods, smiling so softly that something inside my heart shifts again. "Okay."

"I'll see you," I tell her with a wink.

Then I'm closing the door and I'm walking back to my hotel room.

Smiling.

CHAPTER SEVEN

MAGGIE

"Sorry, what was his name again?" Sam asks, her nose scrunching up on the screen of my phone as I talk to her through FaceTime.

I sigh and adjust myself on the bed, trying not to get too comfortable. When I'm on the phone with Sam I always shut my bedroom door to get privacy and if I'm on the bed with even a few minutes of peace, I usually pass out. There's been many a phone call or FaceTime session where I've passed out mid-sentence. Luckily, Sam understands.

But I don't think I can pass out today, not with this adrenaline running through my veins and butterflies swarming in my stomach, feelings I haven't been able to shake ever since I dropped the Swede off at the hotel.

"His name is Johan Andersson," I repeat.

"I don't think I like that name."

"Yeah, well it's his name. I call him Mr. Sverige though."

"Mr. Sverige? What are you doing, acting out some weird student-teacher fantasy or something?" She pauses, tilting her head in consideration. "Not that it's weird to have that fantasy. Lord knows we had that about Mr. Strong. Remember Rodney Strong?"

We had a professor called Mr. Strong. I can't remember his first name because we always called him Rodney since Rodney Strong was the wine we drank the most in the evenings when we'd sit crammed in my dorm room, complaining about men.

My heart pangs at remembering the good ol' days.

"When I first saw his driver's license, I thought his name was Swedish Driver's License," I explain. "Sverige means Sweden or Swedish. Anyway, you had to be there."

"It sounds like it," she says. "If I wasn't so good at reading you, I would have thought the whole thing was made up."

"What?"

"First you walk in on what sounds like an impossibly tall, hunky Scandinavian god naked, then you see him at the bar, when, by the way, you never go out. Then you proceed to take him home, so he can sober up. The next day he wakes up and gets in a fist fight with that loser your sister is dating, knocks him out, you fix him up and then he asks you out on a date." She pauses to brush her hair out of her eyes. "All the while he's exceedingly rich."

"I never said he was exceedingly rich," I tell her, although when I told Pike about the kind of car he had, he'd told me it was worth a hell of a lot of money. Plus, there's that whole heir to a pharmaceutical company thing.

"I'm going to assume he is," she says. "If you don't have sex with him Maggie, I'm going to be so mad at you."

"Whoa," I say, laughing, my cheeks flaming. "Who said anything about having sex with him?"

"Oh give me a break. You want to pretend that this isn't where it's going?"

I shake my head, but my mouth keeps wanting to creep

up into a smile. Sam is usually the first one to call me on my bullshit. Not only have I been thinking about it since I first saw him—I mean, who can blame me—but all those thoughts and feelings and urges have been put through the ringer ever since he insinuated it.

Because he *did* insinuate it, didn't he?

He looked right at me with heat in his eyes and talked about taking me back to his hotel room. If that wasn't a hint that he was planning to seduce me after dinner, I don't know what is.

Don't get ahead of yourself.

And yet it's so damn hard not to.

"Wow," Sam says. "You are a smitten kitten."

I roll my eyes, making sure my face isn't betraying me with any longing looks. "Oh I am not."

"Fuck, dude. You can be a smitten kitten all you want. When was the last time you went on a date? Here, right? And when was the last time you were going gaga over someone? Never. Never, Maggie. I've never seen you get this look in your eyes before."

I frown, trying to make my eyes turn to hardened steel. "What look?"

"Maggie, it's okay to want this guy. I think you should get dressed up and make yourself feel sexy. Shave your legs. Shave your lady bits. Put on makeup. Wear a dress. Heels. Go out with this Viking god and have a wonderful date. Forget about your brothers and sisters. Forget about April and all her shit. Forget about everything except that you're out with this guy that you want to fuck and then you go back to that La Quinta and you fucking fuck him."

I swallow hard. "It's not that easy."

"Oh my god." She sighs and does a mock fall back away from the phone.

"What? I just…I just met this guy."

"You've already seen him naked," she points out.

"I know but that wasn't sexual."

"It doesn't matter. You saw him naked, you rescued him drunk, you bandaged up his wounds like Florence Fucking Nightingale. Go and get those Swedish meatballs, girl!"

I burst out laughing. "Stop!"

She's laughing too. "I'm sorry, I was waiting this whole conversation to sneak that in there. Believe me, I've got a joke about his Swedish berries as well."

"Sam."

"I know, I know. I can't help it." She sighs happily. "Anyway, I'm just saying. Stop worrying and just enjoy it. You know he's not going to stick around forever."

"I know. I think that's what's putting a damper on this whole thing. Here is this hot as fuck, sexy, rich, funny, smart, exotic beast of a man and he's only here because his car broke down. Soon, maybe even tomorrow, he'll be off to LA and then home. And I'll still be here."

"At least you would have gotten some food and orgasms out of it."

"And a broken heart."

"Oh please. This is all about your vagina. There's no need for your heart to join the party."

I giggle. Apparently, I'm immature. "I miss talking to you, you know."

"Well call me more often and not just when you're about to get laid, okay?"

"I'm still not sure about that."

"Either way, you should at least prepare like you're going to get his cock. None of this Bridget Jones reverse psychology bullshit. Put on your sexiest bra and underwear. Shave."

"You already told me to shave."

"Well shave again because I have a feeling you're in for a lot of yard work."

I sigh. "God, if I do sleep with him, it's going to suck when he leaves."

"So, just follow him to Sweden. You can get a Swedish travel article out of it and sell it."

"Yeah right. Do you remember what my life is like now? Even if I could go, I couldn't. And I can't even convince the local newspaper here to hire me. I don't get it. I'm a good writer. What I did at NYU was good shit."

"It was, but they probably just can't hire anyone right now. Your best bet is to stick to freelancing. Are you doing that?"

"I can't even write," I mumble. "I have zero inspiration. Zero time. Zero motivation."

"Make time."

"Sam," I say, feeling a hit of anger cut through me. "You have no idea what kind of pressure I'm under over here with everything."

She pouts. "I know. I'm sorry. I just want you to succeed that's all. You shouldn't have to give up on any of your dreams or hopes just because of what happened."

"Yeah, well, I have." I exhale, feeling sorrow dampen me. Funny how you can go from excited and elated to defeated in seconds flat. Welcome to my world now.

"Speaking of hot Swedish men, have you seen the Prince of Sweden?" she asks.

"Sweden has a monarchy?" I ask but even as I do so I remember Johan's story about ABBA and the queen.

"Yeah and the prince is fucking hot. There were actually two of them but the other one died a few months ago or something. Sad. He was young too, only in his mid-thirties."

God, I haven't been keeping up with the news at all. Not

that I'd take any notice of anything happening in Sweden of all places.

"How do you know all this?"

"Dude, I'm like a royal junkie. Harry and Meghan, Will and Kate. Those sexy ass Casirahis of Monaco. I am on it." She adds, "I guess all Swedes are exceptionally tall. Your guy. The prince. Alexander Skarsgard."

"Looks like I was born in the wrong country."

"Crown Prince Viktor of House Nordin," she says as she gets up from where she was sitting at her desk. "Here, I think I have the magazine."

"Magazine?" I repeat. "Oh jeez, Sam. You need a hobby."

I hear the rustle of papers as she rummages through something and then returns to the screen holding up a magazine. Through the grainy video I can make out *Royalty Monthly* with Harry and Meghan on the cover.

"Hold on," she says while she flips through the pages. "I was thinking of starting, like, a royalty blog, you know."

"Well it would at least put this obsession to use, though I can't say it's good use."

"Here," she says and then opens the magazine so I'm staring at one of the pages.

The headline says *Prince Alexander and Prince Viktor visit the Stockholm Children's Hospital* with a picture of the princes below it.

Both are tall, about as tall as my Swede. One has dark hair and a paler complexion while the other's hair is lighter and skin more tanned and…

Wow.

Though the picture isn't clear, this guy looks a lot like Johan.

Sam takes the magazine away from my view. "See, they're hot."

"Hey, put it back," I tell her.

She smiles. "I knew you'd like it."

The picture comes back onto my screen. It's so grainy because of the low light of Sam's room so I can't make out the details, but fuck, it really, really looks like Johan. Obviously, it's not, but the resemblance is striking.

"Happy?" she asks.

I shake my head. "It's weird. Johan looks exactly like the prince."

"Which one? The dead one or the not dead one?"

"The one with the lighter hair."

"That's Viktor. He was always the one who kept to himself. He wasn't heir apparent until Alexander died."

"How did he die?"

She shrugs. "I don't know. Something to do with the wrong prescription maybe? Or he had some heart defect? I've read a lot of different things."

"Hmmm," I muse.

"What?"

"I don't know." There's something about all of this that's making me feel off-balance. It's not just that they look the same but it's that...it's that they *really* look the same. There's something here not right here. "Hold on Sam, I'm going to put you in the background."

"Looking them up are you?"

"Yeah well the picture is really grainy and blurry," I say absently as I open up the Google app and enter in Prince Viktor of Sweden.

The first thing I see in the search results is the Wikipedia entry and the headshot of Prince Viktor to the side.

My heart stills. Pins and needles rush up and down my body as I stare at it in disbelief.

"Oh my god," I whisper.

Oh my god.

It's Johan. Sverige. Mr. Swedish Driver's License.

"What? What's happening?"

"It's him," I say breathlessly. "It's him."

"Who?"

I quickly click the images and suddenly I'm bombarded by a whole grid of him. I click through and through and through, staring closely at the photos but I don't have to. I know it's him.

How the fuck is this possible?

"He told me his name was…"

"Johan," she fills in quickly.

"Yeah, Johan Andersson. That's what his ID said. I saw it."

"You think…wait…you think that the rich big-dicked Swede you're going on a date with is the actual Prince of Sweden?" She starts laughing. "Maggie! You're crazy!"

"I know, I know it's crazy but fuck. This is him."

"It can't be."

"I'll get a picture of him tonight and I'll show you."

But she's also right because how can it be him? How could this be true?

"You're seeing what you want to," she says. "I put the idea in your head and now you're thinking it's him. Your mind is warping your image of him to fit this Viktor's. But it's not him. It can't be. He's in fucking Sweden right now."

"How do you know?"

"I don't know, but I do. Look, come back to me. Let me look you in the eyes and tell you how nuts you are."

I sigh and close the Google app and come back to Sam's face. She's earnest, I'll give her that. "You're nuts, Mags."

I shake my head, unable to get rid of that feeling that I'm right. "It's him."

"It's so not. Come on. You know I'm your biggest supporter and I think you're one fine hot piece of ass, but I can guarantee you that if the Swedish prince were in your town for some fucking reason, you wouldn't be walking in on him naked. Staying at the fucking La Quinta!" She barks out a laugh. "And then he wouldn't be alone and drunk and drugged at a bar and he wouldn't, I repeat, he wouldn't fight your sister's thug boyfriend. You're hot but you're poor in small-town America and he's a fucking prince from Europe, okay? Think about everything I just said."

I know what she said and it all makes perfect sense.

But...

"What if it is him?" I ask hopefully. I hate sounding hopeful but there it is.

"It's not."

"But what if it is? What if I take a picture of him and then send it to you and then you're all like, shit it is him. Then what?"

"Then don't tell him that you know. Keep that shit to yourself. And write a fucking article and sell it to the gossip mags. Sell it to Royalty Monthly. Forget the, whatever your town is called, forget the paper there and go big. You could get a fucking ass-load of money for an article or interview with the Prince of Sweden, the heir to the throne." She pauses. "But it's not him. K?"

I nod slowly. My brain refuses to accept it, but I'm just going to have to wait and see. I'm sure the moment I see his face I'll realize that I've been mistaken.

"So forget all of that and just go have fun tonight. Get laid. Be loud. Make him go down on you and don't you dare get Rick-Rolled. And then call me tomorrow and tell me all about it."

I laugh softly. "I will. Bye, Sam."

I hang up the phone, watching her face disappear, and stare at my closet full of second-hand clothes. Luckily men don't notice the brand of a dress and I have a couple that look fairly new.

I sort through the rack, pull out a simple black sleeveless

one with lace overlay, put it down on the bed and start getting ready for my date.

He's not the prince, he's not the prince, he's not the prince, I tell myself.

But, god.

What if he is?

CHAPTER EIGHT

MAGGIE

I'm a nervous wreck.

I can't remember the last time I was ever this nervous.

I've changed outfits enough times to make anyone crazy. I've gone from the black dress to jeans and a blousy top, to a long sundress, to black pants and a tank top, and all the way back to the black dress again.

Now I'm pacing my bedroom, both trying to break in these three-inch heels I picked up in New York but never wore and trying to dispel all the nervous energy that's been building up inside me to dangerous levels.

A knock at my door.

I pause and then run over to my window that looks out onto the street. No cab yet. I glance at the clock on my wall. It's five to seven. He could be here at any minute.

I'm going to be sick.

"Maggie," Pike says from the other side of the door. "What are you doing?"

"Getting ready."

"Still? He's going to be here any minute."

I sigh, shaking out my hands as if that will dissolve my nerves, and go over, opening the door a crack.

"I'm busy."

Pike frowns at me. "Nice makeup."

I glare at him. "Are you being sarcastic?"

"No," he says. "I've just never seen you wear it before."

He's right. I rarely wear makeup, certainly not the whole shebang like I'm doing right now. Apparently I'm a bit sensitive over how I look at the moment.

"Are you naked?"

"No." I grimace, wishing my brother wouldn't use the word *naked* around me.

He puts his hand on the door and shoves it open, causing me to take a step back and almost bail in these damn heels.

"Jesus, Mags," he says with wide eyes. "Just where are you going again?"

"The Bullshed," I tell him, my vulnerability morphing into defensiveness. "Why? What's wrong with what I'm wearing?"

"You just look a little dressed up, that's all. I mean, heels. When have you ever worn heels?" He looks completely confused and flabbergasted.

"When I lived in Manhattan," I snipe, hands on my hips. "You know in other parts of the world, people actually dress up when they go out for dinner."

"Yeah and this ain't those parts of the world."

"Pike, do I look nice or not?"

"You look nice. *Jesus*, you're touchy."

Was that so hard? I snatch my purse off the bed and head out of the room.

"He's here!" Rosemary yells from downstairs.

Oh god.

I practically keel over, my hand going to my stomach as I lean hunched against the doorway.

"Are you okay?" Pike asks.

I nod frantically, my eyes pinched shut. My nerves are so razor sharp it feels like I'm being sliced in half. "Bad case of nerves," I manage to say.

"Why?"

God, brothers are so fucking dense. "Never mind."

Next to my room the door to April's room opens and she pokes her head out to see what the commotion is. Sees me, goes "Uggggh," rolls her eyes and then slams the door shut.

"Don't worry about her," Pike says putting one hand on my back and shoving me out into the hall. "Don't worry about anything."

"Yeah right."

"You're nervous about going on a date with this guy? He's just a guy," he says, ushering me toward the stairs. "A tall fucker with a funny accent who beat up Tito Jones. But still, a guy."

Is he just a guy?

Even if he's not the Prince of Sweden, he's definitely not "just a guy."

My heart feels like it's literally lodged in my throat as I walk toward the front door, sweat breaking out on my palms. Shit, what if he tries to hold my hand? I frantically start wiping my palms on my dress then take the deepest breath possible before I open the door and step outside into the fading sun.

There the cab is waiting, and I see the Swede climb out of the back seat and hold the door open for me like a true gentleman.

He's smiling, that movie star smile with those perfect white teeth, the cocky twinkle in his eyes.

And I know in my heart of hearts that there is no wondering or questioning or dreaming anymore.

This is him.

He might still be Mr. Sverige by default but he's not Johan Andersson at all.

He's His Royal Highness, the Crown Prince of Sweden, Viktor of House Nordin.

And he just rolled up to my house in a yellow cab.

"Hey," he says to me, gesturing to the cab with his arm. "Your chariot awaits."

I grin at that. A nervous grin. A stupid grin.

I can't believe this is happening.

Viktor–*Viktor*, god how he suits the name Viktor–isn't as dressed up as me, but he still looks amazing. Leather jacket, a rust-colored V-neck tee that makes his blue eyes pop, dark jeans, dark boots.

Sam isn't going to believe this.

I barely believe it myself.

A knocking sound comes from behind me and I whirl around to see Pike, Rosemary, Thyme and Callum at the large, kitchen picture window, waving and motioning me to get in the damn cab.

My eyes then trail up to April's bedroom window.

She's there, watching.

Gives me the finger.

I roll my eyes at her, turn around and hurry toward Viktor before anything else happens.

"You look beautiful," he says to me as I approach him, and I'm so mesmerized by the way he's staring at me, like he's stripping the clothes right off me with his gaze, that my left heel wobbles and suddenly I'm pitching over like a tree, my fall to the ground inevitable.

Without even moving much, Viktor's hand shoots out and he grabs hold of my arm with a grip so strong he could probably break my bones if he wanted to.

"Falling for me already," he says, waiting patiently until I get my footing again.

I giggle mumble "sorry" and "thank you" in response. Then add, "Johan!" a little too loud.

He frowns at me. He thinks I'm nuts. "I think I liked it better when you called me Mr. Swedish Driver's License."

I slide in the back of the cab, conscious of the fact that my dress is riding up higher and higher on my thighs as I do so. Viktor gives my legs a burning glance and then shuts the door, coming around to the other side and getting in.

"Where to?" the cab driver asks. He eyes me in the mirror, does a double take, and then turns around to look at me. "Maggie McPherson?"

"Yeah," I say cautiously.

"I forgot this is where you lived," the cabbie says. "I'm Earl. Earl White? I used to know your father. Anyway, real sorry about what happened. Such a tragedy. You poor kids. All on your own. Man, I hope they execute the punk that murdered them, give him a taste of his own medicine."

I nod and smile politely, trying to work down the lump in my throat. Well, that's one way to have my nerves disappear– have someone bring up not only my parents being murdered but the monster who did it.

I don't look at Viktor. I don't want him to read my face.

But he does reach out and puts his hand on top of my hand.

Wraps his long, strong fingers around mine.

Gives it a comforting squeeze.

Thank god my palms aren't sweating anymore.

"So where to?" Earl says again.

Viktor lets go and my hand now feels naked and alone without his.

I clear my throat. "The Bullshed. Please."

"You got it," Earl says and drives us off.

Viktor chuckles.

I glance at him quickly out of the corner of my eye. "What?"

"I thought you said The Bullshit," he says, leaning back in his seat. "And I thought that was a brilliant name for a restaurant."

His comment makes me relax, just a little. Despite who he is, he's really good at putting me at ease. Or at least trying.

The thing is, my body was already tight and jittery around him before I figured out who he was. Just being in his presence, in the backseat of this cab with his massive frame and long legs and those large hands and that strong jaw and those eyes, those eyes that hold so much in them, hold back so many layers that keep touching the surface, I am nervous. Nervous. He is so much larger than life, worldly, and fuck, he's *noble*. Not just as a characteristic but in a literal sense.

And then there's me, who could barely get a date in New York, who is chained to tragedy, drowning in responsibilities I'll never live up to, stuck forever in this town and…

"This is a beautiful town," Viktor says, and he says it with such earnestness that I have to look at him, my brows raised to the roof.

"Are you poking fun? Do you Swedes have a word for that like the Brits do, like taking the piss?"

"I'm not taking the piss," he says. "It's pretty here. This light. These hills. We don't have hills like this in Sweden. We barely have any hills at all."

I look out the window at the houses we're passing by, at the rolling hills in the distance beyond the town that are catching the last rays of the sun. I force myself to see the town through his eyes. Maybe it would look more promising to me if such awful things hadn't happened here.

"Actually, it's beautiful if you drive in from Bako," I concede. "That's Bakersfield, to the west. You're driving on this ugly highway and it's just desert, but not the kind of romantic desert like you get in the Mohave with all the Joshua trees, but this dry, dirty, broken-down kind of land. And then these hills appear in the distance, like brown and tan velvet and the highway starts winding up through them. When the sun hits it just right, it feels like you're driving up to heaven."

"That sounds beautiful," he says softly.

"Yeah, and then your heaven quickly turns to hell."

"Do you ever think about leaving?" he asks. "Moving? Seeing the world?"

I laugh dryly. "Every second of every day. But I can't."

"I'm sure it's not impossible though."

I give him a sad smile. "But it is. It is. And you know what…I might think about it, but I also try not to spend too much time complaining either. It is what it is."

He nods. "It is what it is."

With our conversation taking a rather serious turn by the time the cab pulls up to The Bullshed, a steak house around the corner from the hotel, at the edges of "downtown," I've nearly forgotten all about the new development.

You know, that I'm going on a fucking date with the Prince of Sweden.

No big deal.

Still, I know that I'm going to need some kind of proof. I need Sam to tell me I'm not crazy and I need to prove to her I'm not.

I need a picture of him.

We walk into the restaurant, and even though it's Saturday night, the place doesn't look too busy. As Viktor requests a table for two and the hostess disappears around the corner to check, I bring out my phone.

"Here, let's take a selfie," I tell him, sidling up to him and holding the phone out in front of us.

He balks, seeming visibly uncomfortable.

"What?" I ask him, but I don't lower the phone. "You don't like having your picture taken?"

I press the shutter, subtly taking one anyway even though it will be a pic of us looking at each other, both frowning.

"No, it's fine," he says and flashes the camera a forced smile.

I take another one and hope that it didn't make things weird.

"Sorry," I tell him, slipping the phone in my purse. "I figured after this you'll be on your way and I'll look back on this as if it were a dream. I'll need proof that it was all real."

Lame, Maggie.

But he nods, seeming to buy that cheesy justification.

The hostess comes back and leads us to the table. As we walk through a row of booths, Viktor puts his hand on the small of my back. It's possessive, letting everyone here know that we're together, and it causes heat to tingle in the pit of my stomach.

It says, *I'm his*, even if it's just for tonight.

We're seated at the end of the row, which thankfully gives us a lot of privacy. A small candle is lit between us, the lights overhead dimmed and warm.

"This is very nice," he says, giving the restaurant an appreciative glance.

"Well it's not Manhattan," I tell him. "And it's still too good for me." Before I can get settled, I get up, grabbing my purse. "I'm just going to quickly use the restroom. Order me anything you wish."

He cocks his brow. "Anything? You know in Sweden, we're rather fond of aquavit."

That must be some type of water. "That's fine," I say brightly. I can always order some alcohol after.

I steal away from him and head into the restroom at the

opposite end of the restaurant, go straight into a stall, lower the lid, sit down, and bring out my phone.

My heart is going so fast it's making my fingers fumble and I'm barely able to send the two pics of us through to Sam.

I add: **CALL ME NOW. Right now. Not on FaceTime.**

I see the pics get delivered and seconds later, the phone rings.

"Sam," I whisper, answering it.

I hear a choked sound on the other end, then, "Fuck. FUCK!"

"It's him, isn't it? It's him," I say, getting more convinced by the second.

"Oh my god, I can't…it looks just like him. He is fucking fine, Maggie, holy fuck, if you don't tap that ass, prince or not, I will come over there and tap it myself."

"But it's him right? You agree?"

"It looks like him. I've never seen him in a leather jacket but yeah it's him."

"I know it's him."

"Where are you now? Are you with him?"

"I'm in the bathroom of a restaurant. We're on our date. That's why I don't want to FaceTime, pretty sure that's illegal if someone is sitting on the can."

"Listen, listen," she says, "you have to interview him. You have to. Oh my god, Maggie, this could end all your problems."

"How?"

"How would you interview him or how would it end all your problems?"

"Both."

"Well for one, if you got an interview then you could sell it like we discussed."

"I don't think that's legal."

"Of course it is! Didn't you learn anything in school?"

"It's…unscrupulous."

"Not many things in life are *scrupulous*," she says. "Even if you don't feel comfortable writing an article, you could at least do it all as an anonymous source. Seriously you can make big, big money."

I ponder that, though I'm disappointed in what the idea of having more money does to me. "How much money?"

"I don't know. Enough to make you and your family's lives easier for a few months. Don't you have a toilet that needs fixing? Look, he's the heir apparent now. He will be king one day. The King of Sweden! And you have the inside track right now. My god, Maggie, don't you see the possibilities?"

I do see them. I just wish my moral compass wasn't spinning so wildly right now. "How would I interview him? I can't remember anything and he's going to notice I'm taking notes."

"Don't you have a voice recorder on your phone?"

"It's an old iPhone."

"You should still have it. It comes with the phone. Open it, then press record and have it out while you're having dinner. Just don't let him see. Easy peasy."

I can tell it's not going to be easy peasy.

But it's worth a shot.

"I'll do that now," I tell her. "I'll text you later."

"Wait, wait," she says. "Can I just tell you one thing?"

"What?"

"You two make a damn good-looking couple."

I sigh, hating how my heart just glowed at those words. "Don't tell me that."

"It's true. Maggie, he wants you."

"You can tell that from a picture?"

"Yes. The way he's looking at you, my god. He wants, no, *craves* you."

"I'm the only person he knows here, and he barely knows me at all."

"Maggie. He wants in your pants. Okay? Now go get that interview and go get those Swedish berries!"

I hang up and I think I hear her swearing in awe as I do so.

Shit. Now I feel like dry-heaving again.

Can I do this? Am I okay with doing this? Is this the kind of person my mother raised me to be?

Then again, my mother also raised me to put family first. And if I have a chance to put food on the table and buy things we really need for my brothers and sisters, then I don't think I have much choice.

I quickly find the voice memos app, open it and then press record. I hold the phone close to my side and step out of the stall, grateful that there was no one in the restroom to hear all of that.

CHAPTER NINE

MAGGIE

When I get back to the table I notice two glasses of water out for us as well as what looks like highballs of vodka. I slide into the booth, ever so careful of keeping my purse at the end of the table and my phone face down on top of my purse, recording in secrecy.

"I ordered an appetizer for us," Viktor says. "I hope you don't mind. I'm afraid I've taken quite a liking to your onion rings in this country."

"I can't blame you." I clear my throat and jerk my chin to the drink. "Vodka?"

"Aquavit," he says. "Didn't you know?"

"Of course," I say, taking the glass in my hand.

"Cheers then," he says, raising his. "Or as we say, skål!"

"Skål!" I say, noticing the way that his eyes never leave mine, even as he sips his drink. *I guess he takes the seven year's bad sex superstition seriously*, I think to myself as I take a drink and... *ah* –

Oh god!

The burning!

The aquavit is fucking acid on my tongue.

I start coughing, choking. *Dying.*

"It's strong," he says, trying not to smile.

I just keep coughing, reaching for my water. Shit. I thought with all the tequila shots I did in college I would be able to handle this, but this drink is on another level.

"I'm fine, by the way," I manage to say between gulps of air. The smell and taste of licorice seem singed in my senses, and no amount of water will wash it away.

"I know you're fine." He calmly takes another sip. "Like I said earlier, you're tougher than you look."

I cough again, my eyes watering. "Holy crap," I tell him, my hands braced against the edge of the table. "I think I saw Jesus."

He chuckles, the sound warm and rich. He's still looking at me like everything I do greatly amuses him.

"But you're more relaxed now, no?"

Actually, he's right. The drink was strong, but I can already feel it washing through me, this languid warmth, like sinking into a hot bath.

"Did I seem tense before?"

He gives a light shrug. "A little."

"Yeah, well don't go getting yourself a big head. I haven't been relaxed in a very long time."

"Big head?"

"You know, like an ego."

"Oh," he says. "I see. I thought you meant like a big cock. And you can contest that I already have one."

Phhhhhhhffff.

The gulp of water I had in my mouth just goes flying across the table in a spray.

"Oh my god," I gasp. "I am so sorry."

I frantically grab my napkin and start wiping down the surface.

"It's quite alright," he says nonchalantly as he dusts the

spray off his shoulders. "This seems to be the normal reaction from you when my penis is involved."

My hand goes to my mouth this time to stifle the laugh and anything else that wants to come out. I know my cheeks are burning up, but I think they've been burning up ever since I had that aquavit.

"I like it when you blush, you know," he says, eyeing me. "It makes me wonder what else I can do to make you turn so rosy."

"Stop," I cry out playfully, averting my eyes.

"Oh, I can go all night long."

I shake my head. He is unbelievable. His accent makes everything sound light and flirtatious but the wicked gleam in his eyes tells me he's serious.

If I wasn't hot and bothered before, I definitely am now.

Don't forget who he is, I remind myself. *Don't forget you're recording all of it.*

I wince at the thought of playing this all back later.

"You okay?" he asks me, leaning in a bit.

"Oh yes, fine," I tell him. "I mean, aside from spitting on you and nearly choking on the drink. What was even in that? Tastes like burning licorice and, like, dill."

"Caraway seed," he says, having another sip. I watch him swallow, my eyes resting on the hollow of his throat. God, he's got a sexy throat. I can imagine his neck muscles all corded and tense when he's coming and–

"*Smaken är som baken, delad*," he rattles off in Swedish, interrupting my fantasy. "Taste is like your bum…divided."

"Excuse me, what? *Tasting my bum?*"

"Only if you're into it," he says, a tiny, knowing smile crossing his lips, like he knows exactly what's happening later. The thought makes me squeeze my thighs together.

Then he clears his throat. "Actually, it's a saying. Taste is like your bum, divided. It means that…well, not everyone likes aquavit."

I don't think my body will ever stop feeling like it's on fire. "How many more sayings are there?"

"We have quite a few," he says. "We even have a family motto."

Ah, here we are. Here is the segue. Here's where I can get this on track to something like an interview.

"Does it involve bums or cows?" I ask warily.

That gorgeous smile widens. "I'm afraid not. Our motto is alltid mer, aldrig mindre." He pauses. "It means *always more, never less*."

"Always more, never less," I repeat, louder, for the recorder. "I like that."

"So do I. In the past…in the company, things were rather formal and stuffy, you might say. Everything was just for show. There was no…warmth. But my parents, my father, but especially my mother, they decided to do things a bit differently. More time with the public."

"Public?" I ask.

"Clients," he says smoothly. "More time with the clients. More time getting to know them. More time doing charity work and being involved with the community. Always more, never less. Always go all in, always give more of yourself, always do your best. Never settle, never cheat, never withdraw."

It's so weird to hear him talk about his family and job like this because I know what his actual family is, his job, his role. I could probably get a lot out of him this way, just asking questions and twisting his answers around to apply to the monarchy.

The waitress comes by with the onion rings and then takes our orders. I haven't had a steak in ages, so I ask for a nice juicy rib-eye with a baked potato and asparagus. My mouth is practically watering even ordering it.

"It's nice to see a girl who likes to eat," he remarks.

"Hey, most girls love to eat," I point out. "But I do especially because it's so rare I get to eat something this good, like a steak. God, I can practically taste it already."

"Do you do most of the cooking at your house?" he asks.

"Yeah, usually," I tell him, picking at the onion rings. It's taking great restraint not to devour them all. "If not, Pike does. It's usually more me than him but he helps out."

"Must be lucky to have his support. He seems old enough."

"He's eighteen," I tell him.

"How old are you?"

"Twenty-three." And though I know how old he is because I spent all day Googling him, I have to ask. "And you?"

"Thirty," he says. "And your brothers and sisters, how old are they?"

I dip my onion ring in and out of the ranch dressing and list off their names and ages.

"Wow." Viktor sits back in his seat, running his hand through his hair. "I admire you."

I shrug it off. He means well, but I hate that term. "There's nothing to admire. I'm just doing what I have to do. Anyone in my position would do the same."

"No," he says and a darkness flits across his eyes. "They wouldn't. People are inherently selfish at heart, even with family. They'll push others away in order to save themselves."

I pause with the onion ring and stare at him, wondering what brought this out. Despite the always more, never less motto, were there problems in his own family? Did it have something to do with his brother?

I know I probably shouldn't ask this next question but in

journalism school we were taught that the dangerous questions are the right ones to ask. "Do you have any siblings?"

He looks like I just slapped his face and he pales before my eyes, a world of pain crushing his features. I instantly regret the question.

He opens his mouth to say something and I don't want to put him on the spot. "Have you always lived in Stockholm?" I ask quickly, trying to cover it up.

"Yes," he says quietly. "To both. I was born in Stockholm and while I've traveled around Europe, it has always been my home base. And yes, I had a brother."

I swallow uneasily, looking away from his eyes. They've turned so haunting, I feel haunted in return. "Had?"

"He died just over a month ago."

"I'm so sorry," I tell him.

"Thank you," he says. "And thank you for not asking how."

I manage a weak smile. Even though a journalist would ask how, especially since the real reports are conflicting, as someone who lost loved ones, I know better. If we want people to know, we'll tell them. "I understand."

"I know you do," he says. "Maybe that's why…"

"Why what?"

He shrugs and finishes the rest of his drink. "I don't know." He puts the glass down and shoots me a furtive glance. "I feel drawn to you, Maggie. In ways I can't quite explain. And maybe that explains it."

Drawn to me? If we weren't just talking about something so serious I think I would be swooning in my seat.

"You know the other day," he says, "I was in Vegas. I'd always wanted to go, and it was a natural stopover on the highway. But I barely made it into the hotel. There was a wedding, and everyone had these flowers and the smell…"

"White lilies," I whisper absently, the images of them in

front of the caskets clouding my mind, bringing with it all the memories of pain.

"Yes." He frowns and sits up straighter, leaning forward on his elbows. "How did you know?"

I take in a deep breath and blink. I don't want to cry here, not now.

"It's okay. You don't have to say anything," he says.

"No, it's fine. Really. I just needed a moment. Sometimes I think I'm always needing a moment." I let out a shaky breath. "We had white lilies at the funeral for my parents. It's common here. It's the symbol of innocence and I guess people think there's innocence in death, even though the way my parents died was anything but innocent. Anyway, I can't smell them either without being transported to that day. They're forever tainted to me. And the problem is, a lot of flowers smell similar to lilies, at least to me."

"So what you're saying is, you're not a girl who loves getting flowers."

I let out a soft laugh. "No. That's never been me."

The smile fades from his face. "Well, now I know how it affects me too. When I smelled them, suddenly I was brought back to everything I've been running away from and I had to get out of there. That's how I ended up here, with extra medication in my system and a lovely girl who took pity on me."

"You've been running away?"

He nods, his hands slowly twisting around his empty glass. "I am on vacation but the reason for the vacation is that I needed a break."

"If you just lost your brother, that's understandable."

"Yes. I suppose. But in this business, we don't have time to grieve. You see, I wasn't poised to take over the company. My brother was. Alex was his name. Is his name. See? Fuck. Sometimes I'm not sure if he's alive or dead."

The sight of Viktor pretending not to be Viktor and yet suffering this loss all the same is breaking me up inside. No matter how hard he's trying to be someone else, the pain doesn't take a vacation. The pain remembers who you are. Like Liam Neeson, the pain will always find you.

"Anyway, it was always Alex's job and not mine and now, well everything has changed." Around and around the glass goes. "Now the job is mine and I'm stuck with it. Drowning in it, if I may be so honest. I'm just not...not good enough or strong enough for it."

"I highly doubt that. I know we don't really know each other but I think you might be the strongest, most capable man I've ever met." He doesn't seem to believe it. I go on, "But if you don't want the...job...can't you quit?"

"People in this line of work don't usually quit. Not unless it is a danger to their health. And, well...let's just say I've seen firsthand what that danger is. I see what awaits me."

"Another drink?" the waitress says cheerfully, interrupting our conversation like someone shining a buzzing fluorescent light in a dark room.

"Could I get a glass of the house red?" I ask her.

"Sure thing." She looks to Viktor and he just nods and taps his glass.

She walks off, leaving us alone again.

"Are you going to finish that?" He nods at my nearly full glass of aquavit.

"No," I tell him, pushing it across the table toward him. "It seems the bum is still divided on this one."

"It's too bad I'm not here for that much longer. I think you'd be quick to pick up Swedish."

"Yeah," I say softly, my heart dipping inside my chest. "It is too bad. So when do you think you'll go to LA?"

"When the car is fixed. I ordered in a part today from a

store in Bakersfield. Should come up on Monday. I can just get it in there and go."

"You could use Pike's garage, I'm sure that will be a lot easier than tinkering in La Quinta's parking lot."

"I might take him up on that. But that still leaves me tonight and tomorrow. Tomorrow is Sunday. Do you want to spend your Sunday with me?"

Yes. Yes I want to spend Sunday with you and every day after that.

"I have work."

"What time?"

"Seven to three."

"So then I can't keep you out too late tonight, can I?"

I think you're worth all the sleep-deprivation in the world.

"Or maybe," he continues, his eyes lazily drifting down from my gaze toward my lips, then down my neck, then sliding across my chest. My skin dances from the intensity of it all, at the way he so easily affects me. "Maybe you'll spend the night at work. You won't even need to go home. Can't promise you that you won't be exhausted though."

Damn.

Damn.

"Here's your drinks."

Damn it!

The waitress appears, sliding a glass of wine toward me and another glass of aquavit toward Viktor, and while I smile politely my eyes are telling her she's interrupting something really important.

I think she gets it because she gingerly says, "I should let you two know that the food will be out shortly." Then she scurries off.

"So what was it like growing up here?" Viktor asks and everything inside me just sinks. We were so close to getting into that flirty sexy talk, the kind that teases with everything promising to come, and now he's reverted back to small talk.

But I like talking with Viktor. About anything, even small talk about my boring life. Even though he's pretending to be someone else, and even though I'm pretending that I don't know he's pretending. I just like being around him, period.

And honestly, I don't really care that he's a prince. I easily buy into his fake persona because that other stuff doesn't interest me. As someone who is just passing through town, everything else that he is to the world doesn't matter because for right now he's here and he's with me and this is the first time in a long time, maybe ever, that I actually feel like someone wants to be with me, wants to talk to me. And yes, wants to sleep with me. I just hope he's not pretending that part too.

Then dinner is served, and I tell him about my life and he tells me more about his, and then it slowly dawns on me that I absolutely can't betray this man. I know that an article would pay for things we desperately need, I know that it would kickstart my career, the one that's been put on the back burner. I know it would change things for me, for my brothers and sisters, in a positive way.

But this man…this gorgeous, funny, sweet, cocky, forward man, I can't do that to him. Even if he leaves in a day or two and I never have contact with him again, I can't betray his trust, even if he doesn't realize he's trusting me with something so big.

The minute I decide that, the weight lifts off me. Something in my chest becomes lighter. Now I can just relax and enjoy the rest of the night, which now seems to be dessert in the literal sense.

"Chocolate lava cake," the waitress says, sliding the plate toward us.

We're doing the cheesy couple thing where we're both

sharing the one piece, with the one plate in the middle of the table between us.

"I didn't think I'd be able to have a bite after all that steak but now that I'm looking at it," I tell him, my fork poised to dig in.

He takes his fork and taps my fork out of the way.

I look up and meet his eyes. He gives me a wicked smile.

"I only want a taste," he says, his voice growing low and rough, causing my stomach to flip.

Cue the innuendo. "Is that so?"

"I don't want to spoil my appetite for later."

I feel my brow lift.

He just keeps giving me that panty-melting grin. He knows exactly what he's doing.

He slices into the cake with zeal, chopping off the corner.

Silly Swede, don't they have lava cakes back home?

I slice right into the middle, the best part.

With a little too much zeal.

Some of the hot melted chocolate in the middle goes spilling outward on the table, edging toward my lap.

"I've got it," he says, reaching over to the end of the table where a stack of napkins is behind my purse. He yanks them out of the holder, passing them to me, and the movement causes my purse to jerk forward, the phone to flip off the top of it and land on the table, right beside the cake.

Face up.

Showing the voice memo.

Recording us.

Oh.

Fuck.

No.

My fingers grip the napkins and suddenly I've forgotten all about the cake.

Fucking hell. Fucking hell, please don't let him see that, please don't let him realize what that is, please don't.

"What is this?" he asks, his brows coming together as he stares at it, watching the counter roll onwards, the red waves dancing on the graph as they record the sound of his voice. He glances up at me and there's fear etched all across his face.

I think I must look the same. Because I am scared shitless.

"What is this?" he repeats, picking up my phone, staring at it. He presses the red button to stop and then displays the screen to me. "Why were you recording this for…" He looks at it again. "The last hour and a half. Our entire dinner?"

No, no, no, no, no, no.

"It's an accident," I tell him feebly. Not the best excuse but the only one I have.

He stares at me so deeply, with so much bold ferocity, that I shrink back.

"You're lying," he says. His eyes may be made of fire right now, but his voice has turned cold.

I feel that cold in my bones.

"You're lying," he says again, his grip tightening around my phone. "I can tell. Why were you recording this? Us? Tell me, Maggie."

I lick my lips. My mouth feels like sand.

I'm trying to think fast but the evening and the wine and the steak and everything and I'm just…I've got nothing.

It was an accident. Tell him it was an accident again.

But he won't believe it. I know he won't.

He's seeing right through me. Right to my rotten core.

"I didn't mean to," I whisper to him. "I'm sorry."

"Didn't mean to? How did you not mean to?"

"I…okay, so I was but then I decided not to. I decided not to."

"Why. The fuck. Were you. Recording us?" he asks, his

words sharp blades hitting between all my ribs. "Do you know who I am?"

I can only blink at him. My eyes tell him everything.

"Well, fuck," he swears, pushing himself back against the seat, arms braced against the table, the muscles in his forearms popping like he's holding himself back from something, a vein in his forehead looking dangerous. "You know," he says to himself. "And you *knew*. This whole time, you knew who I was."

"No," I say adamantly, finding my voice. "I didn't know. I swear, I didn't know. You have to believe me."

"Bullshit, Maggie," he says. "And fuck your bullshit."

"Viktor, *please*."

His eyes flash as they fly to mine. "Oh my god. And you just called me Viktor." He shuts his eyes, shakes his head. "So much for everything."

The waitress comes by with the bill and before she can get close I give her the look that she better not dare come here right now. She gives me a *yikes, girl* look and then gladly leaves.

"You knew," he says again, rubbing the palm of his hand up and down his face. "You knew."

"I didn't, I swear. I only found out this afternoon, after you left, I promise."

"Your promises mean nothing."

I balk at that. I shouldn't be bothered by it, but I am. "Hey, I never promised you anything, okay? And by the way, it was wrong to record it and you can decide whether I'm telling the truth or not, but you've been lying to *me* this whole time."

"Don't you dare flip it around on me."

"I'm not flipping anything, I'm just pointing something out. You told me lies first."

"I had to," he says, practically growling at me. "I had to for my own sake and my family's sake."

"Okay, well, I'm just saying."

"And I'm just saying, we're done here."

"Viktor."

He shakes his head sharply and taps his fingers on top of my phone. "Delete this, please."

"Yes, yes, of course," I tell him. I grab the phone and though it takes me a moment because my hands are shaking so hard I nearly drop it, I figure out how to delete it. "It's gone." I show it to him.

But he doesn't look relieved. He doesn't look anything except pissed. And while I had been treated to the Viktor who minds his manners and has funny sayings and loves innuendo, I'd also witnessed the Viktor today that had no problems knocking out Tito several times with complete ease, a man he didn't know and a problem that wasn't his.

Maybe I don't know this guy at all. Maybe Johan Andersson was someone totally different than Crown Prince Viktor and maybe now I'm seeing who he really is.

But I don't think that's the case. I think Viktor is as multi-faceted as anyone is and what I'm seeing now is a man who is suitably angry because I broke his trust.

"The way you looked after me," he starts to say and then trails off.

"I didn't know," I tell him, desperation running through me like wild horses. "I swear I didn't know. Everything I did, I did for the very same reason you gave me earlier. That I'm drawn to you. And I just wanted to help. That's all. You have to believe me, I had no idea who you were until tonight. *Please.*"

That seems to get through to him, seems to sink in. His shoulders drop a little, his breath comes out long and hard. Then, "You said you were a journalism student."

Ah, fuck.

"So I guess you were recording us for, what, a tell-all article?"

I don't say anything. Clamp my mouth shut.

He shakes his head. "How much would they have paid you, huh?"

I inhale deeply, trying to catch my breath and to stop shaking. "It would have been enough for everyone to get new clothes and school supplies for the fall and for a plumber to fix our downstairs toilet," I tell him. "It's been broken forever and even Pike can't fix it."

I'm not trying to guilt-trip him or anything, it's just the truth. But even so, it reaches him.

He stares at me. It feels like eternity. I hate the way his eyes have changed, especially as the fire hardens to steel, to something forever cold.

"I'm sorry," I tell him softly, my words breaking, because what else can I do? Inside I feel the big black pit of shame starting to pull at me, dragging me down under into its depths. To say I feel embarrassed is an understatement.

He doesn't say anything. Just raises his hand to get the attention of a passing bus boy and asks for him to call him a cab.

There are tears burning behind my eyes, but I manage to keep them at bay. I get my purse and fish out my wallet. I know whatever money I have in there is for groceries for the week, but I won't let him pay, not now.

Suddenly his hand reaches out and grabs my wrist, holding me in place. "Keep it," he says gruffly. "I know how much you need it."

Then he brings a wad of cash out and throws it down on the table. "Come on," he says to me as he gets up, pulling on his jacket. "Cab will be here soon."

"I can get Pike to pick me up," I tell him feebly, staring at his money on the table, wishing I had enough pride that I would still pay. But I'm not that proud. I have no pride, not anymore.

"You're getting a cab." He jerks his head toward the front doors. "Come on."

I take in a shaking breath and get to my feet, walking behind him with my head down, afraid to look at the other tables. Though I'm sure our argument wasn't heard or witnessed by anyone, I still feel like everyone is looking at me and pitying me.

There goes Maggie McPherson, they'd whisper to each other.
Poor thing.
White trash.
Such a shame what happened to her parents.
Now she's in charge of all of them.
She can't do it on her own.
That man is way too good for her.
Sugar daddy.
I think she's a prostitute now.
How desperate she must be.

I follow Viktor out of the restaurant and into the night, the stars above us like tiny lanterns but I find no beauty in it. If only I could turn back time, we could have avoided all of that. We could have stepped out of here drunk and full and happy and maybe he'd say something romantic about the stars, or maybe he'd say something about sex and then we'd still get a cab but instead of standing apart like two strangers, maybe we'd be falling into each other. Smiling, laughing, touching, excited for the night to come.

If only I could turn back time, the two of us may have embarked on a very different future, maybe one that involved us together.

But I can't turn back time. I wished with all my might that I could the night my parents died, and I wish it now, but it hasn't worked, and it will never work.

I am stuck with this new reality.

I am stuck, period.

The cab pulls up and to my relief it's not Earl White again, just some old guy.

Viktor strides over to the driver and hands him a wad of cash through the window and then, then he somehow still has his manners, and he opens the back door for me, gesturing for me to get inside.

"Get in. He's taking you home. Or wherever thirty dollars will get you."

Now this, *this* feels like a walk of shame. Deep shame. "I'm so sorry," I tell him as I get in the backseat.

"Goodbye Maggie," he says without even looking at me and then slams the door in my face.

That door slamming was like the closing of a prison door on every dream and hope and *what if* I had blooming inside me tonight.

Now that bloom has wilted, dead.

The cab drives off, the driver asking where he's to take me.

But all I can do is just sit there.

Sit there and think about how royally things got fucked up.

I burst into tears and cry all the way home.

CHAPTER TEN

VIKTOR

Fuck.

It's past midnight.

I've not been able to sleep for a second.

I've been tossing and turning in bed, then watching TV, then pacing up and down the room. I have a nest of hornets in my heart, buzzing around viciously, their barbs stinging the same wound over and over again.

She knows who I am.

Maggie, this girl of sweetness and light, was hiding a secret just as big as mine.

I was such an idiot to think she couldn't see the truth. Of course she knew the truth, had ulterior motives. Why else would she have come to my rescue like that at the bar? Did I really think it was from the goodness of her heart?

I feel like an idiot. I *am* an idiot.

I was so blinded by her beauty, her body, the way she looked at me, the way I wanted nothing more than to bury my head between her soft legs and make her cheeks go that rosy pink, that I didn't even consider she could have had another motive.

Fuck.

Fuck.

I know I shouldn't be so upset about this, that I should have seen it coming. But for a moment there…I wanted to talk about Alex. About how he died. I wanted to share with her parts of me I don't share with anyone, not even Dr. Bonakov. I wanted to unload on her all the vile, bitter things that have been dragging me under into the raging darkness, this darkness that I know I can never escape.

Lilies.

And to think she knew exactly what I was talking about.

But that wasn't for show.

That was the truth, her truth.

Her parents were murdered and the moment I found that out in the cab was the moment I vowed to myself that I would do everything I could to make her life better. If I was drawn to her before, after that I was *affixed*.

Bewitched.

All of that is gone now. That vow shattered like the scant bit of trust I had in her.

But perhaps I had more trust in this girl, this stranger, than I thought I did.

Maybe it's why this hurts so much.

This betrayal feels bigger than it is because she was starting to mean more to me than she should. Like she had never been a stranger to begin with.

And maybe that's why I can't help but cringe when I think about the way her face fell, the open remorse and embarrassment and shame in her eyes when I found that recording. I'd never seen someone crumble like that right in front of me. Her hope and joy disintegrated in a second.

I was angry. Disappointed. I still am.

But I could have acted like more of a gentleman. I didn't have to slam that cab door on her. I could have handled all of this with more grace and understanding. Always more, never less.

I'm nothing close to being the prince I need to be.

I sigh and sit down on the bed, head in my hands. I need to talk to someone, but I don't have many people to talk to. I felt Maggie could have been–or *was*–that someone, but I was wrong. There's always Freddie but he's so clinical with the way he handles me. And my parents–forget it.

I pick up my phone and check the time. It's past midnight here so it's morning in Europe. Though I haven't talked to him other than a few texts here and there since I left on this trip, I call Magnus.

Magnus is the Crown Prince of Norway. Heir to the throne, oldest brother of four wild sisters. Doesn't help that he's quite wild himself, showing up in the tabloids practically every day. No wonder everyone in that royal family drinks too much.

It takes a few rings before he answers.

"Hello?" he mumbles, sounding half asleep.

"Magnus. Did I wake you up?"

He groans, switching to Swedish. "No. I mean yes. But I suppose I should get up."

"Are you alone?"

I can practically hear him grin over the phone. "I am now. She left in the night."

"Doesn't that get a bit awkward?" Magnus is a bit of a playboy, to put it mildly.

"They understand," he says through a yawn. "Less paparazzi waiting outside when it's the night. My driver takes them right home. No harm, no foul." He clears his throat. "How is your trip? When do you come home?"

"My flight out of Los Angeles is in a week."

"And your trip is going…?"

"Honestly, it's been life-changing. The best experience I've ever had. I never once wanted to come home. Until now."

"Uh oh. What happened? Wait, don't tell me. It's about a woman."

I hesitate. I hate that he's right. "It could be."

"Viktor," he says, sounding delighted. "The fucking moose comes out to play."

Moose. I haven't heard that nickname in a while.

"It's not what you think. At all."

"Okay then tell me. What did this woman do that made you want to come home? Suck you off the wrong way?"

"I think you're mistaking me for you."

He laughs. "Okay, then what?"

I explain the situation as best I can, starting with me getting stuck in this town, then going to the bar, all the way to me sitting here in this hotel room, the very hotel she works at, on a long-distance call.

When I'm done, he lets out a long, low whistle. "That's complicated," he says. "Far too complicated for a vacation."

"Right, well it's what happened."

"So now you're going to what, just get your car fixed and go to LA and forget all of this ever happened?"

"That's the plan."

"That's the plan?"

"I guess."

"You guess."

"Stop that."

"You're just going to leave this girl and not talk to her again."

I really don't like the sound of that but…"Yes."

"You're lying."

"How am I lying?"

"I know you. You may pretend to not give a fuck, but you always give a fuck. You're noble, you big moose, far more noble than I will ever be. This girl sounds like she's been handed the shittiest hand in life and you're just going to up and leave her?" He laughs. "Tell me, don't you think there's a chance she might be telling the truth?"

"About what?"

"That she didn't know who you were before that evening."

"How would I be able to tell if she's telling the truth or not? I don't even know her. That much was made apparent."

"Hey, I know you don't always think with your dick the way that I do, but if you're hung up on her because you just wanted a quick fuck, then obviously you should just give up on that and head to LA where I'm sure plenty of women will be willing to suck you off just like they are clamoring to do back in Sweden." He pauses. "Which, by the way, I don't understand how your name isn't always in the papers like mine is."

"Because I'm discreet about who I fuck. A little discretion can go a long way, Magnus."

"Yeah, yeah. You sound like…well, everyone. But okay, so this girl, if you want something more than just a fuck, if you feel something else toward her like you seem to, well then I don't think you're about to up and leave."

"I barely know her," I remind him. "What can I feel toward someone I've known for twenty-four hours?"

"I wouldn't know," he says. "But I imagine it's possible. And I've never had you actually pick up your phone and call me over a woman before."

He's right about that. But it does nothing to extinguish the flames in my chest.

"Look," he says. "I think you know whether she's telling the truth or not."

"Then what if she is? She still recorded me, without my

knowledge, for an article or a gossip magazine or whatever. She still did that."

"But she told you she wasn't going to use it in the end and you have to decide whether you believe that or not. The girl sounds like she was desperate and desperate people do things they normally wouldn't do. Shit, if I had a kroner for every time a girl I slept with sold me out for the tabloids, well, I'd have a lot more money than I have now."

"I think you have enough money, Magnus," I say dryly.

"Not the point, *Moose*. Besides, you never told her who you were. She had to find out for herself. So she put up with you and your fake name and your fake background, spewing your lies. What if she hadn't found out you were Viktor? What if she never knew and you ended up sleeping with her and ended up falling for her? Then what? She'd have to then eventually find out the truth about you, find out she fell in love with a lie, and then your relationship would crash and burn. Jeez, come to think of it, I think what happened to you now was the better option."

Fuck. I hadn't thought about it that way. The fact that if anything had grown between us, it would have been based on the lies I was telling. That one day I would have had to tell her I wasn't who she thought I was.

"Well this is just all shit then, isn't it?" I sigh.

"Sounds like it. Well, if you don't mind, I have to get up and start my day."

"Do you have an important engagement or are you base-jumping off a cliff or something?" Magnus is also a bit of an adrenaline junkie, much to the worry of his parents, and, well, the country.

"Car racing," he says, and I know he's smiling. "Going down to Monaco tomorrow for a race, then maybe some gambling."

"Pretending to be James Bond?"

"Something like that. Hey, good luck, Viktor."

He hangs up and just like that I feel thrust into the silence and loneliness that comes with the middle of the night.

I stare at the phone in my hands, wishing that I had gotten Maggie's number at some point. I honestly have no contact information for her. I just know her address.

I could write her a letter.

But what would I say?

I'm sorry that you lied to me.

No.

I'm sorry I lied to you.

Your lies don't matter, you never owed me the truth.

I just want you to know I don't harbor any bad feelings, just a simmering sadness that I missed a different path to what could have been.

But that path would have been based on lies anyway.

I'm sorry that it had to be this way.

Good luck with everything.

Fuck.

Good luck. I hate that term. I know that Magnus just said it to me but what it really implies is that you will need luck. And you only need it if you can't make it on your own.

I can make it on my own.

I don't have to tell Maggie good luck and then be done with her. I have control here, over my future and hers.

I step out of my pajama pants and into a pair of jeans, throwing on a sweater, then grab my wallet and phone and head downstairs to the lobby.

The night clerk has that glazed zombie look that most shift workers have.

"Is it too late to get a cab?" I ask.

The clerk shrugs. "We'll see," he says, monotone, as he picks up his phone and dials.

Turns out it's not and ten minutes later a cab pulls up outside the hotel.

It's that damn Earl White guy from earlier, the one who knew Maggie.

"You again," the guy says as I get in. "How was your dinner?"

"It was fine. I, uh, forgot something at her house. Do you mind taking me there?"

"It's pretty late, pal."

"Yes, well, you know jet lag."

He frowns at me and shrugs, starts driving. "Sure. Just tell me that you're looking out for that girl."

"Maggie?"

"Yeah, Maggie. I can tell you're not from around here so I'm not sure you know the details but what happened to her parents is the worst thing this town has ever seen. Now you'd think being a prison town that we'd be used to it, but frankly, that was above and beyond what's normal."

"And what happened, exactly?"

"She hasn't told you?" He eyes me in the mirror.

"No," I tell him. "I don't blame her."

"I guess that's not exactly conversation for a date, is it?"

I just give him a tight smile, hoping he'll continue.

He does. "Well, shit, it was about a year ago. You know, I knew her father because he'd often go to the bar after his shift. He was a prison guard and they're heavy drinkers. Can't blame them, handling all the shit that they do," he says, wiping his nose with one fat, hairy hand. "So I used to drive him home a lot. He was a good guy though, didn't drink and drive as you can see, worked hard to put food on the table. Wasn't the smartest with his money, had a bit of a gambling problem but we all have our vices. I mean, I'm no angel."

"No one is," I offer politely.

"Anyhoo, I guess there was this punk at the prison, a

real troublemaker, violent, messed up, and he had it out for her father or maybe her father had it out for him. Either way, they were always at odds. Then one day this guy gets out on parole. Comes over to their house. Shoots both her father and mother in the head while they were watching TV. Shot the dog too. Thank god that she wasn't home, that none of the kids were. They would have been killed too, I know it."

I have no words for that. Alex's death traumatized me and yet here was Maggie and her brothers and sisters having to lose both parents in such a way. I just can't fathom it.

Suddenly I'm more confident in what I have to do.

"So are you dating her or what? You her boyfriend?" he asks me.

I shake my head. "No. Just a friend. Just passing through."

"Ah, that's too bad," he says. "She's such a pretty girl. Funny with a smart mouth on her. I like her. It would be nice to see her get some support. I know her brother helps out from what I hear but even so, you know, how tough that's gotta be."

I nod, and we lapse into a silence for the rest of the ride until we're pulling up the street of her house.

"Hey, do you mind parking here and waiting? I'll pay for your time."

"How much time?" he asks, the light from the streetlamp glinting off his balding head.

I hand him fifty bucks. "As much time as this buys me."

He looks at it, his eyes narrowing. "Ten minutes?"

I glare at him. Give me a break.

My look changes his mind. "Okay, however long you need."

I get out and walk over to her house. The lights are all out and the way the moonlight is hitting it, accentuating the peeling paint and missing boards, makes it look like a haunted house. In fact, now that I know her parents were actually murdered in the house, it only adds to the feeling.

I shouldn't knock on the door because I don't want to wake everyone up, and unfortunately, she has her window closed.

I stoop down and scoop up some pebbles, stand underneath her window, trampling over some weeds, and start tossing them at the glass.

Shit, I hope this is her window. If I get her sister April's, I'm in for one hell of a tongue-lashing.

I wait and look around, feeling like a stalker. The street is quiet, sleeping, no sign of life except for the cab driver sitting in his car, pretending not to watch me. After a minute, when nothing happens, I throw the pebbles up again.

Finally, I see Maggie's face in the window, her skin pale, eyes darker than the night, looking ghostly in the faded frame.

I wave for her to come down, hoping that she will.

She disappears from sight, and my chest tightens. I wait.

The front door slowly creaks open and she steps out onto the porch. She's barefoot, wearing a white robe that hits her mid-thigh and nothing else. She still has this aura around her—pale, fragile, cautious as she takes me in, her dark hair drifting around her shoulders on a soft breeze. I yearn to reach out and run it through my fingers.

It's only then that I notice the emblem on her robe is the La Quinta logo.

"Present from work?" I say in a low voice, nodding to it.

She looks down and then wraps her robe around her tighter. "Why are you here?" she whispers, frowning.

"Because I wanted to apologize."

She looks even more puzzled, her lower lip pouting slightly. The sight of it is forcing my brain to go in a different direction, my skin to feel hot and tight.

"What would you need to apologize for?" she asks, incredulous. "I'm the one who betrayed your trust."

I nod. "You did. But I betrayed it first, by starting out with a lie. And I could have ended things better instead of being so stubborn and sending you home in the cab like that. I wasn't raised to act that way."

She seems to relax at that, eyeing me with sympathy. "You're only human," she says softly, sticking out her leg so the robe falls away from her white, creamy thigh, and she points her slender foot at me, tapping me on the side of the knee. "You're allowed to be human, to be angry, to react."

I swallow hard, trying not to stare at her thigh as she retracts her leg. I don't know if it's the moonlight, the fact that it's just the two of us talking in whispers, the fact that I don't know what's underneath that robe, but I have a sudden urge to reach down and grab her under her thighs. Feel the smoothness of her skin squeezed between my hands then pick her up and press her up against the house, letting that robe fall open, sliding to the ground, leaving her breasts bare. I bet under the moonlight she would glow.

"What?" she asks me in a furtive hush.

I blink up at her, aware that I've been staring at her hungrily. My heart beats loudly in my head, sabotaging my ability to think, and I'm forgetting the whole speech I had prepared on the ride up here.

She cocks her head, studying me, still a wary look on her brow but her eyes are curious now, waiting for what I have to say.

"Anyway." I cough. "I should have handled everything better than I did. And for that I'm sorry. But I have to know, and please be honest with me, did you know from the very start who I was?"

"No!" she says emphatically, then glances up at the windows and quickly lowers her voice. "No, I didn't. I swear.

I saw you in the hotel room and I thought you were just an average guest." I raise my brow. She smiles. "I mean, above average, obviously. We've already talked about the size of your, uh…"

"Cock," I fill in.

"Yeah," she says, and fuck do I want to hear her say it. But I bite my lip and let her continue. "But still, a guest. Then I saw you at the bar and I don't know. Maybe I was already drawn to you in ways I couldn't explain, maybe it was because I'd already seen you naked, but there you were. And it was like fate was bringing us together or something. Okay, not as lame as that sounds, but you know what I mean. And I just knew I had to help you. So I did. I didn't know who you were."

She's talking a mile a minute and waving her hands around but in her eyes I see her truth and in her voice I hear her honesty and I know she had no idea.

She continues, "I can't say that everything I did for you was because I was selfless. I think in some way, I just wanted to get to know you."

"It worked."

"Kind of," she says, scrunching up her face. "Except I only got to know you as Johan. I never got a chance to know Viktor."

"Would you like a chance?"

Her eyes narrow. "What do you mean?"

"Why don't we start all over again?"

She stares at me.

I stick out my hand. "Hello, I'm Viktor."

A shy smile lifts the corner of her mouth and she extends her hand. "Hello, I'm Maggie."

I grasp it, giving it a firm but warm shake. "And now we start again."

I know what I want to do, how I want to start. I want to

keep holding her hand and then slide my palm up her arm, to her neck, wrap my fingers around the back of it and hold her tight. I want to pull her into me, suck that pouting lower lip of hers into my mouth until she blushes. I want to see if she tastes like vanilla ice cream. The creaminess of her skin makes me believe she does.

It takes a lot of self-control to keep myself in check, to focus on my plan.

I take in a deep breath and hope she doesn't notice how badly she affects me.

"Maggie, I've been thinking that despite the last twenty-four hours, we don't really know each other. You definitely don't know me. So I'm offering you a chance to get to know me and to make some money at the same time."

This whole time I've been speaking she's been nodding attentively but now that I've mentioned money, she immediately tenses up.

"What are you talking about?" And the way she says it makes me realize she might think I'm talking about prostitution.

"Don't worry, I'm not going to pay you to have sex with me."

Her eyes widen. "Uh, I wasn't thinking that. But now I am."

"Look, what if you still did the article you were going to do, but this time you have my permission. This time we're doing it on my terms, all out in the open."

"The article?"

I look over my shoulder to see if the cab is still there, and it is. I look back to her. "Yes. What you were recording. You were going to write that up, weren't you?"

She gnaws on her lip, doesn't say anything.

"So just do it again. Officially. You can take pictures, whatever. As long as I get to approve what you write before it's sent wherever you were going to send it. We can even send it to the Swedish tabloids. You know they would pay top kroner for it."

"How many kroners?" she asks.

I laugh. "Enough. Enough to get all those things you need for your family. More than that. I'd say fifteen or sixteen thousand kroners."

"Oh my god, that much!" Her eyes nearly bug out of her head.

"It's about two thousand American dollars," I explain. "Still good though."

Her shoulders slump a little as she tries to grapple with the idea. "But…why would you do this?"

"Because you helped me. Now I'm helping you. That's how these things work."

"You think I'm charity."

"No Maggie," I tell her, grabbing hold of both her hands. "I think you're beautiful."

Her stare lingers on my mouth for a long, agonizing moment until she blinks up to my eyes. She looks scared, unsure, a tiny line forming between her brows. I can't tell if it's because of what I just proposed to her or if it's because I called her beautiful, but I'm not willing to rock the boat.

"Look," I say, letting go of her and taking a step backward. "You can call it My One Week with the Prince. Everyone will eat it up."

"I just…" She looks away, her eyes searching the darkness of her front yard as if she'll find something lurking there.

"Or call it whatever you want," I say quickly. "I just want to help, and I think it would be fun. For both of us."

"I work so much this week. Every week. And you're leaving."

"I don't have to leave. I'll go to LA and fly out as promised but I can spend the rest of my time here until that happens."

"My work," she says again.

"Luckily you work where I'm living."

"But I can't be seen with you."

"It doesn't have to be difficult. Just let me into your life this week and I'll let you into mine. We don't have to distract from your family. In fact, why don't I come by tomorrow night and cook dinner for everyone? We can have the interview after."

"You would cook for everyone?" she asks in disbelief.

"I can make more than Swedish meatballs," I say.

At that she starts giggling, her cheeks flaring. Wonder why.

She looks over my shoulder, noticing the cab. "Is that... Earl? Is he waiting for you?"

"He's fine. I think we're friends now," I tell her. "Just tell me you'll do it."

She's torn. But I can tell she's leaning toward the side I want.

"I want to help," I add. "And before you protest again and tell me it's charity, I'll tell you it's because I like you. And then when you say that it's too much, I'll tell you that's what I do. Always more, never less. There is no too much with me."

She sighs, relenting, her eyes going up to the stars for a moment and it looks like she's having a silent conversation with God.

Then she gives me the sweetest smile, the kind that makes you melt right there and then on the spot and under that moon she says, "Okay."

I break into a grin, elated. "Okay." I jerk my thumb toward the street. "Well I better get back to the hotel and you better get back to bed. I know you have to work early."

"Yeah," she says, "I guess I might see you around tomorrow."

"It's going to be hard not to know you," I tell her.

She gives me a small wave, just a few fingers, and then turns to walk inside her house.

I stand there for a few moments wondering if I should go in after her. Wondering if when I said we were starting over, if we could fast forward and go straight to the middle.

But I lose my nerve. It's the middle of the night and we've both had quite the day. Then there's the cab, its meter running.

I look up at her window hoping to catch a glimpse of her and when I don't, I head back to the cab and get in.

CHAPTER ELEVEN

MAGGIE

"Maggie, get out!" April yells at me from the other side of the bathroom door and before I even have a chance to yell back, she starts pounding on it, rattling it on its hinges.

I close my eyes, counting down to ten, hoping to rein in this permanent caldera of frustration I seem to have whenever she's around.

"I'll be a few minutes," I tell her as I grab a towel, having literally just stepped out of the shower. "Go use the other bathroom."

"You would say that, wouldn't you?" Her animosity flows right through the door.

The other bathroom is the one in Mom and Dad's room. The room no one likes to go in, unless I have a drunk Swede passed out in there.

Which I don't. Not today.

Last night I was shocked that he showed up like that in the middle of the night, throwing rocks at my window nonetheless. I'd only been asleep for a couple of hours after I'd spent a lot of time sobbing into my pillow and generally feeling sorry for myself, when I'd heard the clatter on the windowpane.

It took a lot of effort to wake up and notice the sound was real and happening and then I was at the window and looking down at Viktor.

I thought I was dreaming.

Viktor bathed in the moonlight, pebbles in his hand, looking up at me like every romantic movie scene you could think of. But this wasn't make believe, even though it felt like it, and it wasn't a dream. It was like high school all over again when my old boyfriends would throw shit and yell up at my window, so I could sneak downstairs and go have sex with them in the back of their car.

Except Viktor is the antithesis to every boyfriend I've ever had and he wasn't at my doorstep because he wanted to have sex with me.

Although, there was something carnal and hungry in the way I caught him gazing at my mouth and body a few times…

Regardless, he was there with an apology and a proposition, neither of which I felt were owed to me.

But I still accepted them. I accepted them because I'm a weak, weak woman who is okay with feeling like charity as long as it benefits others.

And yet it wasn't just that. I accepted his apology, his willingness to start over, his offer to be the subject of the article because I like him. I want him. I want to be around him, as much as I can before he leaves forever.

I want to get to know Viktor as Viktor. It's not about the article anymore, though of course that money will help immensely. It's about finding someone else who seems to understand you in ways no one else does, even if you don't understand yourself all that well.

I mean, I was not only humiliated after what happened at

the restaurant, but my heart felt crushed too. Every naïve and silly hope I had inside me, the ones I kept buried, those moved to the surface like bones through a freshly-dug grave. They were exposed, bare, and felt every lash of the consequences.

This time I won't fuck up.

Which is why I'm taking a shower right now, trying to get all gussied up for the date tonight. Okay, so I'm not sure if it's really a date anymore. Things seem kind of odd now between us and we're technically starting over.

Except that he wanted to kiss you last night. You know he did.

I ignore those thoughts.

Anyway, there's nothing wrong with looking your best for a fucking prince, that's for sure. In fact, I wish I could get everyone else in the family to dress up a little bit and behave. I know that Viktor's already seen our side of crazy but now that I know he's a prince, we could try a little harder.

Only I haven't told anyone yet who he is. I did tell them his name is Viktor and I had been mistaken earlier, but I've left the prince part out. They definitely don't need to start losing their shit and fawning all over him and with April being my sworn enemy these days, I hate to think what she'd do. She'd be the one contacting the local paper, or at the very worst, Tito and his crew. I'm sure they'd love to fuck up Prince Charming.

And you'd love to fuck Prince Charming.

I push that thought out of my head too.

"Maggie," she whines, still hitting something against the door, maybe her head now.

"Argh!" I yell and quickly wrap my towel around me, whipping the door open. "Fine, it's yours!"

I storm past her and she storms into the washroom and the door slams shut, and I slam my door shut, and now I've officially regressed into being a teenager again.

Knock, knock.

My door now.

"Oh my god, what?" I cry out.

"It's me," Pike says, voice muffled on the other side.

"I am naked this time, okay? Go away."

"Does the Swede know that Callum is allergic to shellfish and peanuts?"

Argh, fuck. I should have mentioned he has allergies. "No. I'm sure it will be fine!" I yell.

"Okay," Pike says. "Well I'm going to skip out on dinner."

I clutch my towel tighter around my chest and go over to the door and yank it open, wet hair in my face. I blow a strand away. "What? Why?"

Pike looks bored as he leans against the doorframe. "I have a date."

I cock a brow. "You...*you* have a date?"

"Oh fuck off," he says, clearly way too insulted by what I just said. "You think I can't have one?"

I just shake my head. "It's fine Pike. Go on your date. We'll save you the leftovers."

"So what's his deal?" he asks as I'm trying to close the door on him.

I pause. "Who, what deal?"

"The Swede. Why is he cooking for you, for us?"

I shrug. "I guess that's a thing they do in Sweden. Haven't you heard of Swedish hospitality?"

"I've heard of IKEA and Stieg Larsson and that's about it."

"Well it's a thing. They like lots of candles and throw pillows and little painted horses and they like to cook dinner for people, okay?"

"I'm not sure I trust him," he says, looking off down the hall as if he's smelling something.

"You can trust him," I tell him, trying to close the door again.

"He just seems too good for you, Maggie. Too good for us."

Again, I pause. Let out a painful sigh because damn if I haven't been thinking that this whole time and Pike doesn't even know the half of it.

"You can't second guess everyone's intentions," I say to him. "That's not the way to go through life."

"No?" His eyes darken. "That's the way Dad thought. And look what happened to him. To Mom. You give someone the benefit of the doubt and you've given them too much. They trusted too much, and it got them killed."

Well, fuck. Way to forever inject paranoia into my life, Pike.

"I know," I say softly. "But I'm fighting really hard to let this guy in. I can't stay an island forever. I can't stay a rock. I want to be soft for once."

Pike rubs his lips together and looks away. Finally, he looks back and says, "Just be careful. I don't want to see you get hurt. When you hurt, we all hurt."

Then he turns and walks away. "I'll be home late," he says over his shoulder. "Story time is on you tonight."

I know Pike is just looking out for me as any good brother should (watch Callum when he gets older, he'll throw me right to the wolves), but I wish he wouldn't worry that much.

I'm also annoyed that I have to do story time. Story time is what I like to call the brothers bonding session. Even though Callum can read (better than most kids, actually), Pike has made it a habit to read to him from a book every night. Looks like I'll be on duty and I know that Callum is going to make it hard on me, just because it's fun to get me all riled up.

There's no time to dwell on that though, not when Viktor is coming by in an hour.

I quickly get dressed in jeans and the blousy top I tried on last night. It's silk or fake silk and this brilliant blue and shows off just enough cleavage without being trashy. I spend time doing my makeup again, putting just gloss on my lips in case he feels like kissing me, and then dry my hair so it falls around my shoulders in long dark waves.

Is it touchable? I run my hands through it. It's touchable.

I won't have any excuses for him not to touch me.

Then it's time to start on the house.

Because it's Sunday and I worked all day, the kids have been home and I haven't been here to pick up after them. As a result, the house is an absolute disaster.

I find Rosemary and Thyme downstairs in the living room, both of them on their phones scrolling through websites, both looking bored out of their minds, and enlist them to help me.

With bribes, of course. They can both choose a meal for me to cook later in the week. It was something my mother used to do. We didn't have the money for allowances or special rewards so what she would do is bribe us all with food. If we did X amount of work, then we could choose the dinner. As long as it wasn't steak or lobster or something crazy, we could have it and it always worked. At least for me. I worked my ass off for my mom's lasagna.

The twins are easy though, thank god, and within no time the entire house has been dusted and vacuumed and tidied. I take in a deep breath as I lean against the broom and wipe the sweat off my brow, admiring my work.

There's a knock at the door.

I immediately shove the broom away and smooth down my hair.

"The Swedish Chef is here!" Callum cries out excitedly from the kitchen. "Bork, bork, bork!"

"Oh my god, Callum!" I exclaim. "No. Please stop."

I hurry past him and open the front door before anyone else can.

Viktor is standing there in a suit.

A fucking black suit, white shirt, black tie.

He didn't even look like this yesterday when we went out for dinner.

And in his hands are flowers.

Lavender, to be specific, in a small pot.

"These are for you," he says, smiling at them as he hands the pot to me. "And for me too, I guess. I know our aversion to flowers and lilies now and figured lavender not only smells very different and calming, but it's an herb as well. My mother has them all over her garden at her…house…and it brings good memories."

I've only gotten flowers once, from my dad when I graduated high school, and yet somehow this little plastic pot of lavender means just as much.

"Thank you," I tell him, subtly sniffing the purple ends. Their soothing, herbal scent fills my heart and I know this smell will forever remind me of him.

He holds up a tote bag from the local grocery store. "And here is the dinner."

I step aside and usher him in. I may have been able to ignore the dirty thoughts I was having earlier, but I can't ignore the way he makes my body feel. How my hair stands on end and shivers roll down my back and how just him brushing past me lets loose the butterflies that were caged in my ribs.

I follow him down the hall and into the kitchen, both mesmerized by the sight of him in his suit and the scent of lavender filling the air.

"You look amazing," I gush.

"And you look outstandingly beautiful," he says, his eyes drinking me in until I'm squirming on the spot. He places the tote bag on the kitchen table and Callum immediately runs over to him. "Hi! Bork, bork! If you're making lobster or crab or shrimp, I will die, you know. I will literally die."

Viktor looks up at me in horror. "Oh no," he says slowly. "Really?"

"It's okay," I tell him quickly. "Callum can eat mac and cheese."

"I'm just kidding, Miss America," Viktor says, breaking into a grin. "I didn't bring shellfish of any kind."

"But I want mac and cheese now," Callum whines.

"Who says I'm not making mac and cheese?" Viktor says teasingly to him. He starts bringing out items from the bag, placing them on the table. "Let's see, we have fresh pasta. We have hard cheddars and parmesan. We have chorizo and prosciutto. Onions, garlic, rosemary, and…"

"Me!" Thyme yells from the living room. Obviously eavesdropping.

He grins. "Not quite. Paprika." He looks at me with the most adorable gleam in his eyes. "You don't have a sister called Paprika, do you?"

"No, you've met them all," I tell him. Despite what Pike had warned me about earlier, I immediately feel at ease with Viktor. The fact that he's a prince, that I'll be interviewing him later, barely crosses my mind.

Well, it does a little.

Enough so that I'm doing a quick glance around the kitchen, making sure there isn't anything out of place. Everything looks tidy and spotless, except the fridge, which is absolutely covered with drawings and report cards and calendars and notes with a plethora of magnets holding them all down. For a second I feel a burst of pride, knowing that the fridge looked like that before my parents died and it still looks like that now. Perhaps I'm doing a better job than I thought.

"Do you need any help?" Callum asks Viktor as he sorts things.

Callum has never asked to help me in the kitchen before.

Viktor smiles at him appreciatively and I'm aware of how charmed they are of each other. It warms my heart.

"Well let's see," Viktor says and takes off his suit jacket, hanging it on the back of the chair, and starts rolling up his sleeves. His tanned, muscled forearms pop against the white fabric as he folds it around his elbow. Hot damn. Forget about warming my heart, this is warming up other places.

"What are you good at Callum?" he asks.

Callum taps his finger against his chin in thought. "Math."

"That's great. I meant in the kitchen."

"Slicing things," he says with a big smile. "Or stabbing things." Evil giggle.

Viktor's eyes widen briefly. "Okay, so we'll keep you away from the knives." He looks at me for help.

I shrug. "Beats me, he's never wanted to help me in the kitchen."

"Because you're not James Bond," Callum says.

"Well *sorrrrrry*," I tell him. I can't blame the kid. Viktor in his suit in our kitchen is probably the most exciting thing to ever happen to us.

"Have you ever grated parmesan, Callum?" Viktor asks him while rummaging through the drawers and finding the cheese grater. He raises it up triumphantly while I silently shake my head. A cheese grater is just a knife with scales.

"Never mind," Viktor says quickly, placing the cheese grater far away from him. "How about you just sit there and sing me songs? I rather liked your rendition of *Dancing Queen*."

Oh god. Now that I know "Dancing Queen" was sung to his actual mother the night before she became queen, by ABBA themselves, Callum's version seems even more crude.

"I forgot the lyrics," Callum says with a shrug. "But I can rap." He clears his throat like he's about to sing an opera. "I like big poops and I cannot lie."

I roll my eyes and give Viktor a warning look. He asked for this.

"Can I help with anything?" I ask coming around the table beside him.

"An apron would be great," he says. His hands are already floured from handling the fresh pasta, so I grab an apron hanging in the pantry–one that has chickens all over it, my mother was obsessed with chickens–and bring it over to him.

We smile at each other as he lowers his head so I can slip the top strap over his neck. With his head at my height, I take a moment to run my hands through his hair under the guise of fixing it.

My god. This is what heaven feels like. His hair is so thick and lush and silky, the ultimate sensory experience. I get a whiff of his shampoo, something woodsy and herbal that makes me want to drool. How I want nothing more than to just grab a few strands between my fingers and give it a sharp tug. I want to see the easy-going expression on his face become something raw and wild.

He sneaks a glance up at me and I realize how inappropriate I must be touching him like this.

"Your hair was a little messed," I say quietly, then I go behind him and tie the straps around his lower back. Damn, if Callum wasn't sitting right there and watching this whole scene, I'd start running my hands up and down his back, feeling every hard, taut muscle, and then climb him like a jungle gym. He's just so tall, his shoulders so broad and wide, that I feel like I take up no space at all next to him, like Viktor commands every atom in the room when he's around.

But Callum *is* watching, very intently I might add, and

whatever intimacy I had conjured up by putting on an apron vanishes.

I take a few steps back from Viktor and decide to go and tell the girls to help set the table. The pasta shouldn't take too long. I bring out a bottle of red wine for the adults.

When Thyme and Rosemary are done, they sit down at the table and start grilling Viktor as he stirs the pasta and cheese on the stove, asking a million questions about Sweden. At least it prevents Callum from singing.

"What's Sweden like?"

"Do you have the biggest IKEA in the world?"

"Do you know Alexander Skarsgard?"

"Do all girls have dragon tattoos?"

"Is it snowing there right now?"

"Does everyone have funny names?"

"Do you have a nickname?"

At that last one Viktor laughs.

"Actually, I do," he admits, grating some more parmesan into the pot. By now, it's almost ready.

"Well what is it?" I ask, hoping it's embarrassing because it would be nice to see Viktor look flustered for once. He's always so poised and regal.

My mind goes back to my fantasy about hair-pulling.

He says a word that sounds like "elk" but if, like, a sick person said it.

"What?" Callum asks, scrunching up his nose.

"Älg," he repeats. "It means elk, but it's not the elk that you know. It's actually a moose."

"So your nickname is *moose*?" Thyme asks.

"Like in the Archie Comics," Rosemary says.

"Why moose?" I ask.

He grins at me. "Have you ever seen a moose, especially a young one? They're all legs with a big head. Growing up, that was just like me. Of course, now that I've gotten older this head is…" He trails off and looks at the kids. "Well, my head, seems pretty normal."

"Except what's in the inside," Callum giggles.

"Callum, please," I beg.

"No, he's right," Viktor says good-naturedly. "Long legs, big head, a little crazy. Seems like a moose to me." He takes a step back from the pot and wipes his hands on the apron. "Hey, Callum, how about you add the paprika at the end, the finishing touch?"

Callum looks so proud to be chosen, he can barely get out of his chair fast enough.

Viktor holds a mound of the red spice in his hand and lowers it for Callum who carefully takes a pinch. For one long, agonizing moment I swear I can see the wheels in Callum's head turning, evil wheels, ones that are telling him to blow the mound of dusty paprika all over Viktor's pristine white shirt.

Please no, I think to myself.

And Callum actually looks over at me with a tiny smile like he can hear what I'm thinking and suddenly I'm struck by how much he looks like that creepy kid at the end of *The Omen*. I swear I hear the demonic Latin chanting, *Ave Satani!*

Then he stands on his toes and sprinkles the pinch of paprika into the pot.

"Voila," he says proudly. "Mac and cheese by moi."

"Your French is very good," Viktor says. "Now we eat."

I breathe a sigh of relief and get up to start helping him serve.

"Sit, Maggie," Viktor commands.

"Yeah, sit Maggie, woof," Callum says.

"Not what I meant," Viktor chides him and then nods at me to sit down as he grabs the pot from the stove. "Maggie, please. Just relax for once. There's no cow on the ice tonight."

"Cows?" Callum asks.

"It's, what do you call it, an inside thing between us," Viktor explains.

I sit down, both loving and hating the feeling of him doting on me. I'm so used to doing everything all the time that to actually just sit and be served food like this makes me feel like *I'm* royalty here and not the other way around.

And once again I'm reminded that, holy shit, he's a fucking prince.

"Where's April?" Thyme asks, grinning up at Viktor like she's got a mad crush on him as he doles out the incredible looking pasta onto her plate.

"April!" I holler. I know I heard her get out of the bathroom a while ago.

I guess the strength of my bellow surprises Viktor because he says, "Wow. That's a set of lungs."

"Comes with the territory."

"I'll get her," Rosemary says, getting out of her chair and running up the stairs. By the time Viktor has poured the two of us wine and the kids all have juice, she comes back, alone. "She's not coming."

I sigh heavily. This hurts. I don't know why this does in particular but I feel like this is her way of telling me to fuck off again. It's obvious I like Viktor and that it means a lot to me that he's here and doing this for all of us.

"Should I go talk to her?" Viktor says, poised to get up.

"No," I say quickly at the same time Rosemary says, "*Big* mistake."

"I think she's sore that you beat up her boyfriend," Thyme offers.

"He wasn't her boyfriend," I tell her. "He was just a big jerk."

"That's one way of putting it," Viktor says under his breath. Then he smiles at everyone and raises his wine glass. "*Smaklig måltid!*" he says. "Which means have a nice meal."

We all raise our glasses and clink against each other's and I look into Viktor's eyes and he looks into mine and I hope he can see just how touched, just how happy I am, that this is happening. I know April and Pike aren't here, I know I felt like charity at the beginning but now, now I just feel what it's like to just be normal for once.

Of course the food is absolutely amazing. I know you wouldn't expect too much with mac and cheese, but with the spices and the chorizo and the parmesan, it's melting me inside.

"I think you really are the Swedish Chef," Callum says after a few bites, cheese dripping from his mouth. "Hurdy schmerdy!"

"It's really good," Thyme says.

"Can you cook for us every day?" asks Rosemary. She's serious too.

"Sadly, Viktor has to leave for LA at the end of the week," I tell them. "He's flying back to Stockholm."

In unison, all of their faces fall.

"Bummer," Thyme says.

"But," Viktor says, wiping his mouth with a napkin, "we still have a lot of time to get to know each other. You were asking me questions earlier, so I think it's time I ask you the questions."

And then he proceeds to ask the twins and Callum questions about themselves. Mainly trivial questions, but questions nonetheless. The kids feel important, that much I can tell, and even though the food is incredible, there's more talking at the table than eating.

The way that Viktor listens so intently to each one, his focus completely on them, makes my ovaries want to explode. Add in the fact that he cooked us this damn meal, he's wearing a suit, his forearms are golden and rippling with strength and I now know what running my fingers through his hair feels like, it presses a small ache in between my ribs.

I want this man *so* much, I don't even have words for it.

And I'm not sure I'll even get a chance to have him before he leaves.

He doesn't belong to me.

He belongs to another country.

And I'll be left behind in mine.

As if sensing my thoughts, he turns his head to look at me and once again the breath is knocked out of me. He is so damn gorgeous it makes me want to cry.

"And you, Maggie," he says to me. "What's your favorite flower?"

Is this where the conversation turned?

But I don't even have to think.

"Lavender," I tell him, my eyes falling on the pot I put in the middle of the table. Forever lavender.

When we're all finished eating I tell the kids to go in the living room and watch some TV while Viktor and I clean up in the kitchen.

They take off like rockets. Usually I have them help me with clean-up but since Viktor is here, I want time with him alone.

"I suppose I should have brought dessert," Viktor says as he starts filling up the sink with dish soap and warm water. We've never had a dishwasher, so you can imagine the amount of dishes there always were to do in this house. "Your brother and sisters would have liked that, maybe a pie of some kind."

I grab a dish towel and lean back against the counter beside him, ready to dry. "You did enough," I tell him. "Those kids are over the moon with you."

He glances at me with a smirk. "Over the moon?"

"It means to be, I don't know, not quite in love but…

enamored. Charmed. In such a huge way that the moon somehow gets involved."

He chuckles softly, the sound spreading warmth through me. "And you, are you over the moon with me?"

Well that puts me on the spot.

I give him a shy smile. "The moon doesn't seem big enough. I might be over the sun."

He studies me for a moment, his gaze sinking deep into mine. I see enough longing and heat in his eyes that I don't feel silly for my admission. "I don't think anyone's been over the sun for me before," he muses.

"I'm sure they would be if you cooked them a meal like you did."

"The way to your heart is through your stomach," he says with a nod. "I shall keep that in mind."

You've already found your way to my heart, I think and for once, the thought doesn't scare me. Tonight, I feel emboldened.

Yet when he hands me a wet dish, my eyes focus on drying it, afraid to look at him. He's so close, his elbow and arm brushing mine as he works, and that gorgeous scent of his mixed with the lavender and the lemon dish soap are burning a memory in my head. My skin feels tight and hot and the nerves in my stomach dance in a constant conga line. Every part of me feels alive.

The fact that I think I'm falling for him doesn't scare me but what does scare me is what happens after that.

"So, when does the interview start?" he asks after a long bout of silence.

Oh right. *That.*

The truth is, I don't want to write about this dinner even though that was his intention. I feel like what I witnessed tonight, the quiet charming moments between him and my family, I want to keep that just for me.

"Tomorrow," I tell him. "It starts tomorrow."

"So then what is tonight?" There's gravity to his voice, the low tone making electricity burn in my stomach.

I look up at him and try to read his gaze. "I guess we're just getting to know each other," I say. Because what can I say? That this is a date? A date with me and my brothers and sisters? I don't think so.

He nods in response, hands me another dish.

We work together in silence, but it's comfortable. It's the kind of silence that lets you be lost in your head without having to explain your thoughts, the kind that tricks you into believing you're deep in the stages of domesticated bliss.

And I am lost in my thoughts. Thoughts about him, the kids, my life, my future, that it takes me a moment to notice that we're done and Viktor is taking off his apron. He's standing right in front of me, folding it in his hands, and staring at me with such intensity that I feel like I might have missed something, like he was saying something before and I didn't hear him. Something heated. Something I *want* to hear.

He tilts his head, his eyes settling on my lips for a moment before he looks up to meet my gaze again.

"Can I kiss you?" he asks, his voice low and smooth.

Oh my god.

Did he just ask if he could *kiss* me?

I knew the guy was a gentleman, but I didn't know how much of one he was.

I swallow the brick in my throat, fireworks going off in my heart.

"Of course," I say softly, wishing my voice was steady.

This is it. This is it.

Fucking finally.

I close my eyes, my lips parting open, just enough.

I wait.

Nerves on fire.

Heart dancing.

Lips aching for him...

No kiss.

And I don't feel him come any closer.

I open my eyes and look at him.

He hasn't moved. Instead he's just watching me, wearing the cockiest smirk I've ever seen.

"I didn't mean now," he says. "I just wanted to know for future reference."

My eyes narrow, my body growing hot with embarrassment and sexual frustration. "You're a jerk."

He laughs playfully. "Someone has to keep you on your toes."

I shake my head and snatch the apron from his hands, bringing it to the small hamper we have in the pantry and tossing it in there.

"So your nickname is Moose, huh?" I say, trying to cover up the awkwardness. Even with my back turned to him, I can tell he's still grinning. "Maybe your nickname oughta be *dick*."

"Who's to say it isn't?" he answers.

Once everything is dry, I tell the girls to do their homework and tell Callum he has to get ready for bed. Like I thought, he makes a huge fuss, not wanting to miss out on what's going on with Viktor and the "adults."

Then I bring up story time.

Then, to my surprise, though honestly, I don't think I should be surprised by *anything* he does now, Viktor volunteers for story time.

And suddenly Callum is racing to his bedroom to put on his pajamas and get in bed.

"Do you even know what story time is?" I ask Viktor as we go up the stairs.

When he doesn't say anything I look down at him over my shoulder and see that his focus is completely on my ass.

His eyes flit up to mine. "Sorry," he says, not sounding very sorry at all. "And story time, that sounds like when you make up a story, a bedtime story."

"Callum usually has Pike read from a certain book."

"Nah, I think I'll just make something up," he says.

"Suit yourself. He's a tough critic," I tell him as we step into Callum's room. He's already sitting in bed, a big grin on his face, in his faded Superman pajamas. Viktor pulls up a chair from the desk and I sit down on the end of the bed because there's no way I'm not going to be here for this.

"I know you usually have a book read to you," Viktor notes, "but I have a special Swedish story to share with you. Do you like trolls?"

Callum shakes his head.

Viktor looks at me, trying not to smile. "Okay, do you like dragons?"

Callum shrugs.

"What about dragons and Vikings?"

Callum sits up straighter. "Are there battles and axes and swords and blood?" he asks excitedly.

"Of course," Viktor says to him and then looks at me. I'm shaking my head. *No*. Not a good idea before bedtime.

"Or maybe not," he corrects himself.

"Awwww," Callum whines.

"Or maybe a little." Viktor nods at me. "Your sister can just cover her ears at that part."

I raise my brow and try to bite back a smile.

So Viktor launches into a story about a Viking prince named Erling. At first I know he's making it all up off the top of his head, but the more he gets into the story, the more it seems natural, real, and the more I get involved in it. Soon both Rosemary and Thyme are sitting together on Callum's bean bag chair, listening intently to the battles and the wars and the Viking boats and the dragons and even the fair maidens that need rescuing. There's an evil king and a supernatural queen and a witch and flying whales.

By the time it's all over–almost an hour later–Callum is both wired and half asleep. And out in the hallway is April, skulking around outside the door, having listened to most of it even though she would never dare admit it.

Now it's late and everyone is tired and Viktor says he should get going.

I want to protest, but he's right.

The cab is called.

I follow him out in front of the house, waiting with him for the cab. After that whole "can I kiss you" thing, I'm feeling a little slighted but still hopeful. Maybe this is it. Maybe he was waiting until we were really alone.

I gaze up at him, the moon rising behind him. He gazes down at me. But the moment I start to think it might happen for real, Viktor's eyes fly up to the windows behind me.

I turn around and look up to see everyone watching us from the bedroom windows, goofy smiles on their faces. I wave, sigh, and look back at Viktor with a wry smile.

"Always an audience, huh," I say.

"I'm used to it," he says just as the cab pulls up. "So tomorrow we'll get more…professional."

Professional? Fucking great.

"Of course," I tell him, pasting a smile on my face. "Thanks again for dinner."

"It was my pleasure," he says and does a little bow.

I curtsey to him in return which makes him burst out laughing. Then he gets in the backseat and the cab drives off.

CHAPTER TWELVE

MAGGIE

"I don't think you give yourself enough credit," Viktor says, seemingly out of the blue. We've been talking about Swedish football (you know, soccer) for what feels like forever, so this change of conversation throws me.

"What are you talking about?" I ask, folding my legs up under me, careful not to knock over the bottle of wine between us.

It's Wednesday evening, and after two days of Viktor and I having rather "professional" meetings after work, either in coffee shops or in the minivan, I decided that enough was enough. I wanted to have some fun.

Actually it was Viktor who decided it. Maybe he could tell the interview was coming out stiff and formal after a while. Maybe it was because I was so damn rusty at it, maybe because I don't actually like interviewing Viktor. I like talking to him, having an exchange of ideas, being honestly invested in what he says, because I want to, not because I have an article to write.

To be honest...I don't think I want to do the article anymore. I haven't completely vetoed the idea but I'm leaning toward it. Even with the formalities of asking rote questions and listening to the playback to make sure I got it all, scribbling notes when something strikes me later, I keep feeling the same feeling I had when he made us dinner. That our relationship, whatever it was, our time together, it was just for me and him. No one else. I want to keep it close to me and protect it like the fragile and precious thing it is.

And so today after work, Viktor picked me up in his sweet Mustang, now fully-fixed thanks to some help from Pike, and we're here, sitting on top of the highest hills to the south of town, a plaid blanket I found in the garage laid out beneath us.

We have a bottle of wine. Actually two. Plus, tubs of olives, slices of cheese, an onion and fig jam, and crackers. The sun is setting to one side of us, bathing us in gold that shines on the soft fresh grass of the rolling hills below us. From here it looks like Tehachapi is another world, a beautiful world. Viktor wanted to go somewhere enchanting and this was the only place I could think of.

Right now, it feels like we're the only two people left in the world.

Right now, it's perfect.

He sighs and leans back so he's propped up on one elbow, one of his long legs stretched out, the other knee bent, and though he has sunglasses on, his gaze is focused on the setting sun. "I'm talking about everything, Maggie. Everything you do."

"We're not talking about me here," I tell him.

"We never talk about you," he says. "It's been nothing but me the last two days. Frankly, I'm boring."

"You were the one who suggested I interview you," I point out, popping an olive in my mouth. *And you're never boring.*

He looks over at me. "I know. But tonight, it's all you."

"Then why have you been talking about soccer this whole time?" I ask with a teasing smile.

He takes his sunglasses off to give me a steady look, the blue of his eyes popping like cornflowers against the sunset. "It's called football, my dear."

"My dear. So formal."

"Did you ever want kids?"

He just lays that question in my lap, just like that.

I blink at him. "Excuse me? Did I ever want kids? Shouldn't the question be, do I want kids? No, wait"—I wave my hand dismissively—"why are we even talking about this?"

"Because I'm curious," he says gravely. "Because the last two days I've been talking, and I've wanted nothing more than to hear you talk. Because I want you to tell me the things you keep inside. I want to be the man that you confide in, that you trust, that you want to let in."

If that's what you want, what even are we?

But I don't ask that. Instead I run my hands over the plaid blanket, the scratchy wool pricking the sensitive skin of my palm. "Kids? Honestly, I never gave them much thought. When I was younger, having a family wasn't on my mind. All I wanted was out of this town. I wanted to be the journalists you read about, the ones out there getting the important stories, making a difference in people's lives, shining light on injustices. That's what I wanted. I thought that getting out of this town and going to New York would change everything. So no, I never really wanted kids, I guess. I certainly didn't think I would be saddled with five of them, that's for sure."

"And did it? Change everything, that is."

I shrug, trying to ignore the pangs of regret, the disappointment. "It might have. I was never really given the chance. You have to understand, one minute I was just a student at NYU, studying for classes, partying with friends, just trying to figure herself out on her own. The next I was here, and I was in charge of my brothers and sisters. I lost my mother, my father, hell, my dog. It's only been a year. I've had no time to adjust."

"I think you have," he says.

I can't help but glare at him. "You have no idea," I snap.

His forehead creases in sympathy. "I know I have no idea. I have some idea, but not to your extent. I just don't think you see yourself the way that I do, the way that others see you. That you've adjusted more to this than you think you have."

I gnaw on my lip. I want to ask how he sees me, but I don't have the courage right now. Suddenly I'm his focus. I think I've always been his focus but now he's looking at me like I'm some puzzle he has to get to the bottom of and he won't stop until he does.

And I should open up to him because he's a stranger. No, he's not a stranger anymore, he's Viktor. He's not the Crown Prince of Sweden either, he's just Viktor. But Viktor leaves in a couple of days.

He leaves in a couple of days.

And I both want to let him in so I feel like someone out there knows me intimately, knows who I am and what I'm made of, and I also want to shut him out because if I let him in, a piece of myself will leave me and I'll never get it back. I'll always think back to this and think, there's a man out there, a prince, and he knows my deepest thoughts and feelings and it might be freeing or it might be the opposite. Giving Viktor my heart might just put me in a cage.

It doesn't seem fair to have someone get to know you right before you never see them again.

"So, how do you see me?" I whisper.

He stares at me for a few long moments, taking in the different corners and features of my face. In this light, with the sun setting behind him, the gold in his brown hair glows like a halo.

"I see a young girl, a strong girl, who had to give up her dreams and everything she wanted in life in order to do the right thing. I see a woman who made a choice to do the right thing, which was to take care of her family. Her brothers and sisters who mean the world to her. She decided to step up and be their guardian, the one to protect them, the one to raise them. I see a woman whose strength not only lies in the day to day but in the choice to be there forever."

I look away from his gaze, feeling like he's peeling back too many layers and only seeing what he wants to. "I had no choice."

"Of course you did," he says. "You had a choice to tell the courts that you weren't capable of raising your siblings. Legal guardian or not, they would have taken one look at you and seen how young you were, seen your lack of experience and education, maybe even the trauma that you had gone through when you lost them. They would have given them to a state worker or whatever you call them here. But that didn't happen. That wasn't even an option for you, was it?"

I shrug. "It had to be me. There was no one else."

"You wouldn't have done it if you didn't think you were strong, if you didn't think you could handle it. You would have quit. But you didn't, Maggie. That's strength unlike any I have seen. And, in time, maybe you'll see it too."

"I don't feel strong though," I tell him. "I just feel like I'm constantly *trying*."

"There is great strength in trying. It's like working a muscle. The more you try to do something, the more you try to do better, the stronger you'll get."

A silence falls between us as the last of the sun disappears. Dark blue seems to drift down from above.

"I'm only strong because I've been lucky so far. I don't

know what's around the bend, especially with April. And I don't know if I'll be able to handle it. I never asked for any of this."

"I know. But that's life. Life is about making the best out of what you've been given."

I stare at him, sometimes so lost in the beauty of his face that I forget to see the sadness swimming beneath his eyes. Somehow it seems even more apparent in the dusk. "It sounds like that should apply to you, too."

He gives me a slow nod and looks away. "You're good at switching the subject."

All of our conversations the last couple of days–or at least the questions I've lobbied his way–have been quite shallow and safe. They have to be. Something painful and in-depth, Viktor would never agree to that. He's as guarded to the others back home, the public, his family, as he is to me here.

"You're good at avoiding the personal questions," I rally back.

"You've never asked me any personal questions."

"Okay, then I will," I tell him, adjusting my position to pour myself my second glass of wine. "You had told me on our first date, well, our only date,"—he frowns at that—"that you were running away from something. What was that?"

"Is this on the record?"

"Of course not," I tell him before I have a sip of wine. "This is between you and me."

"All right," he says. He turns over so he's on his side, facing me, his face open. A breeze ruffles a few wisps of hair. He clears his throat deeply. "My brother committed suicide."

I still, the wine nearly slipping out of my hands. I place it down on the blanket and hold it upright, my grip tight on the stem.

I had no idea this was what he was going to say.

He goes on, voice lower, maybe trying to mask the tremor

in it. "He took a bunch of medication our doctor prescribed him. I was the one who found him. Not his guards, not his secretary, not his parents. Me. I found him because I wanted to check up on him. You see…" He trails off, looks off, wrestling with a bitter smile. "He had actually called me a few days before saying he needed to talk to me and I blew him off. I couldn't even tell you why. Maybe because I was going through a rough patch myself, maybe because Alex was always the strong one, the perfect one. Of course we all knew better. My parents pretend they didn't know, but they all knew *fucking* better."

I'm holding my breath as he tells me this, feeling like if I make it seem like I'm not here, it might be easier for him to talk, to continue. At the same time, I don't want him to relive any pain, I don't want him to hurt.

He takes in a shaking breath, his nostrils flaring. "Alex never wanted to be on the throne. He never wanted to be the direct heir. It's not that…okay, the job, the role itself, it's extremely stressful. It might not be what it used to be, but at the same time it's not for the weak, not for the timid. There are rules, there are obligations, your freedom and your privacy are stripped. I personally think the roles should be appointed and not through birth. Appointed to those who want them, who earn them. If that had been the case, well Alex would have never been prince and I wouldn't be either. But here we are."

He reaches for the bottle of wine, unscrews the cap in one motion and then pours a big, messy glassful before downing half of it in one gulp. After that, his breath seems to slow.

"Alex," he says, after letting out a deep exhale, "was a perfectionist. Always was. My parents can be tough. He had a lot he had to live up to. From an early age he cared very much about being perfect. About being strong. Unfeeling, even. The more he did that, the older he got, the more shut off he became. He had a…an inner world, if you can imagine. A world I didn't understand. I tried to but he wouldn't let me in. He wouldn't let anyone in, which is probably why he never married, never had a serious girlfriend for long. There were rumors, of course, that he was gay, but that wasn't the case. It was just that Alex started to separate that inner world of his from the outer world and the more disconnect that happened, the harder he had to appear normal and perfect. The pressure crushed him in the end. That's all it was. The pressure. God, how alone he must have felt. So alone that he reached out to me and I came to him too late."

He closes his eyes, pinching the bridge of his nose, shoulders slumped. He breathes in and out and I wish there was something I could do or say. Putting my hand on his back and telling him how sorry I am feels so trivial.

And yet I have to think about how I wanted people to be around me right after my parent's death. People always meant well but pithy remarks never meant much to me. What mattered was knowing that someone was there for me. That I wasn't alone.

Viktor has been nothing but alone in this.

"I understand," I tell him, my words so soft they almost disappear on the breeze. I won't share with him what I want to, how I can relate, that I blame myself sometimes for my parents death. It's absurd, I know, I was on the other side of the country. I just think that had I not been in New York, had I been at home, it wouldn't have happened.

But I know that comparisons don't help. Every death is different. So I inch closer to him and I put my hand on his back and though it feels trivial still, like it's not enough, I can only hope it is.

"Maggie," he says, voice choked.

"I'm here," I tell him, bringing my knees in closer so I'm now hugging him from the side. It's an awkward angle, I'm not quite comfortable, and yet I'm not going anywhere. I hold onto him as if I can somehow absorb all his grief and combine it into mine. Maybe I don't think I'm strong enough to be me but right now I'm strong enough for him.

"I know this isn't like the old days," he says, moving his face so it's nestled in my arms, his words muffled. "I know that the monarchy doesn't hold the power that it once did. But I am so afraid of taking this role. My whole life I lived with knowing it didn't matter, that I would never likely be king. I was the one no one paid attention to and I liked it, I fucking liked it, because I could fail on my own and no one would notice. But now a whole country is watching. A whole country is measuring me against Alex. They never knew the truth about him, other than that he was poised and perfect. They *never will* know the truth. But with that comes the fact that I'll never be *enough*. And that was fine before when no one cared…but now…"

"Viktor, Viktor," I whisper to him, cradling his head, feeling his soft hair under my hands. "My moose." I feel him smile faintly against me. "You are more than *enough*. So much more. You live by your family's motto so well. Always more, never less. You are the always more and you…you fucking astound me. You know, growing up, as a little girl, you have fantasies about princes. Blame it on Disney, blame it on the fairy tales. You want that man to be noble and kind and powerful and oh so good-looking." I let out a soft laugh. "Man, I thought Prince Eric was such a babe."

"From The Little Mermaid?" he mumbles into me.

"Yes. Him and Prince Phillip. The way he slayed that dragon for her…anyway. These princes were ingrained in our heads as children and as we got older, we not only realized that Prince Charming was never coming for us, but that we didn't want him. The real princes seemed so stuffy, so cold. Don't get me wrong, I love Prince Harry and I guess

William is okay, but in general, the term *prince* lost its meaning. It no longer conjured up the fantastic. But you…you Viktor, you are a prince in every way shape and form. You embody the word, you are selfless and kind and proud and smart and noble and you care, more than anything, you care. You're the prince that every girl had a fantasy about but you're more than that, because you're real. You're so real. And you're here right now and you're with me and I can't…I can't thank you enough."

He raises his head to look at me. His eyes search my face as if he's found something he's lost and he has to double-check that it's still his.

"What about Prince, the musician?" he asks and though his voice is hoarse, there's a flutter of amusement in his eyes.

I can't help but smile. "Different prince," I tell him. "Everyone wants *that* prince and to be that prince."

Viktor stares at me, giving only the subtlest of nods. I'm very aware that my arms are still wrapped around him from the side but I can't figure out how to let go or if I even want to.

I never want to.

"I'm going to kiss you," he says as he gazes up at me, heat burning through whatever sadness was there before.

I laugh sharply. "Is that so? Because I don't—"

What I was going to say was *I don't believe you*.

But all of that falls away the moment he places one large, warm hand against my small face and presses his lips to mine.

For a moment I'm stilled. I'm reduced.

Every atom around us slows and slows until the world focuses on just one thing.

His lips.

My lips.

Then…

His mouth.
My mouth.
Then...
His hunger.
My hunger.
His step into this great unknown.
My leap off the cliff.

Viktor is kissing me, his lips moving against mine in a long, sweet, soft embrace until my own lips are dancing with his. He tastes like wine and salt and something I never knew I needed, never knew I craved, until right now. He kisses me with confidence, like he knows how to kiss me already and somehow he already does. As our kiss deepens, our mouths open in unison, our tongues tease and touch and lick like we are discovering who the other is for the first time.

Then his fingers press into the side of my face and another hand comes up to grab the back of my neck and I'm pitching backward onto the blanket. I know that food and wine and plates and knives are below me but I don't care. I will roll around in a sea of wine, I so don't care.

But he has me, his grip strong as ever and he lowers me back gently to the ground, brushing away anything in the way until I feel the wool blanket scratch at the back of my neck.

Now he's partially on top of me and I'm so conscious of the weight of him, how big he is, and then I'm conscious of how much I've craved this. Craved this feeling of being under him, being dominated, no matter how slightly, of being wanted, needed.

Consumed.

Because now his kisses are consuming me, not just his soft lips and the wet warmth of his mouth moving hungrily against mine, but that he holds me, as if I might blow away in the breeze, the way he presses into me. I can feel the hard, long length of his cock dig into my thigh.

I've needed this. I didn't realize how badly until now, the fact that he has me in his grasp, that I'm feeling every single part of me scream to life. It has me shaken to the core and...

His lips trail away from my mouth, places soft and hard kisses along the length of my jaw, then down the side of my neck. I can tell he's eager from the way he's rushing, his stubble cutting across my skin, the way he bites me just sharp and quick enough. Then he's battling himself, a low moan escaping him, the kind of moan that makes me wet in a second. His breath becomes labored as he struggles to regain control, tries to slow down. The bites turn to licks, long wet swaths of his tongue in an attempt to soothe his damage.

But I want to be damaged. I don't want the poised and regal Viktor that I've seen lately, the one in the suit, the one who always knows the right things to say. I want a Viktor that's raw and messy and wild. I want him to fuck me up before he fucks me, fuck me up *while* he fucks me. I want to see him lose all control and struggle to regain it back.

He groans into the hollow of my neck, his hands gliding down the sides of my waist. I buck up into him, aware of how desperate I must seem and yet I don't care. I want him, all of him, fast and hard, I just want to be free of this constant craving I have, an itch that I'm begging to be scratched.

Set me free, the thought shoots through my head like jagged lightning.

He's trying. His hand slides between my thighs, his knee parting my legs, and I curse myself for wearing jeans, for the thick wall of fabric between my sensitive flesh and his willing fingers.

My phone rings, the sound shooting between us like a lancer.

I ignore it. I have to. Nothing is more important than this, than having Viktor settle between my legs, than wanting to slide my hand into his jeans, feeling him pulse in my hand.

But something is.

Something that Viktor realizes.

He pulls away, breathing hard, his eyes glazed with hunger and lust that only turns me on more. God, I'm so fucking wet I swear that I'm drowning.

"Your phone," he manages to say, pressing the tips of his fingers into my cheek.

I nod. "It will go to voice mail," I say breathlessly, my hands going behind his neck, trying to bring his face back to mine, to suck on those plush lips of his.

Not that I ever, ever check voice mail.

Viktor frowns and I know that he won't relent until I answer it. He thinks it could be the kids.

And one glance at the phone tells me that it's Pike.

Shit.

I roll away from under Viktor and put the phone to my ear, trying not to sound like I was moments away from having sex. "Pike?"

"Maggie we have a problem."

Oh shit fuck.

"What?" My heart was already getting a workout, now it's stepping it up a notch.

"April went back to Tito's."

I groan, closing my eyes. Just the other day I had tried to talk to her about why a guy like that was bad news, not to mention he could go to jail if it continued between them. She wouldn't have any of it, not even when I started pleading with her to at least use condoms and birth control if she's going to do it anyway. Even when I was fourteen and I got my first boyfriend, my angst levels weren't cranked that high.

"Shit."

"I'm going after her," Pike says.

"Do you need back-up?"

"No, I have the cops," he says. "One of the guys who comes into the shop regularly is an officer. I told him what was happening and he said they're all very aware of the guy. Not sure if we can prove anything but at least this way it'll scare the both of them."

"Yeah until April decides to be a martyr or something."

"Anyway, I'm going over there with the officer. I need you to come home and watch the rest."

I know if I really wanted to I could bring up the fact that Rosemary and Thyme are old enough to take care of Callum and had recently volunteered. But I know I'm needed. As much as I want to, I'm not going to continue to roll around on this hill with Viktor while all this other shit is going on.

"I'll be right there," I tell him. "Thank you for getting her, for doing this."

"No problem," he says and hangs up.

"What is it?" Viktor asks. He's now sitting up, watching me with concern.

I sigh and adjust myself, adjust my clothes. "April. As usual. She's back with Tito but Pike is going over there with the cops. Maybe he'll end up in jail. Tito, that is."

Viktor nods. "I'll take you home."

Something inside me sinks. Suddenly. Like my heart has been weighted down with concrete. The idea that he's going to take me home after this, after I'd finally gotten a taste of what we could be, how good it could be, feels so…finite. He leaves so soon and it's like every second we have together counts.

Actually I'm hating myself for spending the last two days interviewing him for some article when I could have been kissing him. Fucking him. Being with him on so many different levels, so many ways that count. From the first moment his lips met mine I knew that *this* was what was supposed to have happened all along. This was how we were supposed to know each other.

"Hey," Viktor says softly, reaching over to cup my cheek. "There's no cow on the ice."

I can't help but laugh. It's a sad laugh because, shit, I can't let this be it for us. And it's a warm laugh because here he is, always trying to make me smile.

But after he leaves for good, I'm not sure how I'll ever smile again.

CHAPTER THIRTEEN

VIKTOR

When I wake up the next morning I struggle to remember where I am. For the first time since I ended up in this wayward town, I feel like a different person. I wake up feeling like I've gone somewhere else entirely, not just inside my mind.

But I'm still here. Lying on the hotel bed. A bed that's made every day by Maggie McPherson. I've learned to go out to the lobby or into town for a walk when she's in the hallway with the maid cart, coming to clean the room.

It's so damn weird, to be honest, to see her doing that role. It seems to diminish her. Not that being a housekeeper is anything to sneeze at, it just seems like such a constricting job choice for someone so dynamic. Maggie is smart and bold and strong and effortlessly funny. Here she keeps her head down. Cleans the rooms to meticulous standards.

Pretends not to know me.

That part kills me. I know why she has to do it. I know she's afraid that the hotel will find out and have problems and fire her. I also know that it's just something she's doing to get by and that if she lost this job, she thinks she would lose everything.

But I don't think she would lose anything, she would only gain.

I have a little fantasy that I keep to myself.

It doesn't involve Maggie in her maid uniform, although that's always a plus.

It involves me asking Maggie to come back to Stockholm with me.

To start over with her life there.

But that fantasy is as far-fetched as most are. That's why they are fantasies and not dreams. Dreams are attainable. Fantasies are in another galaxy all together.

But in a fantasy, there are no rules and so you can imagine whatever you wish.

In mine, Maggie comes to Stockholm. With her whole family.

Everyone gets uprooted.

She lives with me in one of the palaces that I'm supposed to move into upon my return. The kids live on the other end of the property, attended by nannies and teachers and anything they need.

None of them will ever have to want for anything. They won't have to struggle or worry. Their futures will be open, they'll have all the money they need. There will be no guilt, just the security of knowing they will be taken care of for the rest of their lives.

And Maggie will be a queen.

Not at this moment, but eventually.

A princess

Then a queen.

And she will rule (as much as a modern queen would rule), making the changes that are so sorely needed. Sweden may be one of the best countries in the world to live in with the best healthcare and education and social services, but there is always better work to be done.

The fantasy is so realistic it almost borders on a dream.

Except that it's all crazy to even think about.

Maggie and I don't know each other enough.

We aren't in a relationship.

She would never come to Sweden for me.

I don't think she'd go in general.

She'd never agree to pull everyone out of school to move them there.

It just wouldn't work for a million reasons.

So I tuck that fantasy away, knowing that one day I'll draw upon it and pretend it happened and feel, for once, that I'm living the life that I'm supposed to, a life that I want to.

But this morning, the fantasy is in full-swing. It won't leave.

Maybe because last night I finally kissed her.

It wasn't that I found the nerve. It's that I couldn't wait a second longer.

The way she held me, the way she told me she understood, I felt it like I'd never felt it before. To be seen. To be heard. To have someone dig deep enough to try and figure out what you needed to hear, what you needed to feel.

What you need in every cell in your body.

I kissed her and it was like my whole life became condensed to that little flashpoint. Every kiss that came before was obliterated and every kiss that comes after will never measure up, so as long as it's with someone other than her.

That kiss undid me in ways I didn't see coming.

And so now I'm here, I'm sleepy and I'm yearning to have her in this room with me. I know she's out there in the halls somewhere doing her job.

But grabbing her and pulling her in here and having my way with her won't be enough. It's not what I really need.

Always more, never less.

I get up out of bed and slip on my pajama pants and robe and then head out into the hall. It's 9 a.m. which means she's cleaning the third floor at the moment, so I make sure the coast is clear and then head up the stairs.

I look up and down the hall until I see a cart and then I quickly head toward it.

There's a chance, of course, that it's not her cart but I peek my head into the room with the door open and I see Maggie sorting out the curtains, the sun shining through them like clouds.

With her back turned to me, I sneak inside the room and wait for her to notice, a surprise much like the one where we first met.

She turns around and then opens her mouth to yell.

Thankfully no words come out.

I quickly stalk over to her and grab her, pulling her to the side of the bed so we're just out of the line of sight from the hallway.

"God morgon," I murmur to her in Swedish, one hand holding the back of her thin neck like you'd handle a delicate flower stem, the other hand slipping down to the small of her back.

Before she can say anything, I kiss her softly on the lips, pulling back just enough to hear her protestations.

"What are you doing here, you can get me killed!" she hisses at me.

I smile, raising a brow. "Killed? Is that how it is in this country?"

She narrows her eyes at me. "Fired. If I get fired, you're paying for me for the rest of my life."

Little does she know that's something I would love to do.

"I have another proposition for you," I tell her, my eyes drifting between the depths of her brown eyes and the peach sheen of her lush lips.

"Another interview?" she asks dryly, her eyes flitting to the door and back, her muscles tense.

I pull her over until I'm against the wall and I'm holding her to me. "Come with me to LA."

She stares at me for a moment before her chin jerks back. "LA? Now?"

"Tomorrow," I explain. "Or tonight. Come with me. The car is fixed, it'll be an easy drive, we'll get a hotel…"

I was hoping that last bit would pique her interest but her expression hasn't changed.

"I can't go to LA," she says, shaking her head.

I ignore the sinking feeling in my chest. "Why not?"

"Because I have a job, Viktor," she says thumbing at the collar of her uniform. "An actual job that I need in order to support everyone."

I won't be deterred. "Don't you have vacation days in this country?"

"Yeah, we do, *I* do, but it's so last notice."

"Maggie," I say gently, licking my lips, "you work six days a week. No human can keep that up in the long run. So not only are you owed this vacation but you need to take this vacation. It's just a few days, regardless. Tonight maybe, Friday and Sunday. You have Saturday off, yes?"

"It's such short notice," she says again but I can see something in her eyes is relenting.

"But it doesn't hurt to ask, does it?"

"But the kids. Who will take care of them?"

"Pike?"

"He works."

"If you're suggesting they come too, well, I know I sound

completely selfish Maggie, but I want you all to myself. Every single inch of you."

My hands disappear into the soft strands of her hair and I have to hold myself back from kissing her mid-sentence.

"I guess I could ask my friend Annette," she says after a moment. She saws her lower lip between her teeth. It makes me fucking hard. I want a taste. "She always says she'll look after everyone if I wanted to go away for a weekend."

I raise my brows and stare at her expectantly. "So then…"

She starts tapping her foot against the ground to some invisible drum solo as she looks around the room, thinking.

I let her think. I take a step back from her, giving her space.

Finally, she shoots me a worried, yet hopeful, glance. "Do you think I should?"

I grin and grab her arms, pulling her so she's flat up against me. I press my hands on both sides of her face, holding her still, forcing her to look at me with those big beautiful eyes of hers. "We only have a few days together until I leave. And until I leave, I want to spend every single second of the day with you by my side. From the moment I wake till the moment I sleep." I lean in and rub the tip of my nose against hers, inhaling deeply. My eyes close. "I'm not going back home until I know what you feel like from the inside, until I've tasted every sweet inch of your skin."

She stiffens under my grasp and when I open my eyes, her cheeks are tinged with pink. I've minded my manners, I've stayed noble, but when it comes to taking her in the bedroom, all of that is gone. I won't be royal. I'll be a savage instead.

"You drive a hard bargain," she whispers and then bites her lip coyly when she realizes what she's said.

I take her hand and press her palm against my cock, already thick and straining to escape through the button-up fly of my pajamas. "You have no idea," I say through a groan as she grips me, cautious at first and then with an eagerness that makes her eyes shine.

"I have some idea," she says, her words taking on this throaty, sexy voice that strips away another layer of refinement, so close to unearthing the rough, raw instincts inside me. "But we can't do this here," she says, shaking her head as if to shake some sense into herself.

She removes her hand and takes a step back from me and I grind my teeth together, fighting the urge to grab her and throw her on the bed. I don't fucking care whose room this is.

But I don't. I control myself.

I give her space.

"Ask," I tell her, clearing my throat. "Please. Now."

She lets out a shaky breath. "Okay," she says in a quiet voice but I can hear a tinge of excitement in it. "Let me ask Annette first," she says, quickly pulling out her phone and scrolling through her contacts.

I notice the whole bottom half of the screen is cracked. "You need a new one," I point out.

She gives me a wry smile as she texts. "I need a new everything."

From outside in the hall there is the sound of footsteps, the rustle of someone's clothes as they walk. It reminds me of home, the way the officials stride down the palace hallways, always so full of pomp and business.

Her eyes widen and she pauses texting. She looks to me in fear and I quickly step into the closet, just in time for me to hear someone say sternly, "Maggie?"

"Yup," Maggie says and through the slats of the closet I see her slip her phone inside her pocket. She walks over to the door.

"Are you still working on this room?" the voice, a woman's, asks.

"Almost done."

"Good girl," she says and I can tell she turns to walk away.

"Wait," Maggie cries out softly. "Juanita, I have a favor to ask you."

A pause. "Yes?"

"I know this is such short notice but I'd like to use my vacation days and take the next few days off work."

"What? Why, what's going on?"

"I, uh, I have a friend who wants to take me to LA this weekend, just to give me a break. Since I haven't taken any of my two weeks since I started working here, I figured I might as well before I get burnout."

"I don't have a problem with that, Maggie. I do have a problem with such incredibly short notice." She sighs. "Luckily one of the housekeepers who just started has been asking for more shifts."

"Oh thank you, thank you." I can hear the smile on Maggie's face which makes me smile in return.

It sounds like Juanita walks off and Maggie takes her time slowly walking back over to the closet. She brings out her phone and resumes texting.

"Can I come out yet?" I whisper.

She just smiles, teasingly, like she likes having me in here. Finally she sends through the text and then opens the door.

"Looks like you're going to LA," I tell her. I know she hears the joy in my voice, sees it right there on my face, but I don't care. I'm not going to pretend that this doesn't mean the fucking world to me right now.

"I can't believe I'm doing this," she says nervously. She glances at the phone. "And I don't know yet if Annette will go for it."

"Is this the woman who helped you carry me from the bar?"

"That's her."

"She sounds like a good friend. I'm sure she'll say yes."

At that her phone beeps and she glances down at it.

From the moment I first saw Maggie smile I thought she had the most sexy, innocent and joyous smile I'd ever seen but I've never seen it as big and pure as it is right now.

That smile is for you, I tell myself. No one has ever smiled for you like that before.

"She said she'll do it," she cries out doing a little dance.

I grab her by the waist and yank her into me, kissing her hard and quick on the lips. If I don't get out of this room with her soon, there is going to be trouble.

"I'm going to start packing then," I tell her, heading toward the door. "How much time will you need after work to get ready?"

"Maybe an hour?" she says. "Better make it two."

"I'll come get you at five," I tell her. "We can get a bite to eat on the road."

"Okay," she says, her eyes dancing.

I poke my head out into the hall to make sure no one sees me and then head to my room to pack.

Originally I had made my reservations for tomorrow night at the Hollywood Roosevelt hotel, so I call them and move it up a day, securing one of their cabana rooms that overlook the pool. With Maggie with me, I'm pulling out all the stops to make this as memorable as possible.

Then I make an extra special secret request with the hotel, the kind of crazy thing that only a fool in love would do.

But I'm not a fool in love.

I'm not in love.

And I don't think I'm a fool.

I don't know what I am.

I just know that the woman of my dreams, of my heart, of my life, is spending the new few days with me. Just the two of us. And when I get on the plane on Sunday and fly back home, I want to make sure she never ever forgets me.

I know I won't forget her.

The thought of having to leave her kills me a bit inside but I push it aside and get busy packing.

After I've checked out and spent the good portion of the day hanging out in the lobby of the hotel, reading a Swedish thriller that I've been flipping through for the last three weeks, I head on over to pick her up. I have to admit, it's kind of bittersweet to say goodbye to this hotel. I feel like I've lived a lifetime already in this past week. I'll especially miss their waffles.

I'm right on time but Maggie is already standing outside the house, a duffel bag slung over her shoulder.

She smiles broadly at me and then throws a wave over her shoulder to her family who are all gathered by the front door. She runs on over to me before I even have a chance to turn off the engine and open the door for her.

She tosses her bag in the back seat and then gets in, arm poised and hanging out the window. She slips on her sunglasses and taps the dashboard.

"Let's go," she cries out happily.

"Your wish is my command," I tell her, giving a quick honk at the house before peeling out onto the street. "You seemed ready to get out of there," I comment as we cruise through the streets toward the highway.

"Oh yeah. Once it hit me what I was actually doing, where we were going…who I was going with, I couldn't pack fast enough."

"Do they care that you're going?"

"The kids don't care. April is probably jumping for joy,

especially after last night. She thinks the cops threating Tito was all my idea of course, even though I was with you the whole time," she pauses. "Pike wasn't too happy about it."

"I get the impression that he doesn't like me. I was surprised he even helped me with the car." In fact, all while he was helping with the carburetor I was afraid to turn my back to him, thinking he might try and whack me over the head with a wrench.

"He's...distrustful."

"What does he think I'm going to do?"

"I suppose he thinks you'll take me to Sweden and I'll never return."

I swallow, feeling bricks in my stomach.

Would that be so bad?

"Wouldn't that be something," I say, trying to sound ever so easy going.

"Mmmm," she muses. I have a feeling it's something she would never even entertain. "I just can't believe I'm going to LA."

"You must have been before," he says. "You live so close."

"When I was younger, but I don't remember it too well and you don't really give a shit about LA when you're a kid. I think we went for a wedding or something. All I really wanted to do was go to Disneyland but of course we could never afford to do that."

"Well, I've never been to Disneyland either. I think we should go."

She stares at me, her brows raised. I know her eyes under those glasses are wide and round as saucers. "You're kidding me."

I shrug. "Why not? There are no cows on the ice this weekend, Miss America. Only you, only me. And we can do whatever the fuck we want to do, starting right now."

She laughs, loud and bright, a sound I feel will be burned forever in my head.

"Okay. First stop then is In & Out Burger in Lancaster."

"In & Out?" I repeat. "That sounds kind of...*lewd*."

"Well, the taste is orgasmic, that's for sure."

"All right. First stop. Orgasmic burgers."

She seems to get all quiet and blush at that.

Probably because she's thinking the same thing I'm thinking.

Neither of us can wait for dessert.

CHAPTER FOURTEEN

MAGGIE

"So this is Los Angeles," Viktor muses as the Mustang cruises down the freeway, the valley disappearing behind us, the city in front of us beneath a layer of smog.

Being it's Thursday evening, there's quite a bit of traffic, but we've managed to miss the worst of rush hour thanks to our stop at In & Out. I think I took too much pleasure in watching Viktor wolf down his animal fries, cheeseburger and chocolate shake. I don't know where he puts it all, but it's apparent now that whatever Viktor eats immediately gets transformed into muscle. A steak? He just added an eight pack to that six pack. Must be a Swedish thing.

We're staying in Hollywood at the famous Roosevelt Hotel, right across from where the Oscars are held and the Grauman's Chinese Theatre (which now has a new name but old habits die hard). I know most tourists come to this area and that's probably why Viktor picked it but even though I haven't seen Hollywood first hand, I do live in SoCal and so I do know it's a cesspool of human garbage and gaudy commercialism.

"Oh," Viktor says as the Mustang cruises down Hollywood Blvd, eyeing everything like he's made a huge mistake. "I didn't quite picture this."

"What, the guy taking a leak on the Starbucks door, the woman across the street yelling at people, or Captain Jack Sparrow who seems to be fighting a saggy-assed Spiderman over a quarter?"

He nods as he takes it all in. "Yes. All of that."

"Welcome to Hollywood," I tell him. "May we never leave the hotel."

"May we never leave the hotel *room*," he says, glancing at me. Though there's the telltale smirk on his lips, his eyes have taken on an edge. The kind of edge that makes my stomach flip.

I tried not to think about it on the drive down in case I was going to psych myself out, but there was no mistaking what this weekend was about. Yes, it was about hanging onto Viktor for every last moment that I got.

It's also about having Viktor in every single way I can get.

In New York, the handful of dates I'd gone on, some of them had ended in sex. Sometimes the first date, often the second. And I was nervous for each one. Worried about everything from how the guy was going to judge my body or my performance, to whether it was going to be any good, what kind of protection we were going to use, if it was going to be weird to be intimate with someone I didn't know well. Sometimes I even worried if the guy would be an asshole if I decided to say no.

But with Viktor…it's different. Every single thing about him is different. He's nothing like the guys I've dated or slept with. What we have, whatever it is, is nothing like the relationships I've had before.

Don't get me wrong, I *am* nervous about having sex with him. I want everything to be perfect, I want to make it so he'll never forget me. I want him to strip all my inhibitions away and turn me into a wanton, greedy woman. But at the same time, it feels like it has to be this way. I mean, the first time I laid eyes on this man, he was buck naked. After that, everything sort of fell into place.

I know my cheeks are hot right now under his gaze. My body has been doing nothing but betraying me this past week.

He pulls the car around to the back of the hotel where one of the valets cheerfully takes the vehicle, gushing over the make and model and all that car stuff. The Mustang is a gorgeous blue, the color of the deep Pacific, and a few middle-aged women waiting for their rides, big sunglasses taking over their face, are admiring it.

Or maybe they're admiring Viktor. Everyone here seems to be somebody and Viktor definitely is. They might not recognize him as the Crown Prince of Sweden but with his stature and his ridiculous good looks, they probably assume he's a movie star.

Of course I feel out of place at the Roosevelt. It's not abundantly fancy but it's got this hip, young Hollywood vibe, and let's face it, the place is way too cool for me. I wish I had put more thought into my clothes on this trip instead of slipping on jeans, a tank top and Converse but I pretend that I'm so famous, I don't even need to dress up.

"Here you go, Mr. Andersson," the smiling receptionist says to Viktor as she hands him the key cards and for a moment I'm confused until I remember that he has to travel under the fake name and only I know who he really is.

The receptionist then seems to wink at me and gives me an impish smile. Jeez, they sure are friendly here. You don't get that kind of greeting at my hotel.

Viktor waves away any help with the bags, which is odd because I assumed that he's used to having people do stuff for him. I mean he told me he not only has a private secretary but a butler as well.

We walk through the hotel toward the pool area, past a cool little outdoor bar with Turkish rugs, a multitude of dangling lights all over the place. People are drinking, socializing, some are jumping in the pool. Again, not the type of hotel I'm used to working in.

"I was going to get that room for us," he nods at a door as we pass it on the second floor. The walls here are white concrete or brick, giving you the feel of being somewhere exotic. "It was Marilyn Monroe's suite. Unfortunately, someone had already taken it."

"Jerks," I mumble under my breath. I love Marilyn but I'm just so damn happy to be here, I would have taken anyone's room.

"Here we are," Viktor says as he pauses at one of the doors. I could be wrong, but I swear he looks nervous.

He takes an anxious look at me, as if to say *here goes nothing*, and then swipes the key in front of it, opening the door.

We step into the room.

He flicks on the light.

It takes me a moment to take it all in. It's a really nice room for sure but that's not what grabs my eye, causes my hand to fly to my chest and makes me *gasp*.

A trail of purple flowers leads from where we're standing at the door all the way to the bed, the white bedcover absolutely covered in them.

Then the smell hits me and my eyes adjust better.

Lavender.

Instead of rose petals, the room has been sprinkled with lavender.

I stare at Viktor in disbelief. "Did you do this?"

"Well, I had the hotel do it, but yes."

I'm completely dumfounded by this.

He did this.

For me?

"Do you like it?" he asks tepidly, and now I see why he was so anxious before.

"Viktor," I say, his name comes out breathless as all my emotions rush to the surface. "This is the most romantic, beautiful thing that anyone has ever done for me."

He shoves his suitcase and my duffel bag off to the side and then places both of his hands on either side of my cheeks. I love it when he does this. His hands are so large, warm, strong; my face so small in comparison. I feel protected and adored.

Wanted.

Captive.

His.

The heated glint in his eyes spear me, holding me in place as much as his hands do, and he looks dangerously handsome, the lights in the room showcasing the sharpness of his cheekbones and the hollows underneath. He has a face that you could see someone like Da Vinci trying to paint, forever trying to capture his beauty but never getting it quite right because it's Viktor himself that takes your breath away, it's his spirit and soul that shines through the symmetry of his features.

His gaze drops to my lips, his gorgeously long lashes creating shadows against his golden skin.

"Mitt liv, mitt allt," he murmurs in Swedish, his voice so low and rough it makes shivers shower down my back. "Min Maggie."

I don't understand what he's said, all I know is that he means it.

His thumb runs across the edge of my jaw, pausing at my lips.

"I could kiss you for a thousand days and it still wouldn't be enough," he says. "I could gaze at you for a million days and it wouldn't be enough. I could touch you, taste you, be so deep inside you that you're fused to my skin, do this forever and it still wouldn't be enough. Forever with you isn't enough."

Tears prick at the back of my eyes. I swallow, trying to stay strong. This shouldn't be so hard. This shouldn't feel like this. I shouldn't be so lost, so head over heels over heart for this man.

We should have stayed strangers.

That thought sends a jolt through me. On one hand, had we never gotten to know each other like this, it wouldn't hurt so much to have him leave. On the other hand…fuck. I wouldn't have known *this*.

I've never had this before.

I'm not sure if I will again.

He's right. If forever wouldn't be enough, these last few days sure as hell won't be.

"But," he says, leaning in and softly places his mouth on mine, dragging his top lip over my top lip. Somehow he tastes like lemon drops. "We both know I don't have you forever. Only for a few days. And I am going to spend every moment with you, trying to stretch it out into infinity. I want to feel your lips burn on mine the entire plane ride back home. I want the taste of you still in my mouth as I fall asleep at night." He brings his face back just enough as one of his hands slips down to the hem of my top, tugging at it impatiently. "I would like to get started now."

I laugh at his sudden formality. "Well okay then," I tell him, raising my arms above my head so he can pull the top right off. "Let's get started."

He grins at me and yanks the top over my head, leaving me in just my bra. My best bra though, in racy red lace. In the past maybe I would have covered up my breasts, feeling insecure or on display, but it's impossible to feel anything but *desired* with the way Viktor is staring at me.

I shift backward and undo my jeans, shimmying out of them, so I'm standing in just my thong and bra. I feel like I'm burning up under the heat of his gaze, a look that both terrifies me and gives me courage. Feigning confidence, I hook my thumbs around the lacy sides of my underwear and start to pull them down.

"Wait," Viktor says hoarsely. "I want to take them off with my teeth."

Well, jeez.

Yes.

He gestures to the petal-strewn bed and starts unbuttoning the short-sleeve dress shirt he's wearing. "Lie down. On your back. Legs over the end."

I raise my brows. "Wow, demanding much?"

My defiance makes his eyes flicker. Gives me a quick, cunning smile as he steps toward me and places one hand on my chest.

"Lie down," he whispers gruffly into my ear, giving me a small push downward until my knees are buckling and I'm falling, the lavender pressing into my spine. "On your back."

He then reaches down and grabs both of my hips with bruising strength and yanks me so that my ass is on the edge of the mattress. "Legs over the end," he repeats.

I haven't seen this side of Viktor before and I'm taken aback, staring at his broad throat where his pulse ticks. I blink up to meet his eyes and I see fire crackling along the glacial blue, a wildness he's kept so well hidden beneath his stately demeanor.

I like this side of him.

No, I *love* it.

He gives me that wicked smile again and then I'm met

with a hard, punishing kiss that takes my breath away. I arch up for him, lacing my fingers around the back of his neck to keep from falling further back as his hands slip across my stomach, down between my legs. His fingers glide over the fabric of my underwear.

"This all for me?" he murmurs against my mouth. "All so wet for me?"

Everything is for you, I think.

The pressure from his fingers deepens, ripping a gasp from my throat.

God...*oh*...that feels nice.

Nice in a way that makes me realize how fucking hungry for him, for this, I am. I have no doubt that he won't take long to make me come.

He pulls back and brings his mouth down my neck, over my collarbones, my breasts, the sides of my waist. He's both kissing and nipping, sweet sharp pain that creates jolts of electricity between my legs.

His teeth raze down my hips and he takes the strap of my underwear in his mouth, his tongue curling around, and pulls it down. I bite my lip and bring my legs together to help him get it off. It doesn't look that easy but it looks sexy as hell.

He manages to pull my underwear halfway down my thighs with just his mouth until he gets impatient and basically tears the strap, snapping it in half.

"Hey," I tell him, looking up. Those were my only nice ones!

He stares at me with raw impatience. "I'll buy you another pair."

"From where? Disney–" but the rest of my sentence dies on my tongue because he yanks my thighs apart and buries his head between them, his hands on my thighs and pressing hard enough to leave bruises.

I immediately stiffen at the first contact of his tongue and then I start to melt.

Oh...I'm melting.

Right into his mouth.

He flicks the tip of his tongue over my clit and instantly I am dissolving into a sea of stars while a galaxy at my middle whirls tighter, tighter.

No, this won't take long at all.

"You taste so perfect," he moans into me and I instinctively grab the top of his head, my fingers winding in his hair and holding his head against me, though I think I couldn't pull him away even if I tried. "So sweet, so beautiful. A lavender ocean. I could taste you forever."

His words trail off into grunts and little moans, telling me how much he's enjoying this, enjoying me.

"Oh god," I cry out, feeling like I'm losing oxygen already as his tongue plunges deep inside me. My hips rock and I feel like I'm being too demanding for wanting more but from the way he's gripping my hips, squeezing my delicate skin and pumping his tongue in and out of me, I know he wants to give it.

Something hot and electric starts to build in my core, working its way up my spine, and I'm growing more frantic for my release. I want to come so badly it's driving me crazy and yet I want this to last forever, the sight of his head between my legs, his mouth wet and open and ruthless as he licks me out.

I am being devoured.

I am being ravaged.

I am...

God. "I'm coming," I say, breathless, and the world pauses in that heavy, silent, slow-motion moment before the bomb goes off. "I'm–"

A cord is pulled deep inside me and I am yanked into

another world, a shooting star made of fire and livewires and I'm calling out his name, "Viktor, Viktor, oh god, *so good*," and I'm practically whimpering as I come back to earth, my body convulsing, my thighs squeezing both sides of his head.

"Was that good?" he asks a moment later.

I'm still struggling to catch my breath, my body oversensitive, my heart so loud and fast in my head that I can't think straight. I look to see him staring at me eagerly, framed by my thighs, his mouth wet, glistening on a curved smile.

There are pieces of lavender in his hair.

"Yeah," I tell him. "Yeah…I…"

There are no words.

But he has words.

"That was for you," he says, his voice taking on this low, guttural tone. "This is for me."

He stands up at the foot of the bed and starts stripping.

The shirt that was partially unbuttoned is now thrown to the floor.

His shoes are kicked away. Socks peeled off.

His hands go to his pants and he unbuckles his belt with stealthy confidence. My eyes go from his face to his chest to his abs to now his underwear as he pulls down his boxer briefs and steps out of them.

I know I've seen Viktor like this before. Naked.

But I've never seen him like *this* before.

Cock extended, large and hard.

For me.

I still stand by what I thought the first day that I saw him naked, that I would love to suck his dick like a fucking porno.

He can tell, too.

Perhaps he wants to pretend it's that day all over again.

I bring it up as he walks toward me, his cock hard as it

juts out between us. I'm barely able to take my eyes away from it.

"Pretend you were that stranger on the first day?" he questions. He shakes his head and stops right in front of me. "No. I don't want a stranger to suck me off. I need it to be you. I've dreamed about that lush peach mouth of yours for days."

Fuck. He doesn't mince words. I wonder how dirty his thoughts are in Swedish.

I sit up and he wraps his hand around the base of his cock and holds it near my lips. "Suck," he demands. "*Min lilla persika.*"

I swallow hard, unsure of what that means, unsure if I can fit him all in my mouth but I'm more than willing to try. I reach out and hold him in my hand, feeling his hot, smooth shaft pulse in my palm.

I'm wet again in a second.

I look up and meet his eyes and he's staring down at me with a look that can only be called carnal, his eyes urging me to go on.

My grip around his cock tightens and he lets go and slowly pushes his hips forward until his cock slides in my mouth. The salt of him hits my tongue, creating another wave of need through me, and as he pushes through my lips, his hands glide into my hair.

He groans and I can feel him grow even harder, like steel. In my mouth he feels fat and swollen, and sometimes when he's pushing in, it's impossible to accommodate all of him.

But I try, licking and sucking, the suction sounds and wetness filling the air and I'm pumping him into my mouth faster and faster, occasionally razing him with my teeth which only makes him moan louder.

"Fuck," he says and then mutters something in Swedish as

he abruptly pulls out. "I'll come in your mouth later. Now I want to come in you."

The thought, as much as I want it, makes me pause.

"Condom?" I ask. "I mean do you have one?"

Do we need one? That's what I'm really asking.

He looks at me with glazed eyes until he blinks some clarity back into them. "I do." He clears his throat. "I am clean though. I get tested regularly, it's well, *they're* very adamant about health check-ups. Are you on the pill?"

I nod. "Yes and I've been tested. Recently. When I came back to California." I pause, not sure if I should continue or not. "I haven't had sex since I came back. For over a year."

He barely reacts. "Then I should make this worth your while."

You already have, I think.

And then he's pushing me back on the bed again, kissing me, licking me, consuming my whole body for the second time, his cock pressing against me here and there as we find our spots in the sheets.

He grips under my ass, pulling it up toward him and then gets between my legs, determination on his brow.

I'm so wet still that the slightest movement forward and he slips in.

Oh...*fuck*.

"Maggie," he groans, pinching his eyes shut as he buries his head into my neck and I can feel his hot, ragged breath, already struggling for control. "The things I want to do to you, I don't think I can do them all this time."

"There will be other times," I manage to say, my hands sliding over his shoulders, down his arms, pricking him lightly with my fingernails as he pushes in further and I'm spread around his thick girth. I've never felt so...full.

So taken.

So his.

"Yes, tonight," he says and the way the words hang in the air I realize tonight and tomorrow and the next night are all we have to do all the things we want to do with each other.

Life just isn't fair.

"Don't think," he whispers in my ear before taking my lobe in his teeth and tugging. I feel like a million sparks are raining down my spine. "Don't think, just feel."

I am feeling.

Everything.

"I feel," I tell him. "Just don't ever stop."

"Fuck," he growls and then he slams his hips forward until he's pushed all the way in. It feels like he's pushed the air right out of my lungs.

I gasp loudly and he presses his hand over my mouth, over my cheek, holding my head down with force as he starts to fuck me at a punishing pace, his hips strong and relentless as they drive his cock in and out. My breasts jostle from each thrust, the bed starts to creak and move, I can hardly focus on anything, my grip digging in tighter in a wild attempt to hold on.

"You feel so good," he grunts into my neck, one hand now pinning my arms above my head, while the other slides between us and starts tapping my clit. "Come for me again, I want to see your face as you're coming. I want to see what you look like when you call my name, when I'm fucking you so good. *Helvete.*"

Holy shit, this dirty-talking Swedish bastard is going to be the death of me.

He hisses and then stabs forward, sinking in so damn deep I'm not sure where he ends and I begin. I feel like I'm being folded in half. I cry out, half in pain, half because it feels so amazing that nothing, no one, will ever satisfy me again.

"Oh my Maggie," he says before cursing some more in

Swedish. "You were made for me, weren't you? This, your amazing cunt, it's so perfect, too perfect." He groans, his head thrown back, sweat trickling down his throat and then snaps forward again, faster, harder. My hands trail down to his hips, his ass, grabbing on desperately.

Lavender is flying everywhere.

My thighs start to shake and the pressure from his slick fingers increase. There are no neat and tidy circles, instead it's sliding all over the place with every relentless pump into me but I don't need much.

"You like this, don't you my Maggie," he growls at me, staring at me with the wild eyes of someone completely raw and primal, operating on the basic instinct to fuck and fuck. "You love my cock, how it fills you, how deep I am inside you."

I can't even answer him. My world is spinning tighter until there's nothing else but him and me. No hotel, no bed, no people in the world outside. Just us and the smell of musk and lavender.

My eyes shut and I grow tight and then it's just "Oh god!" and my orgasm crashes over me again and I'm no longer myself, no longer in my body, the only thing I am is this boneless thing that's spouting off words and sounds that make no sense at all.

"You're so beautiful when you come," he says and slips out of me. "Like your innocence is banished in front of my eyes."

I'm still not quite here so it takes me a moment to realize he's pulled out and then I'm disappointed and bereft at his absence.

But when I open my eyes, he's hovering over me, slipping an arm underneath my back and flipping me over on my stomach.

"Up, to the wall," he says gruffly and I feel his cock press against my ass for a moment. "On your knees."

My legs are jelly and I don't have much strength but I somehow manage to crawl to the top of the bed and get on my knees, facing the wall, my palms flat pressed against the headboard.

He comes up behind me and I look down to see each sinewy thigh capture me on either side, then he pushes down between my shoulder blades until my back is arched into a U and my ass sticks out against him.

I feel his fingers slide between my legs, then position his cock.

He enters me in a single long push and I'm flat up against the head board again, gasping. From this angle, I'm feeling him everywhere.

"Can you come again for me?" he whispers in my ear as he begins to pump. He wraps a hand over my throat. "What if it's rougher? Would you like that?"

Yes, please. Anything. I would give this man anything right now.

I nod and the grip on my throat grows tighter as he starts rolling his hips into me, faster, harder. I can feel my ass jiggle with every thrust, the bed shakes and I can barely breathe and I'm overwhelmed and overheated and...

"Fuck, this, this," he hisses at my ear. "You fuck so good."

His thrusts become brutal and I feel like he might just break me in two or shatter me into a million pieces and he has lost his mind to me or I have lost my mind, my body, my soul to his.

Then his fingers slide over my belly, finding my clit once more, swollen and wet and wanting and needing and greedy, I'm so greedy for him, to come again, to...

I come in an instant and his grip on my neck tightens and I'm seeing stars.

And I'm loud.

The kind of loud that gets you noise complaints but in

this second it doesn't matter. I am stardust and delirious as the orgasm rips through me once again, turning me inside out. The world starts to blacken a little at the edges and I'm vaguely aware that he's still choking me, still pounding me, with this ruthless force that causes the headboard to slam again and again.

Then his hand becomes a vice, just for a painful second as he pauses and then he completely let's go of me, his pumps slowing.

I gasp for breath and he cries out, a rough and ragged bellow that fills the space around us like a battle cry. Right now he is more of a Viking warrior than he is a Swedish prince.

He collapses against my back and I'm pressed flat against the headboard and wall and sweat pools off his body and onto mine. He's breathing hard, I don't even know where I am. We take a few minutes to come back and when my thoughts and clarity return, I swear I'm a different person altogether now.

He pulls out and runs his hand down my damp spine before giving my ass a little slap. Then he falls to the bed, grabbing my arm so I collapse beside him.

"Was that okay?" he asks me, pulling me toward him so my back is to his chest, kissing my ear. "I don't wish to be too rough with my Maggie."

"You weren't too rough," I say. My heart is still a marching band in my chest, the sweat on my body starting to cool. "You were…you were good. You were *making me come three times* kind of good. Which is a lot better than good."

"Always more, never less," he says.

I smile at that and everything inside me seems to smile too. Beams of light and butterflies and happiness. I'm sated and content and I love how he goes from a wild man bent on fucking the hell out of me to one adoring and doting me with his tenderness.

"Next time, I will last longer," he tells me, pulling me closer still so I'm nestled under his arm, my head on his chest.

"How much longer can you last?" I chuckle.

"For you? I want to last forever. I never want this to end."

Damn.

That kicks me in the gut.

Now that the throes of orgasm are wearing off, I'm back into this sticky reality, the one in which the two of us only have a few days with each other.

There is no forever with us.

There never was.

I close my eyes and breathe him in.

He smells like lavender.

CHAPTER FIFTEEN

MAGGIE

Having lived almost my whole life only two and a bit hours away from LA, you'd think that I would have been to the City of Angels a lot. But as I had told Viktor, the only time I remember was for a wedding, some relative on my dad's side. I remember seeing Venice Beach and being enamored by the sand and the seagulls and that bright blue Pacific, but that was about it.

What I really wanted was to go to Disneyland. There were multiple kids in my grade with annual passes, I remember thinking they were the richest kids in the world, practically royalty.

Now I'm with actual royalty. Funny how life works.

Standing outside the gates to the Magic Kingdom, with an actual god damn prince by my side, a prince who outshines any of the ones in the park, a prince who would have his own kingdom, his own country, one day. A prince who…

Is smoking a joint?

I thought Viktor was right behind me as we were walking toward the ticket booths but now I've turned around to see him off to the side and smoking a joint, a puff of smoke falling from his mouth and wafting around him.

"Really?" I ask him, coming over. "Pot?"

He nods and squints at me, taking the joint away from his lips. "I smoke quite often at home. When no one is looking, of course. Usually if I happen to visit Magnus. He's the Prince of Norway," he explains.

Pot smoking princes, huh?

He tries to hand it off to me but I shake my head. I'm no angel but I'm about to step into Disneyland. I don't need that shit. I'm going to get high on churros.

"Where did you get it anyway?" I ask him.

He nods over at the busy intersection. "Bought it from the homeless fellow on the corner."

My mouth drops open. "You did not!"

He smirks at me and has another drag. Blows out the smoke. God he looks sexy with his eyes all squinty like that. "I picked it up in Colorado on the way here."

"You're lucky it's legal in California. The last thing you need is for your ass to be thrown in jail. What kind of a headline would that be?"

"Not a good one," he says and then stubs out the joint, flicks it in the nearest wastebasket and holds out his arm for me. "Let's go."

Because this was a last minute addition to our agenda, we're only at the park for one day which sadly means that we have to choose one park instead of both. As much as I want to go to California Adventure and ride the Grizzly River Rapids or California Screaming, we've decided on just visiting the OG, Disneyland.

Honestly though, it was a hard decision to come here at all. With only so many days left with each other, part of me didn't even want come. I wanted to stay in the hotel room with Viktor and continue to have him fuck my brains out.

Though we fell asleep right after last night, both of us exhausted, especially me for having come three times, this morning we woke up and blindly groped for each other in the dark and got back at it. Sex in the shower followed right after.

But Viktor was looking forward to Disneyland too and I know we can't do all of our getting to know each other in the bedroom. As much as my body wants to get to know him better, my mind still wants to know his on the same level.

Either way, this trip will be a memory neither of us will ever forget. If someone ever brings up Disneyland in the future, I can think back and go, "Oh yeah, I went there once with the Prince of Sweden."

But who am I kidding? I won't forget a single second of our time together, even just the boring stuff like standing in line forever at In & Out and talking smack about everyone else in front of us.

We didn't get a chance to order our Disney tickets online, so we end up in yet another line to get our tickets (thankfully it wasn't as long as the one for burgers) and then we're into the park. In seconds I am smitten. The sounds, the sights, the smells…god, all of Main Street smells like heaven.

"Oh my god, it's Pluto," I cry out, pointing at the character with a line of kids waiting patiently for their pictures to be taken with him. Then I spot Goofy. "Oh my god, it's *Goofy*!"

"I don't know what's worse," he says.

I blink at Viktor, ready to go on the defensive if he says any shit about either character. "What?"

"How fucking adorable you look right now or how much this is turning me on."

I smack him across the chest playfully, my hand bouncing back like I've slapped a bunch of bricks. "You can't get turned on at Disneyland. It's gotta be a rule."

He shrugs. "You obviously don't know me. I can get

turned on anywhere." He flashes me a wicked grin. "I bet I can turn you on anywhere too."

"Oh hush," I tell him, grabbing his hand and leading him further into the park.

It's almost summer and even though kids are still at school, the park is crowded. Maybe it's always this crowded. Everywhere I look there are people, large families, couples with babies, couples without kids, people that look like they're about to run a marathon through the park, old people on scooters, Donald Duck. Normally crowds of this size would give me some anxiety, but here it doesn't affect me, not when I'm hanging onto Viktor. His size and presence seems to command attention and make people part in from of him.

"Where to?" he asks as we pause at the end of Main Street.

I don't even have to consult the map. I nod at Sleeping Beauty's castle.

"The castle."

He looks at it and squints. "You call that a castle?"

"Hey, when am I ever going to have an actual prince in this situation after this?"

He shrugs. "I'd hope never."

He takes my hand and we walk over the bridge, the castle getting a lot smaller the closer we get.

"My mother would like it," he muses, looking around as we go through the entrance and into a courtyard full of shops and children running everywhere, most of them in little princess costumes.

"Oh," I gasp. "I want one. Do you think they have adult sizes?"

He gives me a funny look. "You want to be a princess?"

"What girl doesn't want to be a princess?" I ask and then I realize the question probably holds some real meaning to him. "I mean, as a kid, of course you do. It's a fantasy."

"Am I a fantasy?"

I look him up and down, looking impossibly handsome as he always is. "You're my fantasy, yes. Definitely."

He seems to think that over as we head into one of the shops. "You know, if you came back with me to Sweden, and married me, then you could be a real princess."

Oh my god.

I stop dead in my tracks.

My heart lurching to a stop.

"You do not joke about that," I manage to say, my blood thrumming hot through my veins.

Oh my god.

What if he isn't joking?

But I see the sly glint in his eyes, the hint of a smile and he is joking.

Thank god I didn't take him up on it.

"Hey, I'm not desperate to be a princess, thank you very much," I tell him, picking up a crown from a display. "Why should I be when I have all that I need to be one right here."

I can feel his eyes on me, watching me intently. "I think we should buy you a crown," he says after a moment.

I smile at him sweetly. "You're really hell-bent on making me a princess."

"Actually I have a better idea." He ducks around the corner and comes back holding a stuffed version of the reindeer from Frozen.

"Sven the reindeer?" I ask as he puts the plush toy in my hands.

"No," he says, almost annoyed. "It's a moose. Viktor the moose."

"But it's a reindeer," I tell him and show him his name tag. "And his name is Sven."

Viktor takes the animal from me and rips the fabric nametag off his collar, hiding it between a pile of Olaf slippers. "Now it's Viktor. The moose." He shoves it back in my hands. "Now when I'm gone, you'll still have a Viktor of your own."

Well, fuck. If this isn't one of the cutest things ever.

Even though he just vandalized a Disney toy at Disneyland.

I look down into the reindeer's big eyes and will myself to think of it as Viktor the moose.

After we buy the reindeer–*moose*–and the clerk wanted to double-check with us that we were okay with buying a defective toy, we head over to Splash Mountain, because the wait times seemed somewhat reasonable.

That was a lie, of course. There are no reasonable wait times in the park, so Viktor and I are yet again stuck in a long line.

But I guess stuck is too strong of a word. The thing is, I'm positively delighted with just standing beside Viktor and doing nothing but waiting. We talk, about everything we can without getting too personal, because who wants to get personal surrounded by a bunch of strangers.

I lean back against his chest and he wraps his big arms around me and we shuffle forward, not wanting to be apart. He tells me about his pet rabbits he had while growing up, how he was so obsessed with *Watership Down* at the time that he named them after the characters and was convinced they were going to have an uprising when he wasn't looking.

I tell him about my family's tradition of giving weird names. Rosemary and Thyme, and Pike have always gotten the brunt of it, but Callum's middle name is actually Danger, April has two, May and June, and my full name is Margaret Mayhem.

"Margaret Mayhem?" Viktor laughs loudly, the sound soaring over the crowd and making a few people in line turn their heads. "I'm sorry but mayhem means…"

"Mayhem means a little chaotic and crazy," I say with a sigh. "Apparently both me and Callum were handfuls when we were born."

"Or perhaps you both grew into your names like, what is it called again? A self-fulfilling prophecy."

"That might be true for Callum but I am *not* chaotic or crazy."

He raises his brow at me. "Well…"

I punch his chest. "Hey."

He grabs my fist and kisses my knuckles. "You were a little chaotic and crazy last night," he says in a low, silken voice.

I immediately blush and my body knows all too well. I've felt the ache of him between my legs all day and I know I'm walking a little differently.

Even though we end up boarding the log flume ten minutes later, my body is still feeling a bit hot and needy, especially as we end up sitting squished at the very back of the log and my ass is pressed into his crotch.

I glance at him over my shoulder, my eyes turning sly. "You comfortable?" I ask, wiggling my ass into him.

He just shakes his head, his jaw growing tense in playful warning.

As it turns out though, a lot of the ride is in the dark.

Now, I know that the dark in Disneyland is only dark to you. The place is famous for the amount of cameras they have set up, eyes on you at all times. They can always see you clearly, no matter what.

But from the way we're sitting at the back, so squished together with his long legs bracketing mine, it's almost natural for Viktor's hand to be in my lap.

Unbuttoning the top of my jean shorts.

Slipping his fingers into my underwear.

"We could get caught," I turn my head and hiss at him,

hoping all the singing from the animatronic animals drowns out my voice from the other people in the log. Thankfully they are all adults.

"So?" he says lazily, sliding his fingers around and around.

My eyes close briefly.

This is *so* wrong.

But, god, it feels *so* good.

"So we could get banned for life."

"That's okay," he says. "I live in Sweden."

I'm about to tell him to stop, that it's wrong, that we're in public and we're violating laws and probably Disneyland's innocence but then the log starts to climb up the final hill and the gravity thrusts me further back into him.

And Viktor has skills.

He keeps his fingers going, rubbing me expertly, and with the *tick tick tick* vibrations of the log as it's cranked up the hill, I'm coming just as the log flume hits the crescendo. The world is open and bright in front of my eyes, all of the park in front of me, and my mouth is open, crying out his name.

And then we're dropping straight down, down, down into the water.

Nothing like a cold splash hitting you in the face to bring you back on track.

After the ride we're both soaked, me in more ways than one, and we pick up the large photo of us they took during the final fall.

Viktor is grinning like an idiot in it.

It looks like I'm screaming from fear.

Only the two of us know the truth about that photo.

That thing is going up on my wall.

When we finally get back to the hotel from Disneyland, we're both exhausted. The traffic from Anaheim to Hollywood ensnared us for hours, so bad that even the Waze app on his phone couldn't shortcut us out of there.

Our hotel room is freshly cleaned and passes my inspection (a housekeeper always knows what to look for) though I'm sad that the last signs of the lavender flowers have been swept away. I still detect a hint of it in the air, or maybe I'm forever smelling it like a memory that won't go away.

"Get naked," Viktor says, taking his shirt off over his head, displaying that hard, bare torso of his.

"You aren't tired?" I ask him, my fingers already obeying his commands before my mind has a chance to argue. I take off my tank top, one that says *Powered By Pixie Dust* that he bought for me in the park and I couldn't wait to change into, then I start unbuttoning my jean shorts. He strides over to the curtains that have been left open and pulls them shut just as the shorts fall to my feet.

"I don't care if people see," I tell him. After what happened on the ride, I feel like I've dipped my toe into the life of someone else, someone footloose and fancy free. I want to live like I don't give any fucks left to give. I want to get into a fuck bankruptcy.

I want to do that with Viktor, live this whole other life in this hotel room.

But when I lie down on the bed, naked, and he joins me, the exhaustion takes over the both of us. Viktor wraps me in his arms and pulls me toward him, his leg hooking over mine, so that we are a tangle of limbs and warm skin.

"Just a nap," he whispers into my ear, even though it's nearly midnight already. I didn't think I would feel as comfortable just lying here naked with him as I am when I'm fucking him, but in seconds my mind and body start to drift away.

I'm awakened by the scrape of a lighter, a puff of smoke filling the air.

I open my eyes to see Viktor sitting up in bed, smoking.

It's cinematic, with the courtyard light coming in through the crack in the curtains like a spear, lighting the edges of him up. There's another light coming from the bathroom but the main one is off and we're mostly in darkness. I don't remember turning it off before I fell asleep.

"What time is it?" I ask.

"Sorry," he says to me, glancing over his shoulder with a warm smile. "I didn't want to wake you. But I knew if I went on the balcony, someone would see me. There's been a party out by the pool all night."

It's only then that I notice the dull thump of music and the occasional laughter.

"I couldn't sleep," he explains, lying back down on the bed, facing me. "I thought this would help."

He holds it out to me in offering and this time I take it, looking up at the ceiling as I do so. "Won't this set off the smoke detector?"

He bites back a grin. "No."

"But we could get in trouble, I don't think they allow smoking of any kind."

He studies me for a moment, his expression soft, amused, content. "We'll be okay."

I shrug at that, trusting him. After we gave new meaning

to the word Splash Mountain this afternoon, smoking in a hotel room shouldn't have me so worried.

I have a puff. Hold the smoke in my mouth, probably for a bit too long, probably because I'm trying to show off in front of him, and he has to take the joint back from my fingers.

"And for a moment there I didn't think you smoked," he muses.

"I don't," I tell him and then start coughing violently. Point proven. "Honestly. Very rarely. Sometimes Pike has some but that's about it."

He nods, puffing back. "I understand," he says, smoke falling from his mouth. "You have a lot to worry about, a lot to be ready for."

I pull the edge of the blanket over my chest, tucking it under me. I like the whole lying around naked thing but a girl has her hang-ups. "To be honest, I rarely drink. I can't afford the hangover for one, not when I have to work so early, and I feel like I have to always been *on*. Like, with my parents, they were always drinking. I mean, not in a bad way, but it was a common sight. I think back now and I'm like, how did you do that? How did you let yourself be loose and relaxed and just know that everything was going to be fine?"

I catch myself and then reach out and grab the joint from him as a way to start blurring memories. "Of course, it wasn't fine in the end, was it?"

"It will get easier, Maggie," he tells me as I inhale. "I promise."

I take a moment before I exhale. "How would you know?" I cough.

"I don't know. That's what people tell me. I suppose becoming a king and becoming a parent are similar in a lot of ways."

"I guess," I say. "But with you, you have a system in place. You have, like presidents or prime ministers or something to actually pass rules and do all the dirty business. If you're a parent, all that dirty business is on you."

"You're right," he says, taking the joint back. "I can't pretend to know. I can only say I understand."

I know he does. We're in such similar situations. Very different situations, mind you, but similar all the same. Saddled with responsibilities that are bigger than we are, overwhelmed by the change in our lives, grappling with loss.

I sigh and fall back on the bed. The pot is starting to affect me already and I hope things don't get weird. "Tell me about your brother, Alex."

Viktor exhales sharply through his nose and I can feel him tense up.

"I don't mean anything bad," I say. "Let's just forget, just for tonight, that we've lost them. Pretend they're still here. Pretend we're at a party and people want anecdotes about them. What would you tell them? What are some of your best memories?"

The room has grown silent except for the sound of my beating heart and the dull thud of the music outside. Viktor then lies back on the bed beside me and we both stare up at the ceiling.

"Alex was always a bit of a weirdo," he begins. "But I never had a problem with it. He was totally fascinated by the strangest things. Things like trains, for example. He loved trains. He was obsessed for years. I know it sounds silly, but being my parents and all, we had a massive playroom for all of our toys and at the end of it was his train collection."

He takes another hit of the joint and lets the smoke float above us like fog.

"He'd spend hours in there, even when I got to an age where toys no longer interested me, he was still fascinated. But it wasn't the locomotives or the tracks or the romantic quality of trains that kept him going. It was just the wheels.

Of all things, there was something he found comforting about the wheels turning. Give him a train without a track and he didn't care for it. Give him a track and he would spend hours and hours watching it make the rounds around the room. Even now the sound of a toy train brings me back."

"Sounds like a nice memory."

He looks at me in surprise, as if it hadn't crossed his mind. Then a small smile tilts the corner of his mouth. "Yeah. It is a nice memory. It was something about him that I found peculiar but so essentially Alex."

"What else is a nice memory?" I ask, wanting to know more.

"Christmas," he says. "Christmas is a big deal in Sweden. As you know, Santa comes from Lapland. We also celebrate Christmas Eve instead of morning."

"So when do you open your presents? I mean, how does Santa get them to you without you seeing him?"

He smiles. "Well that's the thing. You have to have a pretty sneaky Santa. And we did. You'd never see him. Until one day I rigged a trap."

"A trap? You set a trap for *Santa*?"

He shrugs and then puts the joint out on the notepad beside the bed. "I was curious. Anyway, I made it so that he would trip over a wire which would then send all these metal things, like the fireplace poker and an ashtray and a tin box, stuff that was hard and noisy, onto the floor. We had hardwood floors in the living area where the tree was, so you would hear it. And I knew that we were always sequestered for some convenient reason in another room the same time the presents would appear."

"I see where this is going." I can't help but smile at the thought of a super curious and devious Viktor rigging a trap for Santa. It reminds me of Callum for some reason.

He nods, still staring up at the ceiling with a dreamy look

on his face. "Oh, yes. So we were all in the study because my mother had to show us something, who knows what, and then CRASH. There was a huge bang and commotion from the other room. So I raced out of there first and my mother managed to hold back Alex, or maybe Alex already figured it out by then and he didn't care. Either way, I ran into the room to see my *father* dressed as Santa, a sack of presents at his feet, along with all the other crap I had set up scattered on the floor. Do you know what I did?"

"What?"

"I looked into my father's eyes and for once I saw a father. I know that sounds silly, of course he's my father. But he's also the king and he often has that mentality first, father second. The fact that he dressed as Santa himself and didn't have a palace worker or butler do it, that meant the world to me. Meant that he actually cared. So I looked at my father and I said, 'So sorry to disturb you Santa, thank you for the presents.' And then I ran out of the room. To this day my father still thinks he had me fooled but the thing is, I wanted to be fooled. I never wanted him to know that I knew, it would take all the magic away."

"That's actually really sweet," I tell him, running my fingers over his chest.

"What about you?" he asks. "What do you remember from your childhood that was good?"

"Honestly? Everything." I don't have to think too hard. "Even though we grew up fairly poor, you know, and yeah I was upset that I didn't get to go to Disneyland like other kids did, or I didn't have the toys everyone else had or I didn't have new clothes, my childhood was pretty happy. I don't know, it wasn't until I was much older that I realized we lacked. Even so, I loved my parents and they loved me, I know they loved me, you could feel it, they showed it, you knew, we all knew their love and…"

The tears hit me like a slap in the face. I thought I was going to be fine talking about this. I should be fine by now.

Viktor reaches out and pulls me to him, holding me tight.

"I'm fine," I say, but I'm not fine. I can't even find the words to go on, the tears just keep flowing and flowing. "I... I'm..."

"It's okay," Viktor says. "I'm here."

I know you're here. You're here for me. And then you'll be gone. They were here for me and they're gone. Everyone I love leaves me.

Everyone I love leaves me.

"I miss them so much," I cry out, sobbing so loudly that it hurts my chest. My mouth is open, gaping as the choked, silent wails try and escape me. "Oh god, oh god. I miss them so much. It hurts, Viktor, it hurts me."

"My Maggie," he whispers, kissing the top of my head over and over again. "I hate to see you hurt. I wish I could take this pain from you, I would give anything to do so."

I dig my fingers into his shoulders, hanging on tight, afraid to let go. If I hold on tight enough, maybe I won't have to be alone.

"I just want to see them again," I whimper, my words garbled. My heart is so heavy I'm afraid it might pull me down so low that I'll never get back up. "I just want to tell them how much I love them. How much they meant to me. How much I need them. I don't think I'll ever stop needing them."

I try and hold my breath, try to suppress the sobs, but it doesn't work.

I cry and I cry, feeling like I'll never be free of this.

"I don't think we're supposed to stop needing our parents," he says softly, smoothing my hair with his palm. "I think that's what love is, always needing someone. Needing doesn't have to be a bad thing or a weak thing. It's just part of living. We need air to breathe and food to eat. We need certain people in the same way. In the end it's what keeps us alive."

I nod, sniffling in to him.

"Hey, it's okay," he tells me softly. "I'm here and I'm not going anywhere."

"But you are," I manage to say. "You're leaving me too. And I need you, Viktor, I need you."

He exhales, long and shaking.

"I know, Maggie, I know."

Silence passes between us and the dark of the room seems to press in on us. The crying has dragged the life out of me and suddenly I'm so tired I feel I could sleep forever. Every part of me feels poured in concrete.

I've almost completely drifted off when I hear Viktor whisper into the dark.

"I need you too."

CHAPTER SIXTEEN

MAGGIE

There's something different about the way you wake up when it's a day you don't want to face. Even if your first thoughts upon waking are jumbled from sleep, you still know, deep down, that something is going to happen. It's like sadness hangs in the air above you, a heavy hand that holds you down and reminds you that you will need all the strength you have to get through the day.

Even though I'm wrapped under sheets, with Viktor's strong leg hooked over mine, the back of my head resting in the crook of his arm, I'm immediately hit with a pang of sorrow. Any other day and I would wake up blissful after these two beautiful days we've had with each other, the fact that I fell asleep, entangled in his arms.

But as safe as I feel with him like this, he won't be able to protect me from the pain that will come later, a pain that will make this anticipatory one seem like nothing more than a scratch.

"*God morgon*," he says to me in Swedish, his breath warm on the top of my head. There's something so beautiful and peaceful about his voice in the mornings. Normally it's so deep and strong and polished. Refined. As it should be. He has a lifetime of public speaking ahead of him.

But in the mornings it's ragged, raw, groggy with sleep. It makes him seem less of a prince, more of a young man.

"How did you sleep?" he asks. "I passed right out I think."

"I slept like a baby," I tell him, turning over on my stomach and facing him.

Yesterday was our last day and we were so exhausted from Disneyland the day before, that we literally stayed in the hotel room and by the pool, only venturing out onto Sunset Blvd to grab a meal at a trendy restaurant. The rest of the time, well, let's just say there was a lot of sex. I am thoroughly worn out but in the best way possible.

"Good." He gives me a soft smile, his eyes warm as he stares at me, and reaches over, gently brushing my hair off my face.

We stare at each other for a few moments, the moments you know you will remember, the moments that become scenes that become memories. To just stare openly at someone like this, to have them stare at you, to not need words to say, I like this. I like you.

I'm falling for you.
I've fallen for you.
Please, please don't go.

But those might just be in my head. I close my eyes, scared for a moment that he'll see those thoughts, that they won't match his.

"Breakfast," he suddenly says. "I think we need breakfast." He sits up and I see him look at the clock. He doesn't say anything about the time but we did sleep in a bit longer than we should have. He does have a plane to catch.

"What would you like?" he asks, getting up and walking over to the desk. My eyes are draw to that tight round ass of his, looking extra taut with his slight tan lines. I wonder where he got tanned. Being a prince in Europe, he probably spends winter in the Mediterranean, sunning on giant superyachts.

There's so much more that I don't know about him and there's no more time to find out.

I think I'm going to be sick. My appetite is completely gone.

And when *my* appetite is gone, then you know it's serious.

"I'll just have toast," I tell him.

He glances at me over his shoulder, picking up the phone. "You sure?"

I nod. "And coffee."

"Well naturally," he says then says into the phone. "Ah, yes, good morning. This is Vik…this is Mr. Andersson in room 219, I would like to order room service. A pot of coffee," he looks at me and mouths *cream?* I nod. "With cream. Some toast with jam and all those fixings and I'll have two soft boiled eggs and a side of bacon."

"Soft boiled eggs?" I ask him. "Interesting choice."

"Very common breakfast at home," he says as he hangs up the phone. "Served alongside some crisp bread, ham, and of course, pickled herring."

I scrunch up my nose. "No."

"Oh yes. Quite good," he says. "You'd grow to love it."

I swallow the lump in my throat. I won't have the chance to.

It's not long before there's a knock at the door. Viktor quickly slips on a robe and throws me one and once we're covered, opens the door for the room attendant.

"I hope you tipped him well," I say to him after the guy leaves, closing the door behind him.

"What am I, an animal?"

Viktor looks offended.

"No, it's just, well in Europe you don't tip, do you? And

also no one ever tips hotel staff enough. And also, yes. You are a moose."

He grins at that. "All of that is true, except that most of us in Europe know how tipping works over here. Do you want to sit on the balcony?" he asks, as he picks up the tray from the room service cart.

I look through the curtains at the bright sunshine, hear the faint splash of people in the pool right below.

I shake my head. "I'd rather eat in here."

Out there I know I'd be sharing him with the world. We have hours, minutes, left with each other and I can't bear to not have him all to myself in this beautiful dark world we've created in this hotel room.

"Me too," he says, wincing at the beam of white light coming in through the curtains. "I think I've had enough of the California sunshine."

But have you had enough of me?

He places the tray in front of me and gets on the bed, both of us sitting cross-legged on the messy sheets. He pours me a cup of coffee, then adds a splash of cream.

"That enough?" he asks.

This isn't enough.

But I nod. "Yes, thank you." I clear my throat as he hands me my cup and pours himself one, black. "You don't put cream in yours?" I ask.

His head shakes. "No. We drink it black in Sweden. Puts hair on our chest." He pounds a fist against his pecs in a mocking gesture. "Apparently it works."

Viktor does have hair on his chest but it's the perfect amount, just enough to make him look like some Nordic Viking god, not so much that looks like a caveman.

We both fall silent and sip our coffees and the room seems to hum with this energy of all the things we aren't saying to each other, of all the goodbyes that loom on the horizon.

"What is it?" he asks me after studying my face for a good minute.

I give a small shrug. "I was just thinking."

"I can tell," he says. He brings his brows together until a deep line forms between them and he runs his finger along it. "You get *this*."

"It's called resting bitch face here in America," I tell him.

"I've heard about this face," he muses. "Sounds too harsh for you."

"What would you call it then?"

He takes an easy sip of his coffee and seems to think about it. "Thinking sexy face."

"Sexy face?" I laugh. "How is that sexy?"

"Because it's sexy when you're all mean looking. Makes me think I did something wrong and you're going to punish me."

I roll my eyes. "Stop."

"It's true. But I think all your faces are sexy. Especially the ones when you're calling out my name. Your mouth drops open like a ripe peach. It reminds me of other places. You know what we call a peach in Swedish? *Persika*. I'm very much in love with your sweet persika."

I'm blushing. Oh yeah, I'm blushing, probably the shade of a *persika*. I think he even called me *min lilla persika* the other night.

But...

Did he just use the L word? It was just to describe a body part—or two—but even so.

I look at him with big eyes but he only smiles at me. If he said something he didn't mean to, he's not showing it.

I swallow. "Is that so?" I manage to say.

He leans forward, and with one swift move, pulls the sash

around my robe so it opens and my breasts are exposed, and since I'm sitting cross-legged, my *persika*.

His eyes rest between my legs and I can practically see his mouth watering which makes me wet in return. "If you take a picture it will last longer," I try to joke, feeling so bare and exposed. Vulnerable. Yet there's no fear in being this way with Viktor. It's natural.

"That must be a saying," he murmurs, his eyes trailing up my stomach now to my breasts and I swear my skin burns in their wake. He moves the tray to the side. "I would love to take many pictures."

I stiffen at the thought and he smiles gently at the worry on my face. "I'm also taking pictures in my mind. They will be there forever. You know how couples carve their name in the bark of a tree? The sight of you, the smell of you, the sound of you, the taste of you, it's all etched in my head. It won't be smoothed away with time."

My heart swells in my chest, pressing against my ribs.

I won't be smoothed away.

I won't be forgotten.

"You know I can't get enough and I won't get enough of you," he tells me, taking the cup of coffee from my hands and setting it down on the tray. "Not with the time we have left, not with all the time left in the world. But I will take my time now, enjoying every inch of your sweet skin while I can." He then picks up the small pitcher of cream. "Lie back."

I raise my brows, stare at the cream. *What?*

"Why?"

He gives me a look that says, *just do it*, and so I do. I'll do anything he tells me to.

Apparently even if it involves cream.

He breaks into a carnal grin and takes his time slowly tilting the pitcher, so the cream splashes out delicately onto my breasts.

I gasp.

"Is it cold?" he asks, amused.

"No." I just think most people would gasp in this situation. I stare at him curiously. "What are you doing?"

"Going to have breakfast with you."

"With me or on me?"

"Both."

He pours a bit more, biting his lip.

"Fuck. Your skin is just like the cream. You have no idea how hard I am right now."

"I might." My hands reach around below, grabbing at his robe and tugging at it, trying to expose him, to feel him, but he shifts just so that I can't touch him.

"I like to torture myself," he explains before running his hand between my breasts and slowly licking the cream off of his finger, his long tongue riding up the side, his eyes never leaving mine.

"I think you might be torturing me while you're at it," I tell him, my hands going into his thick hair and giving the strands a pull.

His eyes close with a groan and he starts massaging the cream over my breasts, my nipples hardening into tight little peaks, so sensitive that every time he brushes over them I want to scream.

This man, this man, he's undoing me.

There will be nothing left of me when he's done.

Nothing left of me when he's gone.

He lowers his head, his stubble scraping along my skin and bringing me back around to the here and the now.

All I have is here and now.

His mouth dips down to suck my nipples into his warm mouth, making my back arch. "Fuck," he moans, the vibrations running through me until I am so fucking wet. "You're so perfect."

His hands spread the cream down over my stomach and between my legs, dragging the wetness over my clit.

My grip tightens in his hair and I gasp again, my hips bucking up automatically, desperate for friction, for purchase. "Come inside me, please." The words nearly choke on my tongue.

"I've only started feasting," he says, sliding his finger inside, his thumb rubbing my clit. I clench around him, hard, until he pulls his finger out. "Do you see the way you taste to me," he says, licking his finger again.

Jesus.

"Better now," he says. "You make it sweeter. And yet it will be sweeter still."

He reaches over and grabs the small jar of honey that came with the toast, unscrewing the cap and dipping his finger in. He brings his finger to my lips, rubs the honey over them before sticking his finger into my mouth. I can taste myself, taste the sweet honey. Most of all I can see the lust in his eyes, the raw, sensual desire he has for me.

No one will ever look at me like this again.

I shut my eyes, trying to drown out that voice.

"What's wrong?' he asks.

"Nothing," I tell him, opening my eyes. He looks so concerned, he might break. "I'm just…"

Trying to hold on to the moments we have together.

Trying to ignore what's about to happen.

Trying, trying, trying.

"Make me come," I tell him, my voice coming out ragged. "I want you inside me, I want you to make me come."

Rip me from my mind. Make your body salvage my body. Damage me until I can't think, until there's nothing left to feel but you.

"I want to paint you with honey," he says, moving back to paint squiggly lines of honey down my breasts and stomach.

"I want to paint you with my tongue. I want to take my time."

We don't have time!

You have a plane to catch.

A country to return to.

But I manage not to say it because I don't want to ruin the last time we have together.

The last time.

"Take your time," I say quietly, lying further back into the sheets, closing my eyes.

I can feel him hesitate before he slowly, teasingly, licks the honey off of me.

Off my breasts, my collarbone, my stomach, my hips, my inner thighs.

My body tenses with each pass of his warm, hot tongue. It's so decadent and rich the way he devours me, like I really am a feast to him.

He settles between my legs, his fingers pressing into my thighs, pushing them further apart.

"Now that you're all clean," he says, "I'm going to get you dirty again."

My eyes fly open.

His robe is discarded behind him and his massive body is prowling between my legs like a big cat stalking its prey.

I will never get tired of this sight, of his bare, hard body hovering over mine.

The ease in which his hands work me, like I'm an instrument being tuned.

The way that he pushes inside me, always with this breathless gasp that turns into a moan that turns into sweet nothings that shake with his want.

The sounds of his skin slapping against mine, the feel of his sweat dripping on me as he works me so fucking hard, his face creased with the effort of it all.

The moment he brings me to that razor edge and I willfully fly over it.

The world spins before I tumble, shaking and twirling through spasms that put me upside down and up again. I'm wild, I'm crazed, I'm disoriented, I'm spent, I'm...

This is...

As the intensity of the orgasm wanes, the intensity of my emotions slam over me like a wave.

This is it.

I keep my eyes closed, fighting back the tears. I hate that I've cried with him already this trip when I opened up about my parents, I don't want to cry again, not during sex, not now.

But the hot, damp knot in my chest grows and grows until I have to gasp for breath.

I'm not sure Viktor notices. He's coming too, groaning and grunting and swearing in my ear, those feverish sounds that I love so much.

"Maggie," he whispers through a ragged breath, kissing me roughly on the lips. "Maggie, I..." he breaks off and exhales so hard the bed shakes. "This, just this," he says. He wraps his arms around me, holding me tight.

Time seems to slow with our heartbeats.

The sweat on my skin cools.

Someone outside, so far away, jumps into the pool with a splash.

I want to lie here forever.

"Maggie," Viktor whispers to me. "I am so sorry but I have to go. We have to get going."

I nod. Forever isn't enough. "Of course."

I practically drag myself out of bed. No point in makeup when I know I'm going to cry it all away. I put on the same clothes as yesterday, brush my teeth, slick on some deodorant, pull my hair back in a ponytail and I'm ready to go.

I take one last look at the hotel room and realize that it changed me. The person who stepped in here, nervous, anxious, on Thursday night is not the same person who is walking out of here on Sunday morning.

We get his car from the valet, the blue finish sparkling under the sun, and after a few wrong turns and wanting to strangle the Waze app, we get on the right freeway heading to LAX.

There is so much tension between us, so much worry and sadness, that I don't even have the words to talk. I'm afraid to, afraid to say the wrong thing, to say something that will make it harder for both of us.

The thing is, as much as Viktor whispered sweet nothings to me this morning, as much as he's told me how hard it will be for him to say goodbye, I don't think he can possibly feel the way I do. I'm even surprised I feel the way I do. I'm a rational person. I use logic. I've had enough of life slapping me upside the head to have a jaded and cynical outlook on it. I err toward the negative rather than the positive.

I don't believe in love at first sight, in soul mates, in happily ever afters.

But with Viktor…he makes my soul feel brand new. Not something tired and weathered and trampled upon. I feel as if just being with him has scraped off all the rust, letting a part of me, all of me, shine. Maybe for the first time he's helped me discover who I really am.

Maybe there is no logic in love.

Maybe you just have to let it in when you see it, when you feel it.

Maybe you just need to believe in it.

On paper, it looks like I barely know this man and therefore I couldn't possibly love this man. But I'll burn that damn piece of paper to ash.

I do love him. My heart knows it, I know it, and even if I

pretend otherwise, even if I tell myself it's impossible, it won't change a damn thing.

I look at Viktor, at his hand on the steering wheel, the glint of his watch, the way his sleeves are rolled up to his elbows, the tan of his skin. He's wearing his sunglasses, the wind coming in through the half open window and mussing up his hair. His eyes are on the road as far as I can tell and every so often he worries his bottom lip between his teeth.

Then he looks at me. "Taking a picture with your mind?"

I nod. Clear my throat. "Listen, uh, I can't remember. Am I taking like an Uber you arranged back to Tehachapi or is it a shuttle or…?"

He frowns at me. "Uber?"

"You know, a cab."

"I know what an Uber is. Why would it take you back home?"

"Because you said you arranged for my transportation back. Is it a Greyhound? I seriously don't mind."

A smile spreads across his face. "Maggie, Maggie." He shakes his head. "Miss America. *Min sota lilla persika.*"

"What?"

"You're taking the car back."

I stare at him. Blink.

"Huh?"

"The car," he says, smacking the dashboard. "She's yours."

"What?"

No way.

No fucking *way*!

"What did you think I was doing with the car?"

I shrug, trying to find the words but it's coming out all flustered. "I don't know. Selling it?"

"I don't need the money. And you could use an extra car. And if you don't like it, sell it. Keep the money. Just make sure Pike does the sale so that you know what it's worth."

"Viktor…I can't possibly accept this car."

He's nonchalant. "It's a gift and I want you to have it. In fact, I need you to have it."

"I…I don't know Viktor…."

His car. His sexy, beautiful, incredibly rare car. I couldn't possibly take it. And I would look like an idiot driving around town in it.

"Sell it," he implores me. "I know what you're thinking. Sell it and you'll make your family very happy. You'll have money in their savings, money for college, money to get that damn toilet of yours fixed. You deserve it. You all do."

"Viktor, it's too much."

"No," he says, his voice taking on a harder edge. "It's not too much. It's not even enough but it's the best that I can do without…" he sighs. "Please Maggie."

I rub my lips together while I try and wrestle with the knot in my stomach. I need my pride to take a hike again, I need to believe what he's saying. "Are you sure?"

"Always more," he says. "Never less."

Oh, Jesus.

"You're unreal," I whisper. "How did I get so lucky to find you? All the people in that hotel room I could have walked in on and I walked in on you."

"All the maids that could have walked in on me, I'm sure glad it was you and not Juanita."

I let out a sour laugh.

"I am joking of course," he says quickly. "Perhaps now isn't the time for it."

"There's always time to laugh," I tell him but he's kind of right. I feel all humor drain out of me the closer we get to the airport.

He parks the car in the short-term lot, gets his suitcase out of the trunk and places the keys in my palm, folding my fingers over it. "Yours."

I grip the keys with all my might. I'm starting to think I might have to build a shrine to him. Viktor the moose and this car and the Splash Mountain picture. And lavender. Lots and lots of lavender.

I follow him into the terminal, stand by him anxiously as he gets his ticket and drops off his bag and the whole time I feel the seconds slipping away from us.

Why is time so cruel?

Why can't we just hold it in our hands and keep it for ourselves and never let it let us go?

The walk over to the security line is brutal. I feel like I'm being led to a sentencing.

It shouldn't be so hard, I tell myself. *You're just overemotional.*

But I can't rationalize my way out of this one.

We stop in front of the the agent who is scanning boarding passes and I know I can't go past any further.

"Well," he says, turning to me, grabbing my hand.

I shake my head because no, no. This isn't it.

"This is it," he says. He squeezes my hand and gazes down at me with such tenderness that my knees are moments from buckling. I'm barely keeping upright.

"I hope you have a good flight," I manage to say, my voice starting to break.

"Maggie," he whispers, running his thumb over my lip, his eyes searching mine, so beautifully pure and blue and warm. This man is so warm, his heart, his soul, his everything. "Come with me."

God.

My heart almost explodes.

"Viktor..."

"You could come with me," he says, swallowing hard. A look of desperation comes over him. "You could come with me. To Sweden. We could be together. Just for a week. You could do it. We could do this."

No.

"Please don't ask me," I plead, the tears brimming in my eyes, making it hard to see. "Please don't ask me."

Because if he asks me, if he tries to convince me anymore, I'm so afraid I might say yes. This man means so much to me that I'd be willing to throw everything I have away, just for the chance to be by his side, even if just for a few more days.

"I don't want to leave you," he says, clearing his throat. "I can't say goodbye. I'm not ready."

"Viktor, please," I cry out softly.

I see him break right before my eyes.

Then he's grabbing me, pulling me into his chest, putting his arms around me so tight and then I'm breaking too, shattering and splintering and it's only his strength that's keeping me together.

"I will come back for you." He kisses the top of my head, pressing his lips hard. "Just you try and stop me."

He then lets go and steps back and I nearly fall to my knees.

I can't breathe.

I can't feel my heart beat.

I can't feel anything but the loss of him walking away.

"I will come back for you," he says again, his jaw tight. His eyes don't leave mine, even as he hands his ticket to the guard to be scanned.

Then he has to turn and walk away, swallowed by the line.

Then he's gone.

He's gone.

PART TWO

SIX MONTHS LATER

CHAPTER SEVENTEEN

VIKTOR

STOCKHOLM

"One more question, your highness," the journalist asks me and from the way her heavily-shadowed eyes twinkle, the sly twist to her bright pink lips, I know this one is going to be something I won't like. They always save those questions for the end, so if the interviewee doesn't answer it the way they want, they can always cut it out.

I'm used to it though. Since I've been back, I've been fully immersed into my role as heir to the throne, which means countless interviews as my country and the world starts to accept me. It's all just a formality, a public relations move to ensure that Alex's legacy is never forgotten and to assure the public that I'm someone they can trust. Maybe even like, although it's hard to say if I'm winning them over or not. According to my mother I am, according to my father I'm not, and Freddie, dear Freddie, is as diplomatic as ever.

None of this has been easy but I've risen to the challenge. I've adapted to the schedule and the new life. I've learned, for the most part, how to protect my privacy and deal with the paparazzi's newfound obsession with me. The Swedish journalists and photographers, they're a lot easier to handle and I'm starting to know a few of them by name. Swedes in general are fairly reserved and that extends to the tabloids.

The Brits on the other hand are a fucking nuisance. They practically run over babies and kick kittens in order to get their perfect shots and ask the most moronic questions like "Is it true your brother was in a Satanic cult and was sacrificed?" and "Is it true he was gay?" and "Is it true that you're having an affair with your butler?" and "About those sex tape rumors…"

I have no idea what the sex tape rumors entail but I have a feeling it involves a butler.

As much as leaving Maggie behind in California killed me, my parents and Dr. Bonakov were right to suggest that leaving Sweden for a while would get my head on straight. I came back from America different, changed. I can't say if it was having weeks of freedom on the open road, of being completely anonymous, or if it was all Maggie.

Who am I kidding, though? It *was* all Maggie.

It will always be Maggie.

"What is the question?" I ask the journalist, who also happens to be British. I'm on camera for a British TV show, which, thankfully, isn't live.

She shows off her blinding veneers. "The other week when you opened the School Leaders Forum in Malmö, a reporter had asked if you met anyone special and you replied, *yes, I did once*. Can you elaborate on that? Who is the special someone and what happened?"

I groan inwardly while keeping the smile on my face. I remember saying that. I don't know why I did. It just came out. I'd been asked that for six months straight and every time I dodged it except this one time. I'm lucky I walked away from that reporter without divulging any more information.

Of course now, here I am, caught in the cross-hairs.

"There isn't much to elaborate on," I say and I'm already regretting that because I should have just said something like "it meant nothing" or "my personal life is my private life."

She nods eagerly. "So what can you elaborate on? Who is she? Or him?"

I have to fight to not roll my eyes. "*She*'s…someone I met once. That's all. There's really nothing else to discuss."

"Christmas is coming next month. You won't be spending it with anyone?"

I give her a steady look. "No," I tell her as politely as possible.

The journalist isn't having it. "But you have to understand, Your Highness, that you're one of the most eligible bachelors in the world. On top of that, you're very handsome. You do know how good-looking you are, right?"

I cock my brow and give her an awkward smile. "Honestly, I spend so little time thinking about it."

"About your looks or being single?"

"Both," I tell her. I glance at the producer off to the side and then to Freddie who has been watching this whole thing. "I think I am done here, right?"

"Of course," the producer says while Freddie nods.

"Jesus," I say to Freddie after I leave the building and get in the back of the car, flashbulbs following me right to the window. "Did you know she was going to ask that?"

Freddie shakes his head. "No, sir, I did not."

The driver pulls away, leaving the shouting reporters behind. I glance at them through the narrow window at the back of the car, shaking my head.

"Though I did mean to ask you, sir," Freddie says. He's

been calling me sir more and more now. "What special someone were you talking about?"

I glance at him. He stares right back at me through his glasses, not the slightest bit chagrined for asking such a personal question.

"I met someone when I was in America," I tell him. I have to admit, it feels good to get that off my chest. I haven't told anyone about Maggie, not counting Prince Magnus.

"I figured that," he says matter-of-factly and goes back to scrolling through his iPad.

"Wait, what do you mean?" I ask, twisting in my seat to face him. How could he have known? "Did you read my letters?"

"Letters, sir?" he repeats.

When I first got back to Stockholm, I was so busy being thrust into this new life that I barely had any time to talk to Maggie. When I did end up having time to talk on the phone, the time zones came into play. Sure we had texted each other a lot but I had a sneaking suspicion that my emails weren't as private as they might seem. The thought of opening a private one, not tied to the palace, had me wary of hackers. You hear those stories all the time too.

So I started to write her letters. I told her not to write me back because there's no way someone wouldn't find it but instead she would text me her thoughts and feelings. Our conversations were always delayed but at least I was able to get out to her what I was feeling.

And I was feeling a lot. More than I imagined I could. It wasn't just her that I was missing, (needing, *craving*) either. I talked a lot about my job and Alex and my parents and everything I needed to express because she is the only one I feel who really understands me.

Lately though, I haven't had the time to send her anything and in response, she hasn't texted either. I know long-distance relationships are hard. Hell, I don't even know if what we had or have can be considered a relationship–but I think it's something worth fighting for.

I just haven't figured out how to fight for it.

"What letters?" Freddie repeats.

"There was a girl. I wrote her letters."

"What was her name?" he sounds genuinely curious.

"Maggie," I tell him. "Maggie Mayhem McPherson."

"Pardon me for asking, but was she by any chance a stripper?"

I glare at him.

He gives me a small smile. "The name, you see."

"She was definitely not a stripper," I tell him. "She was very real. Got handed a terrible hand in life, so yes, I could also see with a name like that and her background, stripping seems like a viable option. But no. She's one of the hardest working, strongest people I know."

"She hasn't come to visit," Freddie points out. "Or has she?"

I shake my head. "No. It's just not possible." I really don't want to get into Maggie's history with him, but I think it's the only way he'll understand that she's not like everyone else. "She's twenty-three, from a town you've never heard of. Her parents died, were murdered actually, a year or two ago and she's been the legal guardian of her five siblings ever since. Works as a maid to make ends meet."

For once, Freddie looks impressed. "Wow."

"Yeah, that's what I thought. I mean, that's how she won me over at first. I was just…fucking impressed."

"You sure it wasn't her looks?"

"I never said she was hot."

"Sir, I am betting she's hot."

I can't help the stupid smile spreading across my face. I look away. "She's beautiful."

"Of course."

"But the more I talked to her, the more I got to know her…in many different ways…the more I realized how alike we were."

"Well, I must say it's a shame I can't meet her."

"Yes, it is," I say with a sigh, staring out the window. If Maggie were here, would she even like Stockholm? It's dark now as sin, and the forecast tonight calls for snow. Even though it's the end of November and technically autumn, it's been cold as fuck and it's only going to get worse. Sweden is a far cry from California.

By the time the car takes me back to Haga Palace, I'm tired and climb the three floors up to my bedroom to retire early. It's a far cry from the palatial apartment I had before. The apartment, though it consisted of the entire top floor of one of Stockholm's grandest buildings, was very private and rather homey. I had Freddie down the hall in his own apartment, as well as guards and my butler, Bodi, in theirs.

But while I was away in America, my parents decided to have me moved, unbeknownst to me. It's a fucking shock when you get off a plane, dealing with no sleep, jetlag, and a broken heart, to discover that you no longer live where you thought you lived and all of your belongings have been moved elsewhere.

I know Haga Palace is the place where Swedish nobility live and raise their families, but because neither Alex nor I have families, we were able to live in apartments downtown. I don't know if moving me here is a hint for me to hurry up and start a family (that seemed to be on the journalist and Freddie's mind too), or, after Alex, they just want to keep an eye on me, but this is the place to do it.

It's just too big for me, too formal. Rooms after rooms after rooms. There are chefs and maids and butlers and Freddie and Bodi, and guards and more. The estate stretches on and on and I swear the furnishings came with the place when it was built in 1802. It's vastly impersonal and though it's still in Stockholm proper, it's in a park outside all the action.

Which is another thing I'm still having a hard time coming to terms with that comes with the new territory. Before this, I was able to do what I pleased, and no one cared much. Not that I was out a lot, but I liked the freedom. Now, I can't. I can't even leave this place without being driven out and the number of guards and secret police around twenty-four seven has doubled.

Of course, it's selfish of me to lament such a change, the loss of my freedom, when it's all because of the loss of my brother. It's his loss that always weighs on me more. It's his loss that always will.

It's only been eight months or so since he died.

Most days I'm too busy to grieve and then I think that maybe I've moved past it and I'm going to be okay. I think to myself "I didn't think about Alex today" or "I thought about him and I didn't feel that razor kick to the gut" and then I both feel like I'm finally pulling myself out of this spiral while at the same time feeling guilty for not thinking about him.

But there is no one way out of this.

One day you might feel fine.

Other days you're reaching for some brandy, reaching for a pill to make you sleep.

Reaching for Maggie.

How could it be that I was only with her for a week when I swear I was with her for a lifetime?

How come having her in my bed for three nights felt like she'd be in my bed forever?

Why is it that I felt more alive with her than I did in all my days before we met?

There's a weariness that strikes me this time of night, when my thoughts turn to her and all we could have had. If only I had tried harder to convince her to come to Sweden, if only it was a plan from the start and not something I impulsively blurted at the airport.

But I know that's not how any of this works.

That's not how love works.

It's not something you plan.

Love is mercurial and goes where it wants, when it wants.

It's not something you choose.

Love is something that happens.

Like an accident or a stroke of fate.

It happens to you whether you want it to or not.

It happened to me and I've spent a long time grappling with what I was truly feeling for her. I didn't believe it was possible to feel what I did. I didn't believe in a lot of things before I met her.

In the end, I didn't want to debate myself anymore.

I gave in.

I accepted it.

And here I am. Lonely as hell, holed up in a room at the top of a palace, trying to wrestle with so many demons I don't know which one to tackle first but I know now, after so much time, in the deepest seat of my heart, that I love her.

I still love her.

And there's just no fucking cure for that.

So I have a glass of brandy, pour myself another, and I sit down at my desk. I pick up my pen and I write.

DEAREST MAGGIE, *Miss America, Margaret Mayhem,*

I WAS GOING to start this letter by calling you min lilla persika but

I decided that it might be inappropriate since I can't see your beautiful face in front of me right now, and I'm not sure if those peach-like lips would smile or not.

I've been missing you lately. I miss you all the time but as it gets so cold and dark here and winter approaches, I'm dreaming of sunny California and your wonderful laugh. I know I'm not a comedian but when I was with you, it was a game to me to try and make you laugh as often as I could. Maybe game is the wrong word—it was a challenge. When you smiled, when you laughed, it was like the sun was shining straight out of my heart. It's like I found the angels inside of you, devils too, an interesting mix when you think about it, but all the best people are interesting mixes. It's like going to a party and seeing people with wings and people with horns and you think to yourself, damn this is going to be a good one.

I'm probably not making much sense so please pardon me. I'm drinking brandy and I've had a hell of a day. What was it that you say in California? Hella?

I've never felt so alone as I do now.

I just had to write that down.

I want to talk about Alex with people, but I can't.

I want to talk about you with people, and I can't.

You were the only one to really understand me.

I don't really think you have any idea of what you did to me, do you?

I'm not sure you ever will.

Words aren't enough.

I have to show you.

If only you could come here. You will grow to love pickled herring, I promise you.

Everyone is so boring.

So proper.

Being a prince is the loneliest job.

Or maybe that's not true.

Maybe it's just lonely being Viktor.

Sometimes I imagine you beside me when I go to the balls and galas and dinner parties and other places I'm carted off to each day and night. I pretend you're there, like a ghost that only I can see. I can almost hear your voice as you comment on what people are wearing and try the appetizers being passed around. I know you look beautiful in your gown, and if people could see you, they'd wonder how I got to be so lucky.

I am so so lucky to have known you.
Been with you.
And I refuse to think that our luck has run out.
I always said I'd come back for you.
I hope you're not wondering why I haven't.
I'm not sure why I haven't.
I'm going to have some more brandy now.

ALLTID MER, aldrig mindre,
    (always more, never less)

Viktor
    (The Moose)
    (Mr. Johan Andersson)
    (Mr. Sverige)
    (Mr. Swedish Driver's License)
    (Mr. Sex God)
    I swear you called me that once.

I FOLD UP THE PAPER, slide it into an envelope that I keep in a stack in my desk drawer, then I drink.

A WEEK later and Magnus has come to visit.

I haven't had time to prepare.

You see when Crown Prince Magnus of Norway shows up in Stockholm, I usually need a few days to put together an itinerary. This is not a man who is happy sitting in my study with me and talking by the fire with a few snifters or cognac or perhaps aquavit. Believe me, I like to go out but for Magnus it's a requirement. Royal policy, as he often calls it.

As usual, he's staying with me. The driver drops him off right at my front door.

When I jog down the stairs to greet him, he's got a bottle of aquavit in one hand and has his arm around my butler, Bodi.

"Viktor!" Magnus exclaims. "You're here!"

I pause at the bottom of the stairs and raise my brow, trying to figure out if he's drunk or not. The flight from Oslo is short and he would have bought that at Duty Free. Booze in Sweden is a lot cheaper than the booze in Norway, not that it matters for Norwegian royalty.

"How much of that have you had?" I ask him.

He shrugs. "Not enough. Man, you have stuffy butlers here in Sweden. I think your old boy here needs to get laid."

The funny thing is that Bodi is not old by any means and he's certainly *not* stuffy. He's forty-five with a shock of red hair and is extremely good at putting people in their place. And by that, I mean he uses his fists a lot. Not on me, but they do say red hair is indicative of temper.

I swear Bodi's face goes rage red to match his hair, so I just shake my head and say, "I've got it from here, thank you."

He nods, glares at Magnus, and then walks away.

"What's he mad about, that we keep kicking your ass at downhill?"

He means skiing and more specifically the Olympics and trials.

"He used to be in the military," I explain. "Which means he's used to putting drunk asses like yourself in their place."

"I'm not drunk," he says again with a heavy sigh. "And you were in the military too, don't forget."

"And I also know how to put drunk asses in their place."

He grins at me. "I heard what happened."

"What?" I frown. This is never a good start to a sentence.

"Oh, you know. Little birds talk, don't they? You never told me that the reason you were sent to America was because you punched your guard in the face."

Right. Poor Gustav.

I give him a tepid smile. "We all have our moments."

"And we shall have some more." He pats his monogrammed suitcase. "Let me get settled first."

"Louis Vuitton?" I muse as I look at the suitcase, trying not to laugh. "Since when do you wear designer anything? You're usually found in, well…"

"Usually nothing, right?" He starts lugging it up the stairs to the second floor. "A girl I was seeing has stock in the company. Or her family does. Long story short, she was pretty hot, but the free suitcase was the better end of the deal." He pauses. "Same room as last time? I thought you would have put in an elevator by now, my god you're a terrible prince, aren't you? No wild demands or anything."

I follow him up the stairs and would offer to help him with the suitcase, but Magnus is a big guy and can more than take care of himself. Not as tall as me but about six-foot-two and absolutely *shredded* as they say in America. He has to be for all the crazy sports shit that he does.

He busts into the guest bedroom and tosses the suitcase on the bed with one hand, still holding onto the bottle with the other. He then pushes his shaggy dark hair off his face and holds out the bottle for me.

"Skäl, Viktor," he says, his wild eyes imploring me to do a shot straight out of the bottle.

So I do.

I haven't had aquavit in a while and for a moment it reminds me of my date with Maggie.

Fucking Maggie.

I can barely get through the days without her haunting me.

"What?" Magnus frowns, taking the bottle back like he's been personally insulted by whatever look I have on my face.

"Nothing."

He shakes his head, has another glug from the bottle. "You are the worst liar, Viktor."

"What?"

"This is the second time I've seen you since you got back from America and you still have that mopey stupid look on your face."

I instinctively run my hand over my features and then try to give him a blank look. "Better?"

"No." He sighs and looks around the bedroom at the ornate poster bed, gold threaded bedding and the cherry wood details. "Christ, it looks like set decoration from a bad play, doesn't it? Where's the Scandinavian charm?"

"There is no charm in this place," I tell him. "And don't forget, all of Swedish royalty originally came from France."

"Those fuckers. So what do you have planned? If it doesn't involve pussy, then I'm going to be very disappointed."

"So crude. Didn't your mother ever teach you manners?"

"Yes. She did. These are her manners. Crude as fuck. All hail Queen Crude." He heads over to his suitcase, opens it and pulls out a dress shirt. "Okay, so let's go."

"Where?"

"Where? I can tell you didn't plan anything, so I say we just go to a club and find some women."

"You know we can't just do that."

"You don't know the right clubs."

Apparently I don't. Even though it's just past dinner, I get dressed into a black dress shirt and jeans, something more club-friendly I suppose, and we arrange for a limo to take us to some fancy place downtown.

"Are you sure about this?" I ask him.

"Yes," he says with a sigh. "There's a back entrance and I've used it many times before."

"I bet you have."

He just grins at me.

"Besides, you know we're never alone," he adds. "We have guards tailing the both of us constantly. They won't let people within a foot of our blindingly masculine radius. I'm sure in the end they'll end up closing down our section and we can just pull a few hot girls from the floor and a few bottles of champagne and that's the end of it."

He's right too. He knows Stockholm's nightlife better than I do. If anyone lives by the philosophy of *there's no cow on the ice*, it's Magnus.

Except once we do get in the dark club with the thumping bass and the smell of drugs, and once our guards have gone around and confiscated every phone from those who wish to stay in the area, the conversation turns serious.

Well, as serious as it can get considering Magnus just brought over a tall blonde for himself and a curvy brunette for me.

While the girls chat to each other, sipping champagne, giggling and stealing adoring glances at us, Magnus turns to me and says, "So you have to get over her. Tonight you shall start. I get Betty, you get Veronica."

"Her?" I repeat, having some champagne and buying time because somehow, I know he's talking about Maggie.

"Yes, her. The girl. From California. The one you called me about and never mentioned again."

"Why do you think I'm not over her? Or that I got under her? All I told you was that I felt bad for lying."

"No," he laughs. "No, no, no. I told *you* that you should feel bad for lying to her. Whatever happened to the article anyway?"

"She didn't write it."

"I see."

"She interviewed me…and we…it got serious for a few days. But she never ended up doing it."

"Lucky for you."

"I wouldn't have minded," I admit. "It would have brought her money. It would have taken care of her for a bit. But she ended up with my car, so…"

"So, you wanted to take care of her. Do you still?"

I glance at him and for once he's earnest. "I do. But I know she can take of herself."

"Of course they can take care of themselves," he says and then he tips his head toward the girls who are giggling very loudly about something. "Maybe *they* can't. But most women can. It's all about wanting to provide, my friend, and when you get that urge to provide then I think that means something."

"That I've entered caveman mode?" I sigh and tap my fingers against the champagne glass, wishing I wasn't here, where this music—and Magnus—are doing my head in. "Whatever it means, she's there and I'm here."

"Then invite her over. Get her ass in your royal palace. Or is it get your royal palace in her ass?"

I roll my eyes. "I tried."

"Try harder."

I give him a steady look because he has *no* idea. "It's not that easy. She can't just up and leave her life all because I want her here."

"It's as easy as you make it. Right? So go make it easy."

"I don't even know if she wants to talk to me anymore. I haven't really gotten any responses from the last letters I sent."

He blinks at me for a moment, his dark, arched brows slowly coming together.

"You've been writing her letters?"

"Yes."

"Like you live in the fucking 1500s?"

I pause. "Yes."

"And you're wondering why she hasn't been getting back to you?"

I'm not sure what he's getting at. "Yes."

"You are a bigger idiot than I thought, Viktor," he says. "Fucking moose is right. Big dumb moose."

"What?"

He throws his arm out, spilling champagne. "Haven't you seen The Notebook? Or any movie where someone is writing someone love letters and those love letters never seem to reach the person they are intended? This is bullshit." He leans forward and taps his girl on the shoulder. "You've seen The Notebook, yes?"

"Oh I love that movie," she says excitedly in an incredibly nasal voice.

"It was shit," Magnus swears, pounding back the rest of his drink and wiping his mouth with his sleeve. He points at me with his empty glass. "And this boy over here is trying to re-enact a scene."

"Awwww," the girl says, looking at me like I'm a puppy. "That's so adorable."

"It's not fucking adorable," Magnus grumbles "It's shit."

And then he puts his arm around her and starts making out.

I cautiously make eye contact with the other girl, the one Magnus tried to get for me, knowing she's going to expect the same.

"I've seen The Notebook too," she says proudly.

I just nod, finish my drink and put down my glass, slapping a hand on her shoulder. "I've got to get going. Give my regards to Prince Suckface. I'll leave a key in the door for him."

Then, trailed by my guards, I go out the way we came in and get in the waiting limo. I'll make sure it comes back for Magnus later.

Until then, I have a flight to book.

CHAPTER EIGHTEEN

MAGGIE

TEHACHAPI

THERE IS A VACANCY THAT GROWS IN YOUR HEART AFTER someone you love leaves you. When they leave, they take everything with them. All the furnishings, all the artwork, even the flooring, until you are stripped bare. Cold. I am one big empty room that echoes with the loss of him.

At first people indulged me and my heartbreak. After I returned to Tehachapi and after everyone was done losing their mind over Viktor's gift, the Mustang, they put up with my crying and blubbering. Annette and Sam especially consoled me and my grief, letting me talk about him for hours, letting me wonder over and over again if it had been a mistake to go to LA, if it had been a mistake to not follow him to Sweden. Of course I knew I couldn't go but it doesn't stop me from wishing things had been different.

People like Pike would tell me that I was crazy for thinking I was in love with him. They still didn't know he was a prince, everyone just thought he was some handsome, foreign rich dude (except for Callum, who still thinks he is

The Swedish Chef). They thought I was infatuated with him because of his money, because of his promises he must have made me. They thought it was just a crush gone wild and that in time I would realize that it wasn't love at all.

How could you love someone after a week?

It didn't seem possible.

And yet I knew if I even tried to pretend that I didn't feel this way, if I tried to ignore the pain in my heart, the depth of my feelings for him, that I would be hurting him in some way.

So I decided to hurt instead.

And eventually, I wasn't allowed to talk about him anymore. If I opened my mouth about him, they'd switch the subject. Even Sam, Sam who I'd been there for through so much drama and breakups, even she once told me, "You need to get over him right now. That was never love, it was lust and both suck to lose, but if you don't forget about him, you never will."

Everyone thought I would get over it and it would go away.

Everyone thought I *should* get over, at the very least.

But the more that time went on and the months ticked by, the more I thought about him, ached for him, needed him. The more I realized that this empty room I carried around inside me wasn't getting filled. I hadn't even attempted to decorate, there wasn't any point. Nothing would do except for my prince, except for Viktor.

But it wasn't all a loss.

We've stayed in touch for the most part.

I first heard from him a day after he left, when he arrived in Stockholm.

After that weekend, my body and soul felt like it had been dragged through the mud. I looked like hell too. Whatever sex-filled rosy glow I had turned to the pallor of heartbreak.

That first day back at work I'd slept in a little and rushed to get the kids to school. I took the minivan since driving the Mustang felt strange (though it was hella fun to drive), then did what I could to get through the day. It wasn't my best and I knew it, Juanita pointing out some pillow cases I forgot to change, but I got it done.

It wasn't until I got home later and was walking past the Mustang into the house that I heard ringing from the glove compartment.

Puzzled, I opened it and found an iPhone in there.

A brand new iPhone.

Ringing somehow with a Post-It note attached to it.

The note said *Answer Me* and my first thought was of Alice in Wonderland when she's picking up the food and drink. What if I answer it and I'm sucked into the phone, straight to Sweden?

So I answered it.

"Hey," he'd said and hearing his voice, even though I'd heard it twenty-four hours before, nearly brought me to my knees again. His accent, the warmth and polish of it all. I never realized how used to that voice I had got.

"Hey," I said back, suddenly overwhelmed with everything all over again. "You're here. And you're on a phone that was in your car's glove box. Did you mean to leave it in there?"

I heard him sigh patiently. "I told you that you needed a new phone."

"Viktor, I can't accept a fucking Mustang and a new iPhone."

"And a moose, please don't forget that moose."

"I can accept the moose. No one will take him after what you did to him." I paused, rubbing my palm against my forehead. "I just…why are you doing so many nice things for me?"

"Why?" he asked, sounding both shocked and insulted. "Why would you think? You're everything to me, Maggie. I feel like I can't do enough. And, well, selfishly, this way I can talk to you every day. I got you a good calling plan."

"Isn't it late right now?"

"I couldn't sleep. I couldn't wait. Is it okay that I called?"

I'd never talked to him on the phone before this, so it was funny how slightly awkward it was, showcasing just how new we were to each other.

But as time went on, keeping in touch became more and more difficult. Those first few days he was back in Stockholm, he was still adjusting to his new life and getting it all together. Not always easy to do when you get back from a long vacation. And because of it, I think he was given a lot more slack by his family and whoever else keeps him in line. We talked often.

Then the phone calls tapered off and the time difference, and his rigid schedule became more of a big deal, so we started texting. I would text him and it would be eight hours until I got a response and vice versa.

Then there were love letters.

Oh yes, the art of the love letter isn't dead.

And even though Viktor's never mentioned the word love, I felt it in his words so elegantly scribbled on paper I could have sworn smelled like lavender.

This was my favorite way to communicate. Even though he told me he hand-delivered them to the post box and they never had a return address, so I couldn't answer him back, I still felt like his words were reaching into my soul. I was seeing a Viktor that I wouldn't have heard over a phone line, that wasn't so pithy and quick as he was over text.

In these letters he took his time. He took his time writing them, took his time describing how he felt, took his time with all the details, much in the same way he took his time when we had sex. He was so thorough and in return I felt so wanted. So…adored.

But slowly, as summer turned to fall and then now, as fall turns to winter, the frequency of the letters dropped off and I've been too scared to text him and ask why. There's a distance between us now that seems greater than the distance between here and Sweden.

It makes that cold empty room that much lonelier.

"So I've been doing a lot of reading up on your Swedish Prince," Annette says to me over her beer.

I look at her in surprise. After LA, I confided in her that Viktor wasn't just a pretty face but the Crown Prince of Sweden. Though I still haven't told my family and probably never will, I couldn't keep it from Annette. I thought I owed it to her since she took care of everyone while I was gone.

She took it all in her very dry, cynical stride. Which I appreciated. Sometimes a dose of cynicism is needed when your heart is feeling things it shouldn't.

But since it's been months since he's left and I've tried my hardest not to talk about him with anyone anymore, I'm not sure why she's suddenly bringing him up.

Maybe it's because we're at the Faultline again. Annette actually moved to Bakersfield a few months ago. Got a good job, a small apartment. Started dating a guy, a dad of three kids, she calls The Dude because he's like the king of bowling or something. She's in town today because she met with her lawyers to finalize her divorce and we're celebrating.

Naturally, there's only one place to do that here.

"Reading?" I question. "Like, history of the royal family?"

"No," she says. "Like tabloids. Internet gossip sites. Swedish ones. I just use the translate app. I believe everyone thinks he's having an affair with his butler. Assuming butler is butler in Swedish and doesn't mean, like, farm animals."

I frown. "Farm animals?"

She shrugs. "He's everywhere, honey. The press can't get enough of him. Makes me understand better why you couldn't either."

I really wish she hadn't brought him up, my plan for the night was to not think of him for once. It has been a week since we last texted and it was along the lines of "How are you doing?" and "Fine, how are you doing?" and it pains me to feel so much distance, to be reduced to just text on a screen.

Then again, I suppose thinking about him was inevitable since we came here. It almost feels like that night I found him in the bar all over again. The only difference is now, thanks to Viktor's Mustang, I'm the one buying Annette drinks and not the other way around.

"I don't look at those things anymore," I tell her and it's true. For the first month I was keeping up with all things Viktor by looking at the Swedish sites and British tabloids and Sam had gotten me hooked on Royalty Monthly (where I also became intrigued with a few of the monarchs that I knew Viktor had mentioned, such as Prince Magnus of Norway and King Aksel of Denmark).

But after a while there were too many rumors about Viktor that I didn't want to believe, and the press was so intrusive. I also think it added to the distance between us, seeing him in his official royal garb with his hat and his sash and medals at ceremonies, or in his sharp suits at balls and galas. He looked so…untouchable. Unreal. Like I was watching a character in a film instead of the living breathing warm and generous Viktor that I knew.

"Cheer up," she says, raising her beer to me. "Tonight is all about new beginnings. For the both of us."

I pick up my martini and carefully tap it against hers. "Skäl," I tell her.

"So how is it going with April?" she asks.

I sigh and give her a steady look. "It's…going."

"And Tito?"

"Tito, thankfully, is in prison now. Not even here. He went to Las Vegas and got arrested for drug dealing and assaulting an officer or something like that so that shithead is out of our lives forever. I hope."

"And April?"

"April on the other hand…" I shrug. "She pretty much hates me even more now. Blames me for taking him away. She can hate me all she wants at this point, I'm just glad she didn't end up pregnant."

"Until she finds another low-life…"

"You're not helping, Annette."

"I'd always told your mother that that girl was going to be trouble. Even at a young age, she wanted to rebel against everything. But you were both pretty close, weren't you?"

"There's a nine-year age difference between us so we were never as close as I would have liked," I admit. "Maybe when she gets older she'll stop hating me and figure out she can relate to me more than anything."

"You aren't an old fogey like me," Annette says, placing her hands on the side of her face and stretching back the skin. "Do you think I should get a face lift?"

I laugh. "Not if it makes you look like Lady Cassandra."

"Lady Cassandra? Is she a royal too?"

"Never mind," I tell her, knowing she hasn't seen *Dr. Who*. "And stop touching your face like that."

"Hi," the perky waitress says to me, suddenly appearing at our table with a shot of something in her hand. "The gentleman over there wanted to buy you a drink."

"Gentleman?" Annette repeats, looking impressed. "I didn't think there were any gentlemen in this town."

"Who?" I ask the waitress, craning my neck around the booth and looking around.

She points down at the booths by the door. "Just right there. I poured it myself, so you can trust it. You don't have to accept it either. That happens here all the time."

I only see one person at the booths and all I see of them is a long pant leg sticking out the side.

Something about that particular long leg makes my heart pick up the pace.

I look up at the girl. "What does he look like?"

She grins at me. "Handsome like I've never seen the likes of. Has a bit of an accent, too. I'm very jealous," she adds, tapping on the table for emphasis before she walks back to the bar.

A few things happen all at once.

One is that I watch as the bartender and the waitress talk behind the bar and the bartender is narrowing her eyes at the guy in the booth and then she looks over at me in surprise. Same waitress as the last time we were here, the one we did the favor for and had to deal with unconscious Viktor.

Two is that I pick up the shot and smell it and wince at the familiar pungent aroma.

Caraway seeds.

Aquavit.

And three, three is that every single cell in my body is tapdancing on fire. Every nerve is a livewire, crackling and humming and ready to ignite me.

This can't be a coincidence.

"What is it?" Annette asks me, brow furrowed as she reaches for the drink and has a sip. "Good lord, what the hell is this?"

I can only swallow, staring at her with wide eyes. "It's him," I whisper.

"Who?"

"It has to be him."

And now I'm getting up, my body light and I'm moving as if I'm in a dream.

"Maggie?" she says but I barely hear her.

I'm moving down the row of booths, past the entrance, pausing just before I'm about to walk by his.

I'm staring at his pants, how perfectly tailored they look, the shine of his shoes. This man is dressed well, no longer in the jeans and boots I'd come to know.

Maybe it's not even the man you know?

The last thought scares me for so many reasons.

But I keep walking, just a few steps more.

Stop at the booth.

Stare at Viktor.

Viktor.

How could it be him? How could this be?

I have to be dreaming.

"Hello Maggie," Viktor says in that beautiful rich voice, that accent, that everything that seeps right into my heart. "I told you I'd come back for you."

I can only shake my head, staring at him in disbelief.

"How is this…how is this possible? Is that you? Are you really here?"

He smiles and I'm automatically melting at the sight of those white teeth against tanned skin, the crinkles at the corners of his warm eyes, sparkling blue, the scruff of a beard which somehow makes him look both older and more handsome. I didn't think it was possible.

He gets out of the booth and stands in front of me and I have to crane my neck back to look at him and I'm so overwhelmed, I don't know what to do.

It's him.

He's here.

I start to sway on my feet. He's giving me vertigo.

Viktor quickly reaches out and grabs my arm to keep me steady and then seems to hesitate a moment before he reaches out with his other hand, slides it behind my waist and pulls me right to him.

"I've got you," he says, cupping my face in my hands. "I'm here."

"How? How?" I whisper, fighting to keep staring at him because I'm afraid if I close my eyes he'll be gone when I open them. At the same time, the feel of his hands on my skin, the warmth of his body pressed against mine, and my eyes want to close, to let him sink in.

I finally feel at peace.

I stare at him. "How did you know I was here? What are you doing here? Why didn't you call?"

He gives me a wary smile, his hands dropping away from my face. "I didn't know if you'd even want to speak to me. When you didn't answer my letters, when you didn't mention them…I thought it was best if I saw you in person and I didn't want you to have a chance to say no."

"Letters? I got your letters."

"This last month?"

"Well, no. The last one I got was in September?"

"There's been more."

"I never got them."

"Fuck," he swears, running his hand through his thick hair. "Magnus was right. That bastard."

"What?" My mind is tripping back, trying to figure out where his letters could have gone. I was the one going to the mail box on the street every day and checking for them.

He shakes his head. "It doesn't matter. The point is, I'm here now."

"How did you find me at the bar?"

He looks sheepish. "I went to your house first. It was dark. Threw pebbles up at your room but…I got April yelling at me instead."

"Oh jeez."

"She told me you were here."

"Well at least she didn't give you directions off a cliff or something." I close my eyes, rubbing my forehead. It still doesn't feel real. When I open my eyes though, he's still there, still staring at me, maybe with the same amount of anxiety as he did before we walked into that lavender-covered hotel room. "You're here," I say again. "I'm not sure when I'll believe it."

He bites his lip for a moment, his eyes searching mine and then he leans in, kissing me. His mouth is soft and familiar and safe and I find myself melting into him, into this sweet, rich kiss I feel all the way in my toes.

"Do you believe it now," he murmurs against my mouth. "Or do you need more proof?"

His hand disappears into my hair.

He's here.

He's here!

I'm *his*.

"So we meet again," Annette says from behind us, her voice giving me a jolt and causing us to break apart.

I can't be annoyed though. Not with her, not with anything anymore. "Annette!" I practically yell. "This is Viktor."

"Viktor," she says in a posh voice and she gives him her hand. Like, actually gives him her hand.

And being the god damn prince that he is, he takes her hand and kisses the top of it. "The pleasure is all mine, Annette."

Even she seems to swoon, just a little. "I suppose I should call you Your Royal Highness, shouldn't I? Maybe curtsey, too?"

"You could," he says, giving her hand back. "Except we've already met once, under rather messy circumstances, being unconscious and all. I think we're past all the formalities now."

"Now that you're back with Miss Maggie here, you could say that."

"He's not back for good," I find myself saying to Annette. "He's got a country to be all…princely over."

"That I do," he says, standing up straighter as if he's suddenly remembering his role in life. "And I'm afraid I'm not here for long."

I know I expected him to say that but there was a teensy-weensy part of me that hoped he'd counter what I said with "Actually I am here for good. I abdicated, screw the throne, I want to live in Tehachapi."

Needless to say, there's a cold pinch in my chest.

"I've been reading about you," she says, "and I admit I'm surprised to see you here with no guards or anything. I thought you had to have secret police with you at all times."

"I do," he says.

"Where?" I immediately start looking around the bar.

He nods at one gentleman at the bar, then another playing pool and one smoking a cigarette just outside the main doors. "They're with me."

I watch to see the guy at the bar glance over his shoulder at us.

I expect Viktor to wave at him and say "hey, we see you" or something but Viktor's face remains impassive and he pretends not to notice him. No jokes. He's already changed, already been trained.

What have I missed these past months?

So much.

"Wow," Annette says. "So I guess I shouldn't go hit on them and find my own Swedish hunk."

"No," Viktor says, giving her a small smile. "They've all been trained by the Swedish Security Service to be as boring and efficient as possible."

"Efficient gets the job done though, doesn't it?"

I reach out and smack Annette. "Hey, what about your Dude?"

"When you're older, you'll realize you should never pass up opportunities," she says with a sigh. Then she looks between the two of us. "Well I think I'm going to head back to Bakersfield now that you two have found each other. Party is over. Are you going to be okay here or do you need a ride back to your house? Unless you're staying at the La Quinta again, Viktor?"

"We have a ride," Viktor answers for me. "There's another efficient man in the Town Car waiting outside. Try not to terrorize him on your way out."

Annette breaks out into laugher and slaps him on the shoulder. "I can see why Maggie is so head over heels in love with you. You have my blessings." She waves at me before she leaves. "See you, kiddo."

She obviously doesn't see the look of absolute horror on my face.

The fact that I want the floor to open up and swallow me whole.

She just let the cat out of the fucking bag and that cat is running around us like crazy.

Viktor is staring at me intently and I know, I know he heard what she said.

Maggie is so head over heels in love with you.

I want to die.

I want to kill her.

I want to kill her and *then* die.

"She seems nice," Viktor says with a smirk and *oh my god* is he just going to pretend like he didn't hear it, like nothing happened?

I'm not sure if that's good or bad.

I clear my throat. "Yeah I want to kill her. I mean, she's a good egg."

"A good egg?" He looks adorably puzzled.

"She's…fine." I look around the bar because my cheeks are flaring up and ugh everything seems so awkward suddenly.

"Are you ready to go?" he asks. "I paid your bill as well, so we can just leave."

"Viktor," I tell him. "You—"

"Shouldn't have? Yes, well I did. And yes, I tipped them well. That poor bartender, I'm assuming she's the one who had to deal with me before? I can't quite remember."

I nod, and he grabs my hand.

"Where should we go to be alone?"

CHAPTER NINETEEN

MAGGIE

THE EFFICIENT SWEDISH SECRET SERVICE AGENT-TURNED-driver's name is Nick.

I'm sure when I got into the back of the black car with Viktor, that he didn't expect me to strike up a conversation with Nick but as the car weaved through the streets heading toward my house, I not only learned that he has twin daughters the same age as Rosemary and Thyme back home (for the life of me I couldn't pronounce their names), but that this is his first time ever visiting America. I told him to at least go to Santa Monica and ditch Viktor for a day, but Viktor didn't seem too happy about that.

In fact, on the ride back, Viktor's demeanor grew tense and when I looked over at him, there were more shadows under his cheekbones, a grayness under his eyes. He looked worn out and I wondered if he had literally just landed—where, LA?—and come straight here.

All I do know is that he didn't book a hotel room in town, which was fine since I wouldn't have been able to stay overnight with him anyway. Some things may have changed for me and with selling his car, I've been able to have more of a safety net, but I'm still in charge of my brothers and sisters and still have responsibilities, even if I feel like I've grown into them a bit more.

And honestly, a few hours with Viktor in a hotel room would not be enough, I don't care how wild the sex is (because it would be wild, right? Viktor doesn't do *tame*).

I want him with me the entire night. I want him in my bed at home. I want him to wake up and look at the same walls I look at every morning, the walls I've always looked at. I want to be in his arms and feel safe where I live. I want him to become a part of *this* life.

But I'd settle for being a tiny fraction of his.

Nick pulls the car up on the street and cuts the engine.

"Thanks for the ride," I tell him.

He gives me a stern look in the rearview mirror. That's just his face though, stern, with a nose like vulture's beak. Would be terrifying if I didn't know that his daughters are obsessed with Harry Styles and so now he is too and can sing every lyric to his latest album.

"He's not going anywhere," Viktor says to me. "It's his job to stay here and watch me all night."

Nick nods in response.

I stare at Viktor with wide eyes. "He's going to *watch us all night?*"

Nick clears his throat loudly and I swear he blushes. "I'll be in the car, Miss McPherson. Don't worry."

"Oh."

We get out of the car and head toward the house. I glance up at Viktor. "I can't believe these people follow you everywhere. That must get annoying."

"You get used to it," he says in a rather grim voice.

"Must make you appreciate all that freedom you had the last time you were here, huh?"

His eyes take a sad slant. "Yes. It does."

Being after eleven at night, everyone in the house should be asleep except for Pike but his light isn't on and I'm not going to test whether he's home or not. I carefully unlock and open the door and grab Viktor's hand, quietly leading him through the house.

It's funny, I have every right to bring a man home to my room, but Viktor will be the first one since I came back. Sometimes it feels like my siblings are parenting me instead of the other way around or maybe that's just what being a parent is all about. You're both trying to not screw up and get caught.

I open the door to my room and usher him inside. He's seen it before in passing during the times he's been over, but not like this.

His eyes immediately travel to my armchair in the corner where Viktor the moose sits underneath a framed photo of my orgasmic Splash Mountain ride.

I start to explain that it's my shrine to him, but he quickly closes the door behind us and kisses me.

His lips and tongue strike a fire against mine.

His hands disappear into my hair, down my back, over my chest, down my sides.

My hands hook up onto his shoulders.

My body presses against his.

In moments we are engulfed in this flame that seems to take over the whole room and it singes my lungs and the only thing I need more than water is him. I thirst for him like nothing else.

We grope and fumble and lick and bite, standing by the door, clothes ripped off and discarded until we're naked and I'm ready for him to take me right there on the floor.

Instead he takes me by the hand and leads me to my bed, acting so confident and self-assured. I feel all my nerves and hang-ups melt away. Though he may be dominant and rough sometimes in the bedroom, I always feel safe with him and even though the last few months have created some distance, I know this is the way we'll come back together.

He pulls back the sheets and blankets that I had hastily made earlier that day and I crawl inside. I know I should probably take more care in making my bed, being a housekeeper for a living and all, but half the time here I'm just like *fuck it*.

"What are you thinking about?" he whispers as he crawls in the bed after me, his firm naked body sliding in against mine. "Your thinking sexy face is back and right now I don't want you thinking about anything but me." He pauses, reaches down and gives his cock a long stroke. "Or my cock. It's so very fucking hard."

Well, that's definitely the fastest way to get out of my head.

I stare at it for a second, feeling the desire sweep through me, feeling like I'm both in my body and out of it, one moment everything is normal, the next Viktor is here and he's naked with me in this bed and he's whispering dirty things to me, stroking that big dick of his and…

"Think of me," he murmurs, and I can't find the words to tell him that I am. "Think of everything I'm going to do you tonight. It's been so fucking long, *min persika*. My sweet little peach. I want to taste you again and again. I want to make up for all the lost time."

He positions himself so he's lying on top of me, his warm chest pressed against mine, his elbows planted on either side of my head. He peers down at me in such a way it unnerves me, hitting me to the meat of my bones. His eyes are kind, curious, and filled with a deep longing I can feel pull at me. But there's something new to them I've never seen before. A flash of fear. The same fear I saw in the car on the ride over here, his tense demeanor outside of the house.

"What is it?" I whisper while he runs his finger down the side of my face, over my cheekbone, down to my lips. He rubs his finger over them and then opens my mouth, sliding a finger inside.

Instinctively, I suck on it and he closes his eyes, letting out a low moan. "This sweet soft mouth."

Then a faint smile crosses his lips, and though the fear in his eyes doesn't waver, it softens it.

"Maggie." His voice is rough, low, coarse. It brings out a flurry of goosebumps all over my bare skin.

"Come back with me."

My heart slows.

What?

I blink at him. "To…LA?"

"To Sweden," he says. His fingers continue to trail across my face and his eyes go to where his fingers go, coasting over the rest of my face, taking in every detail. Now I'm as fearful as he is.

He licks his lips, his jaw wiggling as if he's trying to find the words. "I told you I would come back for you. And here I am. I know this is last minute." I would laugh at what an understatement that is, but my heart is beating so hard I don't think I can even move. "I know you may need time. But I couldn't wait. I don't have many opportunities to up and leave and I took the first one I got. I have to go back tomorrow. I only came to ask you in person."

Tears rush to my eyes. Tears of sorrow because I'll have to say no, tears of frustration because I wish he had given me warning, because maybe then I could have said yes.

"I can't," I sob, trying to stay quiet. "You know I can't."

"Please tell me why."

"Why?" I ask, incredulous. "*Why*?!"

"Maggie." He exhales, his breath shaking as he stares back into my eyes, searching, searching. "Do you know what it means when I call you mitt liv, mitt allt? Min äiskling?"

A lump forms in my throat and the air around us thickens.

"What?" I whisper after a beat.

I've translated it.

I know.

But I want to hear him say it in my language.

Maybe then I'll finally believe it.

"It means, you are my life and you are my everything and you are my love," he says gently. "You have shaken me to my very soul, rattled the bars around my heart, and I am yours, Maggie, I am yours."

Dear god.

I want to cry again. The emotion is building in my chest, squeezing tight. Heat prickles in my head, tempting the tears, while my heart dissolves into stardust.

Viktor just said he loves me.

I've never felt so free and joyous, both uncontained and grounded. His words, his words, his words. They tumble inside me over and over again until I'm smiling, tasting my tears, and…

God. I want to go with him.

It can't just end like this.

"I love you too," I tell him, my voice shaking. "I didn't have a choice. All this time I thought it would go away, that I could blame what I felt for you on something else, that I didn't know you enough to love you. But look at you. You're Viktor. To know you is to love you."

"I think that's from a song," he says softly, but he's smiling.

"I think when you're in love, everything is a song."

"Then let's play a wilder tune."

One of his hands disappears into my hair, the other trails

up the inside of my leg, soft and teasing, inch by inch over my sensitive skin. Adrenaline from his words is pumping through me and I'm already shivering at his touch, craving him more than I ever have before.

I am yours, Maggie, I am yours.

And I am his, I am his.

No matter what happens to us, I am his.

He keeps his eyes on mine, burning with new lust that seems to be struck from a match, blue flames in the darkness, and I'm so turned on already that I'm wet to my thighs. Suddenly I need him inside me more than I can bear.

"*Min persika,*" Viktor says through a groan as his hand slips down, his fingers finding my clit. I let out a small, anxious gasp as he teases it, his eyes never breaking from mine. "Come back with me."

Even if I could, it would take brain power to sort it out, brain power I don't have right now. My mind is shutting down, my body coming to life.

"Don't think," he says gruffly as he grabs my hips and parts my legs. "Say yes in other ways." He reaches for his cock and runs the crown of it up and down my clit, pausing to dip it briefly inside before moving it back up. The sound is so loud in this room, so wet, I worry for a moment that it can be heard outside these walls.

My eyes close, and I surrender myself to this torturous tease. He's not pushing in—it's just a slow slide, back and forth, but I feel myself opening for him anyway, my body hungry at first, then becoming wildly desperate for more. I'm both languid and tense, surrendering and spurring him on as he rubs against me over and over again.

"Come back with me," he says again, his voice growing even rougher, like my silence is making him angry. "I'm not leaving without you."

"Viktor," I whisper, unable to stop from squirming. I need

him inside me. It's not just about getting off now, it's about feeling achingly empty and incomplete without him. It's another way to keep the fear at bay. The fear that he's leaving. The fear I might say yes.

God, could I say yes this time?

I swallow hard, making a noise that's nothing short of begging. My heart is starting to sound in my head, my skin is hot and tight, my nipples are hardened pebbles as the sheet brushes against them. I'm going crazy and I can't handle the teasing anymore. "I want you inside me. I need it. Now. Please."

"Tell me you'll come back with me."

"I'll come with you, here and now in this bed," I counter.

That seems to satisfy him. He's as feverish and worked up as I am.

With a slow exhale, not breaking eye contact, he leans on his elbows and pushes himself in.

Slowly.

Torturously slow.

My head rolls to the side and I gasp, my hands gripping the sheets because I can feel every stiff inch of him spreading me wide, making me feel so fucking full I don't know how I lived without him inside me.

He murmurs something in Swedish and starts to pick up the pace, his fingers become rougher as they grip and pinch my skin, holding me like he can't ever let go.

"Am I hurting you?" he asks, groaning through the words.

"No," I say, licking my lips. I look at him, caught in the heated vibrancy of his stare. "But you can if you want."

He nods and watches me intently as he thrusts in sharply. His lips part as he sucks in his breath, and his forehead creases in lust and awe, like he can't believe this is happening, can't believe how good it feels, how we're together again.

"Perhaps that is suited for another night, when we have more privacy."

He means so that the both of us can be loud. We must have gotten noise complaints at the Roosevelt Hotel.

"*Persika*," he moans, his hands sliding to my breasts where he pinches my hardened nipples. "So fucking sweet, you feel so fucking good. Tell me you're mine, I need to hear it."

"I'm yours, Viktor, I'm yours."

He's watching me, watching himself where his cock sinks into me, his shaft wet with my desire. He's entranced by the sight, the slow push in, the slow pull out.

So good. God, this is so, so good.

Oh…god, yes. Just like that.

Each rock of my hips, each roll of his, pushes him in deeper, makes us connect like magnets. The way his abs clench as he pushes inside, the tiny beads of sweat that gather in the creases, the dampness of his brow. I reach around and tug his firm ass toward me, wanting more, and he drives in so deep that the air leaves my lungs.

"Viktor," I gasp, feeling the emotions swirl inside me, a whirlpool that I know will overtake me again before this is over. My head drops back, my eyes closing in shock as I surrender. He's in me, in so deep, and I don't ever want him to leave. This feels beyond right.

I can't let him leave.

I won't.

This man belongs with me.

The thought sets off something deep inside, a fire in my core that's slowly increasing, spreading, heating up. It's going to take over, it's going to pull me under, and I've never wanted to come so badly in my life.

"Deeper," I whisper, my voice choked with my sudden need for him. "Harder. Fuck me harder. Make me come."

His eyes nearly roll back in his head at that and he responds instantly.

With a throaty growl he starts thrusting deeper, one hand in my hair, making a fist. He leans down, pressing his damp chest against mine, and kisses me, quick and hot, tasting like sweat. My mouth is ravenous against his, the need inside me building and building.

And then we find our rhythm, our bodies coming together in synchronicity. He's pumping into me, working himself into a frenzy and I know we're no longer being quiet anymore.

I no longer care.

This is my prince.

Right now, he's my king.

The muscles in his neck are strained as the sweat rolls off of him, and his eyes are lost in a fiery haze, his pupils so dark and nearly covering all the blue. He reminds me of a wild animal caught in the middle of the jungle, ready to attack, and the sounds coming out of his mouth are equally as raw and primal.

The bed creaks, shuffling on the floor with each savage pump and I'm so glad there's no one below us. The whirlpool of fire inside me is now at a roar and I can't hold on.

"I'm coming," I cry out, my voice raw and raspy and drowning with desire, trying to hold his gaze. He holds mine back, his eyes watching in torrid fascination.

Then I'm twisting as the orgasm washes over me. My body jolts and shudders and I'm high above this world, fading into the stars, into the black. Only warmth and joy remain as I'm washed up on a far-off shore, pushing all sadness away.

"*Helvete*," Viktor grunts, pulling me out of the haze as he delves into a string of Swedish expletives. His growling, animalistic noises, the slap of his sweat-soaked skin against mine, the creak of the bed, all fill the air.

Then he chokes on a long, raw moan that he desperately tries to tone down, his shoulders shaking as he comes.

The pumping slows.

His grip in my hair loosens.

He collapses against me, his hair damp and sticking to his brow. His eyes take me in, his breath heavy and hard.

"Maggie," he manages to say after a minute, his voice raw. He's still inside me and I'm still pulsing around him, the torrent inside me slowing. "I *moose* ask you a question."

I'm so taken aback by the joke that it takes me a moment before I let out a quiet laugh.

"But I am serious," he says, his hand going to my face as he searches my eyes. "Come back with me. Please."

"You know I can't."

"No," he says with a shake of his head, a drop of sweat beading off the tip of his nose. "*You* don't know that you can."

He then pauses, taking in a deep breath.

"Hear me out."

"GATHER AROUND EVERYONE," Pike yells as Viktor and I hover nervously behind him in the back of the kitchen. "Family meeting!"

I glance up at Viktor and he squeezes my hand in return.

"There's no cow on the ice," he says.

I'm not sure about that one.

Viktor and I stayed up very late last night. It wasn't just that we made love three times (although that was a factor), it was that he had a plan for me.

Me *and* my brothers and sisters.

At first it all sounded a little too simple. A little too good to be true. Then the more I thought about it, the more complicated and impossible it became.

So right now, we're just winging it, throwing shit against the wall and seeing what sticks.

It's Saturday, so luckily I'm not working and the kids are all at home. When we got up this morning, the first thing I did was go to Pike's room and have a talk with him, telling him our plan. He's a big part of it and I needed to prepare him, needed him on my team.

He wasn't overjoyed with the idea at first since it means some extra work on his behalf. But he's a good brother and knows how much Viktor and I care about each other. At least he knows that now. Also, this whole thing benefits him as well.

The only thing we left out was the whole prince thing.

That will come.

Callum is the first to come barrelling down the stairs in his pajamas.

"Pancakes, are we having pancakes? Are we…"

He trails off and stops dead in his tracks when he sees Viktor standing there.

"The Swedish Chef!" he yells, pointing. "Herdy schmerdy bork bork!"

"Yes, herdy schmerdy bork bork is back," Viktor says, making his accent thicker to match the Chef's. "Nice to see you, little buddy."

"Are you making us pancakes?!" He's practically screaming.

"Callum, calm down."

"Perhaps," Viktor says and then looks over his shoulder out the window where the Town Car is parked. He whispers to me, "If I do I should bring some for Janne outside?"

"What happened to Nick?"

"They have shifts."

"What are you guys whispering about?" Callum asks, and now Pike is looking out the window at the car with suspicion.

He raises a brow at me and I make the motion that I'll explain in a bit.

"What's going on?" Rosemary says through a yawn as she shuffles into the kitchen, followed by Thyme. They pause before sitting down at the table, looking in unison at Viktor. "What are you doing here?" they ask.

"I'll explain in a minute," Pike says. "Where is April? She is home right?"

"I'm coming," April snaps from the stairway, appearing in the kitchen completely disheveled. She's the only one who doesn't seem surprised to see Viktor. Then I remember she saw him last night and told him where I was.

Then I remember she shares a wall with me.

I wince and look away, avoiding her glare as she goes over to the coffee pot and starts making some. Fourteen seems young for a caffeine addiction but I have to pick and choose my battles in this house.

"Okay," Pike says and then points at me. "Maggie has some exciting news to share."

And just like that it's all on me.

"Right," I say and Viktor squeezes my hand harder. "Okay, here's the thing. There are going to be some changes happening but they're all fun changes, okay?"

"Are we getting a new dog?" Callum asks.

I wince again. "No. Not that."

"What about a hamster?"

"Bearded dragons are really cool," Thyme says.

"No, we aren't getting any pets. Listen. Here's what's going to happen." I take in a deep breath. "I'm going to Sweden for a few weeks."

Everyone just stares at me for a beat.

"Like a vacation?" Thyme asks.

"Yes, like a vacation. To be with Viktor in Stockholm."

"Who will take care of us?" Callum asks.

"I will," Pike says. "With Rosemary and Thyme's help, of course."

They both nod eagerly. They've been waiting for the responsibility, always bringing up the fact that Mallory in *The Babysitter's Club* was eleven when she started babysitting.

"*Then*," I add, drawing out the word, "it's Christmas break. Which means all of you are flying over to Sweden for the holidays."

Silence.

"Christmas in Sweden!" I try and sound more enthusiastic.

Blink blink. No one even breathes.

"What if we don't want to go to Sweden?" April asks with a scowl. I knew I could count on her to say something.

"Then it's too bad because we're all going," I tell her. "And I promise you guys will love it. I promise."

Callum slowly nods, tapping his fingers against his chin. "I suppose it will do." Pause. Bright smile. "Can I meet ABBA?"

I have a feeling Callum thinks ABBA is one person.

"Maybe," Viktor says.

I punch his arm. "Don't tease him, he'll hold you to it."

"And ABBA knows my mother, I'm pretty sure I could arrange it."

"ABBA knows your mother?" Pike asks.

"Well, yes," Viktor says. "Everyone knows my mother."

Here it goes.

"Why, is she famous?" Callum asks.

Viktor looks at him and nods. "Yes."

"Why, who is she?" April says, sounding more curious than snarky now.

"She's the queen of Sweden," he says with a shrug.

"Shut up," Rosemary says. "Your mother is not the queen of Sweden."

"She is. My father is the king."

"Phhhfff," April says, turning her back to us. "Yeah right. We might be Americans but we ain't dumb."

"That would make you a prince," Thyme points out.

"I know," he says. "I am."

"Shut up," Rosemary says again.

"Rosemary, stop telling the Prince of Sweden to shut up," I tell her.

"Pike, tell them to stop lying," April says.

I look at Pike. His brows are drawn together as he looks out the window, deep in thought. He finally looks at us. "The car that's out there. Friend of yours?"

"That's Janne," Viktor says. "He's assigned to protect me."

"Protect you!" Rosemary exclaims.

"Really?" Thyme says.

Viktor nods. "I'm not joking."

"Bullshit," April says. "As soon as this coffee is done, I'm going upstairs and not listening to your nonsense anymore. And I'm *not* going to Sweden."

"But you would get to live in a palace and meet The King and Queen," Viktor says. "All your desires would be taken care of."

"You're a liar."

"No," Pike says, looking down at his phone. "He's not." He

lifts his phone for everyone to see. It's the Google Images page of Viktor.

All chairs are pushed back at once, the scrape of them filling the kitchen as Callum, Rosemary and Thyme run over to Pike to get a better look.

They look down at the screen.

Look up at Viktor.

Look down at the screen.

Look up at Viktor.

"Holy crap," Rosemary and Thyme say together.

"Holy crap!" Callum yells.

"Yeah. Holy…" Pike trails off. "I can't believe you kept this a secret."

I shrug. "It wasn't my place to say."

"I don't like lying," Viktor says. "But I had to last time. It would have been a security risk if anyone had known it was me." He looks at Callum. "I am still a good cook though. That wasn't a fluke."

And now April slowly comes over to Pike and takes the phone from him. She glances at the screen, doesn't say anything and gives the phone back. "Can we seriously stay at the palace?" she asks Viktor.

"I don't see why not," he says. He looks around the room. "So what do you all say? Christmas in Sweden?"

Everyone exchanges excited glances and then yells, "Christmas in Sweden!"

CHAPTER TWENTY

MAGGIE

A WEEK FLIES BY IN A BLINK.

One minute I'm working my ass off with extra shifts, trying to get the house in order for Pike, to make this job as easy on him as possible, the next I'm boarding the plane for Stockholm, Sweden.

First class!

I even have my own bed and everything. It's almost nicer than the bed I have at home. I even have my own butler, just like Viktor does.

Okay, so the first-class flight attendants aren't servants but they do bring you champagne and whatever else you ask for even before the flight takes off.

There is a sharp twang of guilt that I'm doing this while the kids are slaving away at school, but the guilt disappears when I realize they'll be doing the same thing, albeit in coach, in two weeks from now. Until then, I'm going to be alone with Viktor in Sweden.

Viktor said he was going to try and shield me from the world as much as he could. It feels kind of romantic, being kept in secret like a concubine. He said the only people who would know would be his private secretary Freddie, his butler and a few guards. Eventually he wants to introduce me to the rest of his family, but he seemed pretty adamant about keeping me a secret at the start.

I don't mind. I brought up the fact that Meghan Markle and Prince Harry dated in secrecy for months before even Prince William found out. If they can do it, so can we. That said, we'll both be in Stockholm, not some safari camp in the middle of nowhere, and it's going to get intricately more challenging once the kids come, but we'll cross that bridge when we come to it.

All that matters now is that a choice has been made and I'm on my way.

To fucking Sweden!

Land of aquavit and moose and IKEA and ABBA and Volvos and universal healthcare!

There are a million more things to get excited about but as the plane takes off and the runways of LAX drop away, I'm met with some worry. The biggest one is my job. Juanita would have been fine with me taking two weeks off but over a month? That crossed the line.

We parted on amicable terms, even though she thought I was crazy to do this, and she said she'd give me my job back when I returned but the truth is, until then, I'm out of my job.

In other words, I quit my job for Viktor.

Now I know Viktor has told me many times that he would take care of me and I also know I have savings now that can support all of us if it turns out I have to look for another job (of course those savings I have thanks to Viktor), but it doesn't change the fact that I'm doing something quite irresponsible.

Neither Annette or Sam think it's a good idea either. I mean, they thought it was romantic and they think it will be awesome for the kids to travel for the first time, especially if they are treated like royalty. But I did just quit my job to do this, which is a huge step. And though I love Viktor more than I can bear, there is currently no security in our relationship. It's so brand new.

And that's nagging at me too. As it stands, I'll be coming back with the kids, though Viktor said he has yet to book me a return ticket. He thinks he can change my mind. He thinks I might want to stay. He says it will be his mission over the next month to make me stay.

But as Sam had said on the phone, where is this going? Where could this go? I can't just stay in Sweden, I have kids to take care of and a life in Tehachapi. And even if I did stay, then what? Am I willing to risk everything, and I mean absolutely everything and *everyone*, on love?

I guess the answer for now, is, yes. Quitting my job, a job I needed, for a man, was never something the old Maggie would do, but apparently the new Maggie is just throwing caution to the wind these days for a chance to keep having hot sex.

Hot sex with a prince.

Hot sex with a man that I love.

Maybe quitting my job was worth it.

I don't fret too much more for the rest of thirteen-hour flight because the flight attendant thinks I'm super nervous, so she keeps giving me booze. And then I start watching movies, and after a while, when the cabin lights are dimmed, I actually fall asleep.

I wake up just as breakfast is being served and before I know it, the plane is landing at Stockholm's Arlanda airport.

I look out the window to see my first glimpses of the country and my bleary-eyes are blinded by all the white.

Snow.

There's nothing but snow.

In fact, the runway that is quickly rushing up to meet the plane looks exactly like a skating rink.

Oh my god, we're all going to die.

They forgot to plow the runway!

I look around frantically to see if anyone else is in the crash position or bracing themselves but everyone else looks completely calm.

We land without incident. I'm not sure what kind of snow tires they have on this thing.

Then I'm off the plane and in the very clean and modern airport and it's just like…

I'M IN SWEDEN!

The signs are in Swedish and people are talking Swedish, and everyone looks like a supermodel or the bad guy in a Bond film, and I'm so tired and jet-lagged and overjoyed right now.

And scared. I'm also scared, wishing that I could have flow back with Viktor when he did or wishing he stayed in Tehachapi with me, even though there was no way he could have spared the time.

I go up to the passport control and slide a very unsmiling man my passport.

"What brings you to Sweden?" he asks.

Oh shit. I can't say I'm meeting The Prince. That's all top secret.

"I'm meeting a friend."

He looks past me at someone in the line, like he wants to murder someone back there. "What is your friend's name?"

What?

"Uh, Johan Andersson."

"Where does he live?"

"Stockholm."

"What is the address?"

"Why, you gonna come check on me?" I try and laugh.

His sharp eyes flit to mine. "What is the address of Johan Andersson?"

Oh shit. You don't joke here.

"It's one ten…Skarsgård Way."

He narrows his eyes, studying for a moment.

I hold my breath.

How obvious is it that I just made that up?

"How did you meet Johan Andersson?"

"He stayed at my hotel."

"Pardon me?"

"I met him in California, at a hotel. We went to Disneyland. I fell in love and here I am." I smile awkwardly. "Ta-da."

He shakes his head, stamps the page, and curtly slides the passport back to me. "Have a nice day."

I quickly take it from him and hurry along. Jeez, what was up his ass.

Now that I've gotten through passport control, I have other things to worry about.

What if there's no one to pick me up? What if I have to take a cab and Viktor warned me about the cabs, what did he say again?

I ponder this as I get my luggage from the carousel and haul it through the customs and out into the arrivals part of the terminal.

That's when I see a familiar face.

"Nick!" I cry out when I see the beak-nosed man holding a sign that reads *McPherson*.

"Miss McPherson," Nick says to me, as reserved as ever or I'm starting to think that's how all Swedes are. "Come this way."

Nick is dressed in black like all the limo and pick-up drivers are, like they all belong to the same secret army but only Nick walks like he's leading me off to the barracks.

It feels like that too because holy shit, the moment I step

outside I realize how severely underdressed I am. Viktor had told me to bring my warmest coat and even though Tehachapi's nickname is the Town of Four Seasons (which probably sounds really redundant outside of California) apparently my warmest coat is not going to cut it.

It's colder than a New York winter.

It's colder than a witch's tit.

It's colder than a polar bear's toenails.

It's cold as fuck.

Shivering and quickly buttoning up my shitty coat as I follow Nick to the parking lot, we pass a long line of people waiting outside for cabs, none of them looking the slightest bit put out or shivering like I am. I curse them immediately and the wind picks up in response, throwing snow in my face.

Thankfully it's not long until I'm getting in the back of what looks like the Mercedes version of a Town Car. It's warm in here and then we're on the highway which seems even less plowed than the runway was, except all the cars are zooming along it at top speed. We only slow down when the visibility turns everything in front of us into a white wall and we're still going faster than fifty.

"Is it always this, uh, snowy?" I ask Nick.

"Not always in November but we're getting an early start to winter this year."

Oh great. I can't look out the window anymore, it's giving me anxiety, so I lay back and let the warmth of the car's heater wash over me and the jet lag seep into my bones and then Nick is shaking my leg.

"We're here," he says.

I slowly push myself up and look around. I'm still in the car. Outside it's all white.

He gets out of the car and opens the back door, a rush of startlingly cold air swooping in and slapping me in the face.

He has an umbrella held above me, though the snow is taking no prisoners, and helps me out.

"This is the back entrance to the estate," he tells me, and I look over the car at the tall three-story white building that seems to blend in too well with the snow. "Bodi there will get you all sorted."

A man comes scuttling out of the back door and grabs my suitcase out of the trunk. I've heard of Bodi the butler before but for some reason I imagined him to be dressed, like, well a butler. I suppose it's as much of a stereotype as me wearing a French maid's uniform.

Bodi is balding a bit but has crazy red hair and bright emerald eyes that match his green velvet suit.

"Welcome, Miss McPherson," he says to me, gesturing to the door. "Please follow me inside."

I look at Nick as snowflakes gather in his hair. Even though it's the afternoon here, things already seem to be getting dark, bathing the grounds in this blue-gray glow.

"Where is Viktor?" I ask Nick. I would have thought he would have come out of the door with Bodi.

"He will be back later," he says and then gets back in his car, the tires spinning on the snow for a moment before the car lurches off.

"Miss," Bodi urges from the door.

I nod and come toward him, nearly slipping twice on the snow before I get to the door.

"Sorry," he says, nodding behind me. "It's usually shoveled dry. I know Her Highness wants a heated driveway installed but this is a very old place."

I wave him off, not wanting him to make a fuss. Who the fuck would I be, some poor girl showing up at a royal palace and seeming upset that the driveway isn't shoveled?

I also found it kind of funny that he said "Her Highness wants this" like he's being sarcastic but he's very much not.

Because, that's Viktor's mother. I might not have to call Viktor anything but Viktor, but I can't go up to his mother and be like "yo, what up Mrs. N, what's happening?"

Imagine if you married Viktor, I think to myself as Bodi leads me into what looks like a giant pantry. *Would I have to call my mother-in-law Your Highness? That doesn't seem fair.*

But I brush that thought out of my head pretty quickly because even though I'm currently following a butler through a Swedish palace because I'm dating the prince, that sort of stuff seems very far away and off the table.

After all, we only had one week together in California.

But what happens when we have a month in Sweden?

The palace, in some ways, is exactly as I was expecting. When you think of a palace you think of striped wallpaper and high ceilings with crown mouldings and elaborate designs. You think of antique high-end tables peppered with statues and large oil paintings with gold frames hanging from the walls. You think of velvet chaises and chairs, much like Bodi's suit, and silk and satin and leather. All of this stuff makes up the many rooms of the palace.

It is lacking the Scandinavian charm that I assumed would be here–like an IKEA showroom on steroids–but honestly, I'm so enthralled and amazed by the palace that it doesn't matter.

It's a fantasy come to life.

"This is your room," Bodi says, opening the door.

It takes my breath away.

And not just because I climbed three floors on very steep stairs.

It takes up the whole top tower of the building and the ceilings are at least fifteen feet high. There's a huge four poster bed, a little living room seating area to one side with a widescreen TV, on the other side is a desk by the window that must look out to the front of the palace, then a bar cart, a door leading to what I assume is the bathroom, closets and more.

"This is my room?"

"This is His Highness's room," Bodi explains and I swear the guy winks at me. He rolls my suitcase along and then chucks it up on the luggage rack already laid out for it. "Feel free to explore the house. If the doors are closed it's probably because it belongs to one of the staff. I'd suggest you walk the park and the grounds but not in this weather." He nods to the whiteout outside the window. "Perhaps later in the week."

He does a little bow and then turns to leave.

"Wait," I call out. "When does Viktor get back?"

"It's hard to say," he says with a raise of his brow. He's probably not used to hearing him called Viktor. "He has a speaking engagement at one of the universities this afternoon and I believe he's going to Drottningholm Palace for dinner. Where the King and Queen reside." He pauses by the door. "Just relax and make yourself at home. If you're hungry or you need me for anything, just ring this bell here and I'll be up right away." He taps a buzzer by the door. "Oh and try not to fall asleep until a reasonable hour. It will only make the jet lag worse."

"Okay," I say softly as he leaves, closing the door behind him. "Thank you."

Holy fuck.

So Viktor just has this Bodi guy at his beck and call twenty-four seven? I mean, I get that's what butler's do but I've just never seen one in real life. Or heard of one. I mean, do celebrities in LA have butlers? Do the Kardashians?

To top it off, Bodi seems to want to serve. He seems to love his job. It makes me feel ashamed, actually, for taking no pride whatsoever in what I do. Sure, no one else looks kindly upon housekeepers and maids but that doesn't mean I shouldn't.

What you did, remember. You quit. Past tense.

Fuck. Stupid voice.

That's when I'm hit with a wave of nausea and the room spins. Suddenly it doesn't seem right to have to stay awake anymore.

I force myself though, determined to beat the jet lag. I put all my clothes away in the chest of drawers and the space in the closet that Viktor has clearly created for me. Then I put my toiletry stuff in the bathroom and take a long hot shower, which makes me feel a little bit better.

Oddly enough, I'm not hungry at all, and I go to the window, spending a few minutes looking out of it, trying to see if I can see trees through the whirling snow and darkening light, or if my eyes are playing tricks on me.

I glance down at his desk. A pad of paper is laid out, along with a pen and a small sachet of…

I pick it up and smell it.

My heart melts.

Lavender. It's lavender.

He really was scenting his letters.

I let myself swoon for a moment because *wow*.

Viktor is the real deal.

I sigh happily and then do one of those twirling, smiling, swooning moves across the room like a total Disney princess and then fling myself on the bed.

The moment the soft covers meet my cheek, I know it's a bad move.

Sleep comes for me like a monster and then…

I'm out.

"Maggie?" I hear a voice float into my dreams.

I open my eyes to darkness.

A slice of bare light cutting across my vision like a sword. Then it fades.

I fade.

Another light glows behind my eyelids.

I pry them open to see Viktor standing beside the bed having turned on the side lamp, his pants unbuckled, undoing his tie. It runs through his fingers with a slick cutting noise that stands out to me in this cavernous room.

"I didn't mean to wake you," he says softly. "I'm so sorry I wasn't home earlier."

I mumble something like, "no cow on the ice," but it all comes out in a garbled hush. I clear my throat and try to push myself up onto my elbows, my eyes all squinty, my hair mussed up. I'm still in my clothes.

"What time is it?" I whisper, my voice rough. I need water.

"It's just after ten," he says. "At night. Let me get you some water? Do you need anything to eat?"

I'm still not hungry. I just want to keep sleeping.

"Water is good," I manage to say.

He gives me a warm smile and then walks off into the bathroom. I hear the sink running and I place my head back on the bed.

"Here," he says, and suddenly he's sitting beside me and holding out a glass.

I try to sit up, not as much as before, and take it from him, downing it in three large gulps and coughing wildly at the end.

"Easy, Maggie," he says to me, taking the glass away. "I'll

get you another. I'd offer you some red wine or brandy, but I don't think you need anything."

"No," I say, grabbing hold of him. It takes me a moment to realize that now his clothes are all off and he's just in his pajama pants and nothing else. My fingers curl around the fabric. "Please stay. I don't feel...*good*."

He lets out a low laugh. "Jet lag is a bitch, as they say. It always takes me a few days to adjust when I'm coming back home. It can be really brutal. Did you take any melatonin?"

I shake my head. He did mention it, but I didn't think it necessary. I thought jet lag was something I felt when I went from California to New York. This is a whole other beast altogether. This makes me feel like I'm on a really weird drug bender and not the good kind, the kind that you know will take days to wear off.

He strokes my head and I'm falling into the mattress again. "Just sleep Maggie. Tomorrow is another day. A better day. I'll be here in the morning."

"Then where are you going?" I ask him and suddenly I'm gripping him tighter again.

"To a gala," he says.

I look up at him and squint. It's still my Viktor, looking as handsome as ever. Jet lag doesn't change that. "Okay."

"I'd invite you of course but…"

"But I'm a secret."

"It's better this way, please believe me."

I sigh, nestling my face deeper into the covers. "I believe you. The whole Meghan and Harry thing."

"You don't understand. I want time alone with you. I don't want to share you. Everything is still so new to us and our time together, just us, is crucial."

I smile, my eyes closed. "I know."

And I do. I can feel every single word that falls from his lips, the way they radiate from his heart.

I feel him lie beside me in bed and when I open my eyes, his face is facing mine, cheek against the bedspread. "Look, Maggie, I invited you here because I want you here and I need you here and I'm going to do what I can to make it worth our while. Whatever silly thing I have planned or engagement that's not worth it, I will skip for you. Whatever event I'd rather not do, I won't. I'll stay home. I'll tell people I'm running a fever, I don't know. But I will do all I can to make sure that the next two weeks and the weeks after that with your family, are all focused on you. I will be here by your side, as much as I can. As Viktor, not a prince. As your friend, your lover, your man. You understand?"

"I do. That was a lot of words flying into my head, but I understand," I mumble against the bed, my eyes lazily focused on his. I smile and reach for the waistband of his pajama pants, my hands skimming the taut planes of his stomach, the soft trail of hair. "Do you understand this?"

He grins at me, that same fucking grin that always catches me off guard and frees the butterflies all over again. "I understand very well. But you're in need of sleep, my dear."

He then moves over on the bed and pulls back the covers, and then puts his hands under my arms and practically lifts me so that I'm properly positioned.

Then he starts to undress me. My jeans, my sweater, my shirt. My bra. I'm topless in my underwear and in the back of my head I'm wondering if I smell and then I remember I had a shower earlier. My hair must be such a wild mess right now, I never even had a chance to brush it.

"Sleep tight," he says to me, pulling the sheets over me. "I'll see you in the morning." He pauses. "If you wake up in the middle of the night, feel free to watch TV or whatever. I can sleep through anything."

I don't even get a chance to reflect on that before I'm drifting off again.

CHAPTER TWENTY-ONE

VIKTOR

It's been a couple of days since Maggie arrived in Stockholm.

I would love to say the days have been bright and easy.

But that's not quite the case.

The moment that I showed up in Tehachapi I knew there were two hurdles for me to jump. One was to convince Maggie to come back with me to Stockholm. This, I assumed, was the biggest hurdle of all.

But it didn't take as much convincing as I thought. Probably because Maggie is somehow in love with a sorry sap like me, just as much as I am in love with her. When I finally convinced her, it felt like an anvil was lifted off my chest and that the hardest part of our relationship–the will to continue it–was over.

Then she got here. And already on her first day landing in Stockholm, she was alone. I had engagements and dinners I couldn't get out of without a huge guilt trip and though I'm not always susceptible to guilt trips, I also knew I had to pick my battles. There would be many battles on the horizon.

Even so, I didn't get back home until she was here and delirious with jet lag.

Which of course, because she went to bed earlier, meant she got up at two in the morning and couldn't get back to sleep. When I finally woke up at seven a.m., I found her wandering the halls of the palace. In the dim light after the snowstorm, she looked like a ghost, but she was more than content, just soaking in the history of the place and happy to be here.

It made me realize that she's a lot more interested and excited about my new role, and all that comes with it, than I am.

But as the days went on, I became busier and busier. I tried to shake most things but unfortunately, so many of them were part of my job. Even just showing up counts. You make a speech, you cut a ribbon, you pose for pictures. If you aren't there, the world will notice, and the world will talk, and they won't be saying nice things.

Though Maggie was still coping with jet lag in a big way, she's also very independent. On the days I had engagements, I had Nick take care of her, driving her anywhere she wanted. He became her companion in some ways. Not quite a bodyguard but more like a tour guide. I know in the future that Maggie's freedom here might be more constricted but for now, she could do what she wanted, go where she wanted. Even in -11C weather, even in the snow. She went out and braved it all.

I am feeling bad though.

I'm not connecting with her as much as I would like.

I want her to feel that I'm here with her, not just some tired thing that stumbles in late at night. Someone that's too overworked and overwhelmed to even take full advantage of this beautiful woman in my bed.

I swear it's creating a bit more distance between us than

before. We connect on so many levels, but we communicate best with our bodies. I need to be inside her, need to feel that contact, that love, that desire.

That understanding.

I need her more than I can bear.

I'm in the car, halfway to a lunch I'm supposed to attend with a Croatian diplomat, when my thoughts turn to the creaminess of her skin, the peach softness of her lips, the way she melts underneath my touch.

I can't stand it anymore.

She's here to be with me.

And one day she will be gone.

If I don't take advantage of that, I'll hate myself forever.

I tell the driver to turn around and take me back, all while sending a text to Freddie and telling him I don't feel well. Freddie knows, of course, all about Maggie, even though he hasn't met her yet.

He also knows I'm full of shit.

I don't care.

The need to be with her is overpowering.

Within twenty minutes I'm dropped off back at the palace and storming through the halls looking for her.

"Where is Maggie?" I ask Bodi, who is dusting a painting.

"I believe she's in the study, sir," he says.

The study is on the main floor and actually a living room, just on a cozier scale. There's a desk and a couch, some arm chairs and a fireplace. A large bar cart. It's a place to unwind with guests, so I can't imagine why she'd be in there alone.

I walk inside and see her curled up on the couch with a book in her hand. She's wearing fuzzy black leggings she's calls her long underwear, as well as a soft gray sweater that falls off one shoulder, exposing her creamy skin. Her feet are encased in fluffy slippers.

"Oh hey," she says, putting the book down. "Did you

forget something?"

"Yes, you," I tell her. I stride over to the couch and glance down at the book. It's an old worn classic in English. "Watership Down?"

She smiles sheepishly which makes her cheeks extra rosy. "I remembered you telling me about having rabbits as a child and naming them after the book. When I saw this at a used bookstore the other day in English, I couldn't help myself."

"If you got it in Swedish maybe you could learn the language."

"Maybe. Or maybe you would make a better teacher…"

She doesn't have to finish the sentence.

I could teach her…if I were here.

She tilts her head and looks at me. "So, why are you here? Was it cancelled?"

I nod. "Yes. I cancelled it."

"Why?"

"Because I'd rather be with my lover than with a stuffy diplomat. That's why."

She stares at me for a moment and then takes the book, putting it gently on the coffee table beside the couch.

"Lover?" she questions. "Is that what I am today?"

But I don't even have to answer her because she's already taking off her slippers, then her leggings. Briefly her eyes flit over to the study doors I'd already closed.

"No one will come in here," I tell her, my voice already growing rough with impatience. I have no doubt Bodi knows what's happening behind these doors.

She reaches down and pulls her top off her head. I hadn't even noticed that she wasn't wearing a bra until now.

"*Helvete*," I mutter, taking my dick out of my pants and giving it a long hard stroke as I stare down at her. She stares up at me with those dark, wide, almost nervous eyes, her lips parted, her silky dark hair across her face. Her nipples are hard pink peaks against her full breasts. Her stomach leads smoothly to her hips and thighs that just beg for my teeth to dig into them and make marks along her creamy flesh.

The sweet pink flash of her *persika*.

"I'll do more than that," she says, getting up on all fours and facing me. "I always remember what you said about my peachy lips that you like so much."

A grin spreads across my face. "Which ones?"

I move closer to the couch while she reaches up for my cock, slowly wrapping her long fingers around it. The pressure reverberates along every inch of me, and I let out a harsh groan, the desire slamming into me.

"Lick me, *sakta*," I tell her, my words coming out thick.

She flashes me a wicked smile. "Sakta? Is that Swedish for *suck it?*"

"It's Swedish for *slowly*," I tell her. "As in, go slowly. Please."

"It's been too long, I guess," she muses in a teasing voice, sticking out her tongue and licking around the dark, swollen tip. My head goes back and my eyes close, giving into the feeling, even though I desperately want to maintain eye contact with her.

Her tongue slides down to the bottom of my shaft and everything inside me tenses. I've never felt like this, this white-hot blistering lust that penetrates every last nerve. This is what I get for waiting, sleeping beside her for days on end and being too tired to do anything.

The tension inside me builds and builds into something more than primal, and when I finally open my eyes, practically panting, her sly eyes glance up at me with excitement. With her dark hair spilling around her milky shoulders, she looks like a fucking goddess that men would have died trying to paint.

But she's nothing but real, nothing but here and now as

she takes me into her mouth. Her lips are wet and plush, like a ripe juicy peach.

Persika.

I make a fist in her hair, tugging on it just enough for her eyes to widen, and she sucks me harder in response. It would be so fucking easy to just come hard down the back of her throat and watch her swallow, watch her accept me.

But I'm not about to come now. I want to be inside her again, to feel every hot squeeze of her around me. I need that connection again. I need to remind her of why she's here in Sweden, why she came to be with me.

She came here because I can't be without her and I want to show her just how much I need her.

"Hold on," I pant, pulling back. My cock pops out of her wet, wet mouth.

Helvete.

"Turn around," I tell her, my voice shaking with need.

She does as I ask, and I grab her hips, tugging her back into me, teasing the crack of her bum with my glistening cock. Then I lean over and take a quick nip of her ass cheek.

"Ow," she says, shooting me a deliciously dirty glance over her shoulder.

"Jag är ledsen," I mutter. Which means I'm sorry. And I'm not really sorry at all. She knows how rough I can be.

Even so, I lick over the bite marks, making her relax, soothing any surprise. I want to know how wet and eager she is, so I part her cheeks and stroke my fingertips over her pussy, and I'm nearly salivating over how slippery she is.

I push my finger in and bite my lip at how she holds me. So tight. Her breath hitches and she lets out a breathless moan that shakes me to my core.

You're mine, I think. *And only mine.*
You're here with me.
That's all that matters.

Suddenly the urge, the pure need to be inside her is overpowering and I'm nearly trembling at the hunger pulsing through me. It's this animalistic drive that sneaks up, like I'm being reduced to nothing but basic instinct around her. She's not just Maggie, my Maggie, she's this woman I need to claim, to take rough and hard and fast until I can't remember my name, until I can't remember who I am and what I do.

Until I can't remember the person I'm supposed to be.

But I need to remember the person she thinks I am.

The person she fell in love with.

I need her to fuse to me, bend to me, I need to take her so hard that she knows exactly why she's here.

I need her to know that this place, with me, inside her, is her *home*.

Without realizing it, I've pushed another finger inside her, rubbing eagerly against the right spot, feeling her swell around me.

"Viktor," she gasps, her head down, her hair over her face as she breathes heavily, her body pressing back into me, wanting more. "God, you're so good. So, so good. Never stop, never stop."

Her words are so desperate and urgent.

They're everything I needed to hear.

I have to get inside her *now*.

I quickly withdraw my fingers, rubbing them along my lips briefly, savoring her sweet and salty taste, and then I hold my shaft, rigid and heavy in my hand and angle it into her. I try to go slow, rubbing my head around her soft opening, getting my tip wet before pushing in just a few inches.

But just a few inches are enough to make my jaw clench, trying so hard to keep myself in control.

It's been too long.

And she's so hot and slippery and tight as a fucking fist that I want to slam myself inside of her, bury myself deep. It takes all of me to try and keep breathing, my fingers digging into her sides that I've bruised many times before.

"You're perfect," I tell her, my voice guttural as I push in deeper, watching as my cock disappears into her, her resistance deliciously tight. "So fucking perfect, Maggie."

I pull out in a slow slide and she shudders beneath me before I push back into her, staying cautious. "I want all of you forever. I want every day to be like this. I don't want the distance anymore, not when we're both here."

My words are coming out rough and jagged and I know I should probably stop talking but she makes me want to talk. She makes me want to tell her everything.

She arches her back into me and I slip myself deeper inside her, almost to the hilt. She stretches around me with a loud gasp, her cunt so snug and wet as I roll my hips against her bum. I'm lightheaded, breathless, and the fire inside me builds, licking me until I'm lost in this haze. The world has been reduced down to nothing but pleasure.

Nothing but us.

"Fuck," she cries out. "God, Viktor, fuck me. Harder. Fucking harder."

A growl escapes my lips at her dirty commands and I slam myself into her until she's hugging every throbbing inch. She's yelling my name and I hear nothing but my blood rushing through my head as I bury myself deep inside her. My hips thrust into her, hammering in this driving rhythm and I reach beneath her hips, trying to stroke her clit.

It's wet, messy, and I can barely touch her where I need to but it's enough for her to take over just as the couch starts to inch along the hardwood floors.

She braces herself on one arm and reaches back, and I straighten up, my hands splayed wide around her waist, gripping her harder and harder as I pound into her with reckless abandon.

Then Maggie is moaning, then screaming my name and swearing, and I don't hold back. With a guttural groan, I come, the pleasure ripping through me, turning me inside out. I swear and cry out, coming into her as I go into some mindless, hypersensitive state. In this moment, I'm without thought or self-awareness. I'm just here.

I come back down to earth slowly, trying not to collapse onto her delicate body. I place my hands on the pink cheeks of her bum, leaning on them to keep myself up as I try to catch my breath. My skin is damp with sweat and burning hot, and I feel absolutely liquid inside.

Maggie is breathing hard too, her back rising and falling, having collapsed into the couch with her sweet bum in the air. She turns her head to the side, her face red and beaded with sweat, her eyes heavy-lidded and completely sated.

There are no words to say to each other.

We just know.

We know that's what we both needed to reconnect.

We know that's what we needed to feel whole.

We know that on this earth, no matter the time zone, all we need is each other.

She knows my heart and I know hers.

Sometimes it takes time to find it again.

THE NEXT DAY, our plans change.

They change because Magnus, dear crazy Magnus,

somehow deduced that Maggie was at Haga Palace and then insisted on visiting.

I insisted on him not visiting.

But he's a relentless and charming bastard.

"It's just for a day," he says over the phone. "You know I need to meet her. You know you need my approval."

I don't need his approval but there's no point arguing with him at all. Magnus does what he wants.

"Fine," I tell him. "But just so this gets in your head, we aren't going out. She is a secret, you understand? I will protect her and guard this secret with my life."

I instantly regret everything.

Magnus shows up like he always does. Well, I guess this time he doesn't have a bottle of half-drunk booze in his hands, but he does show up loud and boisterous and ready to party.

For a moment there I forget who Maggie is, forget that she's not some uptight, stuffy, boring noble woman that my parents have set me up with in the past. I forget that in many ways, Maggie is a lot like Magnus.

Hell, they even have roughly the same name.

"Mags," I say to her as she comes down the stairs. I point to him. "This is Mags."

"Hello," Maggie says, immediately charmed just by looking at him. "So nice to—"

And then she's swept off her feet in a second.

Magnus literally picks her up and twirls her around and she's both screaming and laughing and I'm laughing too, trying to ignore the hot coal of jealousy inside me. I know I can be a possessive man, so Magnus isn't helping.

"That was quite the, uh, greeting," Maggie says as she's placed back on the ground. "Is that how all Norwegians say hello?"

"I hope not," Magnus says, raising his dark brows. "And here I was thinking I was original."

I look down at Magnus's bag, now a Formula One race car duffel. "What happened to the Louis Vuitton?"

He shrugs and gives me a devilish grin. "The girl wasn't worth it." He looks at Maggie. "Are you ready to party?"

"Party?"

I had warned her about Magnus but perhaps she thought I was exaggerating.

"Yes, party," he says, clapping his hands together. "You know. I'm saying the word right, yes?" He pretends to boogie down like a lunatic, then mimes drinking and, well, mimes snorting something up his nose.

"There's still the whole issue with us not being seen together in public," I remind him before he gets out of hand.

A look of horror comes across his face. "You mean you're ashamed of me?" He clutches his chest.

"I mean me and *Maggie*," I say with a sigh. "This is still a secret that I'd like to keep and even if we used a back door," he giggles at that, exchanges a look with Maggie, "people would still see us and speculate."

"Relax," he says to me, clapping a hand on my shoulder. "I have thought this through."

He leans down and zips open his duffel bag and pulls out a mask, the type you'd see during the carnivale in Venice.

"Here you go Viktor," he says, waving a gold one at me until I take it from him. He then pulls out a silver one with teal feathers and hands it to Maggie. "And here you go, Mags." Finally, he pulls out a black velvet one for himself.

Maggie turns the mask over in her hands. "It's beautiful."

"Yes," I muse, looking at mine. "But I think this will only draw more attention to ourselves if we go to a club with these on our faces."

"Silly, silly Swede," Magnus says. "You think I haven't

thought of everything? Not only are we going to a sexy little masquerade party tonight, but I've also got five other masks in there for the bodyguards who will no doubt be following us. I already gave mine his and I think he was overjoyed by all the sequins and sparkles."

"You've got to be kidding me," I say.

"*Viktor*," Maggie says as if she's scolding me. "This is the best idea I've ever heard."

Magnus beams at me and gestures to her. "You see this girl here? She's all right. In fact, I think I like her better than you."

"I think you like most people better than me. I have no idea why you come by here."

"Because you never come to Norway!" He looks at Maggie, shaking his head. "There I am in Oslo, all alone."

"Yeah right." I laugh.

"All alone," he repeats, "and he never comes to visit me."

"You know I'm too busy. I'm not used to this stuff like you are," I tell him. "All the engagements and formalities and officials and charities and..."

"I'm not necessarily used to it," Magnus says, straightening up. "I just don't let it dictate my life. I might be a prince but I have my own boundaries. This job does not define me."

Meanwhile, as we're talking, Maggie's eyes are volleying back and forth between us. I suppose it is kind of odd to hear two princes arguing about their jobs.

"Sorry Maggie," I tell her. "Sometimes we forget how good we have it."

She snorts as she tries to slip the mask on. "Are you kidding me? You couldn't pay me to be a princess. Who wants that job?"

She slides the mask on just in time, as if she didn't want me to see her expression as she said that.

I can feel Magnus staring at me. Of course the truth is

that I've thought about her becoming a princess. If we ended up together, and I didn't end up abdicating, that's what she would be. Princess Margaret…Mayhem. And now she's saying I couldn't pay her to do it. I'm sure she meant it in a glib way but I have to admit, that remark bothered me.

"So how do I look?" she asks, adjusting the mask.

"Very mysterious," Magnus says. "Like most women."

"Beautiful," I tell her, tugging it up so I can see her eyes better. "Now even more so."

"So what do you say?" Magnus says. "We have a few hours here before we go out and—"

"Sir?"

We all turn around to see Freddie standing by the entrance to the library.

"Yes?"

He clears his throat and slowly walks toward us.

"Freddie!" Magnus greets him, raising his hand in a high five. Magnus lives to bug Freddie. "What's going on with you, my good man?"

"Hello Your Highness," Freddie greets Magnus and tepidly taps his palm to his before retrieving it rather quickly. He looks to me. "I hate to be a bother but you do have cocktails with your mother and father over at Drottningholm."

"Well I guess tell them I'm cancelling."

Freddie winces. "They were rather concerned, you see, since you've been having so many high fevers recently. They've noticed your absence this last week."

Of course they have. They notice everything now. "Tell them I'm not well yet."

He sighs and pinches the bridge of his nose. He hates lying to them. "Fine. I will do my best."

"Meanwhile," Magnus says, "here!" He throws a mask at Freddie who catches it with one hand. Jeez, I had no idea Freddie possessed ninja reflexes.

"What is this?" Freddie asks.

"You're coming with us!" Magnus announces.

Freddie looks at me. Worried.

"By order of the Crown Prince of Norway," Magnus says, deepening his voice into a bellow, "I command you to attend this masquerade ball with me, this American beauty, and your boss, His Royal Highness, Viktor of House Nordin."

Freddie just sighs. "Do I have to?"

"Yes," Magnus barks. He looks to me with raised brows. "Right?"

I shrug. "I guess."

I know it's Magnus's goal in life to get Freddie good and properly drunk, so perhaps this will finally be the night.

Either way, it's actually a rather brilliant idea on his behalf. I do want to take Maggie out, I do want to show her a good time and have a good time myself without being cooped up in this palace. I want us to have fun and a masquerade ball seems like a pretty good start.

"Okay Freddie," I say to him, reaching over and plucking his iPad out of his hands. "You're off the clock now."

He cocks a brow. "If I'm off the clock, *sir*, then this should mean I can retire to my room."

I quickly give him back the iPad. "Fine, you're back on the new clock and your job this evening is to accompany all of us to the party. You understand?"

He nods. He understands and he doesn't like it one bit.

At least he doesn't until we're getting ready to go to the party and are hanging out in the study, drinking. Freddie has two shots of aquavit and suddenly his face is red and he's laughing like crazy at his own jokes, half of which I don't even understand. By the time we actually leave in a limo to this party that's being held in a grand old building in the old town, Gamla Stan, we're all feeling pretty damn good.

"Shit!" Maggie cries out as soon as we exit the limo in

town, her heels sliding on the snow. I immediately reach for her before she bails on the slippery packed snow.

"You can't possibly walk in those," I tell her and scoop her up into my arms. "Looks like I'm carrying you."

"My prince," she says in her best fair maiden voice, lacing her fingers around my neck.

The winding narrow streets of Gamla Stan are hard enough to walk on when it's just cobblestone but packed in snow it's another story.

"Are you cold?" I ask her as I carry her. She's got a furry coat she found at a vintage store in the hipster area of Södermalm, covering up the long green silk gown that she bought the other day. I feel like Gatsby holding Daisy in his arms, if Gatsby wore a mask. Perhaps I also feel a bit like Batman.

"I'm fucking freezing," she says, but she's smiling broadly. "Does this place ever get warm?"

"Summers are delightful!" Freddie says to her, weaving up the narrow street in front of us. "It's hot and dry and the best place to go is Lake Mälaren where their Majesty's palace is. So many nudists on the beaches, it's incredible the amount of breasts you see!"

I glance over my shoulder at Magnus. "You got him drunk, now it's your responsibility to watch him."

Magnus just grins at me, looking absolutely sinister in his tux combined with that mask.

"I thought Swedes were used to nudity," Maggie says as we round the corner and see the building at the end of a square, a line of masked people waiting to get in, shivering in the cold.

"They are!" Magnus yells, running up from behind us and nearly slipping on a patch of ice. "But Freddie here has never seen a breast in real life."

"Very funny!" Freddie exclaims, awkwardly adjusting his

glasses over his mask. "I'll have you know that I do have a girlfriend."

This is news to me.

"Who?" I ask.

"Is this a real girlfriend or someone you met on the internet?" Magnus asks, elbowing him in the side. That nearly takes Freddie down and he has to lean against a building to keep his balance.

"People you meet on the internet are real," Freddie says, suddenly so serious.

I look over my shoulder to see how the security team is catching up. Surprisingly, none of them were overly annoyed to be wearing masks on tonight's detail. I suppose they would never grumble to me either but I think it's giving them something different to do for once.

The party is held by one of Stockholm's software developers and apparently he also has a rather kinky side because the moment we step inside, we notice all the rooms are quite dark and done up in red silk and there are a lot of half-naked people walking around. Freddie must be losing his mind at all the bare breasts.

Magnus and I separate as to not draw too much attention to ourselves since the two of us together are a pretty recognizable pair, even with masks on. The song "Two Princes" seems to play wherever we go.

I'm also sure there are a few people who know who I am just from the way I walk and hold myself but the real point of the masks is to obscure who Maggie is.

Even though you can't fully see her face, she looks absolutely beautiful. She's wearing this bright red lipstick and her hair is done up in curls that fall softly around her sparkling mask. The slinky green dress shows off every curve and gleams like an emerald next to her milky skin.

It's always been a fantasy of mine to have sex in a public

place with people in the next room, especially if everyone is dressed to the nines and there's a formality about it, but I won't risk it here. Though I'm pretty sure around every darkened corner people *are* having sex, we can't afford to get caught at this point.

So I just hold Maggie's hand and we cruise around the room, admiring people's masks, sipping champagne and stealing kisses. There's something so wonderfully freeing about all of this that it reminds me of being in Hollywood with her again. No one knew who we were, no one cared and it was just the two of us, getting to know each other's bodies, each other's hearts.

As we plunk ourselves down onto a loveseat in the corner of one room, and she nestles into my arm, I realize that this is just the tip of the iceberg. That down the line, I'll look back at this moment and realize that I didn't know her the way that I eventually will. That though we are both in love, there are many steps to love and this is just the first one. My love for her will only grow with time, evolve and deepen.

Or it won't.

That's something a fool in love would think.

The thought strikes me, an ice pick to my heart.

I've tried not to think about our future together, tried to focus on the here and now but I know, lingering just out of sight, like a floating dot at the corner of your vision that you can't quite focus on, that something will change. That these times, this honeymoon period where it's just us two in secret, that it will soon become very real and with that, a lot harder.

We will be tested. And I just hope we have what it takes to pass.

"Are you happy?" I ask her, my fingers pressed against her warm cheek, the dim chandelier lights reflecting in her dark eyes.

She blinks at me in surprise and smiles. "Of course I am. Are you happy?"

"More than I thought possible," I tell her, giving her a soft kiss.

"We have a problem," Magnus announces in a low voice, interrupting us.

I look up to see him standing in front of the love seat, his eyes looking wild beneath his mask.

"What?"

"Freddie's been unmasked. We have to go."

Maggie and I sit up straighter. "What happened?" I ask, now noticing that some people by the door to this room are looking at us and whispering.

"He was hitting on some guy's woman and they started fighting. His mask was ripped off. The guy immediately recognized him as Freddie Vereberg, your private secretary. We have to go. Now."

"Shit," I get to my feet, hauling Maggie up. "Where is he now?"

"Your people have him, don't worry. But the jig, as they say, is up."

I look around and then start pulling Maggie toward the door and down the stairs.

"Don't go that way," Magnus hisses, "that's where the paparazzi are waiting outside."

"Paparazzi?" Maggie squeaks.

"The bastards are quick." Magnus points down the hallway. "The back door is there, exits onto the royal palace of all places."

"The royal palace?" Maggie asks. "Another one? How many do you have?"

"Too many," I tell her as Magnus starts to walk away. A crowd starts to form around us. "Where are you going?" I yell after him.

He does a dramatic twirl and takes off his mask and everyone around us gasps, as if he's just been revealed as a hideous monster and not Prince Magnus of Norway. "I'm going out the front. I know your paparazzi would love to take a photo of a handsome prince for once." He gives me the thumbs up. "Good luck."

I watch as he strides off down the stairs and I squeeze Maggie's hand. "Let's go."

We hurry through the crowd and by now everyone has figured out who I am. A few are taking pictures, some are kneeling or bowing or doing a curtsey, all of which makes me feel extremely uncomfortable and quite weird given their attire.

Thanks to Magnus's distraction though when we burst through the backdoor we only see a bouncer and no one else. Beyond us is the stately façade of the royal palace.

"So who lives there?" Maggie asks as I look around for the best way to get out of here without being caught.

"That's where my office is," I tell her absently. "I thought you were already there, it's open to the public."

"Honestly I don't remember much of those first few days."

I pull out my phone and call Nick, telling him to come pick us up in front of the palace.

"There he is!"

I turn around to see a whole fucking swarm of paparazzi running through the snow toward us, flashbulbs going off.

"Fuck," I swear, looking at Maggie. I've never seen her look so scared and though I'm a fast runner, I'm not sure I can outrun them while carrying her and I know she can't run in those shoes. I don't even know where I would run to.

"Viktor," she whimpers, holding my arm tight, her eyes widening as they approach. "What are they going to do?"

Try and ruin me, I think as I look around, trying to figure out how to get out of this mess.

And then I spot it.

An escape.

I grab Maggie and pull her, slipping and sliding, over to an old Vespa that's parked along a row of bikes covered in inches of snow. I dust the snow off and then pick her up by the waist, placing her on the back of the seat.

"What are you doing?" she cries out. "This isn't yours is it?"

"I'm borrowing it," I tell her, sitting in front of her, hands on the handlebars. "The owner will get it back tomorrow."

"You don't have the keys!"

"Vintage Vespas don't have keys," I tell her and look over my shoulder to see the paps approaching. Shit. I toggle the ignition and after a few sputters the old Vespa screams to life.

"Hang on!" I yell at Maggie and she wraps her arms around me as the snow tires spin and spin before they find traction. We go off with a jolt.

"Ahhhh!" she yells into the wind as the Vespa churns through the snow until it finds a smoother path down on the main street. I weave it in and out of traffic, glad we don't have far to go before we're back at the house.

"I didn't even think you could drive these in the snow," she says, her arms gripping me tighter as we narrowly avoid a snowbank.

"Swedes can drive anything in the snow," I yell over my shoulder.

"And apparently steal Vespas while wearing tuxedos," she yells back. "I guess you think you're James Bond now."

"Well, I'm not Gregory Peck," I fire back. "Come on, let's get you home."

She presses her cheek between my shoulder blades and we leave the chaos behind.

Chaos that I'm sure will catch up to us in the morning.

CHAPTER TWENTY-TWO

MAGGIE

"Excuse me, do you speak English?"

I turn my head to see a Japanese couple with their cameras out, holding them toward me like an offering.

"Yes I do," I tell them. "Would you like your picture taken?"

"Oh yes, please. Thank you," they say, handing me the camera and posing in front of the royal palace. I snap a few pictures and they go on their way, shivering as more snow starts to fall.

It's hard to believe that it was just the other night that Viktor and I were here at the masquerade party and escaping on the Vespa. It reminded me that even though I came to *Det Kungliga Slottet* (the royal palace) right after I arrived in Stockholm (it's one of the major sights in the city) the jet lag seemed to have erased it from my memory. So here I am again, peering at the swords and crown jewels down in what can only be described as a dungeon, then traipsing the "royal apartments" as part of an audio tour.

A lot has happened since that night.

For one, we woke up the next morning to see Magnus,

Viktor and I on the front page of the tabloids and the newspapers. All wearing masks, of course

Some of them reported on the Vespa ride (it was returned to the owner), some reported on the opulent party (calling it an orgy, which is a bit of a reach), some wrote about the fist fight that Freddie got into. That part was true. Poor Freddie still has a black eye.

Everyone speculated on who I was. All of them wrote about the "mystery girl that finally captured Prince Viktor's heart" and now it seems the whole country is scrambling to figure out who I am.

There were a few interviews done with people who were at the masquerade party and they mentioned that "the Prince and her seemed to be very cozy" and "he couldn't keep his hands off her, it was obvious that he was smitten" (I liked that one the best) and "I don't know where she was from but she wasn't Swedish."

I guess in some ways we got lucky but in other ways it's really fucked shit up. The paps are out on full force and have taken to hanging out by the main gates, which is why I've spent the day braving the cold and wandering around Gamla Stan and the Photography Museum, trying to keep myself occupied. I feel like a prisoner if I stay in the palace. I'm just lucky that Nick is able to sneak me out and lose anyone that starts to tail us. His training definitely comes in handy.

And now that the public knows that Viktor has someone serious, his parents are finally aware of me.

That's the scariest part. Viktor went over there for dinner last night (while I ate in the kitchen with Bodi as he explained Swedish soap operas to me) and didn't come home until late. He said it went fine and his parents weren't upset but I know him well enough by now and I could tell *he* was upset.

I also know that since they know the truth about me,

about where I come from, all my baggage, that I'm a commoner to the extreme, that they can't be too happy about it.

I guess I'll find out all that stuff in person tonight.

I'm supposed to meet them.

The King and Queen of Sweden.

At a private dinner party they're holding at their palace for King Aksel of Denmark, who is visiting.

I've been trying not to think about it because the more I think about it, the more nervous I get. I mean I've gone from being sequestered in the house to having to meet a queen and two fucking kings. All at once. I mean, I know meeting your boyfriend's parents is nerve-wracking for anyone but in this case, I feel like I need to be drowning in aquavit just to get through it.

"Don't be so nervous," he says to me later that evening as we're getting ready. "You'll be fine. They will love you like I do."

I give him a look.

"Well," he corrects himself, "maybe not *exactly* like I do."

"You're nervous too, admit it."

He raises his chin and stares down at me. "I will do no such thing."

I sigh and turn to stare at myself in the mirror. I'm wearing the same long green satin dress that I wore to the masquerade party because I don't have anything else that's nice enough. I've put my hair up high and let a few strands of hair frame my face. I'm wearing peachy lipstick that I know drives Viktor wild and soft colors elsewhere. I'm trying for an elegant and classy lady, and though I know I'm anything but, perhaps I can fool his parents.

Oh, who am I kidding? I still probably have *White Trash* written across my forehead. If anyone can sniff that out it's probably a King and Queen.

"So tell me about King Aksel," I tell Viktor as we sit in the back of the car, Nick at the wheel. My leg is bouncing so much that Viktor has to place his hand on it and hold me down. "Is he nice? I looked him up over the summer, he seems kind of young to be a king."

Viktor straightens his tie, peering at himself in the rear-view mirror. "King Aksel is a good guy. A bit reserved, maybe comes across as cold to most people. The Danish press seem terrified of him and loves taking photos of him looking harsh. But I swear, once you get to know him he has a wicked sense of humor. And yes, he's pretty young. I believe he's having a big fortieth birthday bash this year that…" he trails off. "Well anyway, I will be attending."

"Is there a queen? I read that he has daughters."

"There was a queen," he says. "She died last year."

"Oh. Shit. I better not bring that up."

"No. It was a shame too, she was beautiful, perfect. Denmark's answer to Princess Di. Now Aksel has these two daughters, and, well I guess you two might have more in common than I thought."

That makes me feel a little bit better about this king although I'm not going to start up a conversation with him like "I heard you lost your wife, I lost my parents, let's talk about how hard it is to raise kids on your own."

It's not long before the car is pulling up through the gates of Drottningholm Palace and even though it's dark out and a layer of snow is blanketing the landscape, there's no mistaking the in-your-face majesty of the palace.

It's *huge*.

"Wow," I say through a gasp as the car drives around a large statue, "This place is like…the palace of all palaces." I look at Viktor with my brows raised. "And you're going to live here one day?"

"We'll see," he says after a moment and I have no idea

what that means. Why wouldn't he want to live here? The place is so grand and opulent, lit up by dozens of lights against the night sky. Even though I'd never been to Versailles in France, that's what it reminds me of. I tell Viktor this.

"Well, Swedish nobility originated in France," he says. "This palace itself was built in the sixteenth century. It's a UNESCO heritage site. Gorgeous, but not very homey, in my opinion."

"But you grew up here. I can't imagine what that would have been like."

He shrugs. "You know what you know."

It's truly something and honestly has me so awed that for a minute there I forget to be nervous.

That is until I step in through the front doors.

Gold ceilings, massive chandeliers, and columns made of quartz, busts and statues adorning the walls.

I *so* don't belong here.

And in the middle of it all are what seem to be a group of staff. Now here are the butlers and maids and cooks you think about in all those fairy tales and they're all here, hands behind their backs and waiting to attend to us.

One takes my coat, another hands me a glass of champagne and then a tall thin man in a suit with slicked back blonde hair and an iron jaw is whisking Viktor and I over to another opulent room that puts the ones at our palace to shame. I didn't even think that you could compare palaces and have one be better than another but it turns out you can.

"This place is incredible," I whisper to Viktor.

He eyes my champagne glass. Which is suddenly empty. "Thirsty?"

Nervous as fuck, I mouth to him.

"They'll be with you shortly," the blonde guy says to

THE SWEDISH PRINCE

Viktor, seeming to give me a look of disdain before he strides off.

"What's with Dolf over there?" I joke.

"How did you know his name was Dolf?"

I blink at him and laugh. "Are you serious? His name is Dolf? I was making a joke. You know because he looks like that actor, Dolf Lundgren? You know, The Punisher and He-Man and --"

"Dolf Lundgren is a national hero," he says, almost defensively.

Dead serious.

"Is he Swedish?" I ask.

"Who, the actor or my father's private secretary?"

I'm going to assume they're both Swedish. "Never mind."

"His real name is Hans, by the way," Viktor says under his breath just as the doors open and two butlers come in, standing to the side of the doors.

One of the butlers announces something in Swedish.

Oh shit. This got real.

The King and Queen of Sweden step inside the room.

Both Viktor and I immediately get to our feet and I realize he hasn't taught me any of the royal protocol, so I'm trying to do my best impression of a curtsey.

They both walk, no, *glide* into the room and stop right in front of us.

I glance up and they're staring down at me with tight smiles.

Shit. Maybe I'm not supposed to curtsey. Or maybe it just looks like I have a bad back.

"*Mamma, pappa,*" Viktor says before he switches to English. "This is Miss Maggie McPherson."

I straighten up and give them my brightest smile, the one that says, *I'm sweet and normal I swear, please don't hate me.*

"How do you do?" I say and then offer my hand.

They both look down at my hand and then over to Viktor, nonplussed.

In the agonizingly awkward seconds that my hand is just out there waiting, I take a good look at them. I've seen pictures of course, but in person they're just that much more intimidating. More good-looking too. Viktor's father has thick dark hair peppered with gray and a tall, foreboding stature. His mother has delicate features, high cheekbones, a stylish blonde bob that set off her glacial blue eyes. For some reason I expected both to be in tuxedos and gowns but they're both in modest suits, hers pink, his a dark green.

Then, for a second, I'm thinking maybe they don't speak English and they don't know what he's saying or how to talk to me.

Finally, after an exchange of looks between the three of them, his mother—the fucking queen—extends her hand to mine and gives it a firm shake. "So nice to meet you," she says.

"Likewise," I tell her. "Your Majesty," I add quickly.

The king shakes my hand after. "Viktor said you were beautiful," he says. "I see that he is right."

My smile gets shaky. See, that wasn't so bad. The king thinks I'm beautiful and the queen says it was nice to meet me. That could have been worse.

"Thank you," I tell him. "Your Grace."

He looks at Viktor and back to me. "We don't really use that term here in Sweden."

"Oh I'm so sorry!" I exclaim.

"Not a problem," he says to me though he's giving Viktor a look like who is this crazy girl and why haven't you been teaching her anything proper?

I'm about to open my mouth and make a remark about no cow on the ice but I decide from now on I better just shut up.

I tend to talk and babble when I'm nervous and this is no exception.

"Shall we have a drink before the guests arrive?" his mother says and Viktor leads me to the end of the ginormous room where a few couches and love seats are gathered around what looks to be a solid gold coffee table.

A butler comes in and stares at me expectantly.

"What will you have, dear?" the queen asks.

"What are you having?" I ask.

"Just coffee," she says to the butler.

Shit. I guess that means I'm having coffee.

"Maggie will have a glass of champagne," Viktor says, coming to my rescue. "I'll have a scotch."

"Make that two," his father says as the butler replies something that must be the equivalent of "very good" in Swedish and goes to the lavish bar cart in the corner which happens to have an espresso machine.

"So," the queen says as she's handed her coffee. "Viktor tells me you're a journalism student."

"*Was* a journalism student," I tell her. "I studied at NYU."

"That's a very good school," Viktor's father comments. "Do you see yourself pursuing a job in that field at some point? Viktor tells me you're currently a...housekeeper?"

I smile stiffly. "*Was* a housekeeper." I swear Viktor kicks me on purpose. "I quit my job to come here."

"Oh," his mother says then takes a sip of her coffee. "I see."

This isn't going well.

The butler hands me my champagne and I immediately busy myself by drinking it.

Viktor puts a hand on my knee and squeezes it. "I'm sure Maggie will be going back to journalism very soon. She's a natural reporter and a gifted writer. In fact, I think her interview skills are hard to duplicate. Did you know that within five minutes, she was getting all the details of Nick's personal life?"

"No kidding," his father says, seeming impressed.

"Yes, he admitted that his favorite musician at the moment is Harry Styles. Anyway, she has a promising career ahead of her."

I'm glad that Viktor is sticking up for me like this, even though it's not exactly true. I haven't really thought much about journalism lately, especially after I didn't end up writing the article about him. Maybe I'm too preoccupied, maybe I've just moved on. They say whatever you end up studying rarely becomes your career.

I *am* a little annoyed that Viktor is talking for me though. It's a bad habit of his, along with ordering for me and the like. I know he can be bossy and dominant sometimes and I don't even think he realizes it. In this case, though, it's best to let him keep talking. He knows how to work his parents.

After that though, the small talk changes from me to King Aksel, and then some other people I don't know from other countries and I end up feeling pretty excluded and rather bored. I just keep drinking my champagne and wishing we could go back home.

Then King Aksel arrives and we're all hustled out into the hall and everything gets very formal.

I stand beside Viktor, waiting to greet him.

King Aksel is tall and handsome with a cutting jaw sprinkled with stubble, his hair a sandy brown. His eyes are hard and squinty and this gem-like dark blue and he seems to be perpetually frowning. He's almost too perfect except for his nose which is crooked in places and seems to have been broken a few times. I wonder what the story is there.

I'm introduced to King Aksel and I do my best not to fuck it up. I almost do by offering my hand again but before I can move it, Viktor grabs it and holds it to my side with an iron grip. That's when I realize that perhaps you aren't supposed to offer your hand first to royalty.

So I wait for King Aksel to offer his hand first and I barely say anything else other than "Your Majesty" followed by a short curtsey.

This seems to satisfy him but I can't be sure. His eyes flutter with a lot of dark emotions I can't read into and his grip on my hand is crushing. What is it with these Nordic royals and their strong hands?

I'm then introduced to the entourage that follows him in, his sister Princess Stella and her family, plus head secretaries and a few dignitaries and maybe the entire cast of Hamlet.

The dinner is upstairs in what I'm sure is one of many dining rooms and as I climb the stairs with Viktor, hanging onto his arm while making sure I don't step on my dress, I'm accosted with the gorgeous sounds of classical music which makes everything seem extra fairy-tale like and royal.

When I get to the second floor I'm shocked to find a man sitting at a grand piano in the hall and playing the music live.

The queen turns to me and says, "Are you a fan of classical music?"

"Yes!" I exclaim. I mean, I like it a lot. I used to listen to it when I studied. "And I adore Chopin's Waltz," I add, proud that I remembered the name of the piece.

She flinches and lets out a disbelieving laugh. "Chopping?" she repeats.

I nod. "Yes. Chopin."

Viktor groans from beside me.

The queen shakes her head, biting back a smile. "It's not chopping, dear. It's French. It's pronounced *Chopin*."

Like show-pan?

Oh. My. God.

My cheeks go bright red.

The queen exchanges a humorous look with Viktor and then walks ahead.

I glance up at him, ready to crawl into a hole and die. How American must I have just sounded? Chopping? Like choppin' wood? Jesus.

Viktor is trying not to laugh but he fails.

"You jerk," I whisper. "That was so embarrassing!"

"Was? I think it still is."

I punch him on the arm, much to the amusement of some of the other guests as we make our way into the dining room. Whatever, at this point I've lost all credibility. I'm the uncouth American to everyone, watch me blunder my way through this next portion of the night.

But even though dinner looked to be an intimidating affair with this long fancy table and waiters hovering around and five courses and a million forks and knives, none of which I know how to use either, the whole event isn't too bad. It helps that no one really pays me any attention so they just talk about everyone and everything else.

By the time the deserts come out though, people start retiring to different sections of the room and both the king and queen sequester Viktor, leading him out of the room and elsewhere.

Viktor glances at me over his shoulder with a look that tells me not to worry, he'll be back, and then I'm left alone with all these people I don't know.

Fuck. This is the worst part of parties and being with royalty who come from completely different lives than I do, let alone, most people, I just want to shrink in the corner.

But I try making small talk with Princess Stella who is probably in her early thirties and when that doesn't really go anywhere, I start making conversation with her daughter Anya. She might only be six but she's the best talker out of all of them, and she speaks fluent English as well. We get in a discussion about Katy Perry and once again I'm grateful for pop stars, the universal language.

Finally, once the drinks start getting passed around and Viktor still hasn't come back yet, I get up to go and find the bathroom and end up wandering down an endless hallway. Shit, I hope I don't get lost and then end up walking into some forbidden room or something like that. I bet they have a dungeon downstairs that they would gladly stick me in.

"Maggie," I hear Viktor whisper from behind me.

I turn to see him creeping toward me with his finger to his mouth, telling me to be quiet. The fact that he's in a suit and doing this along the ornate palace hallways reminds me of a movie I can't quite place.

"Where are your parents?" I ask him in a hush.

"They're coming," he says.

"Where did you go?"

"They wanted to have a talk with me."

I stare at him. "Yeah, and? What did you talk about?"

"Many things. Nothing to worry about." He jerks his head back toward the dining room. "How is it in there? Has Aksel softened up at all?"

"A bit," I tell him. "Everyone is getting into the brandy and aquavit now. I was just going to freshen up my lipstick. Normally I would whip it out and do it right there but it feels so rude in front of the King of Denmark."

Viktor smirks. "It's so easy to take that sentence the wrong way. Come on." He takes my arm and strides down the hallway, shoulders back, taking long, wide steps, like he's the king of everything. Even though he seems to have hesitations about this place, it certainly suits him.

We walk past several doors and it isn't until he pokes his head in a library and ushers me inside that I clue in to what's going on. He looks back and forth down the hall to make sure no one saw us, then shuts the doors gently.

"What are you doing?" I ask.

"Stealing you away from the party," he says, grabbing me by the silky waist of my green dress and turning me so my back is pressed up against a row of books. "Taking you for myself."

"Sounds selfish," I tease.

"Sounds like the truth," he says. He brushes the loose strands of my hair behind my ears. "I hate having to share you with people. That my parents and other monarchs want a piece, have an opinion. I hate that I can't keep you for myself. I hate that soon, whatever private and precious thing we have will be gone."

"What do you mean?"

"I mean, we can't stay a secret forever, Maggie. People will find out who you are. And I don't want the world to cheapen what we have."

"Cheapen?" I repeat. "Because they'll find out I'm a commoner, is that right? No wait, I'm worse than a commoner. I clean commoner's hotel rooms and live in small-town America, taking care of five kids."

"Maggie," he whispers to me, picking up my hand and kissing my knuckles, his eyes sinking deep into mine. "Don't say such things. You know that it's not true, that you're not cheap. None of that matters. What matters is that I'm public property and I don't want you to be public property too."

I guess I was a bit defensive. I give him a soft smile. "Sorry. I guess I always think the worst."

"Don't think the worst," he tells me. Winks. "Especially when I'm about to give you my best."

I let out a laugh that turns into a gasp as he grabs my hips and hoists me up so that I'm balanced on the edge of a book shelf, my hands gripping the sides to keep me steady. He tugs my dress up so it's gathered around my waist, then crouches down, his head between my legs, my underwear pushed to the side.

I barely have time to compose myself, to prepare, to say "hey, are you sure we should be doing this here?" I don't get to say any of that because he's at me like he's starving, his fingers sliding me apart, his tongue and mouth so soft and warm. I feel every sensation like a bullet, each stroke a hit, radiating outward.

And just like that, any hesitation I had about him screwing me in the palace library melts away. His touch always brings what I feel for him to the forefront. It's how he soothes me, how he tells me that what we have is good and strong and that we're meant for each other.

I want so much from him. But among his satisfied groans and his hungry sounds, I know he just wants to devour me. He wants me to have as much pleasure as he can bring me, because he isn't sure that he's doing enough, making me feel enough. He doesn't want to share me with the world.

But he won't.

I'm all his, always his.

I groan, loudly, and my fingers curl around the edges of the shelf. I'm not sure if this room has cameras and I don't think it has a lock, so what we're doing could get us in big trouble. It's not secret in here that we're together but even so…

My thoughts melt away again, becoming less and less as he licks me out.

His mouth is ruthless. He's tireless. His tongue plunges deep inside me before licking up my clit and sucking me into his mouth. I nearly scream, my body at the height of all awareness, on the verge of overload.

He reaches down with one hand, and two long, beautiful fingers thrust deep inside, curling against me. The heat builds deeper, and my nerves are a million champagne bottles about to burst. It's the slow, twisting anticipation that makes my mouth drop open and my neck arch back until my head meets the books on the shelves.

God, I'm not sure how much longer I can last and Viktor's just gotten started. My legs clench around his face, driving his lips and tongue and fingers against me, inside me, harder, deeper, and he responds by acting as if I'm all he needs to live his life, like he'd die without me.

With impatient hands, he pulls me toward him, his tongue hard and urgent, and the world begins to move, to swing like a pendulum and we're both on it for the ride.

I want to feel him, all of him. My hips rock into him hard. He drags his tongue back over my clit, flicking it so fast, back and forth, over and over, and I can't breathe anymore.

He moans against me, the vibrations shattering my resolve.

And then I let go.

I'm swirling into space, coming into his mouth, nearly falling off the edge of the shelf. His hands grip my waist, holding me up, while he finishes me up with the hard suck of his lips, ripping a cry out of my throat.

I'm loud. I know I am. And at this blissful moment I don't mind if someone in the hallway knows, overhears my cries, because this man is incredible and the whole world should know it.

When my orgasm subsides against his lips, he straightens up, staring at me with feverish eyes. His eyes that say he knows my body better than anyone, better than myself, and he'll never stop proving it.

Instinctively, I grab his head and kiss him, long and soft, the taste of me on his tongue reinvigorating me.

He moans into my mouth, and it's a sound straight from his gut, making my blood run even hotter. "You taste like a peach," he whispers, his lips moving to my neck. "Now you know just how good."

I undo his belt and unzip his pants, fumbling for his cock, grasping his stiff length in my palm, so hot and pulsing against my skin. He moves forward and I guide him in, so wet and ready for him that he slides in like silk, our bodies accustomed to each other with a beautiful kind of ease.

I wrap my legs around his waist, the dress flowing around us, my heels digging into his firm ass as he starts rocking into me, each slow, slick glide igniting my nerves once again.

I whimper as we find our rhythm, like we always find our rhythm. My body aches from wanting him so intensely, and without saying anything, his body responds, always giving me more than I need.

Always more, never less.

"Maggie," he groans against me, breathless, as a bead of sweat falls off his brow and onto my collarbone. He thrusts in harder and deeper, and it feels like the air is being pushed out of my lungs and I'm clinging to his body as his pace quickens.

I press my nails into his back, hanging on for the ride. Our skin slaps together in a violent, thick sound that echoes off the bookshelves. Each push is long and hard, and he grunts with effort until his cock hits me in just the perfect place.

I come hard.

His hips pound against me, brutal, punishing, and he's gone in a flurry of groans, my name whispered over and over as he claws at my hips, releasing every inch of himself inside me, shooting as far and as deep as he can go.

When we've both caught our breath, when our hearts have slowed their schizophrenic pace, he pulls out of me and he grabs my waist, lowering me to the hardwood floor, my ass completely numb.

"Well," I say after a few moments, reaching up and straightening his tie. I'm a bit unsteady on my feet, my legs feeling heavy, my head full of stars and champagne. "Wasn't that a royal treat?"

"I think we both needed that tonight. Just so we can get through the rest of this evening." He grins at me and grabs my hand, squeezing it. "Let's go join the party."

"I think they'll know what we were doing," I tell him as we open the doors and look out into the hall. Empty.

"Let them think what they want," he says.

Though I have a feeling he might regret saying that.

CHAPTER TWENTY-THREE

VIKTOR

"Viktor, we need to talk."

The four scariest words on the planet.

"So this isn't really about skiing, is it?" I ask my father.

The two of us are on cross-country skis on his palace property. My father is hell-bent on staying in shape since his father and grandfather both were victims of heart disease so in the winters he skis around the grounds, doing laps for hours.

Today it's blisteringly bright and sunny and not as cold as it has been, so skiing made a lot of sense when he invited me. I was going to ask if Maggie could come but I also know that if he wanted Maggie to come, he would have invited her. That's the way my father is. Plus, I have a feeling that Maggie has never been on skis a day in her life.

So while I'm here with my father, she's helping Bodi set up the palace for her brothers and sisters. They arrive tomorrow and she's more than excited to finally see them. I'm excited too, it will be nice to have them around bringing a little life into the cold palace.

"It's good to get fresh air, clear your head," my father says, taking a deep breath through his nose, his chest swelling. He looks to me. "You know, I want to apologize for the other day. At Aksel's dinner party."

I wasn't sure if he would, so to have him do it now, even days later, is a relief. While Maggie stayed talking to the guests after dinner, I was taken aside by my parents and giving a lecture like you wouldn't believe.

All about Maggie, of course.

About how common she is.

About how unsuited for the role of princess she is.

About how unsuited for me she is.

My mother brought up countless duchesses and countesses and ladies and whatnot that I could date instead. All Swedes or French or even German. European ladies of refinement.

My father said that Maggie was complicating my job as heir apparent since I'd already cancelled so many appearances and meetings because of her.

They went on and on and on.

I argued back.

I did my best to prove my points.

Love being the biggest one.

But even though they are my parents and I've spent my life arguing, they are so good at turning things around on you and reminding you of their power. You know, as the King and Queen.

Needless to say it all ended on a sour note. My mother softened a little in her stance toward Maggie but my father was rather rude and pig-headed about it. I ended up leaving the conversation and going back to find Maggie. Dragged her into my parents library and had my way with her, as a way to remind her, remind myself, that she's mine and no one can take that away.

I don't say anything, just keep looking at my father. In

this harsh light of winter, he looks older than I've ever seen him and for the first time I realize how much Alex's death must have ruined him. It makes my heart heavy for the first time in a while. The first time since Maggie has been here.

"I was a little harsh on Miss McPherson and I realize that she does mean a great deal to you. We still don't approve, nor do we really understand your desire to be with her, other than her being a pretty face, perhaps a little exotic to us Swedes." He pauses. "But because she means a lot to you and because we have a monarchy to protect, I got some disturbing information this morning."

My lungs ice over. "What?"

"As you know we have many friends in the press. Upstanding journalists and the like. And we've been using them to crack down on unfair reports and speculations at other publications, especially with what happened with Alex's death. So many headlines were cruel and just so damn unfair." His voice breaks at the end there and he trails off, looking away. I'm not the type to hug my father and I'm not sure what to do. Finally he looks back, this time to the palace in the distance, regaining his composure.

"This morning we got word that one of the tabloids has discovered Maggie's identity."

"What?" I exclaim. "Who? How?"

He shrugs, frowning. "I don't know," he says gruffly. "No doubt someone in King Aksel's group. I don't even know who half those people were or why they came but anyway. Must have been one of them. Maybe someone in our own house." He eyes me. "Maybe someone in yours. Whoever it is got a lot of money in exchange for the information. But the tabloid is going to run it in the morning, with the full story on Maggie."

I'm having trouble swallowing, there's so much anger coursing through me. "Do they have pictures?"

"I don't know. But they know who she is, I'm sure they can pull one from her university if they wish."

"Fuck," I say, making a fist, wishing we were closer to the pines so I could start punching them until my knuckles bleed.

"It's going to be tough for you," he says. "And for her."

"And her family," I tell him. "Her brothers and sisters are arriving tomorrow on a SAS flight from LA. If Maggie's picture goes in the paper, people will know who she is. They'll hound her and them. Some fucking welcome. Some fucking trip."

My father puts his hand on my shoulder and gives it a squeeze. "That's why you have to call it off, my son. Do it for her. She doesn't deserve to be put through the media storm that's to come and her siblings don't either. To think otherwise is to be selfish Viktor, and I didn't raise you to be selfish."

You barely raised me at all, I think bitterly. But he has a point. A horrible point.

"What do I do?" I ask him. "About the paper. About all that."

"There isn't much you can do."

"Can't you threaten to stop them?"

"We can only do that if they are defaming her, or us of course, and if intrusive photos are taken, photos that breach privacy laws. Until then, though, we have no power."

"You are the king!" I practically yell.

He gives me a dry smirk. "Yes. I am the king. And we've been fighting the free press for a long time. You should be grateful we aren't in England. We have it good compared to them."

"When I'm king, I'm changing all the laws."

He lets out a sharp laugh. "Oh my boy. When you are king, I won't have to worry about any of this anymore." He sighs noisily. "Let's head back now, shall we? The cook has a wonderful mushroom soup on the stove."

We ski back and I have the soup. My father has to go off to attend to some business as usual so it's just me in the big kitchen and all the while I'm trying to think how to break the news to Maggie and how we can deal with the inevitable. We very well knew that this would eventually happen, that the secret world we built between us would be exposed to the public. I am a prince which means that I serve the country and the people and that sometimes that comes at the cost of relationships, of peace, of privacy.

Sometimes, as with Alex, it comes at the cost of lives.

The other night though, when Maggie asked me what my parents had talked to me about, I lied and said it was nothing to worry about. I didn't tell her their concerns, nor what they said. For all she knows, they like her. In fact, every time she brings up her pronunciation of Chopin (which I thought was adorable) or the fact that she offered her hand to my parents first, I tell her that it only endeared her to them.

That was a lie, of course.

And now I think I have to lie again.

By the time Nick takes me back to the palace I take one look up at the building and see all the lights on, making the place look so warm against the snow, I know what I have to do. It glows because Maggie is happy. She's my warm glowing candle in the cold dark night.

I decide to keep my father's information to myself.

"How was skiing?" she says to me as soon as I walk in the door, Bodi trailing behind her. She stands on her tip toes to place a kiss on my cheek, her own cheeks rosy.

"It was nice," I tell her, handing Bodi my coat. "Cold, but nice. You look all warm. The place looks so inviting and *liveable* with all the lights on."

"I've had so much fun getting everyone's room's ready,"

she says, her eyes shining. "I've been buying so many souvenirs lately that I finally have a place to put them. Everyone gets a Viktor moose, except for Pike of course. He just gets a bottle of aquavit."

"I picked out a good one for beginners," Bodi says, looking rather proud that he's been a part of this.

Looking at Maggie's smile, the joy that's coming out of her, I realize I can't do anything to dampen it.

"Well, show me what you've done," I tell her, offering her my arm. She leads me upstairs.

THE NEXT MORNING, I get up an hour before Maggie usually does and slip quietly out of bed. I make my way downstairs to the kitchen and pull out my phone as I sip a cup of coffee.

I nearly spill it on myself, my hand is shaking so hard.

There it is on the cover of Sweden's *Hänt Extra*.

A picture of Maggie with a bottle of wine in her hand, raised in the air, tits hanging out of her shirt. Her hair is a bit lighter and it's obviously taken in New York and probably yanked from her Facebook page.

The headline says "The Secret is Out! Prince Viktor Has Fallen in Love with an American Party Girl" and the little headlines underneath say "Her Tragic Past" and "The King and Queen Disapprove" with little cut-outs of my parents' heads looking distraught.

It won't let me scroll through the article and read it unless

I buy a subscription and like hell I'm going to support this vile piece of shit journalism. But I have to know what it says about her, if it says anything about the kids.

I call for Nick who appears dressed and ready to go in a few minutes.

"Listen," I tell him. "Something has happened. Are you able to go to the nearest store and get me a copy of this?" I show him the screen.

His eyes widen. "Of course." Then he shakes his head. "We tried so hard to be careful, sir."

"I know you did, Nick, this isn't your fault. I knew this would happen sooner or later, I just didn't want it to happen with the kids arriving today and everything."

He nods. "Should we make extra precautions in case there is a mob at the airport?"

"Maybe have a decoy car ahead of us, just in case. It can't hurt." I pause. "But please, keep it to yourself for now. Maggie doesn't know."

"She doesn't know? Pardon me sir, but you have to tell her. She has to know exactly what she's getting into. It could be dangerous otherwise."

I sigh, running my hands down my face. "I know. I know. Okay. I'll go tell her now."

"Good," he says. "I'll get the paper."

He takes off and I gather up the courage to wake up Maggie with bad news. I pour her a cup of coffee and cream to soften the blow, then grab a small bottle of vodka from the cupboard, just in case she needs it softened a little bit more.

But by the time I open the door to the bedroom, she's already awake

She's sitting up in bed, staring at her phone.

She looks up at me and I know she knows. Her face is drawn and pale, her eyes red, her expression contorted.

"What is this?" she whispers. "Did you see this?"

I sigh and slowly walk toward her with the coffee, not sure how to handle this.

"I made you coffee," I say.

"Did you see this!?" Her words roar out of her.

I swallow my heart. I nod. "I just did this morning."

"How did this happen? How?"

"There was a snitch at the dinner party, that's our best guess."

"Our? Who is *our*?"

This is going to hurt.

"That's what my father told me."

Her eyes blaze. "When did he tell you?" she says through gritted teeth.

"Yesterday."

Boom. The realization explodes in her eyes.

"You knew about this since yesterday? Why the fuck didn't you tell me?"

I shake my head. "I don't know, I don't know. I guess I wanted… I saw how happy you were and—"

"Oh fuck my happiness!" she yells. "Did you read this thing!?"

"Did you? I just sent Nick out to get a copy."

"Oh fuck, he knows now too? I guess the whole world does. I used Google translate on the cover so I know exactly the kind of shit that's going to be inside there, and my god, Viktor, the picture! I was at a dorm party! This makes me look like the biggest piece of trash!"

"It's going to be okay," I say, putting down the coffee by her.

"It's going to be okay?" she repeats bitterly. "Fuck that! And fuck your coffee!" She hits the cup and it goes flying across the room where it smashes on the hardwood floors. "That's just you trying to butter me up, isn't it? Isn't it?"

I've never seen Maggie like this before. Uncontrollable and angry as hell. I guess anyone would be in this situation.

I take in a deep, steadying breath and ignore the shattered porcelain. "I came up here to tell you. To prepare you."

"Oh god." She puts her head in her hands, her dark hair falling over her face. "Oh god," she mumbles. "All of my life is for the world to see now. They know. They know."

"It's…"

"Don't you dare tell me it's going to be okay," she says, her head snapping up. "You have no idea what this feels like."

I balk at that. "I have some idea," I tell her sharply. "I grew up in this role, maybe not as it is now, but I saw firsthand what it did to my brother. I know the dangers, okay."

"Then how come you can tell me that it's going to be all right," she cries out, throwing out her arm.

"Because I choose to believe that!" I yell at her. "I knew this was going to be hard on you, hard on them, hard on us, but I chose to believe that it was worth it. I chose to believe that we would be able to deal with it. And I'm choosing now to think that this is a test that we'll pass and that it's going to be all right."

"A test. This isn't a test. This is just…it's just…" she trails off and looks away at the broken coffee cup. "Fuck. How am I going to deal with this? I hate that the world knows everything about me now. I hate it. It's so gross, it's icky, I'm…ashamed."

"Maggie, please," I say softly, her words are breaking my heart. I come over to the bed and wrap my arms around her. "I made a mistake and I should have told you. For what it's worth, my father gave me the information to protect us and I know he would stop them if he could but he can't. You're fair game and it's unfortunate but it's the reality now. Maybe they'll grow bored of you eventually but for now, you're new and exciting and sadly, I've been such a bachelor all these years that I think they're just excited that I've finally found someone to love."

She snorts into my arms and I can't tell if she's laughing or crying.

I place my hand on the back of her hair and hold her tight. "We knew this wouldn't be easy but we're just going to have to take each day as it comes and remember why you're here. And if there is any silver lining here, it's that now the worst part is over."

"Do you really believe that?" she mumbles.

"I know that I was expecting this day. And yes, maybe this matched my expectations because, I know, it's horrible, but at least the waiting is over. The suspense. You know?"

"So diplomatic," she says after a few beats. "Spoken like a true prince."

I sigh and pull back enough to cup her face in my hands. "We're going to be okay because we're two pretty amazing people if I do say so myself. We can do this. You have to believe me and you have to try."

She swallows hard, wincing. "I hate that they know everything, Viktor," she whispers. "Everything I've tried to hide."

"Everything you've had no reason to hide. Being poor isn't a crime. Having a big family in a small town isn't a crime. Having a blue-collar job isn't a crime. The only crime here is that your parents were murdered but that's a tragedy that you've all faced head on and come out stronger for it. There is absolutely nothing for you to be ashamed of in the life that you have lived. You should be proud. I'm proud. I'm terribly proud of you, Maggie."

Now tears spill out of her eyes and onto my hands. I kiss the sweet salt of her tears and then place a kiss on her forehead. "Maybe this is what it takes for you to believe it but whatever truth they're saying is a truth you need to own," I murmur against her skin. "You're Maggie Mayhem McPherson and the world isn't going to forget you."

At that she laughs, a soft, fluttery little laugh and I know she's pulling in her reserves and trying to be strong.

"I'm so sorry," she whispers.

"For what?"

She looks over at the coffee. "For breaking that. I bet it was a priceless heirloom from the 1600s or something."

"I think it's just IKEA."

She nods. Smiles. "Of course it is."

"Now I know that this isn't the best start to the day but let's not forget the big picture here. The fact that Pike, April, Rosemary, Thyme and Callum are in the air right now, on their way here. That's something worth concentrating our energy on."

She nods and I can see her wrestling with wanting to be excited and wanting to fret over the evil tabloids. "Is it going to be safe to get them?"

"I think so," I say. "We'll have a decoy limo just in case but this story just broke. It will take a few days and a few more tabloids and newspapers, unfortunately, before people start recognizing you. If we're lucky, they might not even recognize the kids at all."

Of course it was impossible to say how that luck would turn out.

"HERDY SCHMERDY BORK BORK!" Callum yells as he zooms around the kitchen and out into the hallways, running at the speed of light with a wooden spoon in his hand. He must have grabbed it off the counter when I wasn't looking.

I exchange a look with Bodi who is trying not to laugh.

"He's doing an impression of the Swedish Chef," I explain.

"I gathered that much, sir," Bodi says, eyes twinkling. "Very enthusiastic young child."

"He's something all right," I comment.

Pike snorts.

I look over at him as he leans against the counter scrolling through his phone, a glass of the aquavit we got for him in his other hand. "You can say that again," Pike says, not looking up. "I've had to take care of him for the last two weeks. Just be glad you don't have a tricycle in this place because he'll be re-enacting scenes from The Omen pretty quickly."

"Ah, that's who he reminds me of," Bodi says, snapping his fingers.

I laugh. "Damian?"

Bodi doesn't look the slightest bit reprimanded that he called Maggie's brother the anti-Christ. "And a little bit of myself when I was younger."

That I can believe.

Pike and I are helping Bodi in the kitchen with some cocktails and late-night snacks. The kids got off the plane earlier today and they're all fighting through jet lag and no one feels like eating a large meal. In fact, I think the twins are already in bed asleep. I have no idea where April is but I probably should find her.

I've been drinking. I probably shouldn't since I have a breakfast tomorrow morning at the Ethiopian embassy, but it's been a stressful day. The fact that Maggie's identity was blown has thrown a wrench into our original plans. Originally, Maggie wanted to take them to Gamla Stan tomorrow and show them around the old town but with the press reporting who they are, it's not such a good idea anymore.

We're just fortunate that when we went to the airport, they weren't harassed. Airports are so busy and chaotic anyway, I'm sure Maggie and crew blended right in as everyone got into the limo without a problem. Of course I stayed in the limo waiting for them and it was such a nice surprise to see all their faces again, even April's who seems to have softened just a bit. Or maybe that's the jet lag.

"Where is April?" I ask them as Bodi arranges cheese on a platter. "Is she with Maggie?"

Pike shrugs. "I don't know. I think Maggie went to bed."

"What? She's not the one with jet lag."

Pike finally looks up, his brows pinch in disapproval. "I think this whole thing with her life story being flashed on the cover of every newspaper is a little overwhelming for her."

And I think her brother just put me in my place.

He goes back to looking at his phone and I exchange a look with Bodi. Then I grab a bottle of scotch from the counter and head out of the kitchen.

I can hear Callum running around on the second floor and even though it's only eight at night, I wince thinking of anyone who might be trying to sleep.

Including Maggie.

Poor girl.

I have never been one to pity her because Maggie never wants anyone's pity but I know how hard this has to be on her, how violated she must feel. There is no guidebook for this and we'll have to take it as it comes and this is just day one of it all but all I can do is hope and pray that we'll be able to get through this.

The thought of it becoming too much for her, the thought of her leaving…

Because she might do that, won't she? Leave with the kids when it's time to go. I thought my chances of convincing her to stay were slim, but I always assumed she would eventually come back. That we could make this work as a long-distance relationship if nothing else. If it became official.

But now…now the fear is building in my chest, one brick on top of the other, getting higher and higher until I can't breathe.

She might leave me and never come back.

No matter how I ask her to stay.

Even if it's forever.

And remember forever isn't enough.

At that I slug back some of the scotch and make my way into the library.

The lights are off so I flick them on and I'm surprised to see April sitting in an arm chair in the middle of the room, a glass of something beside her.

"Why are you sitting in the dark?" I ask her suspiciously.

She shrugs. "I don't know. Felt like it."

"You're not tired? It's late enough now, you can go to bed."

Another shrug. "I'm not tired."

I pause, take another swig of the scotch which catches her attention.

"Can I have some?" she asks.

I peer at her glass. "What's in there?"

"Some Swedish apple drink," she says, eyeing my bottle pleadingly.

I exhale heavily, feeling like I've already fucked up today so why not.

I walk over to her and she holds out her glass and I pour the smallest amount possible into the remains of her drink. "It's scotch," I tell her. "I don't think you'll like it."

"As long as it's not too peaty," she says, taking a small sip. "Probably better on its own but it will do."

I frown at her, taken aback. "Not too peaty? May I ask how you know all these things? You're fourteen."

If looks could kill. "Just because I'm fourteen and I'm from a small town doesn't mean I'm not worldly. I know my scotch."

Jeez. Okay.

"I guess I had you pegged wrong," I tell her.

"Most people do," she grumbles.

"Mind if I sit down?"

She shrugs. "Whatever."

I sit down beside her and put my feet up on the coffee table, place the bottle to my lips and have another gulp, swallowing that beautiful burn.

April's eyes are on me. "I've never seen you drink like this."

My turn to shrug. "Maybe you've pegged me wrong too."

She seems to think this over. "Maybe."

"So how were things at home with Maggie gone? Must have been nice," I say, knowing how well they don't get along.

She narrows her eyes at me. "Must have been nice?"

"Yes. I'm assuming you get along better with Pike."

She studies me for a few moments, then has a quick sip of her drink, smacking her lips together. "I don't know," she says slowly. "Pike isn't any better."

"Well I can tell you that both Maggie and Pike are trying their best. They're trying very hard."

"I know," she says sharply and then sighs, falling back into the couch. "I know they are and I wish they would stop."

"Why?"

"Because it's not their job. It was Mom and Dad's job."

"April, your sister is your legal guardian."

"But she's not my mother!" she snaps and before I know what's happening, tears are streaming down her face. "She's my sister and I miss my sister. I miss having her as a sister. I miss our real mother. I miss my father. I miss them so much!"

She starts sobbing and I gently put my arm around her, pulling her into me, shocked that April is breaking down and opening up.

"I just want things to go back to the way it was," she cries. "I want everyone to be happy again. I know that Maggie is trying and I feel awful for her, about everything she's lost, but we've lost so much too. We're all hurting and we're all trying to get through it. Callum cries himself to sleep sometimes and it breaks my heart and it makes me so angry. It makes me so, so angry and nothing changes! Nothing happens. We're stuck like this forever." She starts to shake slightly. "I just miss them and I can't handle that they aren't here."

"It's okay. I understand."

"How can you understand?" she cries into me, sniffing. "You're a fucking prince! You don't know what it's like."

It then occurs to me that Maggie has never told her family about Alex. In a way I'm touched that she's kept that so private.

"I know what it's like, April," I tell her, my voice grave. "I lost my brother earlier this year. He was the heir apparent, he was the next in line for the throne and I was always in his shadow. But he wasn't well and we were all too selfish and busy to realize it, to really take it seriously. He committed suicide." I pause, taking in a deep breath, trying not to cry either. There's something about talking about it, reliving that moment that I can never get past.

"I found him." I swallow the growing lump in my throat, feeling my lungs squeeze together. "I can never forget the sight. And sometimes I feel just like you and Maggie and everyone else because there's no way around it. There's no changing it. We're stuck like this. Death is a truth that doesn't move an inch."

She sighs against me and I give her shoulders a squeeze. It's nice having her with me like this, a side I've never seen, but I think she needs to show it to Maggie.

"You should tell Maggie all of this, you know. Don't bottle it up inside. She thinks you hate her."

"I don't hate her," she grumbles, pulling away and wiping the tears from her eyes with her fingers. "I just hate that she tries to be my mother."

"You know she doesn't have a choice. If it wasn't her it would be someone else."

"Like a nanny? I think I'd like that better. Then she can just be a sister again."

"Well if you ever end up moving here, you can pick your own nanny."

She blinks at me. "Moving here? We're moving here?"

"Well, no," I tell her. "That was premature of me."

"But you've obviously thought about it. Is that why we're all here? A test run?"

I take another swig. "I don't know. Would you want to move to Sweden?"

"Sure."

I jerk my chin inward. "Really? Just like that? No thought? I mean, you just got here. Us Swedes are a strange bunch. You haven't even tried pickled herring yet."

"Whatever. I hate school, I hate my friends, I hate all the boys. I wouldn't mind starting over. And I know why we haven't been able to move and I know that the others like living there because it reminds them of our parents, but I fucking *hate* living in that house. So yeah, I'll move here and eat pickled fish if that's what it takes."

One thing you have to appreciate about April is that she doesn't hold anything back.

She raises her brow as she looks at me carefully. "Have you talked about this with Maggie?"

"No, not really." I clear my throat, not sure if I should tell her this or not. "I, uh, was actually planning on proposing. On Christmas Eve. I have the ring and everything." Freddie and Magnus helped pick it out. I know that there are heirlooms in the family but I'm doing this without telling my parents. They can either approve or disapprove after but if she says yes, we're getting married and nothing can stop that. I don't care if it means I'm disowned and have to abdicate.

"Can you marry a…a *commoner*?" April asks.

"We can. Things aren't as stuffy as it used to be."

A tiny smile flits across April's face which she immediately tries to hide with a drink. "Well then I hope she says yes." Then she frowns as a guilty expression comes over her. "I think I should tell you something."

"What?" This can't be good.

"You wrote Maggie those letters, right?"

Uh oh.

"Yes. My very personal love letters."

"Oh, I didn't read them," she says quickly and I think I believe her. "But I started going to the mail box and hiding them before she could get them."

I shake my head. I had a feeling but I hadn't wanted to say anything.

"Just like The Notebook," I mutter.

"I'm really sorry," she says. "I was just angry and jealous and I don't know, I guess I also didn't trust you."

"But you do now?"

"I do now."

"Do you think Maggie will say yes?"

"She's an idiot if she doesn't."

I laugh and then lift my bottle. "Here's to that then."

"Here's to that." She lifts her glass and clinks it against mine.

I catch another hint of a smile which she quickly buries with a frown but having April's blessing in all this is a big step in the right direction.

I just hope that Maggie and I can survive whatever happens between now and Christmas Eve.

CHAPTER TWENTY-FOUR

MAGGIE

Hounded.

The word never had much meaning to me until I was hounded. Until I was the fox running through the woods, frantically trying to find a place to hide, a place to stay alive, while packs of hounds chased my tail, threatening to rip me to shreds.

How cruel it is to the fox.

How cruel it is to us.

When Viktor first asked me to come with him to Sweden and bring the kids, he warned me that it could get ugly. That the paparazzi might follow me. That there might be pictures and articles and rumors. He said there would be a media frenzy, much like the ones I'd seen in the news when Prince Harry or Prince William got engaged.

At the time it didn't matter. It seemed like a worthy trade-off to be with him. And honestly I just didn't think it would be that bad. This is the Prince of Sweden and outside of his own country, I didn't think he mattered. And then there was me. I couldn't matter at all. What could people say about *me*?

Well, it turns out, a lot. It turns out everything.

I went into this relationship, into this journey, willing to sacrifice a lot in order to have Viktor. He was worth quitting my job over, he was worth uprooting the kids, even if for a vacation. He was worth giving it a shot because who knows where it might lead.

He is still worth all of that.

Viktor is still my rock.

And while we've been hounded every single time we leave the house, he's there by my side. He doesn't leave us alone. He's the protector of my family as much as I am, and I love him all the more for it.

I'm also protected by Nick and a score of special agents, all who know my safety and the safety of my brothers and sisters are of utmost priority. They no longer follow us everywhere, they are *with us* everywhere. They're walking in front, blocking the cameras, they're pushing photographers out of the way, they're making sure that no one touches us.

But it doesn't stop the photos. It doesn't stop them from digging into my once very private life. It doesn't stop them from making shit up either. I mean, after all the shit I've gone through, the obstacles and the heartache and the sorrow and yes, the damn tragedy, you would think they wouldn't need to make up a thing. This shit writes itself.

And yet there are articles saying I used to be a stripper. Or a prostitute. I've read that I faked my grades to get my NYU placement. I've read in one British tabloid that I murdered my parents to collect on their insurance.

I've read a multitude of horrible things and though none of them are true, they each kill me in thinking that others might believe it. Hell, even the truth kills me, all my dirty laundry is spread out for the world to see.

It's been nearly two weeks since the news broke and the

kids got here and we've probably only gone out into Stockholm a handful of times. Sometimes if the kids get really bored of making snowmen outside or wandering the halls, we pile in a couple of cars and Nick and another driver will take us outside of Stockholm to one of the many estates that the family has spread throughout the country.

Once we even went to a private ski hill on the border with Norway so that Rosemary, Thyme and Pike could try it out for the first time (Callum was happy sledding and April was happy flirting with the lift attendant).

Luckily, for the most part, the kids don't really care. Unless they're cranky, in which case everything bugs them. Being the oldest, Pike knows the harm that the press can do but when I've talked to him he says it doesn't really matter what anyone says because he doesn't live in Sweden, so who cares. He's also more likely to go into Stockholm by himself (albeit with a guard). If people bug him (and he draws stares because of his tattoos anyway), he takes it all in stride.

Callum loves the attention, of course. Rosemary and Thyme are pretty chill. It's April that hates them the most, to the point where she's started fingering the photographers and honestly, I let her do it. I'm living vicariously through her. In all the photos of me you can tell that I'm using all my power not to throat punch someone.

I haven't had a chance to meet Viktor's parents again and neither have the kids but tonight is Christmas Eve and we're invited over to celebrate.

I was worried there for a moment that we wouldn't be. I know it's not exactly the height of sophistication and elegance to have a bunch of foreign kids running around a palace. I also know that this is the family's first Christmas without Alex and I hate to intrude on a time in which they might want to mourn in private. The first Christmas after our parents died was the hardest and this being our second, I know it's not going to be easy either.

In fact, there's been more than a few times these last few weeks that I've desperately wished for my mother to be at my side. She'd give all the right advice, have all the right guidance. She'd approve of Viktor so much and love him as much as I do. She would encourage me to follow my dreams, just as she did when she was alive, even if my dreams are of love.

Love is the best dream you can have.

A knock at the bathroom door snaps me out of my forlorn thoughts. I've been soaking in a hot bath with a glass wine, trying to prepare for tonight. I guess I've been in here long enough because I'm starting to wrinkle like a prune.

"Can I come in?" Viktor asks.

I can't help but smile at his politeness. "Yes," I tell him and he pops his head in the door. "What happened to the Viktor that would barge in and take me in the bathtub?"

He grins sheepishly and comes inside, holding something green from his fingers. "This Viktor has been under a lot of stress lately," he says.

"What is that?" I say, frowning up at him as he comes over to the tub.

He holds it above my head. "Mistletoe," he says. He leans down and kisses me softly. Then he pulls back and holds it above his crotch.

"You are the worst!" I yell, playfully splashing him.

He moves out of the way, narrowly missing getting soaked. "Hey you wanted to be taken in the bathtub," he points out.

I'm almost considering it. He is half dressed in his boxer briefs and an undershirt, and he does happen to have a rather delicious-looking erection. "What time is it?" I ask him, wondering if we have room for a long overdue quickie.

"Actually it's time to get out," he tells me reluctantly. "Sorry, we have to leave in ten minutes."

"Ten minutes!" I startle, water splashing out of the tub. "I can't get ready in ten minutes!"

"You're going to have to try," he says. "Sorry, I didn't want to disturb you and then Callum ensnared me with some riddle and then I realized we're running out of time."

"Argh," I grumble, getting out of the bath and snatching the towel that he's holding out for me. I hate, hate, *hate* having to rush, even though it happens to me more often than not, but I really hate having to rush before I meet his parents for the second time. Plus, it's Christmas, so I have to look extra sweet and I have to make sure the kids look good as well.

I quickly dry off in front of him, no modesty here. "All you need to do is just put on a suit, right?" I tell him.

"Yes. And don't worry, I'll make sure everyone looks presentable." He leaves me in the bathroom and starts to throw his stuff on while I get myself ready at lightning speed.

Somehow I'm only two minutes late by the time I'm grabbing a clutch and heading down the staircase. Everyone is at the bottom of the stairs and it makes me pause halfway down and fish out my phone.

I frantically wave for everyone to squish in together by the Christmas wreath and decorations in the foyer and I quickly take their pics. God, if only Mom and Dad could see them now, Thyme and Rosemary in dresses that match in style (though not color), Callum in an adorable vest, Pike in a suit and April in a little strappy number with a faux fur shawl. I'm not sure if this is what people wear in Sweden for Christmas Eve and maybe we've gone overboard, but I've honestly never seen my little family look so good before.

They look happy, too. Despite the crazy situations we've

been in, they've been kept safe and sound, so far. Maybe it's even been an adventure to them.

At the very least, they're getting to meet the King and Queen tonight, and it's Christmas, so their excitement meter is off the charts.

While everyone goes out the back door and piles into the waiting limo, Viktor grabs my hand and pulls me toward him.

"You look beautiful," he whispers to me.

I couldn't decide what to wear in my rush so I picked something I thought was both fancy and homey, festive and not, a black satin pencil skirt and a white mohair sweater adorned with faux pearls. Red lipstick, nails and an updo to finish it off.

"You don't look so bad yourself," I tell him. He's in an ice-blue dress shirt that matches his eyes and black pants. It's probably the most casual I've seen him in a long time since he's almost always wearing a suit and tie these days.

He leans in and kisses my cheek just beside my lips, not wanting to ruin my lipstick. "I'm so proud of you," he says, his voice low. "I know how hard this has been for you, for everyone."

I nod, swallowing the sawdust in my throat. I don't want to think about it tonight. "I'm just surviving," I admit.

He frowns. "You shouldn't be surviving anymore, Maggie. You should be living."

And he's right. I was surviving back in Tehachapi. Going from day to day just trying to stay alive. Have things really reverted back to that? Did I mean what I said?

"It will get easier," he says, as he's said a million times before. "I promise."

"How?" I can't help but blurt out. "When will they ever leave us alone?"

He sighs. "They won't. But it will get easier to us. We will get used to it. Soon it won't matter anymore because it's just a part of the job."

"I never signed up for a job, Viktor. I love you and I want to be with you no matter what but that's not a job, that's a choice."

He stares at me for a moment, his eyes searching mine as if he can find something to convince him. "It will get easier. You'll be fine. There's no cow on the ice."

"No cow?" I repeat. "Oh, there's a cow. A big fucking fat heifer and she's seconds from going through the ice."

He closes his eyes briefly, exhaling a shaky breath through his nose.

"Not everyone is fine with this lifestyle, Viktor, not everyone can *handle* it," I add, and he knows I mean his brother.

Which explains the sharp look it brings out of him. I probably shouldn't have used him as an example.

A throat is cleared behind us and we break apart to see Bodi standing by the back door and looking at us with raised brows. "Sorry to interrupt, but they're ready to go."

I can hear Callum doing a Swedish Chef impression from somewhere in the limo.

I sigh and nod at Viktor, giving him a small smile.

He doesn't smile back, just turns and heads into the limo.

Oh great.

Merry Christmas to me.

The rest of the evening there's a strain between Viktor and I, which isn't the best feeling to have on Christmas, let alone with his family. I need to feel like he's on my side and when he barely looks at me, it feels like I'm in an isolation chamber.

Fortunately, Viktor's parents are quite accommodating with the kids and I would go as far as to say that they're charmed by Callum, rather than terrified, which is nice for a change.

The kids love it, too. The palace would be jaw-dropping to them on a normal day but with Christmas decorations everywhere—the fancy kinds, like real gingerbread stars hanging from the tree, and candy cane adorned wreaths, plus butlers walking around with trays of hot mulled wine and cider—they are in heaven. Even April is impressed, and she's hard to please.

Unfortunately, I still think his parents aren't that impressed with me. Though his mother has warmed up a bit and has started to go out of her way to ask me opinions on things (even if it's just "does this cardamom cake have too much cardamom?" to which you say, "you can never have too much cardamom!") or to include me in conversations (usually about cake for some reason).

His father though, well, he acts like a king in every way. I think to him I don't really exist and why should I? I'm nothing like the girl that he imagined would be sitting on the throne beside her husband. Because that's what they have to be thinking, isn't?

I'm not here with my brothers and sisters because Viktor is just a fling.

I'm here because we love each other.

And because we love each other, our relationship is serious.

Do I want to marry Viktor?

Of course I do.

God.

Yes.

If he asked.

Does Viktor want to marry me?

I hope so.

I hope that's why I'm here.

He wouldn't invite me all this way for nothing.

I'm here because this is the next step.

This is a trial, to see if we're compatible in the real world, in this very big, scary, important world of Viktor's, and not just one flirtatious week in Tehachapi, to see that we can work.

So…can we?

Honestly, before the paparazzi showed up, I had no doubts. Now, well, those doubts are in my head. And it's not just the paparazzi and being in the middle of a media storm. It's his parents, too.

Yes, I know that he can marry a commoner.

But can a commoner like me ever feel welcome in this family?

Will I ever feel like I truly belong?

Will I ever fit in?

I used to hate working as a housekeeper, not because of the actual work, but because of the way people looked down on me. Now, here, it's like that all the time. It's not just the media writing shit. It's the people who matter, who will matter if we stay together. The King and Queen.

Viktor has always made me feel worthy of him.

But ever since coming here, my worth seems to be sliding through my fingers, like sand.

Viktor had told me once that his father dressed up as Santa every year. I didn't expect that this time since they normally don't have kids over for the holiday, but to my surprise there was a Santa sneaking through the house. Probably one of the butlers or servants, maybe even Dolf Lundgren. It was timed so that when the kids were leaving out *risgrynsgröt* (which is like rice pudding) for him (they do this instead of milk and cookies), they happened upon him finishing up with the presents.

I'll never forget the sight of the kids running to the

window to stare at the red-cloaked figure running through the snow and disappearing into the trees of the endless gardens. If I had actually seen reindeer flying through the air, I think I would have believed it myself.

All in all, the kids had a wonderful time, especially after opening their presents.

But when it was time for us all to go to bed, I was still in a rather nasty mood from earlier and all the sweet hot glögg didn't help either.

Viktor and I retired to his old bedroom while the kids went to theirs, and all I wanted to do was just pass out on that bed and sleep until noon. All the formalities, food, alcohol and being on my best behavior were bearing down on me.

"Do you think your parents had a good Christmas Eve?" I ask Viktor as I pull out my nightgown from my overnight bag. "They seemed to be doing okay."

He sighs and walks over to his side of the bed, getting in. I hate how quickly he gets ready for bed. He just discards his clothes and walks on in, meanwhile I'm washing my face and putting on moisturizer and flossing and brushing my teeth and getting changed and I swear a million years seem to pass between us.

"My mother was crying in the kitchen," he says simply.

"What?" I quickly slip on my nightgown and don't bother with anything else. I get into bed. "I didn't know that. Really, she was crying?"

"You think she isn't human?" he says and his tone has an edge to it.

I should tread carefully here. We're both tired and our nerves are frayed.

"Of course she's human. This is the first Christmas without Alex for you guys. I think for us it all felt a little unreal being here but I'm sure tomorrow it will sink in that our parents aren't here…"

"Yes, well she was upset. I could tell my father was as well. It's harder on him in some ways because he can't show any emotion."

"Is that a rule?"

He narrows his eyes at me. "He's the king."

"Don't kings have emotions?"

"I can't tell if you're joking."

"What? Just because you're a king…"

"You wouldn't understand," he snaps. "It's a tough job. Why do you think I go and see Dr. Bonakov once a week? You have to be strong at all times, never show weakness. Why do you think King Aksel has gotten even worse since his wife died?"

"Because he's grieving?"

"Because he can't show weakness."

"Rule with an iron fist, that sort of thing?"

He cocks his head at me, jaw tense. "You know I will be king one day."

"So you're going to turn into an emotionless robot too?"

Fire flames in his eyes. "Did you just call my father an emotionless robot?"

I shrug, regretting that but feeling stubborn. "Can you blame me? He seems to hate me."

"He doesn't *hate* you, he doesn't know anything about you," he says. Our voices are starting to rise. "And no, I hope I won't turn into an emotionless robot, but you of all people should know what that's like. You said you were surviving this last year. You did everything you could to not feel. Don't be a hypocrite."

"I am not a hypocrite," I say sharply. "I'm calling it as I see it. And your parents don't like me at all, just admit it! Admit that I'm not princess material! Get it out in the open and not this buried wedge between us."

"They like you Maggie…"

"Then how come when they look at me, all I see is their wish for me to be something else."

"You're seeing what you want to see. You're amazing and you know it."

"You're a prince!" I cry out. "You're a prince and I'm *nothing*."

"Don't you dare say that," he hisses, twisting in the bed to grab me by the shoulders. "You are not nothing and never will be nothing. Do you understand that?"

"You are nobility. You are royalty. And the public, your country, they all look at you and they admire you and respect you and want to be you and who am I? I'm no one. I'm just some girl, just a girl."

"You're a girl but you're the strongest girl I know. Strongest *person* I know. You should be admired and respected because of all the things you do and everything you've survived. Any other person in your shoes would be crushed but you rose up and you made sure that you would not go down without a fight. I don't care if you don't see it that way, that's how I see it. That's how everyone should see it."

"But they all expect you to marry someone better. Richer, skinnier, prettier, more educated, more European. You're the most sought-after man in this country, you're the one who everyone wants, you're—"

"I don't care who I am to everyone else! All that matters is who I am to you. Who am I to you, Maggie? Please, tell me." He shakes me lightly and I can see he's struggling to keep his voice under control. "Am I your lover, your friend? Your boyfriend? Soul-mate? What? What am I to you?"

I sigh, my heart heavy. "You're everything to me."

He's getting so worked up that I feel terrible about even trying to fight with him. We shouldn't be doing this, not now.

And he looks like he doesn't believe me. "And you're everything to me. I'm not sure what I can do to convince you of that but it's the truth, Maggie. Sometimes all I can offer you is the truth."

I nod, pulling the covers over me. "I'm sorry. I'm sorry I'm being a pain."

"You're never a pain, Maggie," he says, reaching over to kiss me on the forehead. "I guess this is just part of us trying to fit into each other's lives. Everything you say and feel, I understand. Okay? I do. I don't want you to ever think that I'm not on your side, because that's exactly where I am and where I'll always be."

God. He has such a way of soothing me.

This man.

I give him a soft smile. "Merry Christmas, Viktor."

"Merry Christmas, Maggie."

The light goes off and he lies back in bed.

I hear him let out a long, disappointed sigh just before I fall asleep.

EVEN THOUGH CHRISTMAS Eve is celebrated in Sweden, there are a lot of activities and events going on Christmas Day, especially for the royal family.

For us, we had to wake up at the crack of dawn for Julotta which was something the kids *really* didn't want to do. I didn't want to either. Don't get me wrong, though I'm not especially religious I do like church on Christmas and Easter, but it was crazy early and I wasn't feeling the best.

Julotta, Viktor explained, was a church service traditionally done in the middle of the night, though as the decades went on, and Midnight Mass became more popular, the old four a.m. wake-ups of Julotta were chucked in favor of more reasonable times.

Though to me, eight a.m. is not a reasonable time to be in church.

Luckily, the fact that it was so early meant the kids were extra sleepy (AKA quiet) and because the sermon is in the church located on the palace grounds, we didn't have to hustle them too much.

It wasn't just for the royal family either, there were a lot of people there (who were mostly upper class or perhaps related to the royal family), and actually, even though I couldn't understand it all in Swedish, it was beautiful with lots of lights all over the church. There was a sense of respect and peace in the air that made me feel warm inside and with Viktor beside me, his strong and handsome face lit by the candle light, I felt like everything we argued about last night was being put to bed. It all had to come out but now it was out and we could deal with it and move on.

I hate fighting with him and I hate how much conflict there is in our lives now. I close my eyes and pray that I can take the peace I feel in the church everywhere I go.

When the sermon is over though, and we exit the church, Viktor decides we should head right back to our place to get the kids ready for ice skating later in the day.

So instead of heading toward the palace, we follow the

crowds of churchgoers out along the snow-packed path that leads to the parking lot.

Everyone is very cheerful and respectful, all wearing fancy hats and suits and pearls, bright festive colors that stand out against all the snow. There's a nice vibe in the air and I don't at all feel threatened by anyone. Sure there are some side-eyes I'm getting, especially from older ladies, who literally look like they're about to clutch their pearls, but for the most part people are friendly to me. Maybe it's the Christmas spirit. Maybe I'm finally being accepted.

But when we go through the gates and into the lot, we're ambushed by a frenzy of paparazzi, dozens of them with their cameras out. They actually burst through the crowd toward us and I don't know where the other agents are and Nick seems too far ahead to help.

I'm scared.

I'm actually scared.

The flashbulbs are flying, they're yelling in Swedish and English, stuff like "Are these all your children?" and "Who is the father?" and "The Swedish people don't want an American princess."

Viktor does his best to make sure they back off and I can tell from the way his fists are curling that he's very close to punching someone out, which is probably a bad move for a prince.

Then April starts to run away and a paparazzi steps right in front of her, taking her picture. The flash blinds her, the camera collides with her head and she's down.

One minute she's there, next I can't see her through the crowd anymore.

"April!" I scream and push through everyone to find her lying on the snow, trying to get up, the churchgoers helping her. She's holding her head and from the looks of it, trying hard not to cry.

"You bastard!" I yell at the photographer and I fling myself at him, pounding him with my fists.

"Maggie!" Viktor yells from behind me but I am a pit of rage. I am an angry mama bear and no one hurts my babies! Not even the snarky ones.

I feel strong hands grip me by the shoulders and arms and pull me away and Viktor is pushing me back so I'm behind him and now he's ripping the photographer's camera out of his hands and throwing it on the ground, stomping on it with his boot.

With April on her feet I grab her hand and pull her toward me. "Are you okay?" I cry frantically searching and feeling her head for any bumps.

She nods quickly but doesn't say anything.

From behind us, poor Callum is crying at the whole scene, red-faced with big fat tears rolling down his cheeks.

Rosemary and Thyme are holding onto each other.

And Pike is doing his best to become a wall against the other photographers, shielding us from them as they try and take pictures of the aftermath.

Then in seconds, the crowd is swarmed by agents and we're whisked away through the crowd to the limo where we're ushered in.

We're all breathing hard as the car peels away, Nick apologizing for not being quick enough, Viktor looking like he wants to punch a hole in the wall, the others looking scared.

"We should take her to the hospital, she could have a concussion," I tell them.

"Will do," Nick says.

"I'm fine," April says. "It doesn't even hurt."

But it does hurt.

The fact that this happened hurts.

And I know there's only more hurt to come now.

I know that this was the last straw.

This is a life that I don't want, a life that endangers the ones I have been sworn to protect and watch over.

This…is it.

This is when it all changes.

"Please don't cry," April whispers to me. "I'm okay."

I sniff, not realizing that a tear had escaped my eyes.

Even if April is okay, I know I won't be.

CHAPTER TWENTY-FIVE

VIKTOR

My fists clench and unclench.

There's a stinging cut on the inside of my fingers, perhaps from grabbing that guy's camera, and yet that wasn't enough. I should have split my knuckles open on his face. I should have made it so he could never operate a camera again.

But these damn rules. It's one thing for Maggie to attack him, which, considering he technically didn't attack anyone, can be considered assault if the court wanted to rule it that way. It's another if I do it.

It looks like that won't be the case. The press was in the wrong. They were in the *very* wrong. There were a bunch of witnesses to tell them what fucking garbage it was for them to ambush us after a Julotta service. Especially when you factor in that a fourteen-year-old girl had to be taken to the hospital.

I'm ashamed.

Deeply ashamed.

I know this wasn't my fault but at the same time, how could it not be? I'm the one who had the idea to fly everyone over here. I knew the risks. I knew that the kids would be subjected to shit like this. I knew that things could go horribly wrong and they have gone horribly wrong.

I've been in the military. I've seen my brother, dead. I've seen countless horrible things but what I saw this morning was something uniquely horrific.

I saw the woman I care about and the children that I now consider to be family, be attacked by a bunch of hyenas with cameras.

This isn't anything new.

This has happened before.

But today, Christmas Day of all days, this crossed the line.

I saw them all in this extremely joyous, open, vulnerable state, having just come out of a church. The perfect picture of their smiling faces and rosy cheeks from the cold and all the color of their outfits against the soft white. We all felt the peace, the sense of acceptance that I know Maggie didn't feel last night.

At that moment, I knew that Maggie was letting her guard down.

And that's when it happened.

The laughter turned to screams.

The peace was eradicated by flashbulbs.

Our privacy and space were intruded viciously, without care.

And April got knocked down.

An accident, I'm sure, but I will go to my grave making sure the laws change here, so that stuff like that never happens again.

But what good will changing the laws do if the person, the people, that I'm trying to protect leave me?

I know that's what Maggie is thinking.

She won't even look at me.

All day the distance I tried so hard to fight against last night increased until the line between us became a chasm.

I think I lost her in plain sight right outside that church.

I think I lost them all.

Now it's after dinner and I'm sitting in the study, waiting for her. We hadn't said a word to each other until I pulled her aside and told her to meet me in here, that we needed to talk.

She only nodded.

I hope she shows up.

April is okay, only a bump. The rest seem shaken up but hopefully not traumatized. Pike is a lot like me and wants to beat the shit out of everyone that was involved.

I look around the study and I remember the last time I was in here. We had sex on this very couch. I was just so happy she was here with me and I'd been missing her so much, craving her, that I cancelled my appointment and came back for her.

At that moment, everything between us was right.

Everything in the world was right.

I can't honestly say that things will be right again.

Not for us.

Not for me.

The door opens slowly and I bring my eyes up to see Maggie step in.

She's hesitant. Looks tired, listless, like she needs endless sleep. Still beautiful though. Always so damn beautiful.

But all that beauty doesn't hide the truth I see. That there's something in her eyes that makes my heart disintegrate.

I can tell that no matter what we talk about, she's already left me.

She's here, standing in front of me, and she's already left me.

"Hi," I say to her.

"Hi," she says in a small voice.

"Please sit down," I say and already it sounds like we're strangers.

How the fuck did this happen?

"I'd rather stand," she says, stopping in the middle of the room and folding her arms across her chest, hunched over like she's cold.

I shake my head and get up. The distance between us is now insurmountable.

"How are they?" I ask.

"Shaken up."

"And you?"

She doesn't say anything. She presses her lips together and I can tell she's trying not to cry.

"Maggie," I say softly, taking a step toward her, wanting to feel her warmth and not this endless cold. "I am so, so sorry about what happened."

"Not your fault," she says, words clipped.

"I didn't expect it. We were at church for crying out loud."

"It's not your fault, Viktor."

But she won't look at me.

I walk up to her, taking her hand in mine and the warmth and pulse that once flowed from her body to mine, the electricity, the sparks, they're all gone. I'm holding a stranger's hand.

"I promise," I tell her through a shaking voice. "That I will never let that happen to you or to them again."

"How?" she asks, glancing at me. "By creating a law that will take years to come into effect? You can't even create laws. You're no king."

Ouch. But maybe she didn't mean it that way.

"I can work with my father."

She lets out a sour laugh. "Your father hates me."

"Please, we went over this. He *doesn't*."

She doesn't believe me. She doesn't want to.

"Look, it might take a while, but it will happen. We just need to deal with it for now. These things take time."

"But there is no more time left," she says, blinking back tears. "Viktor. I'm leaving."

I shake my head trying to ignore the crushing weight on my chest, like my heart and lungs are being poured with concrete. "No. Don't leave. We have so much time before you need to go."

"I need to go now," she says, straightening up like she's finding her resolve. "They need to go. What happened to April could happen again and to anyone of them and I am not going to do that to them. I'm taking the first plane home tomorrow with the kids. I don't know if I'll come back."

I stare at Maggie for a moment, not sure if my ears are deceiving me or not.

It's one thing to run.

It's another thing to say you won't come back.

"Won't come back?" I repeat. "You have to come back. For me."

"No, Viktor," she cries out. "I can't. Don't you see how hard this is?"

She shakes her head, tears spilling down her cheeks in rivulets.

"It's just too hard," she says, crying. "It's just too hard."

"What's too hard, loving me?"

God, please don't say it's loving me.

"Being with you! They're two different things."

"No they aren't! When you love someone you'll be with someone, no matter the cost!"

I can't believe I'm hearing this. After everything she's gone through and *this* is the part that's too hard for her? Being with me?

"After all I did for you," I mutter and the moment the words fall out of my mouth, I know they're a mistake.

Her face falls.

Crumbles.

"So I was charity all along."

I hurt her. I didn't mean to.

I grab her, holding her face in my hands. "Maggie, you were never charity. I'm sorry I said that, I'm just…I can't let you go. I can't let you leave. You were supposed to stay with me like the princess that you are."

"No," she says. "You know I'll never be that. That's not who I am. It's not who I'm supposed to be. I'm supposed to be taking care of those kids and that's my priority. I never wanted to be in this position, the one in which I pick them over you but I have to choose. I have to. You have a duty to your country, Viktor. I have a duty to my family. I just…I…"

She pulls away from me and puts her face in her hands, shaking her head. "I love you but I…I can't let my love for you dictate what I do."

"I guess I should have seen this coming." I can hardly breathe, hardly speak, yet the words are flowing. "Maybe we really didn't know each other well enough. All I know is that I love you and that's always been true and if you leave me, you'll take every part of me with you. I know loss and I know it well but I don't think I'll ever be whole again."

She starts sobbing and looks up at me, her face ravaged by tears. "Don't make this harder on me, please! Please! You know what I have to do. Have the grace of a prince and let me go. Let me do the right thing for everyone."

She's right. I know why she's leaving and I understand it. I'm just so scared of the pain, scared of what's to come, that I'm acting desperate to keep her. I'm making it harder on the both of us.

I'm tired of losing the ones that I love.

I try and swallow. "Okay. I'm sorry. If you want to go, I won't stand in your way. I won't hold anything against you. I won't do anything but love you even though now it will be from afar." I reach out and grab her hand and tears fall from my eyes as I kiss her palm. "*Mitt liv, mitt allt*. Always and forever. Please don't ever forget that, my Maggie. You will always be my Maggie."

She takes her hand away from mine and, crying, runs out of the room.

That night she sleeps in a separate bedroom.

The next morning, she's gone.

All the rooms are empty.

The palace is cold and quiet again.

Like someone reached in and removed the heart.

Never to put it back.

CHAPTER TWENTY-SIX

MAGGIE

HOME.

Funny how leaving changes your perspective on your home.

When I left Tehachapi, there was a part of me that couldn't imagine living anywhere else but here. I mean, I wanted to live in New York but I was so not a New Yorker. I was a small-town girl through and through.

Then when I landed in Stockholm, I started to think that maybe that could change. I started looking at the place, the country, not as vacation spot, or a fun romp with Viktor. I started looking at it all through new eyes, trying to see if I could see myself creating a world there. When I went to little cafes and indulged in the *fika* of cakes and coffee, I tried to imagine making that part of my daily routine. I tried to imagine what it would be like to walk along the harbor in the summer, with a warm sun behind you, wooden sailboats bobbing in front of you. I tried to imagine shopping in all the cute little boutiques and even making friends with the locals, eventually working my way past their reserved facades and winning them over.

I imagined all of that and I liked it. I didn't take into account that if I did move to Sweden, it would be because of a prince and there's a chance I would be a princess and if I were a princess (I mean, how unreal does that still seem), I wouldn't have all the freedoms I just mentioned.

But I would have had Viktor.

And he had my heart.

And I believed, foolishly perhaps, that you could build a home in someone's heart.

Now I've learned that the heart is not enough to shield you from the world. The walls are soft, the pain is inevitable, and you bleed too easily.

Making the choice to leave Viktor ruined me and I'm still not sure if it was the right one because I haven't been able to go one minute without feeling the deep stab of loss, one that reaches in so far deep into my soul that I don't know how I'm still upright, how I'm still living.

It's a loss that had me crying the entire flight home.

It's a loss that has rendered me incapable of doing anything but curling up on the bed or the bathroom floor, much like I did after my parents, like I should have done more of. Perhaps I'm grieving for them too. Lord knows that never goes away.

And now I'm back here.

In this town.

In this house.

And I realize that this isn't my home anymore.

I don't have one.

I'm officially nomadic.

The vacancy inside me has returned but I can't even move in.

"Maggie," Pike whispers from the door.

I'm curled up in bed. I haven't moved all day, not even to go pee. Viktor the moose is tucked up under my arm.

"What?" I ask softly, hoping he doesn't ask me to do anything because I don't think I can.

"I'm taking R and T and Callum to see a matinee," he tells me. He pauses. "I saw an ad in the paper for a job at the movie theatre. I know it'll probably be obsolete in a year but do you want me to suss it out for you?"

"Sure," I say, my voice dull. The world dull. Sure I could work in a movie theatre. Sure I could work back at the hotel. Sure I could try and do a lot of things but none of that seems to matter right now except for this pain that I'm carrying inside.

Why did we have that fight?

Why didn't we just talk it through like rational people?

Why did I push him away like that? Because it got too hard? I've been able to stay strong through everything in my life and yet the moment that love got too hard, I bailed.

What the fuck is wrong with me?

The tears start flowing again.

I guess I fall asleep because when I open my eyes, the sun coming in through the window has shifted.

I should probably go and pee.

I shuffle out of my room, wearing the same PJs as I've worn the last few days, and look at myself in the bathroom mirror. I don't even recognize myself and I desperately need a shower.

When I'm done in there, I shuffle out of the bathroom, planning to go straight back to bed when I pass by April's room. Her door is open.

"Maggie," she calls out to me.

April and I have gotten a lot closer since our time in Sweden, so at least something good came out of me dragging them all there.

I pause at her door and lean against the doorway. She's

sitting cross-legged on the floor with a bunch of letters displayed in front of her.

The sight of them makes my heart lurch.

"Where did you get those?" I whisper.

A wash of shame comes over her. "I took them from the mailbox."

"Are they recent?" my heart jolts at the thought that maybe Viktor has written to me. We haven't said a word to each other after I left, which is another thing that's killing me. It didn't end well.

But if he's written me, if he says he loves me, if he wants me to come back, I'll…

"They aren't recent," she says quickly, perhaps reading the look on my face. "They're from the fall. I took them and hid them because I didn't want you to read them." She pauses. "I didn't read them either, see, they're sealed. But I knew they were from him."

"Why did you do that?" I ask softly, my heart seeming to break all over again.

"Because I was a dick," she says. "I'm sorry. I wanted you to have them. They smell nice still." She picks one up and smells it and then holds it out for me.

I walk in and gingerly take it from her. Hold it up to my nose. Breathe it in.

I breathe in Viktor.

The faint smell of lavender.

The tears start falling. I've been conditioned.

"Aren't you going to read it?" April asks, eying me with concern. She doesn't do well when anyone cries, which is why I'm surprised she's talking to me right now, showing me all this.

I shake my head. "There's no point. I know what these letters would say. They'll just remind me of everything I lost. Everything I had."

"You know we all would have moved to Sweden," she says matter-of-factly.

"What do you mean?"

"I mean Viktor asked us and we all said yes…thinking that you would have said yes."

I blink at her, frowning. "I'm sorry, I don't understand. He asked you all? He never asked me. I mean, not in an official sense."

She rubs her lips together, silently debating something.

"April!"

She sighs. "Okay well I guess he wouldn't care if I told you now. But…he was going to propose."

"What?!"

"He told me. The night we got into Sweden and you were asleep, we stayed up drinking together."

"You what?!"

"Focus," April says gesturing with her hands. "He was kind of drunk but, like, kind of sober at the same time and anyway he asked if I would move to Sweden and I was like, yes please, get me out of the murder house, thank you. Anyway, he then said he planned to ask you to marry him. You know, become a princess and all that. He said we could live in the palace and have nannies and eat pickled fish. I really thought that's what was going to happen."

I can't believe a word of this.

He was going to propose?

"When?" I ask. "When was he going to propose?"

"Christmas Eve," she says. "But you guys were being weird and the next day no one said anything, I guess because of the whole incident, so I assumed it didn't happen."

I put my hand to my head. "Oh my god. He was going to propose and we started fighting and…"

"Yeah so it seems you guys did the opposite. Instead of getting engaged, you broke up."

"But," I say, walking into her room and sitting on her bed, my eyes drifting absently over the letters as my mind tries to catch up. "But…you would move there? What about what happened with the paparazzi?"

"Whatever, I'll deal."

"What about the others?"

"They were all fine with it. Pike wasn't loving the idea but I mean who cares. He's eighteen, he can go and live in LA if he wants to and, like, open a tattoo shop or something while the rest of us live in a friggin' palace. I mean, hello, who gets the better deal here. Not him."

I can't get this new information to settle in my head. All the crying has rendered it useless. "Rosemary and Thyme. Rosemary wouldn't want to leave here, leave all her sports teams."

"Rosemary has fallen in love with skiing," she says. "She was quick to say yes. Thyme has fallen in love with the Swedish death metal music scene." She laughs. "She says it's musik spelled with a K. And Callum wants to become a Swedish Chef now, so there you go."

"Viktor asked all of you? When?"

"The day before Christmas Eve. I don't know where you were. We had a family meeting without you."

I can picture him calling them all around and asking them and…oh, my heart. My heart. This man loves them as much as he loved me.

He still loves you, I tell myself. *It's not too late.*

"But if you guys moved there…the paparazzi, I mean they are ruthless. You know what happened."

"I'm sure they'll get tired of us and honestly, I don't mind the attention."

"You were knocked over!"

"I think that scared you more than it did me. I was fine, wasn't I? And that made them all look really bad, I think they would have backed off after that. Look, I don't like my photos being taken all the time but I don't know, it's kind of fun. Makes me feel like a celebrity. I'll deal with all of that for a chance at a new life. Don't you think we all deserve a do-over?"

April is right.

We do.

I've had days to mourn and stew and grieve and try to sort out my feelings.

And yet now I'm figuring out my feelings in seconds flat.

"I've got to go," I tell her and immediately scamper out of her room into mine.

"Where are you going?" she asks, following me.

I grab a small suitcase and throw it on the bed.

"Where does it look like I'm going?" I ask, glancing at her over my shoulder. "Now help your sister pack."

THIS IS A MISTAKE, this is a mistake, this is a mistake.

"Would you like some water, miss?"

Mistake, mistake, mistake.

"Thank you," I tell the flight attendant, picking the cup off the tray and nearly spilling it on the guy that's squished next to me.

I'm in the back of the plane.

Flying to Stockholm.

Landing in one hour.

I have no idea what awaits me when I land.

There was no time to plan anything.

Okay, well there could have been time but after talking to April, there was a switch in my brain that had always been connected to my heart and suddenly it turned on. It was a light bulb going off, but it wasn't just in my head, it was in the deep-seated soul of me. It was a light that glowed through the darkness I had been drowning in, a darkness I wanted to drown in, maybe because I'd spent so much time in the last year acting like a robot and distancing myself from all the loss and grief and reality. Maybe I fell so deep because I never let myself fall before.

But this light went on and it illuminated everything and in a second I knew that I had to go.

I had to be with Viktor.

At any cost.

That the only thing that makes sense in this world is the two of us together.

Without him, I'm just surviving.

So I packed with April's help and then when Pike got back with the kids, I hastily told them the plan and begged for him to drive me to LA where I could catch a plane. I know Pike wasn't all that happy that I would be using some of our savings on something that might not pan out but by the time the minivan was pulling up to LAX, everyone was chanting *Sweden, Sweden, Sweden!* and that's when I really knew that my family has my back as much as I have theirs.

I never had a chance to tell Viktor I was coming.

Actually that's not true.

I wanted to just show up and surprise him like he did to me but I realized you can't really do that with royalty. I mean, I can't go throw rocks at his window. I'm not athletic enough to scale the fence, nor throw rocks at a three-story window. So I sent him a text just before my plane took off.

Hey we need to talk. I'm coming to Sweden today. Will text when I land.

But by the time I put the phone in airplane mode, it hadn't shown his text as delivered.

And when the plane lands and I frantically switch my phone back on, it's still not delivered.

Shit!

I get my carry-on and go into the airport, checking my phone every minute.

Nothing, nothing, nothing.

I go through passport control with no problem.

I get to the arrivals and expect to see Nick there with a sign, thinking maybe Viktor somehow got the text and contacted Pike or something and got the details about my flight.

But there's no one.

I'm standing here in the airport looking like an utter fool and I swear to god there's a few people here who already recognize me.

Double shit.

What does Viktor say?

Helvete!

I don't have much choice. I go into a bathroom stall and call Freddie, whose number I've always had for emergencies.

He's surprised to hear from me, of course.

"I don't know what to say," he stammers. "His Highness isn't here."

My heart *sinks*.

"Isn't here? Where is he?"

"Uh, he's on a trip."

"Well when will he be back?"

"Uh. Not sure. Look, stay where you are and I'll have Nick come get you, okay?"

"I haven't booked a hotel," I say feebly. "I haven't...I haven't thought any of this through."

"I'm glad you didn't because then you probably wouldn't have come," Freddie says wryly. "And the palace will always be your home. Just sit tight."

Half an hour later, Nick comes striding through the terminal looking for me. I've been hiding in the corner at a coffee shop with a book over my face and giant sunglasses.

"Are you trying to look...what is the word in English? *Inconspicuous?*" Nick asks as he looks me over.

"Not working, is it?"

"No," he says, looking around at the people watching us with interest. "But you're here now. I'm so very glad to see you."

"You too, Nick," I tell him.

He was starting to feel like family to me and when I'm in the back of the Town Car on the way to Haga Palace, I realize that Bodi and Freddie felt like family as well. It was like while I was here, I was gaining more family than the family I had lost. It's like the palace in the end wasn't some strange and stuffy and formal royal life that I couldn't relate to, it was something warm, with so much love and laughter in the walls. I told myself–and Viktor–there was no way I could be a princess and live that life because I couldn't be farther from one, but the truth is...I don't think a title like that defines you. I think you define the title.

The palace is still covered by layers of snow but the moment I walk in those doors, I feel warm and relieved. Is this my home?

Could this be my home?

Will he take me back?

"Make yourself at home," Nick says to me just as Bodi appears around the corner.

"Maggie!" he cries out, throwing his arms out to me and

enveloping me in a big hug until my feet aren't even touching the ground. You'd think that I'd been gone for months, not a few weeks.

"Hey Bodi," I tell him after he puts me down. "What is this, a beard?" I reach out and tug the end of his red scruff.

"Going for the Viking look," he says, mugging for me. "What brings you back here? We hoped we'd see you again but we weren't sure. You all left so fast, so soon."

I wince, wishing I hadn't been so hasty. "Viktor and I…"

"Yes, I know. You had a fight. I can't blame you for leaving Maggie, Viktor is not an easy person to be with."

"It's not that he's not easy. It's just…this lifestyle."

"It takes some getting used to," he says with a solemn nod.

"I just didn't think I was strong enough to get used to it," I tell him.

"Glad to see you're coming around then," he says, patting me on the shoulder. "Because you're stronger than you think. Come on, I'll put your suitcase in Viktor's room."

"Oh, please don't," I tell him as he hauls it up and starts carrying it up the stairs. "I don't want to assume anything. The guest room that Magnus normally uses is fine."

Bodi nods. "As you wish. Why don't you make yourself comfortable in the lounge and I'll bring you some coffee. You must be exhausted."

I nod and head to the lounge while he runs the bag upstairs. You'd think I would be tired since I didn't sleep on the plane at all, but I am so wired that it feels like I couldn't close my eyes even if I tried. I must look like such a freak.

Bodi brings me a cup of coffee and we sit and chat about everything except Viktor. I want to ask him about where he is since Freddie was so vague but I don't dare. It's not their place to tell me and if it turns out he's visiting a girl or something, then I would just die on the spot.

There's a knock at the front door and my heart starts to

race. Is it Viktor? I look at Bodi and he looks surprised more than anything.

"Pardon me," he says to me and gets up, leaving the lounge.

I hear the door open and then Bodi exclaim, "Your Majesty!"

Majesty?

Majesty?!

Holy fuck it's the king.

Seconds later The King of Sweden appears in the doorway, looking down at me with a look on his face that makes me want to shrink in my seat.

But that would be uncouth, I know that much, so I scramble to get up to my feet, to curtsey. He quickly motions with his hand for me to stay put.

"Please, stay seated," he says, striding over to the chair across from me. He sits down, folding his hands over his lap, and looks me sternly in the eyes. "The two of us, we need to have a talk."

CHAPTER TWENTY-SEVEN

VIKTOR

"Do you know what they call a turnip in Sweden?" I ask Callum.

He shakes his head, smiling. I swear I can ask this kid anything and he'll smile. It's especially disturbing when you're talking about something horrific.

"They call it a Swede," I tell him.

"But aren't you a Swede?"

"I am."

"Am I going to be a Swede?" he asks.

"That all depends on your sister. If she were here, I would ask her." I study his face carefully. "Are you sure you don't know where she is?"

He just grins. That gives me nothing.

It's my fault, really, for having such flights of fancy and for it to actually lead me on a flight which actually put me back in Tehachapi, looking for Maggie.

After she left, I spent a long time wrestling with what I was going to have to do to win her back. I knew that just because she was scared, just because we had a fight, it didn't mean that things were over between us. It might have felt like we were over, especially from the way she basically packed up her family and left. They were all gone the next day on the first flight home and I didn't have any time to realize what was going on.

That I had lost her.

I had lost them.

I had lost…*everything*.

With her gone, the media storm didn't die down either. Rumors started spreading. She had been spotted at the airport, people speculated why she was leaving. People started noticing that we were never seen together, or that she was never seen at all.

I ignored it. That's all you can do. And I tried to move on.

I did everything that I thought I was supposed to do. I threw myself into my role and tried to become a better public figure. I tried to pretend that my heart wasn't breaking inside even though it was slowly splintering to pieces until nothing was giving me joy anymore. Maggie had been my joy, my light, my everything. My persika, my Miss America, my mayhem. Oh, her middle name couldn't have been more fitting because she brought mayhem to my heart, my life, turned my world upside down and I was a better man in the end because of it, because of her.

But putting on a mask only works for so long. I should have known that.

Eventually the mask crumbled away.

Eventually the feelings came pouring back in.

Eventually I realized that if I didn't have her, I had nothing.

Without her I wasn't worthy of the crown on my head.

The next thing I knew I was having Freddie find the next possible moment I had a break, and then we were booking tickets and that was the end of it. The plan was to surprise Maggie like I did last time, to fall on my knees and propose like I should have done before when I lost my nerve. To go and not come back unless I had her with me.

So, with my guard and driver Janne waiting in the car outside, I burst into their house hoping I'd run right into Maggie.

What I found instead was Callum, sitting at the kitchen table with a glass of milk and reading a comic book. Rosemary, Thyme, and April were at Rosemary's soccer game while Pike was upstairs napping. Callum said that Pike is too tired to deal with anything these days.

But when I asked where Maggie was, Callum wouldn't say. I know he knows, but he's just not telling me.

"What the fuck."

I turn to look at Pike standing in the kitchen doorway, trying to focus his groggy eyes on me.

"Bad word," Callum scolds him, shaking his head.

"Viktor?" Pike says, blinking hard. "Viktor! What. The fuck. Are you doing here?"

He sounds far more surprised about me being in his kitchen than I thought. It looks like I'm blowing his mind.

"Nice to see you too?"

"He's a prince, Pike, show him some respect," Callum says.

"Yeah, this coming from herdy schmerdy bork bork over here," I mutter under my breath. I look at Pike. "Look, I'm sorry to just drop in like this without any warning but I wanted to talk to Maggie. Face to face."

"Well, I hate to break this to you but a little warning would have been nice."

I frown. "Why, what's going on?"

Pike looks at Callum. "You didn't tell him?"

"Hey," Callum says, "I get to have secrets too!"

"Tell me what? Where is she?"

"Maggie is in Sweden."

The planet begins to tilt on its axis. "What?" I say, my voice coming out in a hush. "Sweden?"

"She went for you. Suddenly decided she was wrong and couldn't live without you, or whatever, and that was that. We drove her to the airport yesterday."

"Oh my god." I groan. I bring out my phone but I don't see any texts from her or anyone. "She would have texted me, right?"

"She wanted to surprise you. Looks like you two both had the same idea. Been watching too many romantic comedies, maybe."

I look at my phone again and then notice that the data isn't on.

Helvete.

I toggle it onto airplane mode and back and this time a million texts come in.

One from Maggie saying she's going to Sweden.

A bunch from Freddie, saying that Maggie is in Sweden and Nick has gone to get her and he doesn't know if he should tell her where I am.

And then a few from my father. Wanting to know where I am, wanting to know why Maggie is at the palace and I'm not.

And then…

The worst text of them all.

My father saying that he went to the palace and had a long talk with Maggie.

He didn't say anything else.

Fuck.

That is *not* good. For all I know he convinced her to leave, that she has no place in the royal family, and now she's on her way back here again.

I send Maggie a text: **I'm in Tehachapi! In your kitchen! Don't go anywhere, I'm coming back for you.**

I wait a few minutes to see if she'll get the message but then I realize with the time difference, it's late there and she's probably asleep.

If she's even there.

"I can't believe the both of you were in the air at the same time," Pike muses.

"I can," I say with a sigh. "This seems like the crazy type of shit that happens to us."

"Do you want to stay for dinner?" Pike asks. "I was just about to get started. The girls will be back soon."

"Can you cook for us?" Callum asks me. "Pleeeeease?"

I shake my head. "Next time. I promise."

"There won't be a next time." He pouts.

"There will be if Maggie agrees to marry me." I eye them both. "You're all okay with that idea still, right?"

Fuck, I hope so.

"Yes, *d'uh*," Callum says with an exaggerated roll of his eyes.

Pike nods. "The idea has grown on me. Still can't say if I would join you out there. I think I'm more of a sunshine and palm trees kind of boy at heart. But you have my blessing. You have all of our blessings."

"Okay." I get up out of my seat, leaning against the table, summoning strength to go through this travel hell all over again. "I guess I have a plane to catch."

THE SWEDISH PRINCE

JET LAG IS A BITCH, as they say in America.

After criss-crossing numerous time zones in twenty-four hours, by the time I land *back* in Stockholm, I barely know what day it is, what time it is and who I am. All I do know is that I have to get to Haga Palace ASAP.

I have to propose to the woman of my dreams.

The future Royal Highness, future Princess, future Queen.

Of course being that my brain is so fried, I realize that I don't have a ring on me. The ring I had chosen for Maggie is tucked away in a drawer in my room. Fuck it, I'll just have to wing it.

Unless…

I tap Nick on the shoulder as he's driving. We're just minutes away from the estate.

"You wouldn't happen to have a ring, would you?"

Nick shoots me a pensive look. "I have my wedding ring."

"Can I borrow it?"

Nick's face scrunches up. "Do you have to?"

"I'll give it back, I promise."

"I don't know. You know it's bad luck to put on someone else's ring."

"Nick. As the Crown Prince of Sweden, I command you to give me your wedding ring. As a subject of, uh, this royal… order…you must obey. Or face the consequences."

I can tell Nick really wants to tell me to fuck off.

He sighs and then raises his left hand for me to pry the ring off. It takes a bit of effort. "When was the last time you took this off?" I ask him, grunting as I finally get it loose.

"I think my wife got it extra small so that I'd never lose it."

"Or you got fat."

"I think my wife got me fat so that I'd never lose it."

"Fair enough." I twist it around in my fingers. It's

tarnished and plain but it will do for now. As for bad luck, it doesn't stand a chance with us.

"If you lose it," he warns me. "Then you have to deal with my wife. And you have to arrange for me and the girls to meet Harry Styles."

"Done. Hey, now you want me to lose it, don't you?"

He doesn't say anything.

I stuff the ring in my pocket, then call Bodi on his cell.

"Viktor!' he exclaims through the phone. "You'll never guess who is here!"

"I know," I tell him. "I'm almost there. I need your help in keeping Maggie away from the front windows."

"What?"

"Just do it."

"For how long."

"Give me ten minutes."

"Okay but—"

I hang up.

Soon we're pulling into the back of the house and I immediately grab the cook, Else, and Nick, and tell them what to do.

I have no idea if it will turn out or not but after I talked to Magnus before I boarded the plane yesterday, he gave me the idea. Considering all of his knowledge of *The Notebook*, and now this, I'm starting to think he's a true romantic at heart. Though lord help the woman who ends up with him.

With Nick running around the front lawn and doing the rough outline with a shovel, Else and I gather branches from the woodpile and then go about laying them on top of the outline. In theory, when Maggie looks out from the top windows, she should see giant words clearly spelled out on the snow.

Now, I know she knows I'm coming. I had texted her yesterday and though she didn't text back, probably because what do you say other than, *oh shit, how did that happen?* I made sure via Nick that she was at home.

I also called my father, and though I didn't ask what he and Maggie discussed, I told him that I was coming home.

I also told him what I was going to do.

I was going to get down on one knee.

And I was going to ask Maggie to be my wife.

And if he had any objections to that, well then he didn't have to give us his blessing, and he didn't have to be here.

So far, he's not here.

Which means what I think it does.

But I refuse to dwell on that right now. My main concern is Maggie.

Is she going to say yes?

Does she want to marry me?

Does she still love me?

I can't assume any of those things just because she's here. I'm going to have to see it all with my own eyes, looking into her heart and soul and seeing her truth, feeling her warmth in my hands. Just being near her will give me all the answers.

"I think we're done, sir," Else says, dusting off the snow from her coat.

I stare at the words. It's impossible to read from here so I can only hope Maggie will see it from up there.

"I think it's time," Nick says to me with an impish smile.

Else claps her mittens together excitedly.

I go inside the palace.

"Maggie?" I call out into the foyer.

The doors to the study open and Bodi strolls out, sweating profusely.

Am I hearing a fiddle?

"What were you doing in there?" I frown and then see Maggie coming up behind him, looking both shy at seeing me and confused by Bodi and whatever he was doing.

"I put on some music and demonstrated our traditional Swedish folk dancing," Bodi says, breathing hard. "I'm a bit out of practice."

I bite back a laugh. So this was Bodi's plan to keep her away from the windows? Poor girl.

I nod at him my thanks and then look at Maggie.

"Hello."

The sight of her is like a balm on every single wound. She soothes me, heals me, reveals me.

"Hi," she says.

"Well, I'm going to leave you alone," Bodi says and staggers off to the kitchen. "I need some water."

"It's nice to see you here," I tell her.

"It's nice to be here," she says.

Oh, I don't want this to be awkward at all.

"Listen, I—" I say at the same time she says, "Look, I'm—"

"I'm sorry," we both blurt out at once.

"I'm sorry," I say quickly, grabbing her, pulling her toward me until I know she's in my hands. She's here now, she's solid and she's real and I need her to be mine. "I am so sorry. I know I should have never…"

"No," she says quickly. "You have nothing to be sorry for. You did everything right. I knew the risks coming here and bringing the kids and I did it anyway because I wanted a future with you. And somewhere along the line I got scared and I lost sight of that. I lost sight of why I came here in the first place."

"Please, you didn't do anything wrong," I tell her, searching her eyes. "So don't apologize to me either. You had to put the kids first."

"But I did it without consulting them. I had no idea that they wanted to live here, that they would have stayed. In some ways, I made all the decisions for them."

"Like a mother would do."

"Yes but that's not what I want to do or want to be. I want to talk to them, value their opinions because I do value their opinions. Treat them like adults."

"But they aren't adults. They aren't your kids either. They are your brothers and sisters. You're doing the best you can and I promise you I don't blame you at all for leaving. Not even a little. You protected them."

"And yet I didn't realize how strong they were," she says. "Stronger than I thought." She rubs her lips together, exhaling through her nose. "I'm sorry I left, Viktor. I know better than to run. I didn't think I was strong enough and it scared me but I am strong enough. You made me believe that, *you did*. You made me believe in myself, that I can do anything, and I can't thank you enough. You mean the world to me. You are my world. *Mitt liv, mitt allt*."

"God, you're sexy when you speak Swedish," I murmur before I kiss her. Her lips to mine light off a thousand explosions inside of me and it takes a lot of energy to remember my plan.

I pull away and she's blushing. "I almost forgot how you make me feel," she admits breathlessly.

"How do I make you feel?"

She gives me a sweet smile. "Always more, never less."

Well, fuck me.

I thought this proposal was going to be hard enough but she's got me all choked up and I haven't even started.

"I have to show you something."

I take her hand and I lead her up the stairs all the way to my bedroom–*our* bedroom.

"Show me something, huh," she says slyly. "It's been a while."

I laugh. "Yes, that's later, I promise you," I tell her, pulling her across the room to the windows.

I face her, my back to the window, blocking her view.

"Are you ready?"

"Uh, for what? Please don't tell me this is some new Swedish adrenaline sport where you jump out of windows into the snow because I've seen the Russian versions of that and they never end well."

"No," I tell her firmly.

Then I step aside and gesture with flourish to the window.

She walks over to it and peers outside.

I glance over her shoulder to see the letters written in the snow:

Will You Merry Me?

"Ah, *helvete*," I swear.

Fucking Nick can't spell.

Maggie bursts out laughing.

I shake my head, my nerves dancing up a storm in my stomach. I'm so mad at Nick, even though it's pretty hilarious. Most of all...*fuck*. How is she going to say yes now?

"Can we start over?" I ask her.

I drop down on one knee and take her hand and suddenly she stops laughing. Maybe she's realizing just how serious this is.

Because I've never been so serious about something in my whole life.

"I had a whole speech planned out," I tell her. "A speech that was supposed to come before, well, *that* but you distracted me, and I realized, if you don't know how I already feel then no speech will convince you. All I ask of you is if you'll marry me. If you'll be my wife. My princess. My future queen. If you'll stand by my side no matter where we are in the world, as long as we are together. If you'll take on my family as I take on yours. If you promise to love me as I promise to—"

"Can I say yes now?" she interrupts me, nodding her head and smiling from ear-to-ear.

I grin at her. "You haven't let me finish."

"And you said there would be no speech. So can I say yes?"

"Yes," I tell her. "Yes you can say yes."

I don't think I've ever felt happier, luckier, in all my life.

I quickly fish out the ring as if she might change her mind and then I slip it on her finger. It's way too big and about to fall off.

"Oh," she says looking down at it and I can tell she's trying to be kind about it. "It's...*classic*."

"It's Nick's," I explain. "I asked if I could borrow it, though now I think I should keep it after that typo. Hold on."

I get to my feet, and still holding onto her hand, I shuffle over to my drawer where I fish out the original ring, the one I had bought for her before Christmas. It's expensive, with rare lavender-colored stones and a lot of diamonds—it's the kind of ring a princess would wear.

I take it out of the box with one hand while still holding onto her hand with the other, and then drop back down on one knee again.

She gasps loudly, the ring reflected in her wide eyes.

"Miss Maggie Mayhem McPherson," I tell her, staring up at her. "Will you do me the honor of becoming Crown Princess Margaret of Sweden?" I pause. "I'm not really sure how the last names work with us, I'll have to get back to you on that," I add.

She laughs, tears in her eyes. Happy tears. "Again, yes. Yes!"

I quickly take Nick's ring off and slip the right ring, her ring, on.

It fits perfectly.

Meant to be.

"I can't believe this is happening," she cries out.

I get to my feet. "It's happening," I tell her, pulling her toward me into a deep, long kiss. "And it was always meant to be."

"I'm so happy I walked in on you naked," she says and I laugh.

"I'm so happy you liked what you saw."

"Ahem."

A throat clears by the door and Maggie and I whirl around to see my father and mother standing there in the doorway. Judging by their faces, they either clearly just heard what we said about being naked, or they disapprove of this engagement.

Or both.

Then my mother walks in, pressing her palms together.

"Did she say yes?" she asks me, a tremor of excitement in her voice, her eyes brighter than I've seen in a long time.

I look at Maggie. "Did you say yes?" I joke. "I can't remember."

"I said yes," Maggie says, proudly showing off her ring. "Always yes, never less."

"That could be a new motto," I tell her, though I have to admit, having my parents suddenly here in our moment is bringing a new wave of tension. I have no idea what they're going to say.

Always more, never less? What if they say more bad things and less good things?

My father strolls in, hands behind his back, going into father lecture mode.

Fuck.

I just hope whatever he says doesn't dampen the joy we're both feeling right now. I won't let it.

"I'll make this as brief as I did with Miss McPherson yesterday," my father says in his deep voice. He looks to me.

"Viktor, I love you. You're my son. You're our son and we want what's best for you. I know we haven't been the best parents but we tried the best we could given the roles that we have. We have done what we can to ensure you have a secure and happy life. Sometimes I think we've failed you and I know that we failed Alex, on many levels. I know we'll never forgive ourselves for it and I know that those scars don't heal."

He takes in a deep breath. "But the mistakes we made with him, we don't want to make with you. Maybe it's too late but it's never too late to try and be better, is it? It's never too late to start over again and we just want you to be happy. And with her, you are."

He glances at Maggie who is smiling at him with shining eyes. "I had a talk with Maggie yesterday about this very thing and it turns out your mother and I have more in common with her than we thought. We may come from different backgrounds, different countries, but our desires are all the same and that is the desire to do better and be better for those around us. Maggie is an exceptional young woman and we're sorry we didn't grasp that until it was almost too late. Seeing how she was at Christmas, seeing how she handled the situation with April with poise."

He pauses and manages a small smile. "Well, an attempt at poise. I wanted to hit that man, too. But in all of that, I saw a woman who wasn't after you for your title or your money. She wasn't after being a princess. She was after love and when she knew she had to protect the others, she left to protect another type of love. I know it was a hard choice and who knows if it was the right choice. But, regardless, the both of you are here together now and that's all that matters. Viktor, you have our complete blessing on this engagement. You couldn't have picked a better woman to stand by your side."

I blink, unable to process this.

I'm so stunned I can hardly move.

The engagement, my father's words, the way that my mother is looking at the two of us adoringly.

Maggie squeezes my hand. "The King just spoke to you, you should say something."

My first thought is to kneel. That's what you do in front of a king, to show your respect. But kneeling is not enough.

I walk over to him, throw my arms around him and hold on tight.

I can't remember the last time I hugged my father but as he just said, it's never too late to start again.

He hugs me back, a quick squeeze, but that means more to me than anything else he's ever done.

"Thank you," I tell him, my words broken with emotion.

He gives me a wry smile and taps the side of my cheek. "You're welcome."

Then he looks to my mother. "We should really leave these two lovebirds alone, Elin." He holds out his arm to her and she takes it with all the grace of a queen.

They walk out of the room just as he turns to her and says, "We'll let them get back to their naked talk. I have a feeling we were interrupting something."

"Oh, Arvid," my mother chides him as the door shuts behind them.

I can't stop smiling.

I turn to Maggie.

"Speaking of naked," I say to her, grabbing her hand and leading her to the bed. "How about I make you feel like a queen?"

EPILOGUE

MAGGIE

SIX MONTHS LATER

G<small>UNFIRE ERUPTS BESIDE ME, MY EARS BLASTED BY THE</small> deafening sound. I scream but I can barely hear it, everything around me is being shaken up and my brain feels like I have rocks rolling around inside it.

I am beyond terrified.

"Get down!" someone yells and I immediately drop to my knees, covering the back of my neck with my hands. A flash bang grenade goes off and I'm blinded.

"Fuck!" I scream. "Make it stop!"

"Sorry miss, but you're going to need to make it out of here alive," the man dressed head-to-toe in camouflage says to me, keeping his automatic rifle at the ready. "Are you able to run to safety?"

I shake my head. Hell no. I've lost a shoe somewhere along the way, maybe when I first escaped the kidnappers, and the stretch of gravel between here, where I'm hiding out by the side of an old, blasted building, and the military jeep that will take me to freedom, looks like it will be murder on my feet.

I don't think I have a choice though. This guy next to me looks like he'll drag me through the gravel if he has to. Not a very nice way to treat a future princess but what can you do.

I quickly slip off my other heel–I hate that this happened while I was wearing heels, so impractical–and hesitate before tossing it behind me. They were nice shoes and I'm sure I can get another pair, but I'm still cringing at the idea of wasted money. Even being engaged to the Crown Prince of Sweden for six months doesn't change the way I look at money.

I can tell we're about to make a run for it when the man across from me lifts his gun and fires another round of ammunition in the air.

Totally unnecessary.

I plug my ears again. "He's supposed to be on our side!" I yell.

"You need to get immune to the sound," the guy beside me says.

"I don't think I'll ever get used to the sound!"

He stares at me, completely stone-faced. This is just a fun day on the job for him, isn't it? Gets to rescue the princess from kidnappers and feel like a hero, all the while I'm screaming and yelling and acting like a loon.

Because, I mean, I'm sorry but if I were *actually* kidnapped, that's what I would be doing.

I know they wanted me to try and make friends with the kidnappers earlier but I think I just ended up annoying them. Which isn't a bad strategy at all. Annoy them until they let you go. That kind of worked for Bette Midler in *Ruthless People*.

"Come on," the guy says gruffly and takes me by the arm and ushers me across the gravel, the stones biting into my feet. A foot bath will be in order after this.

Then the gunfire erupts again, along with some more grenades and my ear drums are blown to smithereens. Thank god I've kept my sense of humor throughout this whole ordeal, otherwise I think I might be traumatized for life. In fact, that's what they warned me of before I took part in the "terror training." Understandably, Viktor didn't even want me to do it.

But his parents were very adamant that I go through it. In this day and age, you just never know what's going to happen, whether some crazy royal fan wants to kidnap the Princess or Queen or if a terrorist takes over the palace, or attacks a royal event, like our upcoming wedding.

So for the last two days I've been part of this program that they promised would give me some skills and frighten the shit out of me, and honestly, it has. I've been fake kidnapped, I've been dropped alone in the wilds of the Swedish North for twenty-four hours, so I know how to survive if I end up there for some reason (note: bring lots of mosquito repellent—this is more important than food), I've had to do drills around guns and grenades and all sorts of crazy shit.

It's been intense, but as I'm booking it across the gravel with Mr. Serious by my side, I know the moment I get in that military jeep and am driven away, that's the end of it. They're driving me right back to the palace.

To my home.

"Woo hoo!" I yell as I reach the jeep just before I'm pushed, rather brusquely, into the back of the vehicle. "I made it! I'm alive! Oh god, I am *alive!*"

Mr. Serious exchanges a look with the other two serious military men in the back. This wasn't part of their job description.

"Hey," I tell them. "You don't want to know what I'd do if this were actually real. I'd probably kiss all of you, Viktor would find out, and you'd be out of a job. So let's at least act fake happy for me being fake happy at my fake rescue."

In unison all three men attempt to smile.

"Yaaaay," Mr. Serious says flatly.

The moment I'm back at the palace, Viktor is waiting for me in the foyer with a bottle of champagne in one hand and a chocolate cake in the other. He knows the way to my heart.

"My god," he says, looking me over, putting the stuff down on the cart and striding over to me with his arms out. "What did they do to you?" The shock in his eyes quickly turns to flames of anger and he's getting that tick he gets along his jaw when he's about to lose his shit over something.

"Calm down, I'm fine," I tell him. "I can't hear very well and I need a footbath." He looks down at my bare dusty and dirty feet. "But I'm fine."

He's speechless, shaking his head, that anger not dissipating. "I knew this was a mistake. You shouldn't have gone. I have been worried sick about you these last few days. They wouldn't even let me get any updates on how you were."

It's touching to see Viktor so concerned. Not that he normally isn't, but we've both been so busy lately with the upcoming wedding that we've been taking each other for granted. Now, with me gone for two days and getting the wits scared out of me, it feels like this might bring us even closer.

"I told you," I reassure him. "I'm fine." I pause, looking around to see if any of the kids or Bodi are lurking and listening. "Though, if you want to help me clean up, I'd be more than grateful."

Heat flares in his eyes again, this time born of lust and desire. He swallows hard, practically has to loosen his tie. "I—"

"You're back!" April says from the top of the stairs before running down them.

As much as I love my sister and as much as I'm glad that she's this happy to see me, she's also being a bit of a royal cockblocker at this second.

She's about to give me a hug but she stops and looks me over. "You look like shit."

"Yeah, well, that's what happens when you get kidnapped," I tell her. I then notice that she has a purse with her. "Where are you going?"

"Out," she says, shrugging one shoulder, back to teenage one-word answers.

"My mother is taking her, Rosemary, and Thyme dress shopping," Viktor says.

"Your mother?" I repeat.

"I know," he says. "But the ball is tomorrow night and this is the first time they're all going to be officially exposed to high society."

"I understand that." I look over at April who isn't even listening anymore. "But your mother? That's the part that's nutty. I can't imagine The Queen going shopping, she must have to close down the whole department store."

He nods. "That's exactly what she does."

"Well, shit," I say, crossing my arms. "I want to go shopping now."

"You already have a very lovely gown," he says, reaching over and picking a piece of plaster or maybe shrapnel from my hair.

"Yeah, but it's like a childhood dream to go shopping in a department store when it's all closed down. Didn't you ever want to be locked in IKEA overnight?"

He frowns. "To do what?"

"I don't know, bounce on the beds?"

He just grins at me like I'm the most adorable little sprite. "You are far too cute for words. English words, anyway. I have many Swedish ones."

"You guys are gross," April mumbles just as Rosemary and Thyme start coming down the stairs.

"Maggie!" Rosemary says as the twins run up to me and give me a hug. "You're alive."

"Barely," Thyme comments as she looks me over. I do a double-take with her. Instead of her usual overboard goth eyeliner, her face has been scrubbed clean and her black hair is pulled high into a smooth top knot. She's still all in black but she looks presentable. She looks like a soon to be twelve-year-old and not the future bassist for a death metal band, which I know she is at heart.

"You look nice," I tell her.

"She wants to look nice for The Queen," Rosemary says.

"We should all look nice for The Queen," I tell them and look down at myself. "Obviously, I'm in no state to go shopping with you."

"And anyway," Viktor says, grabbing my hand. "The girls deserve some one-on-one bonding time with her. You've had a lot of that lately, yes?"

He's so right. Even though it's late June now and the wedding isn't until next April, I've been having weekly meetings with his mother at their palace. I had never put any thought into getting married before, and I have a feeling a normal wedding is super stressful as it is, but a royal wedding? It's insane how many details there are and how big it's going to be. I mean, it's going to be *televised*.

Frankly, I would rather concentrate on my Swedish lessons and helping our nanny, Ingrid, with the kids, or continue going with Viktor to all the public events, than give another minute of thought to the wedding. I would like to pick the dress and see what roles my siblings can play in the ceremony (I do *not* trust Callum to be the ringbearer, that is just a disaster waiting to happen) but other than that, I want to push all decision-making to her.

But she really wants to include me and she's so excited about the whole thing, that really, even with all the bonding we've been doing, it's been worth it. It pains me to think that my own mother won't be here for this, and I often wonder what she'd say or do (probably "Fuck it! Elope!"), but I'm grateful that my future mother-in-law and I are getting along. It's nice to feel like I have a motherly figure in my life again, even if she's a motherly figure to a whole country as well.

"Girls," Bodi says as he strides into the foyer, "Her Majesty is waiting for you."

April, Rosemary, and Thyme all look at each other and grin nervously before following Bodi out of the room.

I breathe out a sigh of relief.

"So you mentioned a bath?" Viktor says, wagging his brows.

I reach up and run my hands over the hard planes of his chest.

Then realize my hands are dirty and are leaving trails of dust.

"*Helvete*," I swear, trying to wipe it off and only making it worse.

"See, swearing in Swedish is so much better," he murmurs, leaning in for a kiss. His lips barely have enough time to brush mine before the front door opens and Callum comes screaming inside.

"Maggie!" he yells and hugs my waist.

I have to admit, it feels really nice to be wanted like this.

"You're back and you smell like pee. Did you pee yourself?"

I laugh awkwardly. "I did *not* pee myself."

"Callum," his nanny, Ingrid, says as she steps through the door behind him and then says something to him in Swedish, which I think is *that's not how we talk to your sister*. Both of us are learning.

But Callum quickly says he's sorry in Swedish, so maybe he knows more than I do at this point. He smiles up at me. "Did you get to fire a gun?"

"No," I tell him, ruffling up his hair which I know annoys him so much. He squirms away from me. "But I saw guns and bombs and a whole whack of stuff that I promise aren't that cool in real life."

I look at Ingrid. "What did you guys do today?"

Ingrid is in her early forties and is pretty much the epitome of a spinster because of the drab way she dresses and her prim and proper manner, but she's kind, patient with the kids, and luckily, not Viktor's type. I trust Viktor completely, but when it was between her and a young and pretty Australian nanny, the queen was adamant we pick Ingrid. I guess nanny affairs are a thing here.

"We went to the zoo, walked around the park," she says in her thick accent, then gives us a wry smile. "He may have had too much ice cream. I'm sorry."

"Never too much!" Callum yells and then takes off running into the kitchen, probably to get more ice cream. I'm just glad he didn't see the cake.

"He's taking the motto too seriously," I tell Viktor. I sigh. "Well, hopefully he'll burn it off soon."

"I've got him," she says. "You go relax, you must have had quite the weekend."

Understatement of the day.

"Come on," Viktor says, pulling me up the stairs. "Let's get you cleaned up."

We go up to our room and as he draws a hot bath for me, I get a glass of scotch from the bar cart and have a few sips, then get undressed and slip on a robe, opening it to inspect my body for bruises. There are a ton of them, scratches and mosquito bites too, but overall, I think I faired better than had it been an actual kidnapping, so there's that.

"I'll give you privacy," Viktor says, holding the bathroom door open for me once the bath is done.

"Thank you, my prince," I tell him, standing on my tip toes to kiss him before I disappear into the bathroom. As much as I want to reconnect with him, as much fun as him washing me would be, I haven't had a shower in days and I'm pretty dirty. Somethings are best done in private.

However, when I'm finally done with the bath and I've had a shower I'm feeling sparkling clean. I puff a shimmery, lavender-scented body powder all over my skin and step out into the bedroom.

Naked.

Viktor is waiting by the bed.

Also naked.

I'm glad we both were expecting the same thing.

And as I hoped, he looks *very* happy to see me.

I walk over to him, trying to look seductive, my dark wet hair curling over my shoulders and breasts. Then he's grabbing me, his large hands running all over my body, over my arms, my waist, my ass. One hand slips up into my hair, the other slips between my legs, and I'm already wet.

"I've missed you," he murmurs, his voice thick. "I've missed this."

He reaches down and slides one finger inside me and it's enough to drive me crazy. Maybe it's all the adrenaline that's been coursing through my body these past few days, maybe it was being so far away from him, maybe I'm just realizing what a fucking *god* my fiancé is, but I'm suddenly starved for him.

As he is for me.

He picks me up, his hands nearly encircling my waist and practically tosses me onto the bed where I bounce, giggling.

Then he's hovering over me and I drink in the sight of his long bare torso, those abs rigid, shoulder muscles straining as he bites and kisses all the way down my body, being more gentle than normal. I guess I do look like a wreck.

But I no longer feel like a wreck.

I pull him up to me and kiss him, then push him back onto the bed. Usually he's the dominant in the bedroom, but today I want to give him a taste of my own medicine.

I stroke his long, hard cock and climb on to him like a wild horse and then I'm riding him, my breasts bouncing, and I thrust my hips, his cock buried deep inside, his face staring up at me in lust and awe, like he can't believe I'm here and this is happening.

Then I'm on my side, my leg lifted over his hip, and he's driving into me, faster and faster, the headboard slamming loudly against the wall. Sweat drips off his body and onto mine, and the room fills with the thick smell of sex and the intoxicating sounds of my greedy moans and his grunts and his dirty mouth as he fucks me into oblivion. When I come, I'm unleashed, and I'm screaming his name, letting everything go. Every fear, every thought, every darkened part of me.

I'm liquid and sunshine and stars in the night sky.

I'm his princess.

I'm his future queen.

And when he comes, he comes hard and he's swearing and grunting my name, and I know I make him feel like a king.

THE SWEDISH PRINCE

Tonight's ball is being held at Drottningholm Palace.

After I flew back to Sweden in January and Viktor proposed (I'm still laughing at the "Will You Merry Me" fiasco, it almost puts my pronunciation of Chopin to shame), I had a whirlwind couple of months. There was a lot of back and forth from Stockholm to California until earlier this month because I wanted Rosemary, Thyme, and April to finish their schooling for the year. Only Callum stayed with us right away since he's young and was going to jump right into Swedish lessons with Ingrid anyway.

So, Pike took care of the girls while I was living here, making sure they got to school and finished, and then when they were done, they flew back here. With Annette's help he put the house up for sale, and at the moment it looks like it's almost sold. When the sale goes through, Pike gets the money and he's going to use it to open up a garage/tattoo parlor in LA. It's sad not having him here, but I totally get why he wants to stay in California. He is going to visit often, though. Who knows, he may even fall in love with a sexy Swedish girl.

But with all that's been going on, the kids haven't really been introduced to Sweden in a public way. Yes, the paparazzi are still plentiful and they do follow us everywhere, but I've noticed they're far more cautious about approaching us now and go out of their way to keep their distance.

Tonight though, the ball is not only a chance for the kids to dress up and feel part of the royal family, but it's all for charity.

Our charity.

Over the last few months, the royal family decided to come out with the truth about Alex's death, to not be ashamed of it. The King's hopes were that more people will speak up about mental illness and suicide. Sweden has a surprisingly high rate that's especially rampant in the far north, so it's something that needs to be talked about to help end the stigma. Viktor especially has become very adamant about spearheading this cause.

I'm proud of my fiancé and the King and Queen for doing the right thing and I think they're rather proud of themselves as well. It's creating a change that their country needs.

"You look like a cake, I could just eat you all up," Prince Magnus says to me with a salacious wink. I look down at my dress. It's gold with many petticoat layers and a bustier. It reminded me of Belle's gown, which is exactly why I got it.

"You don't look too bad either," I tell him, snapping his bowtie against his neck. "For a Norwegian."

"What am I? Chopped herring?" Viktor says, looking between the two of us.

"It's chopped *liver*," I remind him.

"But I love liver."

"You love herring too," Magnus says, then looks around. "Where, oh where, are the drinks? I'd like to get a few in me before all the speeches start."

The ball is underway and I'm standing with Viktor and Magnus off to the side. The King and Queen are about to step out with the kids and give the formal introduction to them and the event.

I look behind me to see Rosemary, Thyme, April, and Callum all in a row, holding hands like they're about to play red rover. They look so nervous, it's cute.

"You guys look great too," I whisper to them over my shoulder, even though I've already told them they look amazing a hundred times. Callum is in a little cummerbund suit, the girls in long gowns. They all literally look like royalty. The Queen did good helping to pick it all out.

Callum grins and starts doing a little dance. "I'm so excited," he squeals. "Bork bork."

"Callum!" I can hear Ingrid admonish him from somewhere in the background.

Then Dolf Lundgren (but not really) strides to the front of where we are gathered and addresses the crowd. "I'm please to present to you His Majesty King Arvid and Her Majesty Queen Elin."

The King and Queen, both in formal royal wear, come out to a microphone, his mother doing the graceful "queen wave" and his father nods at everyone.

The King clears his throat and speaks. "Thank you all for coming here tonight. As you know, this event is for our charity, The Prince Alexander Fund, which we created in our son's honor to help end the stigma against mental illness. Through the tragedy of losing Alex to suicide, we decided that the best way to honor him would be to ensure that no more lives are lost in the same way. We are a proud country, and we have a long way to go with treatment and societal expectations, however, I believe Alex would be proud of us, of all of you, for taking this first step."

Everyone applauds. I look up at Viktor and briefly lean against him. His chin is raised high, a loving smile on his lips as he looks at his father and I know that this moment, this journey, has meant a lot to him.

Queen Elin then steps to the mic to speak. "Thank you, Arvid. We would also like to take this time to introduce Miss Maggie McPherson, who is betrothed to our son, and her brothers and sisters who have made Sweden their new home."

More applause.

Crap. I didn't know I had to go out there too.

Viktor holds his arm out and I take it and now I'm gliding across the floor and everyone is applauding us. I know my cheeks are going beet red because I was not expecting this, so I quickly turn to the kids and beckon them over. They're so scared, they freeze and it takes a nudging from Ingrid (more like a shoving) for them to finally walk out, still holding hands like they're crossing the street.

Now the crowd is clapping louder and the kids are positively beaming at the attention. Especially Callum, of course he's hamming it up and doing strong man poses.

"Nice family," Viktor whispers in my ear as I look them over.

"The best," I whisper back.

He bites his lip and looks me over. "So when can we start one of our own?"

We've discussed having kids before but only in passing. Now he's asking me with the entire room staring at us. Thank god no one can hear him.

"I've made you go red," he goes on quietly, squeezing my hands. "A royal flush. You know I like that."

"I know you do." I raise my brow. "We can start right after this."

"Give you the royal treatment in the coatroom?"

I grin. "Something like that."

Something like that.

THE END

WANT MORE NORDIC ROYALS?
CHECK OUT - THE WILD HEIR

This is Magnus's story…

At first glance I probably seem like any good-looking guy in their late twenties. I have an obscene amount of confidence, a tattooed body sculpted by the Nordic gods, and I love the ladies as much as they love me.

If I'm not BASE jumping or car racing, I'm chasing other devious thrills with the woman of the week. And that's fine if you're the average single guy.

But I'm not the average single guy.

I'm Crown Prince Magnus of Norway and my latest scandal just landed my entire royal family in hot water.

Now the only way the monarchy can save face is for me to smarten up – publicly. If I don't, I'll no longer be heir apparent to the throne. So it's either I abdicate my future role as King or…

I get married.

To a blue-blooded stranger.

Enter Princess Isabella of the tiny country of Liechtenstein.

Quiet, intelligent, and uniquely beautiful, Ella doesn't like this arrangement any more than I do and she's not afraid to show it. She says I'm a womanizer, that I don't take anything seriously, that my ego should be taken down a few pegs, and I think she aims to make me miserable for the rest of my life.

But even as our arranged marriage becomes a war of wit and words, I'm determined to break through Ella's prim and proper façade to find the wild , sexual and risk-taking woman underneath. I want to uncover the Queen inside her.

The only question is – will she let me?

Flip page for the cover and first chapter...

WANT MORE NORDIC ROYALS? CHECK OUT - THE WILD ...

THE WILD HEIR
CLICK HERE to get *The Wild Heir* on Amazon

CHAPTER ONE
Magnus

"You fucked up!" Ottar says yet again.

Not exactly the thing you want to hear mere seconds before you're about to fling yourself off a 3,200-foot cliff and free fall to the fjord below.

But in this case, as Ottar has spent the last five minutes drilling into my head what an idiot I am and how badly I've fucked up my life, hurling yourself off a cliff seems like the right thing to do. Maybe the only thing to do in this situation.

As I run toward the edge of Kjerag Mountain, I keep my eyes focused straight ahead at the fjord cutting through the valley like a blue knife, and let all thoughts, all worries, all self-awareness, melt away.

I jump.

Those first few seconds of free fall are what I imagine being born is like. A terrifying rush as you're propelled from the solid and steady world you know into the cold abyss. There's nothing like it, leaving safety and life for what should be certain death.

Then you're flying, arms out, weightless, a bird in the sky, an angel's descent, a step beyond being human.

Then you're falling.

Wind rushing against your face, pulling your skin back into a smile, rattling your helmet. There's nothing to anything anymore, nothing but you and the wind and the greatest adrenaline rush you'll ever know. Better than sex, even.

Maybe.

The timer goes off, interrupting the rush before my brain has started to blur together. I quickly reach into the chute to deploy it and I'm jerked back, the blast of the free fall reversing for a second as the parachute spreads and the easy descent begins.

Usually this part of the jump is where your heart starts to slow, where you realize where you are, what you're doing—that you made it. You're safe. As you float down to earth, you carry nothing inside you but awe, knowing that you're just a tiny bright-colored parachute soaring toward a cerulean-blue fjord, eagles at eye level.

But there is no peace and tranquility today.

There is none of that sharp focus and clarity that always comes during a jump, where my scattered world seems to pause, just for one wonderful minute as I fall from the sky.

All I can focus on are Ottar's words slicing through my head. *I fucked up.* And it's not just his words either. It's my sisters, it's my parents, it's the press. It's the damn prime minister.

When you're royalty and you do something stupid, everyone in the whole world, let alone the whole country, gets to weigh in on it.

And I'm the Crown Prince of Norway, heir to the throne, and my latest scandal just set the public image of our country back another hundred years.

No wonder it was easier to jump today than most days.

A scream pierces my thoughts and I look up, even though I can see nothing above me but the electric yellow of the chute. That was Ottar's scream. This is only the second time the guy has BASE jumped, and for him, it's one too many. Hell, no sane person would attempt this sport, but I have the nickname "Magnus the Mad" for a few good reasons.

The screaming seems to stop after a bit, which means

Ottar probably pulled his chute, and now I have the ground to worry about.

Focus, fuckface, I tell myself, willing my brain to stop racing around and work before it's too late. Everything is throwing me off. I grab the pulleys in front of me and steer myself toward the people standing on the small peninsula below me, hoping Ottar follows suit. His last landing was about as graceful as a cow being flung from a catapult.

There's only a small patch of grass to land on—overshoot that and you're going to smash into rock or the ice-cold waters of the fjord. Maybe it's because my mind has been so liquid, but the grass is rushing up fast and I know that this is going to hurt like a mother.

My feet strike the ground and my legs immediately crumple, sending pain up my shins. I duck into a roll across the grass and then spring up just before my shoulder hits a slab of rock.

Helvete.

All the bystanders standing around are gawking at me and my not so graceful arrival.

I push my helmet on straighter, adjust my goggles, and give them all a quick bow. "Not a bad landing when the alternative is death," I say with a big smile.

A few of them clap. These people just seem to be tourists, their speedboats pulled up along the shore, cameras around their necks to capture the crazy fuckers like me who do this famous jump.

And Ottar.

He's screaming again, his legs kicking out as he rapidly descends toward us, his arms jerking on the handles, completely out of control. If he doesn't slow down and steer he's going to smash right into a few people, and then the rocks behind them.

This is going to get ugly.

Everyone is scattering, unsure of what to do, and I know this is all out of Ottar's hands now. Even with his goggles covering up his eyes, I can tell they're open wide, his mouth agape as he seems to freeze from terror.

I don't even think. I start running toward him and leap up, crashing into him in the air while trying to wrap my arms around his thighs.

Somehow I manage to pull him down, like I'm plucking a big, fat, hairy bird out of the air, and then he's crashing on top of me, squeezing the air out of my lungs as I smash into the ground.

"Oh my god, Your Highness!" he yells at me, and even though my mouth is full of grass, I'm already mumbling for him to shut up.

He rolls off me, and then I lie back, trying to catch my breath and hoping no one else heard his address.

"I am so sorry!" he goes on, patting my arms and thighs. "Are you alive?"

Poor Ottar. He never wanted to do any of this shit with me. In the past, he was the guy waiting in the car, hovering on the sidelines. Then, with my father having some health issues this year, Ottar started actually going with me on my activities. If I wasn't going to quit doing them, then at least Ottar would be there closer than ever, keeping an eye on me, making sure I was, well, alive.

But now it's not just him making sure I'll survive to be king, it's to make sure I don't run off into the woods and do something stupid. Or more stupid than jumping off a cliff. I have a bad reputation with my family as being slightly impulsive. Ever since I was a little kid, I've been blowing off the bodyguards and royal guards and escaping every chance I could get.

"I'm fine," I tell him, sitting up and looking around. The

people are crowded together, watching us from a distance as if Ottar was a bomb dropped from the sky.

"You saved my life, sir," Ottar says, placing his meaty palm on my shoulder. "I don't know how to repay you."

I eye his hand and then shrug it off me. "Well, you can start by dialing back your Samwise Gamgee."

"Of course, sir," he says, looking a little embarrassed. I think it's more from nearly dying and me having to save him, rather than the *Lord of the Rings* nickname, because I swear he's always two seconds away from calling me Mr. Frodo. "But again, I'm so sorry."

"Not your fault," I tell him. Not my fault either. "You could help me up though."

"Yes, sir," he says, grabbing my hands and hauling me to my feet. I can feel the crowd inspecting us even more now—probably because of the way Ottar is addressing me, like I'm *someone*—and I'm tempted to do yet another bow to play off two bad landings in a row.

But someone has their camera out, aiming it in our direction, and I can't tell if it's because they want to take a picture of the two fools who just landed or if they think I'm someone of importance.

I give the camera a tight smile and look down at Ottar, who is a good half a foot shorter than me. "We should probably get this stuff off and head to the boat."

Down along the shore is a sleek, white speedboat with teak trim, the name *Elskling* written with flourish on the side. The man waiting patiently behind the wheel is Einar, one of my bodyguards and my getaway driver. Like Ottar, he's always nearby, usually trailing me, because I'm trying to lose him. He used to be in the military though, so he's a hard man to lose.

I hear the faint click of a few more cameras coming from the crowd but this time I don't indulge them with a second glance. I quickly get my gear off and then as Ottar is still fumbling with the straps across his chest, help him too.

There's a collective *"oooh"* from the bystanders and I crane my head back to the sky where the next jumpers are descending, three of them in a row. From this distance they look like brightly colored stars that have burned through the atmosphere.

Another *click* steals my attention.

Everyone is watching the jumpers except for two men.

Men with cameras aimed right at Ottar and I.

Men I should have recognized before but with all the commotion, my mind wasn't able to focus.

You're an idiot, Magnus.

"Hey, isn't that—?" Ottar asks, but he trails off as the two men turn around and start running toward one of the waiting boats.

"Shit," I swear, wondering how many photos they got.

It's not that I was doing anything inappropriate, per se, but I had promised my family I would stay out of the paparazzi's eye for the day, and well, those two fuckers are the bane of my princely existence. The whole reason I came out here was to avoid having my photo taken since usually the paparazzi don't follow me all the way out to Kjerag.

But these guys aren't the normal paparazzi. First of all, they're Russian twins who look an awful lot like the T-1000 from *The Terminator*. Second of all, they act like the T-1000 too. They're fucking unstoppable. No matter where I go, those douchebags are there, taking photos and selling them to the highest paying gossip mag or trashy tabloid. I'm not saying that I cry myself to sleep at night over being known as the "hot and sexy single prince," but it sure makes you a media darling.

"We need to go," I tell Ottar. "Now."

Normally I would just let this go, but since these assholes

will without a doubt be selling the first photos of me of what will be known as "The Aftermath" followed with the headlines "Suicidal Prince Jumps Off Cliff (His Personal Secretary Tries to Save Him)" and "Not Fit to Rule," I feel like it's my duty to care as much as it's their duty to treat me like I'm an animal in a zoo.

We start jogging across the grass to the boat and throw our stuff on board, then wade into the ice-cold water up to our knees before climbing in. Einar is at the wheel, frowning beneath his aviator glasses that glint violet and blue like they've been polarized a million times over.

I step beside him, shouldering the brute out of the way and taking over the controls.

"If you don't mind, I think I'll drive," I tell him, glancing over my shoulder at their speedboat which is zooming off, before shoving the gear into reverse and gunning it away backward from the shore.

Ottar nearly falls overboard, holding on to the rail for dear life as Einar grabs the console to steady himself.

"I'm pretty sure your mother would file this under reckless driving!" Ottar yells, trying to straighten back up, only for me to whip the boat forward and take off after the Russian's boat.

"Pretty sure my mother wouldn't want me to be paparazzi fodder either," I tell him with a wink.

"Just let it go," Ottar says with a sigh that's squeezed out of his lungs as he falls into the railing again.

But even though I'm pretty fucking good at escaping from my problems, the fact that they've followed me here says I've got to face them. Head on. Mad Magnus style.

"Let it go?" I repeat. "You're the one who told me I fucked up just moments before I jumped. I fucked up, so now I have to fix it."

"Sir," Einar says, clearing his throat. "Even if his

psychedelic sunglasses weren't covering his eyes, I wouldn't be able to read them. Sometimes I think Einar is built in the same robot factory as the Russians, but his maker decided to give him extra muscle.

"I've got it, Einar," I tell him. "Why don't you make sure Ottar doesn't fall overboard?"

Einar doesn't move, and from the way his mouth is pressed into a firm line, I don't think he likes it when I tell him what to do. I know he doesn't. I can order Ottar around, but Einar is just a bodyguard, there to protect me, not anyone else.

I don't need his protection, but that doesn't stop him from going everywhere I go. Even when I go on a date with a lady, he's somewhere lurking in the background. The only privacy I get is when I'm fucking them and I have to hope he's not spying through a window. Don't get me wrong, the idea of being watched while having sex excites me to no end, but seeing Einar's grave, pockmarked face would totally kill the vibe.

That said, in some ways I wish he had been watching the other week when I'd gone into Heidi's house.

When I'd gone into Heidi's room.

Not necessarily when I proceeded to screw her senseless that first time.

But the second time, when she propped up her phone and said she wanted to record us having sex as a keepsake, a memento.

I'd agreed to it, because, well why the fuck wouldn't I want to be filmed sticking my dick in her? Usually I don't even bring it up with the ladies because their adventurous sides only involve doggy-style and maybe some light choking or spanking. Filming us having sex? Forget it.

And I was feeling bad since earlier that evening I broke it off with her. Not that Heidi and I were anything serious, but we'd been on a few dates we somehow managed to hide from the public—and her father—and I could tell she wanted a lot more from me. As in, she wanted to become the next princess of Norway.

Naturally, I had to nip that in the bud, even though apparently when I break up with someone I still think it's cool to film a sex tape afterward. Just another example of my impulsiveness getting me in trouble.

God, did I ever fuck up.

But that's all out of my control and who knows what's going to happen to me now. Since the news broke yesterday, I've yet to speak to my parents about it, though I could feel their anger simmering all the way from their palace in downtown Oslo.

I'm feeling that same anger simmer through me right now with only one place for it to go.

I increase the throttle on the boat, and now we're steadily catching up to the paparazzi speedboat. Soon we'll overtake them.

"I hope you know what you're doing," Einar says quietly, his eyes focused on the boat as it gets closer and closer.

"Do I ever know what I'm doing?" I repeat, biting back a smile.

And even if this doesn't work, who cares? They deserve it and more.

"Hey!" I yell at the photographers as we pull up alongside their boat. "Get any good pics?"

My voice is carried by the wind but they both look over and in unison raise their cameras.

I proceed to give them the finger and a big fucking smile.

Then I swiftly grab the wheel and yank our boat to the side, creating a giant wake and ensuring a wave of water flows over the side of their boat, soaking them from head to toe.

I burst out laughing and then gun our boat in the opposite direction toward our boat launch at the end of the fjord, leaving the two fuckfaces yelling at us in Russian, sopping wet and shaking out their cameras which are no doubt ruined.

Serves them right.

"Nice maneuver, sir," Einar says after a moment, and I glance at him to see the hint of what could be called a smile pulling at his mouth.

"Thank you, my good man."

"You know they're going to try and sue you for that," Ottar pipes up, slowly staggering up the side of the deck, never letting go of the railing.

"You're a killjoy, Ottar," I tell him. "Let me have my fun."

I know it's the only fun I'm going to have for a while.

* * *

Even though I've always had my pick of where I wanted to live, including various royal palaces throughout Norway, I'm rather fond of my tiny apartment. Okay, maybe it's not tiny by normal standards. It does take up the entire top floor of a corner building in Majorstuen, one of the city's "hip" neighborhoods, and I have more room than I know what to do with, but it makes me feel a lot more normal to live this way rather than in a palace.

Ignoring the fact that the floor below me is where Einar and Ottar and various rotating guards live, the floor below that is an H&M. On the street, trams trundle on by, a sound I find soothing, and people hurry to and fro, shopping and hitting up the bars.

The paparazzi know I live in the neighborhood but aren't exactly sure where. The windows that face the street are tinted, obscuring me from people and when I need sun, I head up to the roof where I have a whole private deck free from prying eyes. And there are more than a few entrances into the building, including a tunnel that pops up a block away in a small gated courtyard.

That's how my mother will be getting here tonight. I feel bad having her go through the tunnel since it was built in the 1800s and it can get pretty dank in there, but she was insistent that she come visit me as soon as possible.

It's all bad news. The fact that she wants to discuss something with me here instead of at the palace where my father and youngest sister, Mari, are says a lot. Like there are less witnesses in case she wants to murder me.

I'm looking around the apartment, wondering if I should hide my knives, or, at the very least, the large Viking axe I have on display on the wall, when there's a knock.

I stride over to the door, running my hand through my hair to make sure it's all in order (my hair is usually messy and longer than she thinks is appropriate), take in a deep breath, and open it.

My mother and her bodyguard, Per, are standing in the hall. I catch a glimpse of Einar in the background, heading down the stairs.

"Magnus," my mother says to me in a curt voice, which is her default voice at any given moment.

"Mother," I say right back. I flash her a smile which used to charm her but doesn't seem to have that effect anymore. I meet Per's eyes, but just like Einar, they give me nothing. More robots in fine suits.

I clear my throat and gesture to the apartment. "Well. Come in, then."

She nods and glances at her bodyguards with an internal message for them to stay where they are. Then she steps inside and I close the door after her.

"You cleaned up," she says, stopping in the middle of the

living room and looking around. It's an open plan apartment which means you can see most of it from any location, and normally it's a mess. Even though I have a housecleaner who comes in here every other day, it doesn't take long for the place to look like a tornado ripped through it. Let's just add Messy Magnus to my list of nicknames.

"I tried to make it fit for a queen," I tell her.

"Bullshit," she swears, shaking her head and eyeing me sharply.

That's my mother for you. She might be the Queen, but she can be as crude and blunt as I can be. While my father is easygoing and gregarious, if not a little loopy, my mother says what she wants, when she wants. She's fearless.

At least she normally is. As sharp as her gaze is tonight as it cuts into me, I can see the sparks of fear behind her eyes, which in turn brings out the fear in me.

My heart starts to speed up and she nods at the two armchairs by the fireplace, an heirloom bearskin rug between them. "Sit down. I have something I need to talk to you about, and for once, I need you to listen."

I swallow hard. "You don't want coffee or?" I glance at the kitchen as if making her an espresso will buy me some time.

"Magnus," she says sternly. "Sit."

So I sit, and she sits across from me. She's a petite woman, only about five feet, two inches tall, but even in a casual silk pantsuit that borders on pajamas, she's formidable.

She doesn't say anything for a moment which ratchets up the tension in the room to an unbearable amount. I finally have to say, "Look, I am so sorry about what happened—"

"Stop," she says, raising her palm. "Just stop. You don't need to apologize. Though I do wonder if you are ever truly sorry about anything."

That was a cheap shot.

"What happened, happened," she goes on. "There's no stopping it. All we can do is damage control, if we can even do that."

"I'm sure the prime minister understands that—"

"The prime minister," she roars, her dark eyes blazing, "does not understand! For crying out loud, Magnus, you filmed a sex tape with his daughter!"

"I was breaking up with her," I say feebly, covering my face with my hands because fuck I don't want to talk about a sex tape with my mother, even though it's all over the fucking news.

"That's how you break up with people?" She's incredulous. I peer up at her to see her shaking her head in disgust. "First of all, what the hell were you doing with Heidi Lundström to begin with?"

"She's a fan," I try to explain. "I mean, she wanted to go out with me. We've met so many times over the years, you know it was kind of inevitable. She'd just broken up with her boyfriend and we were at that fancy charity event for frogs and wetlands or something and…"

"Did you not think for one second that perhaps she was off-limits?"

I shrug. "Well, no."

"Of course not. Because you never take one second to think about anything. Always jumping into everything like you're out of control. You are out of control, Magnus. Always have been. I—*we*—have tried everything to rein you in over your twenty-eight years and nothing has worked."

"Hey," I say, hating that she throws this shit in my face. "I did think. In fact, I thought maybe for once it would be a good match since she has a similar lifestyle to mine and knows what it's like to grow up in a family of power, but she's a lot, uh, more unstable than I realized."

"Well, since you're unstable too, I can see why you bonded," she says, pretending not to notice me wince at the *unstable* remark. "But honestly, a *sex tape?*" She says the words like they're in a foreign language. "You didn't once think about the repercussions of that?"

"Why would I?"

"Because that sort of...*thing*, it always gets loose. Haven't you learned anything over the years with celebrity scandals?"

"That's Hollywood."

"And the same dynamics apply here. Obviously you've learned nothing about being a prince. Instead, you try and shun it every chance you get. Is that what you want? You want to abdicate? Is that why you're self-sabotaging?"

"I'm not self-sabotaging! And I don't want to abdicate."

But my voice trails off at the end of that sentence as it always does when abdication is brought up, when I'm reminded of what a poor choice I am for a king, how terrible I will be.

"Look," I continue, leaning forward with my elbows on my thighs, my fingers laced together as if in prayer. "I made a mistake with Heidi. I obviously didn't want to humiliate her or the prime minister, even though I think he's always hated me to begin with. Can't we do damage control here? Can't we tell the press that it's a fake? Surely someone did hack into Heidi's phone like she says. Can't we say that person made the whole thing up with, like, Photoshop or something like that?"

She exhales through her nose and gives me a steady look. "Not when Heidi has already admitted to the press what happened. Rather proudly, I might add. I think that girl has some, how do you say, daddy issues."

"You don't know the half of it," I mutter under my breath, having a flashback to some rather questionable words Heidi muttered during sex. "So what do I do?"

"I'll tell you what you're going to do, Magnus. And you're not going to like any of it."

I take in a deep breath, wondering what kind of royal terrors await me. "Okay," I say slowly. "What is it?"

She rubs her lips together, taking her time. I know she does this because I'm terribly impatient and hate having to wait. I also know she loves to see me squirm.

"First of all, you're going to have to apologize to the prime minister and Heidi. In person. And then later on camera during a press conference."

"What!?" I exclaim. "On camera? But...the world will eat that up with a fucking spoon. That will make us look weak."

She gives me a sour smile. "We already look weak, thanks to you. The entire monarchy has now been razed to substandard levels. We are the laughing stock of the country, of Europe, of the entire world. Magnus, the damage you've done with this is just the straw that broke the damn camel's back. All respect that this royal family has earned is gone and in a world where monarchies are no longer in vogue nor in real power, this will have lasting effects."

Well, fuck.

"Okay," I tell her, gathering my courage. "I'll do it."

"Yes. You will do it. And you'll do the next thing as well."

"What next thing? It can't be worse than that," I say softly, but from the look in her eyes I can tell it is. I brace for impact.

"The next thing..." she starts and then seems to wince at what she's about to say. "Magnus. You're going to have to get married."

WANT MORE - click here to get The Wild Heir on Amazon and in KU

AFTERWORD

Thank you so much for reading The Swedish Prince. Reviews are much appreciated! They really help the book world go round and help author's out in so many ways. If you leave a review of The Swedish Prince, you'd make my day <3

If you're wanting to check out any of my other romances, I have TOO MANY to list, but here are some of my favourites (and all are available on Kindle Unlimited):

- A Nordic King (King Aksel's story)
- BAD AT LOVE (a quirky friends-to-lovers romance)
- BEFORE I EVER MET YOU (young single mom falls for her father's best friend)
- LOVE IN ENGLISH (the ultimate forbidden romance with the sexiest Spanish soccer star ever)
- THE PACT (two best friends agree to marry each other by the time they're thirty)
- THE NORTH RIDGE SERIES (A trilogy about three rugged mountain men from Canada with very dangerous and thrilling jobs and the women who love them)

-> If you want to connect with me, you can always find

me on Instagram (where I'm posting photos from my recent research trip to Sweden!)

-> or in my Facebook Group (we're a fun bunch and would love to have you join)

-> Otherwise, feel free to signup for my mailing list (it comes once a month) and Bookbub alerts!

ACKNOWLEDGMENTS

Normally my writing is a very close and personal thing. I tend to shelter myself from the elements. I become a rock, an island. I rely on no one but my husband who cooks, cleans and pretty much keeps me alive, and my dog, Bruce, who provides hours of distraction that I probably don't need (but he's so darn cute!)

I usually have one beta read if that (Hi Nina D!) and I have someone who edits and proofs as I go (Hi Rox L!) and I have a multitude of people who I fret to (Nina G, Sandra), but in the end I'm pretty much alone and that's cool. That's how I role.

But with this book I wanted to do things differently. It was a different book than I normally write, had a different feel. I wanted to hit 2018 running with this standalone romance of royal proportions. It was my first royal book after all and with all my inspirations from Roman Holiday and being in Sweden purely for research (and nearly dying from frostbite), I wanted to give an extra oomph.

Bring on the beta readers who gave me helpful and encouraging feedback to make this book the best it could be.

I couldn't have done it without: Sarah Sentz, Pavlina Michou, Imani Hackney, Stephanie Romig, SueBee (especially for her Swedish touch hehe), super Swede Michaela Sirèn, Becky Barney, Renery Gatpayat, Mary Ruth Baloy, Christy Baldwin, Nina Decker, Nina Grinstead, Alison Phillips, Michell Routhier, Sarah Symonds and Heather Pollock. Thank you guys for putting up with me and believing in Viktor and Maggie and being so gentle haha.

Always more, never less.

ABOUT THE AUTHOR

Karina Halle is a former travel writer and music journalist and The New York Times, Wall Street Journal and USA Today Bestselling author of The Pact, Love, in English, The Artists Trilogy, Dirty Angels and over 20 other wild and romantic reads. She lives on an island off the coast of British Columbia with her husband and her rescue pup, where she drinks a lot of wine, hikes a lot of trails and devours a lot of books.

Halle is represented by Root Literary and is both self-published and published by Simon & Schuster and Hachette in North America and in the UK.

Hit her up on Instagram at @authorHalle, on Twitter at @MetalBlonde and on Facebook (join her reader group "Karina Halle's Anti-Heroes" for extra fun and connect with her!). You can also visit www.authorkarinahalle.com and sign up for the newsletter for news, excerpts, previews, private book signing sales and more.

ALSO BY KARINA HALLE

Contemporary Romances

Love, in English

Love, in Spanish

Where Sea Meets Sky (from Atria Books)

Racing the Sun (from Atria Books)

The Pact

The Offer

The Play

Winter Wishes

The Lie

The Debt

Smut

Heat Wave

Before I Ever Met You

After All

Rocked Up

Wild Card (North Ridge #1)

Maverick (North Ridge #2)

Hot Shot (North Ridge #3)

Bad at Love

The Swedish Prince

The Wild Heir

A Nordic King

Nothing Personal

My Life in Shambles

Discretion

Disarm

Disavow

The Royal Rogue

The Forbidden Man

Lovewrecked

One Hot Italian Summer

The One That Got Away

All the Love in the World (Anthology)

Bright Midnight

The Royals Next Door

Romantic Suspense Novels by Karina Halle
Sins and Needles (The Artists Trilogy #1)
On Every Street (An Artists Trilogy Novella #0.5)
Shooting Scars (The Artists Trilogy #2)
Bold Tricks (The Artists Trilogy #3)
Dirty Angels (Dirty Angels #1)
Dirty Deeds (Dirty Angels #2)
Dirty Promises (Dirty Angels #3)
Black Hearts (Sins Duet #1)
Dirty Souls (Sins Duet #2)

Horror & Paranormal Romance
Darkhouse (EIT #1)
Red Fox (EIT #2)
The Benson (EIT #2.5)
Dead Sky Morning (EIT #3)
Lying Season (EIT #4)

On Demon Wings (EIT #5)

Old Blood (EIT #5.5)

The Dex-Files (EIT #5.7)

Into the Hollow (EIT #6)

And With Madness Comes the Light (EIT #6.5)

Come Alive (EIT #7)

Ashes to Ashes (EIT #8)

Dust to Dust (EIT #9)

Ghosted (EIT #9.5)

Came Back Haunted (EIT #10)

In the Fade (EIT #11)

The Devil's Duology

Donners of the Dead

Veiled (Ada Palomino #1)

Song For the Dead (Ada Palomino #2)

Black Sunshine

The Blood is Love